BLOOD & BONES: WHIP

Blood Fury MC, Book 11

JEANNE ST. JAMES

———

Photographer/Cover Artist: Golden Czermak at FuriousFotog

Cover Model: Tyler Caussey

Editor: Proofreading by the Page

Beta readers: Sharon Abrams & Alexandra Swab

Blood Fury MC Logo: Jennifer Edwards

———

———

Keep an eye on her website at http://www.jeannestjames.com/or sign up for her newsletter to learn about her upcoming releases: http://www.jeannestjames.com/newslettersignup

Author Links: Jeanne's Blog * Instagram * Facebook * Goodreads Author Page * Newsletter * Jeanne's Review & Book Crew * Twitter * BookBub

Character List

TO AVOID SPOILERS THIS LIST ONLY INCLUDES THE
CHARACTERS MENTIONED IN THE PREVIOUS BOOKS

BFMC Members:

Trip Davis – *President* – Son of Buck Davis, half-brother to
Sig, mother is Tammy, Runs Buck You Recovery

Sig Stevens – *Vice President* – Son of Buck Davis, mother is
Silvia, three years younger than Trip, helps run Buck You
Recovery

Judge (Judd Scott) – *Sgt at Arms* - Father (Ox) was an Original, owns Justice Bail Bonds

Deacon Edwards – *Treasurer* – Judge's cousin, Skip Trac-
er/Bounty Hunter at Justice Bail Bonds

Cage (Chris Dietrich) – *Road Captain* – Dutch's youngest
son, mechanic at Dutch's Garage

Ozzy (Thomas Oswald) – *Secretary* – *Original* – manages
club-owned The Grove Inn.

Rook (Randy Dietrich) – Dutch's oldest son, mechanic at
Dutch's Garage

Dutch (David Dietrich) – *Original* – Owns Dutch's Garage,
sons: Cage & Rook

Dodge Duke– Manager at Crazy Pete's Bar, did time with
Rook in jail

Whip (Tyler Byrne)– Mechanic at Dutch's Garage (formerly known as the prospect Sparky)

Rev (Mickey Rivers) – Mechanic at Dutch's Garage (formerly known as the prospect named Mouse)

Shade (Julian Bennett) – Works at Tioga Pet Crematorium (formerly known as the prospect named Shady)

Easy (Ethan) – Works at Tioga Pet Crematorium

Dozer – Works at Crazy Pete's (formerly known as the prospect named Tater Tot)

Woody – Works at Crazy Pete's (formerly known as the prospect named Possum)

Castle – *Prospect* – Works at Shelter from the Storm

Scar – *Prospect* – Bouncer at Crazy Pete's

Bones – *Prospect* – Works at Shelter from the Storm

Ol' Ladies:

Stella – *Trip's ol' lady* - Crazy Pete's daughter, owns Crazy Pete's Bar, Liz's sister

Autumn (Red) – *Sig's ol' lady* – Accountant for the club's businesses

Cassidy (Cassie) – *Judge's ol' lady* – Manages Tioga Pet Crematorium

Reese – *Deacon's ol' lady* – Civil law attorney, Reilly's older sister

Jemma – *Cage's ol' lady* – Hospice Nurse, Judge's younger sister

Chelle (Rachelle) – *Shade's ol' lady* – Elementary school librarian

Jet Bryson – *Rook's ol' lady* – Works at Justice Bail Bonds, Adam Bryson's sister

Reilly – *Rev's ol' lady* – Manages Shelter from the Storm, Reese's younger sister

Shay – *Ozzy's ol' lady* – Website designer/graphic artist

Syn – *Dodge's ol' lady* – Lead singer of The Synners, Sig's half-sister

Former Originals:

Buck Davis – *President* – Deceased, Trip & Sig's father
Ox – *Sgt at Arms* – Deceased, Judge & Jemma's father
Crazy Pete – *Treasurer* – Deceased, Stella and Liz's father

Others:

Tessa – Trip's younger sister, Cage and Jemma's house mouse
Henry (Ry) – Judge's son
Daisy – Cassie's daughter
Saylor – Rev's sister, Judge and Cassie's house mouse
Dyna – Cage's daughter
Josie (Josephine) – Chelle's younger daughter
Maddie (Madison) – Chelle's older daughter
Jude – rescued by Shade, Shade & Chelle's adopted son
Dane – Deacon and Reese's son
Maya – Syn's daughter
Liz – Former sweet butt, Crash's ol' lady, Stella's half-sister & Crazy Pete's daughter
Nico, Rex & Eddie - Members of The Synners (Syn's band)
Silvia Stevens – Sig's mother, Razor's former ol' lady
Tammy Davis – Trip's mother, Buck's former ol' lady
Bebe Dietrich – Cage & Rook's mother, Dutch's former ol' lady
Clyde Davis – Buck's father, Trip & Sig's grandfather, deceased
Billie/Angel/Amber/Crystal/Brandy – Sweet butts
Max Bryson – *Chief of Police* – Manning Grove PD, Bryson brother

Marc Bryson – *Corporal* – Manning Grove PD, Bryson brother

Matt Bryson – *Officer* – Manning Grove PD, Bryson brother

Adam Bryson – *Officer* – Manning Grove PD, Bryson's cousin, Teddy's husband

Leah Bryson – *Officer* – Manning Grove PD, Marc's wife

Tommy Dunn – *Officer* – Manning Grove PD

Teddy Sullivan – Owner Manes on Main, Adam Bryson's husband

Amanda Bryson – Max's wife, owner Boneyard Bakery

Carly Bryson – Matt's wife, OB/GYN doctor

Levi Bryson – Adopted son of Matt & Carly Bryson (birth mother: Autumn/Red)

Prologue

LOSING FOREVER

"P-pap! Pap!" Whip inhaled another big breath as he sprinted across the yard and up the porch steps. "P-pap!"

Just as he reached for the screen door, it swung open and his grandfather stood blocking his way. "Why are you out here wailing like a Tom cat who's following the scent of a cat in heat?"

"H-he's b-back!"

His grandfather's wrinkled brow pulled low. "Who?"

"H-him."

"Use your damn words, Whip. Just saying 'him' doesn't work, remember? Form your words and say them clearly."

He was trying. He'd been better about it. Until now. "D-dad."

The old man's spine snapped straight and his cloudy eyes narrowed. "The hell he is."

"Y-yes. He's..." Whip gulped another mouthful of air. "He's h-here."

His pap stepped out onto the wood porch that needed a fresh coat of paint and let the wooden screen door slam behind him, making Whip jump and glance over his shoulder.

The screen door also needed a paint job, but Pap said he was getting too old to do that kind of "shit" and that Whip's mom needed to find herself a worthwhile man to do work around the house and help raise Whip. Instead of the one that she was currently married to, who also happened to be Pap's youngest son.

Blood or not, Pap said both his sons were useless pieces of shit. That was how he actually said it, too. He stated loudly and often that he wished he never had either one.

He also said the only good thing that came out of having those wastes of skin were his grandkids and his daughters-in-law. Whip, Whip's mom, his Aunt Jennie and his two cousins were the only ones left on Earth who made his life worth living.

Whip loved his pap.

Much more than his father. Or his uncle.

Pap called them low-life losers. A lot. Especially when stuff needed to be done around the house or bills needed to be paid and neither of them were anywhere to be found.

Pap said his Uncle Scott, who always insisted on being called Spider instead, was too busy running around on his motorcycle and getting into trouble with the law. While Whip's father was too busy getting himself in trouble with other women.

Whip didn't know why since his dad had a perfectly good one here at home. Maybe if he was a little nicer to Whip's mom, Pap would actually let him stay.

But his dad was never nice.

Not ever.

Not to his mom, not to Pap and not to Whip, either.

Whip actually hated his father. He was mean. Especially when he was drinking.

He had no idea why his mother married him. Whip asked her that once and she said he wasn't like this when she met him. Pap said Whip's dad wasn't a "mean son-of-a-bitch" until his drinking got out of control.

"B-bet he's… h-he's here for m-money again, P-pap."

"Wouldn't be surprised," Pap grumbled. He turned and pulled open the screen door. "Get inside and go find your mother. Warn her that your daddy's here and tell her to bring me my shotgun. The one that's loaded near my bed. I'm going to handle this."

Whip didn't like Pap's tone. It was the one he got when he was annoyed, like when the Steelers lost and he shouted that he was "done" with that "damn team." Sometimes he even threw things at the TV.

"P-pap…"

His grandfather shot him a frown and pointed inside. "Go do what I told you. And don't come back out 'til I tell you, neither. You understand, boy?"

Whip nodded.

"Go!" Pap barked.

Whip went.

"M-mom!" he screamed while running through the house.

"Why are you running?" she asked as she peered around the door from the laundry room. "You sound like a stampeding herd of buffalo." She must be folding clothes again. She was always folding clothes.

"D-dad's b-back."

He wasn't sure if she was frowning at that news or because of his stutter. It had been a while since he'd done it. The doctor said he had finally outgrown it.

Now it was back.

Just like his dad.

"P-pap said g-get his shotgun."

She blinked in confusion. "What?"

"Sh-shotgun."

She rushed out of the laundry room, her eyes wide. "No! I'm not getting his shotgun! Where is he?"

"Out... s-side."

"Where's your father?"

"Outside, t-too."

"Where?" she asked, rushing down the hallway with Whip on her heels.

"P-pap wants his sh-sh-shotgun."

"I'm not giving him his damn shotgun!" she yelled, sounding irritated.

Whip slammed on the brakes and stared at his mother's retreating back as she continued toward the front door. A second later, he heard the screen door slam hard.

Whip turned, ran back to his pap's room and spotted the shotgun leaning against the wall near the head of his bed.

He wasn't allowed to touch it. Not unless Pap was teaching him how to shoot it. Sometimes they did that out in the woods using targets. If he touched it now, he might get in trouble.

But Pap wanted it.

Pap was the man of the house.

Pap would protect them. He promised he always would. He said he would make up for his useless nut seeds. Whatever that meant.

The long gun was awkward but not too heavy for him to run down the hallway with it. When he got to the front door, he heard raised voices outside.

Pap was arguing with Whip's dad.

His dad sounded drunk. Again.

He shoved the screen door open with his shoulder and hurried out onto the porch.

"Let me pass, old man. I live here, too." Bobby Byrne's words were running together and he stunk like beer, even from where Whip stood.

"Get the hell out of here. You're no longer welcome

here. Told you that last time," his pap yelled. "Tonya, you were supposed to bring me my damn shotgun!"

His pap liked to curse. A lot.

He also said he was ornery. Whip agreed once he learned what ornery meant.

"What are you going to do, old man? Shoot your own flesh and blood?" Whip's father shouted, his questions slurred, his face red and his bloodshot eyes narrowed.

Whip didn't like when his face got red like that. It always meant trouble. And not "good trouble" like his pap called Whip.

"If I have to," Pap answered, his face now red, too. He glanced at Whip and held out his hand. "Bring that here, Whip."

"Don't you fucking dare, boy," his father yelled.

"Tyler, take that back inside," his mother ordered, also yelling.

Why was she standing so close to his father? She was within fist range. Didn't she realize that?

"M-Mom!" he warned.

Pap turned on his heels and climbed the steps up to the porch, the hitch in his step worse than normal. Probably because of the arthritis his grandfather complained about often.

He rubbed his hip with one hand and held out his other, the knuckles also knobby from arthritis. "Give it here, Whip, and go back inside."

Whip shook his head.

"Get inside. Now!" Pap shouted at him, grabbing the shotgun out of Whip's hands and pointing toward the door.

His grandfather rarely yelled at him like that. Whip pressed his lips together and rushed inside. He stood just to the side of the door so he could see and hear what was happening, but not be spotted.

He didn't want to get grounded. He hated when he was

grounded because he wasn't allowed to stay up late or play with his friends.

He watched Pap work his way slowly down the steps, putting the shotgun up to his shoulder and pointing the double barrels at Whip's father. "Get out of the way, Tonya. If he doesn't want to leave on his own, I'm going to help him decide otherwise."

Whip's mom stepped in front of her husband, her palms out in front of her. "No, Daniel, he's not worth going to jail for."

"Didn't think you were smart, woman, guess I was wrong," Bobby Byrne said. "He isn't going to shoot me. The old man's nothing but hot air."

"Don't try me, son," Pap warned, taking a step closer with the shotgun still raised. "Tonya, get the hell out of the way. Doing this to protect you and Whip."

"This isn't how to go about it, Daniel."

"Yeah, listen to my wife," his dad sneered, then shoved her out of the way. Whip almost rushed back outside when she stumbled.

A noise bubbled up from the back of Whip's throat when his dad rushed his grandfather. Before the old man could pull the trigger, he got knocked to the ground. Bobby Byrne kicked the shotgun out of reach, hauled Pap up by the collar of his flannel shirt, then hauled off and punched Whip's grandfather right in the face.

His pap fell back to the ground in a heap.

"P-pap!" Whip screamed.

"That's what you get for trying to keep me away from my wife and kid, old man. They're not yours, they're mine."

Whip pushed the screen door open, ran out and down the steps. He sprinted up to his father as he was leaning over to grab Pap again. Whip launched himself onto his father's back and hooked an arm around his neck, choking him as hard as he could. "L-leave him a-a-alone!"

At eight, he wasn't nearly as strong as his father, not even when the man was drunk.

"Get the fuck off me, boy!"

"L-leave us a-alone!" he screamed as he pounded his father on the back.

A hand clamped painfully around his arm and suddenly he was flying through the air. He hit the ground hard enough to lose his breath and see stars.

"Tyler!" His mom's panicked scream filled his ringing ears.

Whip shook it off, pushed to his feet, growled and rushed his father again. When he got there, his father back-handed him so hard across the face, he fell backwards and landed on his ass.

He sat with one hand on his throbbing cheek, waiting for the darkness closing in to pass.

"You said he stopped s-s-s-tuttering!"

Whip tried to blink away the pain in his head.

"He did. Now he only does it when you're around, Bobby."

"You're blaming me for the kid being s-s-stupid?"

"It's all your fault," she screamed, getting in his face. "And stop making fun of him!"

She shouldn't be that close to him. He would hurt her next. "M-mom!"

His father grabbed his mother by the neck and flung her sideways. As soon as she landed on the concrete sidewalk with a cry, he grabbed her hair, yanked her up and back-handed her, too.

"Don't blame me for your fuck-up!" Whip's father shouted.

"M-mom!" Whip cried out, unable to pull his eyes from his parents to see where his grandfather was or if he was hurt.

"You're his damn mother, you caused this." He slapped her again. It was so loud, even Whip could feel the sting.

When she fell to the ground crying, Whip was able to get to his feet again and rush him. "G-get off of her!"

It was like hitting a wall. Two large hands shoved him and he fell backwards, landing next to his mother, scraping his palms on the concrete when he tried to break his fall this time.

"Goddamn defective kid. Starting to doubt whether you came from my loins."

"You want to talk about defective? Have you looked in the damn mirror, jackass?" his pap yelled.

Whip glanced in the direction of where the voice came from and saw his grandfather now standing and wiping away the blood trickling from his mouth. He also saw his grandfather had the shotgun in his hand again. But it was pointed to the ground since Whip and his mother were too close to Bobby Byrne.

They might end up full of buckshot if his grandfather pulled the trigger now.

"He stutters for attention. He does it on purpose. Haven't figured that out yet, old man? He needs it beaten out of him, not babied."

"I know more than you about your own damn son. I take care of them, not you, you useless piece of shit. Wish we never had you."

Whip's father snarled, "Too late, old man."

"I brought you into this damn world and I can take you out, Bobby."

"Do it, old man. Fucking do it. It's nothing but an empty threat."

Pap raised the shotgun.

Whip curled into a ball on the ground, making himself as small of a target as possible.

As soon as he heard his father begin to move, Whip peeked from between his fingers.

Pap had his finger on the trigger. Whip had been taught never to put his finger on the trigger until he was ready to pull it. He ducked his head again, covered his ears and squeezed his eyes shut.

Then his chest exploded as the shotgun went off.

Warm drops splattered his face, his hands, his arms…

None of what his mother was screaming made any sense to Whip. Maybe he wasn't supposed to understand it or maybe it was because his ears were ringing and he could only hear his own thumping heartbeat.

He didn't know and it didn't matter. None of that mattered right now.

Whip forced his eyes open. His father was somehow still on his feet, still moving toward Pap, but now with an arm held across his stomach where the buckshot had hit him and where he was bleeding. His eyes were wide but still held determination. Still remained focused on Pap.

How was he alive or even upright? His shirt was shredded, and so was the now exposed flesh underneath.

He glanced at his pap, who looked like he was in shock himself.

"P-pap!" he screamed in warning as his father closed in on his grandfather.

Did Pap hear him? Or were his ears ringing, too?

Why wasn't he moving? Why was he staring at the shotgun instead of his approaching son?

"P-pap!"

When his grandfather finally lifted his head, his face was so pale and drawn, his eyes empty, but by then, it was too late.

Whip's father yanked the shotgun out of Pap's hand.

"Pap!" Whip screamed as his father lifted the long gun

high into the air and slammed the butt right into Pap's forehead.

It was almost like one of those action movies when things moved in slow motion. Whip watched his grandfather crumble where he stood and land into a motionless heap.

A gaping hole, gushing blood, was dead center in his forehead.

That was when Bobby Byrne fell over, landing on top of his own father.

Whip knew right then that his pap was dead. So was his father.

And during it all, his mother continued to scream.

Chapter One

"Gonna kill the bitch," Sig snarled with his jaw hard and eyes cold as ice. Definitely deadly.

The VP was pacing back and forth across The Barn's floor. His body stiff and his hands jerking as he took long, agitated strides.

Trip had gathered everyone for an emergency meeting. Of fucking course, it was about the Shirleys. Whip wondered if they would even need to have church meetings after they dealt with Hillbilly Hill for the last time.

For patching in prospects? Maybe. But other than that?

The president ripped his black baseball cap off his head and held it crushed within his fingers as he used them to scratch the back of his neck.

Both half-brothers had trigger tempers and right now, their tempers were flaring.

Of course they would be. All of them standing inside The Barn were tired of the Shirley bullshit.

Bone. Fucking. Tired.

The Fury needed to deal with them one final time to end this shit. For good.

Now that winter had passed and the snow was gone,

those redneck roaches were repopulating that mountain. As well as beefing up the numbers in their clan. That had to be the reason they were bringing in "breeders" and "snot monkeys" from clans located elsewhere. Like from Ohio.

Red's mom had been living with the Ohio branch of the Guardians of Freedom with her second husband and, apparently, a bunch of kids. Not just the three she gave birth to, either. Probably more, since the man she married already had kids of his own. The reason he married Red's mom in the first place.

To raise the widower's litter of children and to breed more.

The members of the militia wannabes or sovereign nation—whatever the fuck they were—believed the more children they had, the closer they'd be to God. They figured their way into Heaven was guaranteed by producing tons of snot monkeys.

If that was a requirement to get through the pearly gates, Whip would be shit out of luck.

The problem was, the Shirley gene pool had been so small, the offspring tended to be inbred. Whip wasn't sure about the Ohio group or the rest of them.

It turns out, Red's mother had been persuaded into following those cult beliefs after Red's father died. The woman had been dealing with grief, depression and, at the time, had been extremely vulnerable. As well as lonely.

The perfect target for gaslighting.

However, now the woman was no longer in Ohio, but in Pennsylvania. Apparently to join the same clan she had a hand in sending Red to as a "breeder" against Sig's ol' lady's will.

Kidnapped, restrained, confined and raped.

Red had been so traumatized, she called the baby inside her a "seed." She didn't see it as anything other than that.

Proof the mind did its best to cope with what it had been dealt.

But, seriously, what fucking mother did that to her own damn daughter? Someone who wasn't playing with a full deck, that was who.

No surprise, seeing her mother had put Red, aka Autumn, in a tailspin. And of course, that had put Sig in a tailspin. If the Shirleys tried to grab Red again, the whole world would burn. Nothing but scorched earth would remain.

It would be Sig lighting that damn match, even if he burned along with it. If he had to stop breathing to make sure Red continued, he would do it. No one doubted that. All of them feared it.

His love for Red was so damn intense, it was scary.

The fact that he might sacrifice himself to do so worried his brother Trip.

With Red, Trip, his sister Syn, his niece Maya and now his newborn nephew Rush, Sig had too much to live for. Unfortunately, he was so zeroed in on and in sync with his ol' lady that he sometimes forgot there were other people around him who cared for and loved him, too.

The other day in the Walmart parking lot, Red noticed her mother had three young children with her. She also had no doubt they were her half-siblings because they all had bright red hair like Red, who got it from her mother.

Red knew about Ezrah, now about five, but not about the younger two, who appeared to be around three and one. She had no idea what their names were because they had been born after she'd been kidnapped and traded to the Pennsylvania clan to become a sister-wife for one of the Shirley men.

Red only spotted her mother and her children in the group unloading from the van and didn't see her "stepfather" among them. That didn't mean he hadn't come along.

It could simply mean that the women were tasked with doing the shopping.

The Shirley clan believed women had their "place." Bear and raise the children, and, of course, take care of their men. Most of the men had more than one wife, too.

Red didn't understand why her mother, Alice, would be brought to Pennsylvania. Because by now, she had to be getting to the age where she shouldn't have any more babies. She had to be in her late-forties.

But Alice Haas's age wasn't Whip's problem. Or even where her husband Jeb Haas or his other children were.

None of them gave a shit about that.

What Sig cared about was what Red cared about. First, to make sure they weren't there to force Red into reliving her nightmare. Especially after she'd been kidnapped twice by the Shirleys already. Second, her three half-siblings.

Understandably, Red did not want them growing up in that fucked-up environment. She did not want them becoming just like the Shirleys. Even though she didn't know those kids, she still cared about them.

And because Red cared about them, and everyone in The Barn cared about Red, that meant they all cared about those three vulnerable kids, too.

Now the pressure was on Trip to finally make a move. They couldn't wait any longer to see if the feds stepped in or even if they were still keeping their eyes on the clan. They also couldn't wait to see if Manning Grove PD would get involved.

The Fury had no choice but to stomp up that mountain wearing their boots and take action.

Now it wouldn't only be a war to end the Shirleys so they were no longer a threat against the club and Fury family. It would be a "rescue" effort first, then a complete annihilation after.

Where Whip stood in the middle of his restless brothers, nobody surrounding him disagreed with that.

It was time. No more fucking around. The stakes were so high now, they'd hit the fucking moon.

But Trip and Judge were all about doing it right and not doing it recklessly. That was always the fucking sticky part. It would be difficult to decimate the Shirley clan when their numbers were quickly growing and the Fury's were not.

They also were back to the dilemma of what the fuck to do with the women and children. Could everyone in that damn clubhouse live with women and children being collateral damage?

Sig, maybe. The rest? Probably not.

Before the feds had stepped in and cleared out that mountain, the Fury had been slowly taking out their men. But that method had only been a temporary fix since they bred like redneck rabbits. There seemed to be an endless source. Maybe not on that mountain, but elsewhere. Pockets of them. And those pockets were deep.

This was no longer a "wait and see" situation.

Whip was willing to go along with whatever was decided. He might not have an ol' lady or kids to protect but the sisterhood and the Fury kids belonged to the club as a whole. It was the Fury's responsibility to protect them all.

Once he earned his colors, he did not hesitate to get them tattooed onto his back. That meant protecting Fury property also fell on his shoulders, just as much as it did Trip, Judge or Deacon. Anyone who had their own family to protect.

Because when it came down to it, they were all family. *Real* family.

Every damn one of them.

It was the goal Trip had worked for. It was what Trip achieved.

And Whip felt damn lucky to be a part of it.

He never once questioned becoming a prospect. He never once wondered if he should accept his full set of patches.

All of it felt right. From the day Trip walked into Dutch's Garage to inform the Original he was rebuilding the Blood Fury MC down to this very damn second.

Whip belonged.

Sig's loud rant pulled him from his thoughts. "We gotta get those kids. Red wants them out of their fucked-up hands. So, with or without you all, that's gonna happen."

"Jesus, brother, you can't go off all fuckin' half-cocked. Gonna risk yourself, those kids and don't forget how Red's gonna take it if somethin' happens to you," Trip said with a shake of his head. His signature baseball cap was pulled back in place.

How the man had any hair left when he always wore it, with the way he was always raking his fingers through his hair and with all the stress of being the club president, Whip didn't know. He only knew he wouldn't want to be in the man's boots right now. Or ever.

Whip was a man who could follow orders but wasn't up for being a leader. Not everybody was built for that. He wasn't.

It was probably why he'd hooked up with Billie for a while. They were so damn opposite, they should've been on separate planets.

But Billie was what he needed for a little bit. And, luckily, neither suffered hard feelings once Whip decided he'd had enough, or even after she went from being only in his bed to becoming a sweet butt.

The opportunities she found with Whip's brothers made the sadist happy. It also made some of his brothers happy once they stopped crying when she was done with them.

Once she was no longer a regular in Whip's bed, he stopped hooking up with her. He realized what he wasn't into and discovered he preferred the more accommodating ways of some of the softer sweet butts. The ones who wouldn't leave bruises, welts and brush burns.

Whenever he could and she was available, he had hooked up with Lizzy. But only when Ozzy wouldn't be breathing down his neck about it.

He understood why Oz got so bent when Liz left to be with the Dirty Angel named Crash. The older brother had let a good thing slip through his fingers. However, in the end the Original won the lottery with Shay. The introvert balanced the outspoken Ozzy perfectly.

Liz had been the only sweet butt older than Whip. That was when he found he preferred a woman on the more mature side, too. Unlike Saylor, Syn, Reilly, Tessa or any of the remaining sweet butts.

Fuck, now the women he preferred were more like Chelle and Reese. Even Cassie and Shay.

Those were the women he had fantasies about. But he'd take that shit to his grave. He wasn't a dumb fuck with a death wish.

He liked a woman who had experience but wouldn't leave a hurting on him after they were done. There'd been times after spending the night with Billie, he could barely walk. The woman didn't know how to be or do soft.

Whip wanted soft, but he also didn't want spineless.

Even Red and Syn exuded power under their quiet exterior. Survivors. Both of them. And they weren't the only two in the sisterhood.

Quiet power turned him on, but he didn't like to be overpowered. Like Jet and Reese could probably do to their men.

Though, Whip had seen some of the power exchanges between Jet and Rook. Neither were submissive and he could imagine how hot the sex was between them. The bed probably combusted.

Whip wanted that type of fire, but not for it to leave scars.

For fuck's sake, he needed to fucking concentrate and stop his drifting thoughts. The topic was important.

"We take their kids, it'll also put all of ours at risk again. We wanna gamble with that?" Judge asked, standing tall next to Trip.

Sig paused in front of the club's sergeant at arms and he swore the rest of the room took a step back when the VP screamed in Judge's face, "You're the goddamn enforcer! When the fuck you gonna act like it?"

Judge wasn't having any of that bullshit. "You want those kids out, we'll get those fuckin' kids out, Sig. Why the fuck d'you think Trip called this goddamn meetin'?"

Sig was lucky the Grumpy Green Giant didn't just haul off and pop him in the mouth.

Trip clapped his hands sharply. "Christ almighty! We start fightin' amongst ourselves then we're no better than the fuckin' Originals. Yeah?" He glanced around. "Am I right?"

A bunch of *yeahs* rose up.

"Then let's put our goddamn thinkin' caps on instead of snappin' at each other like we're Cujo."

Whip wondered where that little shit was. Maybe Rook had left the three-pound hairy crocodile with Jet since both Jury and Justice, Deacon and Judge's American bulldogs, were present.

The Chihuahua mistakenly thought he could kick those bulldogs' asses.

He was wrong.

The little fucker was lucky that both Jury and Justice were well-trained and would release the bastard on command every time they had enough of Cujo's shit.

One good shake and the squeaky toy would be a goner.

Truthfully, Whip would not miss him.

"We need to put an end to this—to them—once and for

all. Tired of talkin' about it. Now's the time for action," Deacon spoke up. Deke not only had his ol' lady Reese to protect but now his baby boy, Dane.

"It's been months and the feds haven't come out of the woodwork. Even Jet's said nothin's been mentioned in the Bryson household about Hillbilly Hill. That means it's up to us to get the job done," Rook said. "Deke's right, time to put a period on the end of their sentence."

"Speakin' of sentences, don't want any of us catchin' one," Trip reminded them all. "That's my goal. To keep everyone upright, breathin' and also out of the joint."

"We talked about blowin' up that fuckin' mountain. Think we seriously need to consider that," Ozzy said from where he sat on a stool at the end of the bar.

Sig stepped in front of Trip and faced his brother. "Agreed. That's our best option."

"And how the fuck we gonna blow up a goddamn mountain?" Trip shouted. "Anybody? Does anybody in this goddamn room know how to do that? I sure as fuck don't. And, news fuckin' flash, I'm the only one in this damn room with any military experience."

"Don't gotta blow up the whole damn mountain, just enough to make it uninhabitable," Shade said in his quiet but very effective tone.

Even doing that would still take a lot of explosives. "They're redneck roaches," Whip said. "They might be able to survive the apocalypse. Some of them certainly survived the feds."

"Blowin' up their compound and levelin' their buildings will," Rook lifted one finger, "one, be a warnin' that we're done with their shit." He lifted a second one. "Two, it'll make it so much fuckin' harder for them to rebuild."

"But not impossible," Whip said under his breath. Rook caught what he'd whispered and shot him an impatient look.

"Unless we make it so hard for them to rebuild, it ain't worth their time and they move on," Shade said.

"*Riiiiight.* And a fuck-ton of explosives won't bring the fuckin' feds swarmin', right?" Trip ripped off his baseball cap again and, out of habit, scraped his fingers through his longish hair. "Who in here got explosives trainin'? Who in this fuckin' room can afford the cost for the amount we'd need? Who in here wants to be the one purchasin' the shit needed? I got a fuckin' son now. The fuck if I'll go back inside willingly. And you all know what the hell that means."

A murmur moved through the group because they all knew what that meant and most likely felt the same.

Whip had never spent a day inside and never planned on it. He, Judge and Deacon were the only members of the Fury who hadn't. Mostly because of luck, definitely not because they hadn't done anything to deserve it.

Just the shit they'd done to the Shirleys alone would've most likely caught them a lifetime bid in prison.

Trip wasn't done. "Wanna keep my family safe but also wanna be around to raise my son. Want you all to be around to raise your sons and daughters. What we do affects them, too. Let's not forget that."

"Then, what other solution you got?" Dutch called out from the back of the pack. "We're willin' to hear 'em, prez. I got a grandbaby to protect. They touched Duchess once, they ain't touchin' her again, swear to Christ."

Another grumble moved through the agitated group.

Trip blew out a breath. "Get that." He slapped his hat back on his head and scrubbed his hands down his face. "It's a crazy fuckin' idea."

"Don't know how else to do it other than how we intended to do last time before the feds interrupted our plan. Didn't like it then, don't like it now," Judge said.

"Agreed. It was way too fuckin' risky." Trip shook his

head. "And now there are more homes and kids on this property, not to mention our sisterhood has grown."

"Don't know how else to handle them, then," Deacon said. "Poison their water supply?"

"No, that'll be too slow," Rev said next. "We need to hit them hard, hit them fast and hit them all at once."

"Once we get Red's blood out of there," Sig reminded them. "That's gotta happen first."

"That could create a complete fuckin' shitstorm," Easy said, standing next to Whip.

"Not could. Will," Judge confirmed. "Everyone in this fuckin' room knows that."

"The Originals woulda never let this shit get this fuckin' far," Dutch grumbled.

"And that's why only two of you remain. You forget that part?" Trip reminded the oldest Fury member.

"Might have a solution," Judge said more quietly than normal. He was pulling on his long beard since Jury was out of reach.

The Barn went completely silent.

"Let's hear it," Sig demanded, hands on his hips. "Better be a good one, too."

"Fuck you, Sig." The enforcer's response was louder and half a snarl.

Sig's response was a full snarl, reminding Whip of Cujo whenever he got anywhere near the little rat bastard. "No, fuck you, Judge. Been fuckin' sittin' on your ginormous paws not doin' shit, more worried about your kids than this goddamn club. Time for you to do your fuckin' job or step down."

Everyone surrounding Whip took a collective breath and held it.

"You forget you're the VP, Sig?" Judge jabbed a finger toward the ceiling. "You sit at that table, too. So, shut your fuckin' mouth. You don't think I want all this shit over with?

You want me to act like Ox? That what you want? Just rush up that mountain, wreak havoc and say fuck the consequences? 'Cause that would be super fuckin' easy. But you know who it wouldn't be easy for? Our women and children, if we all end up dead or livin' in concrete containers for the rest of our lives. 'Cause with the record you got, you ain't gettin' out next time 'til they haul your ass out in a pine box, wearin' a toe tag."

"So, what's the damn solution, then?" Sig asked.

Judge shook his head. "Need to make a phone call. Ain't gonna say shit yet 'til I know it's a viable solution. Also need to run it past you and Trip first. Think that's the smart way to do it. Gonna take a shitload of scratch, though. Already know that. Don't know how much exactly but I can tell you our asses are gonna be raw for a while."

"All right then, we'll discuss that first and go from there. But no matter what the deal is with your 'solution', it needs to be a final one. And, like Sig said, we need to do somethin' about Red's siblings," Trip reminded the enforcer.

"Thinkin' that's gonna have to happen right before or at about the same time," Judge said. "We go in, do what has to be done and grab the kids at the same time. If we take those kids and then have to wait for part two? Gonna have a war on our hands. We're gonna have to do this shit wham, bam, fuck you ma'am. We need all those roaches on that mountain at the same time when we hit it."

What the fuck was Judge thinking? Whatever it was, it sounded big.

Truth was, they were at the point where they needed to go big or give the fuck up.

"Say we take those kids, who the fuck's gonna raise them?" Trip turned to Sig. "You think about that? You, brother? You and Red gonna take in three fuckin' kids and raise them as your own? Kids we snatched from their damn parents?"

"Won't have to snatch 'em if they all disappear," Sig said. "Like Judge just suggested, hit 'em hard and take them all at the same time. Chaos is a good cover."

"Chaos is dangerous," Trip muttered.

"Organized chaos," Judge said. "Get the kids and whoever else we think needs to be removed, then…"

Boom.

Judge didn't actually say it but he didn't need to. They all heard it in their heads.

"Gonna finally get Red's revenge by killin' that crazy bitch and her even crazier fuckin' husband. If it wasn't for Red convincin' me not to, it would've happened by now 'cause I owe them that. For fuck's sake, do I owe them. They traded Red like a fuckin' broodmare. Gave her to those inbred goat fuckers against her fuckin' will. She was treated like a fuckin' walkin' womb so she could be bred by those toothless militia wannabes and pop out their spawn."

"Still her mother," Trip reminded his brother.

Though, Whip was pretty damn sure the prez wouldn't shed a damn tear if Sig took revenge on the woman who was supposed to love and protect her own, instead of betray her. Instead of put her in harm's way. Instead of turning her into a birthing tool, no better than exactly what Sig said… a broodmare.

"That bitch lost that title the second she got in with that Ohio cult and betrayed her own flesh and blood," Sig shouted.

"Damn right," Deacon agreed.

They all did. Whip could feel the tension ramping up in himself and his brothers.

He could feel it. The end was coming.

But he sure as fuck hoped it was for the Shirleys and not the Fury.

"Was hopin' the feds would have ended this war for us, but knew that would be too fuckin' easy. One thing I've learned, war ain't ever easy." Trip ripped off his black base-ball cap, shook his head and scraped his fingers through his hair again, as was his habit. "Always gotta be another fuckin' battle. Thought I was done with that shit once I got outta the Marines. Thought I was gonna live a peaceful fuckin' life surrounded by family of my own makin'. But now my family's got a threat hangin' over them. Over all of us."

Cage spoke up next. "You know how I feel about it. Dyna and Jem are my goddamn life. Don't wanna risk them again but also don't wanna let those fuckers just live life free and easy, either, while we're always lookin' over our damn shoulders. That ain't a life and that also ain't the Fury way. And anyway, they'll never be done payin' for snatchin' my baby girl or hurtin' Jemma. Never. Not 'til the Shirley name's extinct."

"Problem is the Ohio clan ain't just Shirleys. It wasn't just one family out there like it was on Hillbilly Hill. It was a much bigger community," Sig explained, "with multiple families. They could blend into society a lot better than those mountain goat fuckers."

"Yep, the Guardians of Freedom ain't just in Pennsylvania and Ohio," Judge reminded them. "Their reach is farther than we know. It's like a whole inbred, hillbilly army."

"Too fuckin' stupid to know what's good for them," Dutch grumbled, out of Whip's eyesight.

"Shoulda just stopped at 'too fuckin' stupid,' old man," Rook told his father.

Trip did a single sharp clap. "All right. The committee's goin' upstairs, gonna hear Judge out and we'll go from there. But, promisin' you now, if his idea ain't viable then we'll figure out somethin' else. 'Cause I vow to all of you right here, right now, this shit's gonna end."

A bunch of *fuck yeahs* rose up around Whip. One even escaped his mouth, too.

"Still gotta remain vigilant." Judge was constantly on their asses about that. "Keep the women and kids close. Keep eyes open, ears to the ground. Dodge couldn't get away from Crazy Pete's tonight, but he's also keepin' his ears open for any talk about those fuckers. So are Dozer, Woody and Scar."

"Before we break, you know what we need to do…" Trip started. "From the ashes we rise…"

The prez raised his arms and the rest of them raised their voices to call out, "For our brothers we live and die!"

Whip hoped to fuck none of them had to die.

He had complete confidence that Trip and Judge would do their best to keep that from happening.

Chapter Two

Whip let up on the throttle of the bike he was currently straddling. He refused to call it a sled because it was a Yamaha. A "real" sled was a Harley Davidson or even an Indian. American made. With a deep rumble that could make a woman squirm.

He grinned as the customer's bike slowed. Leaning over slightly, he listened carefully to make sure the tapping noise from the engine was gone.

Fuck yeah, it was. He was a pro at fixing anything with an engine, two wheels and handlebars.

Dutch always rode his ass by calling him an "idiotic savage" instead of an "idiot savant," even though Whip knew deep down inside the old man secretly appreciated his mechanical skills.

Was he an idiot? Sometimes. But wasn't everyone? Neither Dutch or his two sons, Rook and Cage, were any kind of geniuses, that was for damn sure.

The ball busting was to be expected and nobody took offense. To work at Dutch's, thick skin was required. Actually, more like Teflon. Quick reflexes were also needed to avoid getting clocked by a flying wrench when Dutch lost his shit.

The Yamaha, owned by a long-time customer, was old enough to be a classic and came into the shop regularly. Usually the customer brought it in right before riding season for Whip to go over it from fender to fender to make sure it weathered the winter okay. But this time when he started it, the engine had a little *rat-a-tat-tat.*

Now it was as quiet as a mouse. Dutch would be happy that it had been a quick fix so Whip could move on to the next repair on his clipboard.

Every time one of them had to take a vehicle on a long test drive, they'd been taking it out of town, down Copperhead Road and past the lane heading up Hillbilly Hill.

They didn't drive up the lane but if they spotted any activity from the road, they immediately notified Trip or Judge, who were working on some sort of plan they had come up with after that last church meeting.

So far, they hadn't shared that plan with the rest of them yet.

They said they would once it was solid. Whip had no reason to doubt that.

He twisted the accelerator again and sped out of town. He wore his baseball cap backwards so he wouldn't lose it and dark shades protected his eyes from the sun, bugs and debris as he shot down the back country road, heading toward the mountain.

Every time he approached that dirt lane with the multitude of hand-painted, grossly misspelled "no trespassing or else" signs, the little hairs on the back of his neck stood and ice slithered down his spine. Today was no different, even though the weather was warming up.

Spring was in the air and the organized, now bi-monthly club runs had started back up. Something they always all looked forward to since it was a time to relax and bond with their brothers. Every club run reminded him of a family reunion, especially now that the family was growing like crazy.

He turned onto Copperhead Road and slowed down again, his eyes scanning the woods as he rode. The trees weren't full of leaves yet, but they would be soon, making it more difficult to see anything on that hill.

Even when the trees were bare, the compound was too far up to see it from the road. But for now? They were looking for anything out of the ordinary or even men hidden in the woods with long guns that would poke a few holes through him or his brothers.

Whip already had enough holes in his body, he preferred not to add any extra.

Once the Shirleys were gone, the club should buy the property. He doubted the deed was in the Shirleys' name and if it was, they certainly didn't pay any fucking property taxes since they believed taxation was theft.

Maybe the Fury could buy it from the county for the back taxes owed. He'd have to suggest that to Trip or Sig. If the club owned it, then nobody could rebuild on it. And by nobody, he meant the Shirleys or any other clans from the stupid as fuck Guardians of Freedumb.

Once the mountain was safe and secure, it would be kind of cool to build a place up there in the woods instead of dropping a modular home on top of a foundation in the little neighborhood that was growing on the farm. The field on the other side of the tree line was turning into a mini-suburbia. He expected white picket fences and swing sets to appear next.

Christ, that made Whip's stomach churn. He didn't want to think about settling down like the majority of his brothers. Especially with an ol' lady and kids. He wasn't even twenty-nine yet. Not for another couple of weeks.

So, fuck the house with a white picket fence. A mountain

retreat similar to what Reese owned outside of Mansfield would be so much more badass.

Could Whip afford a place like Reese's? Fuck no, but a small cabin up in the woods might be within his price range. It only needed to be big enough for him. As long as Trip wouldn't have a fit about him moving out of the bunkhouse and off the farm.

The Fury prez might have a problem with the second part more than the first.

Living in the bunkhouse had both its good points and bad. He had easy access to the stocked kitchen and bar, he had constant company if he wanted it, and with only one word he could get a sweet butt to clean his room or suck his dick.

The bad was not much privacy and his room was a claustrophobic box with an even tinier shitter. Basically, he stared at four walls without even a window. Whip imagined it was similar to living in a jail cell. The big exception being he was free to come and go as he damn well pleased. He couldn't imagine not being able to escape when those same four walls began to close in on him.

But currently, he was free with the wind in his face and his knees in the breeze, even if he wasn't riding his own sled. He slowed down further as he approached the long dirt lane, still searching for anything worth reporting.

He saw nothing. Usually he noticed at least an animal or two scurrying through the underbrush. This time he saw no movement, not one new damn thing, not even a squirrel.

At least until he came around the bend close to the spot where they hid their vehicles when they hoofed it up the mountain to do a little spying.

His heart paused before doing a complete reboot at the unexpected sight of another bike. It sat by itself in a narrow, dirt pull-off just prior to their hiding spot.

He didn't recognize it. Dutch's Garage was the only

place the locals brought their motorcycles since that was what they specialized in. This one had to belong to someone passing through.

He glanced up the mountain again. He never once saw one of the Shirleys riding one.

Unless this was a trap.

Fuck.

It *could* be a trap.

He twisted the Yamaha's throttle harder and, as he zipped past the bike and its helmeted rider in case it *was* a trap, more ice slithered down his spine.

That Indian Scout Bobber looked brand fucking new. It shouldn't have broken down already unless that rider beat the fuck out of it and didn't treat such a sweet ride with respect.

Fuck that guy if he didn't. He didn't deserve that ride or Whip's help.

After he shot past the pull-off, he noticed the rider was squatting on the opposite side of the bike.

Who didn't take off a damn restrictive brain bucket once they dismounted, especially when it was warm out? No one he knew.

Unless someone didn't want to be recognized. That made it seem even more suspicious.

He slowed down once he was clear and glanced in the side mirror. The Indian had fiberglass saddlebags mounted on both sides and another large travel bag made specifically for motorcycles strapped to the seat behind where the rider planted his ass.

Definitely someone traveling.

Both the newer sled and the quality accessories screamed expensive. The Shirleys didn't have that kind of scratch.

Then it hit him who did.

The fucking feds.

Did a federal agent pretend to break down? Is that why he still wore his helmet? That pull-off was the perfect spot to keep track of anyone going up or coming down that lane.

Fuck, if it was the feds, they would need to table Judge's "Shirley solution." Whatever it was.

Before the next rise in the road, he slowed to a stop, planted his boots on the pavement and stared into the side mirror on his left.

The person with the bike was now standing, the tinted full face shield pointed in Whip's direction.

"Christ," Whip said under his breath and gave the Yamaha a little gas. He did a U-turn and headed back. "Better not fuckin' regret this."

Maybe he could flush out whether the person was a fed or not. It would be better to know that info before reporting it to Judge or Trip. Especially if the sled truly turned out to be broken down. He didn't want to get them up in arms if there wasn't a good reason for it.

He was a bike mechanic. A knowledgeable one. Out of anyone, he would know if that person's ride was truly disabled or not, or if the rider was lying. Right now it fell on his shoulders to find out who this person was or wasn't.

While it could be risky, if it was a fed, they probably wouldn't place Whip as part of the Fury since he wasn't wearing his cut but the coveralls he normally wore while working at the garage.

Yep, right now, he could pass off as some dumb, but helpful, local hick.

He parked at the far end of the pull-off, heeled the kick-stand down and shut off the Yamaha. Before he was even done throwing a leg over the bike, the "stranded" person was yanking off his helmet.

Only he wasn't a he.

He was a she.

The helmet had hidden a woman and as soon as it was

lifted clear, she shook out her blonde chin-length hair. Whip found himself transfixed as the silky strands swept back and forth.

What. The. Fuck?

Not just any she, either.

His eyes scanned her from head to toe. How did he miss it? It had to be because of the shapeless waterproof windbreaker she was wearing or the fact she'd been squatting down behind the bike when he first passed by.

Or because he really *was* a dumb hick.

Because damn… He now had no doubts at all that the rider was a fucking woman.

And what a woman she was.

She carefully balanced her helmet on top of the travel bag and turned with hands on curvy hips hard to miss now that he was much closer and paying better attention. When her blue eyes hit him, they hit him hard and seemed to rip a hole right through his chest.

He rubbed absently at the unexpected and strange ache.

She was no typical biker chick.

Not even close.

Once again, that made him think she might be a fed. Shirleys would never expect the government to plant a female agent at the bottom of their mountain. To them, females were only good for two things, breeding and raising young, plus taking care of the menfolk.

Sure as shit not riding a beautiful Indian Scout Bobber Twenty, one of Whip's dream bikes. Though, he did have a pretty long list of sleds he wanted to one day own. He had plenty of time and many miles of open road to check those off his list.

He shoved his bucket list to the back of his mind and concentrated on what and who was in front of him. Both the Scout and the woman made his dick twitch. Federal agent or not.

Focus, fool. You need to flush out whether this is a real breakdown or a set-up.

He cleared his throat to make sure his voice didn't crack before he warned, "Ain't smart to be here."

"I'm sure it's not," she murmured, once again squatting down next to her bike and fiddling with something underneath it.

"You should leave."

She released a long sigh. "I would if I could."

He detected a bit of frustration in her words. Was he screwing up her assignment? "Why can't you?"

She remained in a squat but twisted on her toes toward him, lifting a finger in the air.

Fuck. Her fingertip was covered in oil.

Still could be a trap. How hard was it to make it look like your sled was leaking oil? Not fucking hard at all.

Unlike his dick.

He never thought a woman who rode her own sled would turn him on. Guess he learned something new today.

"I was behind a dump truck a few miles back. I realized too late it was losing some of its load." Her face twisted. "A load of stone that wasn't covered, I'll add. I didn't see the large rock flying toward me until it was too late for me to swerve and miss it. It hit the front hard but I didn't think it did much damage." She shrugged. "I expected a dent on the front fender but I guess I was wrong and it did more damage than I thought. Or more than one rock hit us."

Those little hairs on his neck perked up again and Whip quickly glanced around. "Us?" *Fuck.* Was someone hiding in the woods ready to take him down?

"Me and her," she tipped her head toward the bike. "My riding partner, Agnes."

Agnes?

One, who the fuck named their sled? And two, who the fuck named it Agnes? The woman standing before him, apparently that was who. That name reminded him of some old granny who sat in a plaid upholstered rocking chair handing out butterscotch candies, not that beautiful machine she rode.

"Lucky it didn't hit you. Coulda taken you out or at least made you wreck."

"Yes," she said softly, sounding distracted as she stared down at her ride, her mouth tight and her shoulders now slumped slightly.

Disappointed, maybe even defeated.

But it could all be a damn act. He still wasn't convinced yet that she wasn't an undercover fed. "Beautiful sled."

Her eyes lifted and her brow furrowed. "Sled?"

He got stuck for a second on how damn blue her sight balls were. Like the Caribbean, even though he never saw it in person, only in pictures. But damn... They could suck you in and drown you just like that vibrant sea. "Bike."

When her brow dropped low, little creases appeared across her forehead. "I never heard it called that before. Is that a local thing?"

"It's a biker thing."

She digested that for a second as she inspected him from head to toe, then jerked her chin toward the Yamaha. "You don't wear a helmet?"

"Don't need a helmet in PA."

"I know. Just because it's legal to go without doesn't mean you should."

An automatic and sarcastic "Okay, Mom," almost slipped from him but luckily he caught it in time. It was the same damn argument he had with his mother each and every damn time he pulled into her driveway.

"Just think what damage could've been done if I hadn't been wearing one and one of those rocks hit me in the face."

He studied that face. "Yeah, woulda been a real fuckin'

shame," he murmured under his breath. She could have ended up just as toothless as the occupants of Hillbilly Hill. Or worse, dead.

His gaze flicked up the mountain. If she wasn't a fed, where they were parked made them sitting ducks. But he wasn't convinced yet that she wasn't undercover and that the damage wasn't fake.

He was damn sure the feds could set up some pretty realistic traps or undercover schemes. He just didn't want to be the one caught in it.

Because of that, he casually walked around the bike like he was searching for more damage than an oil leak, and while he actually wanted to do that, he also wanted to check out her license plate on the rear.

His eyes flicked to the Illinois plate then back to the blonde still standing with her hands on her hips. She tilted her head to the side and watched him with those eyes that most likely did not miss a damn thing.

Fuck no, he had a feeling it would be hard to get anything past her.

"You could have asked."

Did her lips actually twitch? He smothered his grin and shrugged one shoulder. "Was just curious since you ain't from around here."

"Is it that obvious?"

"Yeah, since I woulda seen you around before. Manning Grove ain't that big."

She looked past him toward the direction he'd come from. "You mean that town I rode through earlier?"

"Yeah."

"It's... quaint."

Among other things. "Certainly is that."

He slid his sunglasses off his face and tucked them into the neckline of his coveralls. He then sidled up next to her and got down on his hands and knees in the dirt and gravel to give her Scout a better look.

There it was. A dent and small puncture in the oil pan that accounted for the leak. He got up, brushed his hands off on his coveralls, then moved around to the front, squatting down and giving it a good once-over. He found a small dent in the front fender, too.

That fucking sucked. Brand new bike and it was already damaged. He could replace the oil pan but he didn't do body work. No one at Dutch's Garage did.

Then he heard it. The slightest hiss.

He ran his calloused fingers along her front tire and found where that was leaking, too.

Christ. A fucked tire and a damaged oil pan. She wasn't taking that sled anywhere except for repairs.

"You're both stuck and fucked," he got back to his feet to face her, once again wiping his hands across his chest on his coveralls, "'cause you got a hole in your tire, too."

She sighed and dragged fingers through her already messy hair making it look like she just had six orgasms and was ready to light a cigarette. Or change the batteries in her abused vibrator. Because he had a feeling this woman didn't invite just anyone in her...

Bed.

He pursed his lips wondering what it took to snag that spot. She probably had way higher standards than someone like Whip. Just by her classy looks, he could tell she preferred older, successful suits that drove cages that cost more than most homes. Not mechanics in grease-stained coveralls with dirty fingernails who lived in a dorm-like room in a shared bunkhouse.

"Do you have any suggestions on what I can do about that around here?"

But maybe she'd be into doing a little test drive. He was

young, pretty damn flexible and willing to take pointers if she was willing to give them.

Normally, he wasn't into short hair even though Billie always kept hers super short. And while the blonde's hair was also shorter than he normally liked, it fit her and didn't look butch. Especially with the way it was cut at an angle to follow her jawline. It was still long enough for a man to get a good handful and pull.

Being in a helmet for hours upon hours had messed it up and the "just fucked" look made it look sexy as hell.

His dick decided now was a great time to remind him that he hadn't taken advantage of the sweet butts in the last couple of days.

He needed to get on that.

It was much easier to find an available one now that the single brothers numbers were dwindling, even with the two prospects being patched over last December. After Liz left, five sweet butts remained, matching the same number of patched brothers available. Him, Easy, Dozer, Dutch and Woody.

And now Crystal was Stella and Trip's house mouse to help take care of baby Rush and no longer considered a sweet butt.

Damn. Only five Fury members were left standing.

It would still be a few months before the three remaining prospects were patched over. If they even were. Castle and Bones would, Whip had no doubt.

Scar? That scary bastard was questionable.

"No?"

No, what? *Ah, fuck.* "Got an idea." One that would work in his favor either way.

One perfectly shaped eyebrow rose. "Want to share?"

"I work on sleds."

She stared at him.

"Bikes," he clarified.

"I understood that part, but I'm waiting for the rest. You said you work on them. Like at a shop? Or in your backyard?"

"At a garage. I'm a bike mechanic. Well, I'm a mechanic in general but I'm good with bikes."

"Just good?"

"Don't wanna brag."

She snorted softly. "I'm sure I'll need someone *great* with bikes."

"All right, then. I'm great."

She smiled and if his dick could smile, it would be, too.

"Own it if you mean it."

That was a good philosophy but he hadn't wanted to sound cocky, but okay, then… "Best in the area."

"Well, then my bad luck just turned," she said.

Maybe Whip's luck had turned, too. As long as she wasn't from the government.

The way she spoke, her confidence, the way her hair was cut… She didn't seem the typical biker chick. Especially with the cost of her sled and equipment. Even her helmet. She had the best. But put her in a suit, heels and some lipstick and she'd fit perfectly in a boardroom full of powerful people.

Not on some back mountain road by herself.

He reminded himself that feds also wore suits. And from what he'd seen, the women tended to have short hair.

Even though he wasn't quite getting that vibe, he shouldn't let his guard down. Not yet. The feds still could've set her up at the bottom of Hillbilly Hill, making it look like the damage had been done with rocks. A hammer and a metal hole punch could cause the same.

His thought process was that if she wasn't, she'd have no problem with him getting her Scout hauled back to the shop. If she was, she'd fight it.

If she fought it, red flags would be whipping wildly in the wind.

"Well," he started, once again glancing around to make sure he wasn't overlooking anything. "Got a solution."

"Yes, you said that already and I'm all ears."

"I can haul you back to the garage on the Yamaha. Then we can come back with the flatbed to take," he couldn't make himself call the damn thing Agnes, "your Scout to the shop."

"I don't want to leave Agnes behind. I can wait with her while you get the flatbed."

Shit.

He slipped his shades from where he'd tucked them, and slid them back onto his face. "Ain't gonna leave you here."

Both eyebrows rose. "I don't think that's your choice."

She was probably one of those women who didn't like a man telling her what to do. Too bad. Right now she had no choice unless she wanted to stay stranded alongside a back country road. Even if she called her own tow truck, they'd drop her and her sled off at Dutch's. All the towing companies in the surrounding area did.

But now he was rethinking the whole vibe she was giving off. He couldn't be too careful. "Look... Got a spot right over there where we can hide it 'til we get back with the roll-back. It'll be safe there."

"Do you think it's safer for me to get on the back of a bike with a stranger than to wait here?"

He glanced up the mountain again. "Yeah. This road's kinda desolate. Never know who might come across you here by yourself." *Like a fuckin' Shirley who could kidnap you, lock you in a damn shed and then strap you down to a damn breedin' bench like they did with Red.*

Fed or not, he kept that shit to himself.

"You don't think I can protect myself?"

"That ain't the point." Federal agents could protect

themselves. He wasn't liking the way this conversation was going.

"Let me get this straight. I'm supposed to trust you but not others who might drive down this road?"

Well, fuck her and the possible badge she wore, then. "I'm offerin' you help. Either you fuckin' want it or you don't. Ain't here to argue about it."

"I don't know who you are—"

He cut her off since he was getting annoyed. And that took a lot for him. "Don't know who you fuckin' are, either."

"It wouldn't be smart to drive off with a stranger."

He pursed his lips and considered that. If he was a woman stranded along a mountain road, he might not hop on the bike of a stranger, either. At least not without confirming who he was first.

He had to admit that *was* smart on her part and a good excuse to give him.

She asked, "What's the name of the shop?"

"Dutch's Garage. Right on Main Street. West side of town."

She pulled a cell phone from the pocket of her windbreaker and held it up. "Do you mind if I confirm that first?"

He shrugged. "Do what you gotta do." *Just get doin' it.*

She tipped her head down and her messy medium-length hair covered her face as she quickly tapped on the screen.

At least Dutch's had a website now that Shay, Ozzy's ol' lady, made them one. The woman could confirm that he worked there just by looking at the large photo on the main page. All five of them had lined up out front while wearing their coveralls for Shay to take the photo. Even dick-dog Cujo had gotten in on it.

Her bottom lip was caught between her teeth when she

lifted her eyes from the screen to him, dropped them back to the screen, then glanced at him once more.

He gave her his signature smirk. The one the ladies liked. "See me in that pic?"

"I do," she murmured.

"See that garage behind where we're all standin'?"

"Yes."

"See that cranky old fuck all the way on the right? He's Dutch."

"Dutch," she repeated softly, glancing back down. She hit the side button on her phone and tucked it back into her jacket pocket. "And you are?"

He jutted out his hand. "Whip."

"Whip?" She placed her much more delicate one in his and shook it firmly. She did not give him one of those damn limp washrag shakes like some women did.

No, confidence oozed from her pores. In the way she stood, the way she spoke and in that handshake.

Again, could that be a sign she was a fed? The real test would be if she straddled the Yamaha behind him.

He pointed to the small oval patch on his coveralls that had his nickname on it. "Yeah, Whip."

Her eyebrows pulled low. "Is that your real name?"

"No. And if you tell me yours, we'll no longer be strangers."

"That's really not how it works," she said with a shake of her head but amusement crinkling the corners of her mesmerizing blue eyes.

"Why? Now you know the name I go by and if I know yours, then that means we know each other."

She barked out a husky laugh and that drew his attention to her mouth. "A simple but very imperfect premise."

If she was wearing lipstick or any kind of makeup it was pretty fucking subtle. Unlike how the sweet butts slapped it on. Whenever the sweet butts sucked his dick, they left lipstick rings around it that were a pain in the ass to remove.

He shrugged and grinned. "Gonna need your name once we get back to the garage anyway when I write up your work order."

"That's certainly true." She tipped her head to the side and considered him a moment before saying, "I'm Fallon. Nice to meet you, Whip."

Fallon. He'd never heard that name before. "That a nickname?"

"No, it's what's on my birth certificate."

"How 'bout your last name?"

"That's on my birth certificate, too."

It was his turn to bark out a laugh. She had a sharp sense of humor. He liked that. Fed or not, he was quickly becoming more interested in her than he should be. Especially since she probably wouldn't be interested in him at all.

Even though he had no idea how old she was, he had a feeling he was younger than her, too.

Not that it mattered, she would be a customer.

And again, by looking at her, she didn't seem to be the type who wouldn't mind spending some time in a small bed in a small room in a bunkhouse on a farm full of bikers.

He was out of her league for sure. *Fuck.*

If he swung that bat, he was sure as fuck going to miss. Or maybe even hit a foul ball. But a homerun? Probably not possible.

Yeah, he was in the minor leagues.

Whip reminded himself his only focus should be on getting the two of them off Copperhead Road, away from the Shirley Clan and back to the garage.

"I still want to know about the name Whip."

"When I was little my grandfather used to call me Whippersnapper and he eventually shortened it to Whip. It stuck."

"You like it?"

"Like that it reminds me of my pap." And "whip" was also slang for a car, something he worked on, so it fit. He also liked it a hell of lot more than Sparky, the name Dutch always used to bust his balls and Trip forced him to keep as a prospect.

She smiled softly. "That's really sweet. Is he still around?"

The sudden ache in his chest made him suck in a breath. "No." He didn't want to get pulled back to that day. That was what usually happened when he thought about his grandfather. After that fateful day, his mother had moved them out of his pap's house and in with his aunt.

"What's your real name?"

Her question drew him out of the past. "Here's the deal... You don't get that 'til after we deliver your Scout back to the shop. Yeah?"

Her lips curled up slightly at the ends. "Oh, I see. A little bit of blackmail."

"Ain't gonna deny it. But here's the rest of the deal... Ain't leavin' you here. Tellin' you it's for your safety to not stay behind."

Her smile disappeared and she glanced around. "This road really isn't safe?"

"Ain't the road, but who lives on it."

"Who lives on it?"

"People who you do wanna remain strangers with. Trust me."

"That doesn't sound good."

"It ain't good," he confirmed.

"Okay," she sighed, grabbing her helmet off her luggage. "Where's this hiding spot you speak of and how do you know about it?"

Chapter Three

He never did explain how he knew about the hiding spot before he pushed Agnes off the road and hid her. That spot was so well hidden with trees, brush and evergreen bushes, Fallon's bike would never be seen if someone drove past.

She had pulled her helmet back over her head and waited for the cute mechanic with the very sexy smirk to mount the Yamaha. Once he did, he waited for her to climb on behind him.

Cute was the perfect way to describe him because he seemed young. His mannerisms, his sloppy speech, his slang, his... She mentally sighed... *everything*.

Young or not, that smirk could make most women's toes curl and panties melt.

Including hers.

And that caught her off guard.

At this point in her life she thought she was beyond falling for a cute boy.

Or cute guy. Or even a handsome man.

Attraction had to do with more than looks.

She wasn't one who was normally attracted to men younger than her, either. In the past, when she'd occasionally dated, she had done so within her circle. Successful businessmen. Men who put their wealth above everything else.

But then, at the time, she had the same mindset, so of course, she'd been drawn to the same. Now, those same men turned her off.

She wanted authentic with a personality, a sense of humor and a heart of gold. Someone easy to talk to and not self-absorbed. A man who wasn't hyper-focused on his success and forgot that a whole world existed outside his bubble.

She admitted she had forgotten that last one, too.

But then, dating had actually become a luxury and not a necessity as she focused on her career and climbing that damn slippery ladder while keeping her eyes on the prize at the very top. Only to take a size ten Tom Ford dress shoe to the chest as they knocked her back down.

Who the hell was she to think she deserved the top spot reserved for a man?

An "overachiever." Someone who was "trying to sleep her way to the top." A "bitch." Those were only some of the whispers she heard. She couldn't imagine what she didn't hear.

Apparently, women never got ahead on their own merits. From their hard work and dedication. From their intelligence and management skills.

Sure.

What a bunch of misogynist bullshit.

Unfair? Of course.

Would it ever change in her lifetime? Probably not. At least not to the extent it should.

All the women who had come before her breaking that glass ceiling and all who would come after her would move the needle. But only a fraction. That glass was pretty damn thick.

What was even more disturbing was other women could

be extremely catty about any woman more successful than them. Instead of being supportive, they were undermining and toxic.

Instead of paving the road for future women leaders, they took a jackhammer to it to create obstacles.

It didn't make any damn sense.

Fallon's road to success had been a threat to both women and men alike.

She knew climbing that ladder would be a challenge, a lot of hard work and dedication. She just didn't realize how many people would want to kick her off that damn ladder along the way.

It didn't matter now.

She was free from all that.

All that she worked for… gone.

Well, not all of it…

She had Agnes. Though, right now, Agnes wasn't feeling herself. She needed a bit of TLC.

She was glad that the Yamaha had a backrest for the passenger, similar to Agnes's setup—what Whip had called the sissy bar—so she wouldn't have to hang on to the mechanic.

She'd never ridden on the back of a bike. She'd never even rode a bike until she bought Agnes and took a safety class. No one she knew owned a motorcycle, so the whole experience had been new.

Freeing.

Perfect, actually. Until now.

Poor Agnes.

Fallon hoped she'd be up and running as soon as possible so they could continue on their journey.

To find her true self.

To figure out what direction she went next.

Or, *hell*, maybe she'd just ride off into the sunset and never worry about her future again.

She'd "just be." Simply exist and do whatever the hell she wanted. She'd follow the wind whatever direction it blew. She'd chase every sunrise and sunset. She'd swim with the tides. Climb one mountain and ski down another.

She had cut those corporate chains that had kept her bound. She was no longer a slave to a computer, to her phone, to anyone.

She'd "just be."

Happy.

Healthy.

Free.

A new Fallon who didn't answer to anyone or anything anymore.

Well, she'd been traveling along that path until she hit this bump in the road.

A bump she could deal with. However, her guess was it wouldn't be cheap or quick. It would take time and money. Good thing she had plenty of both.

This was a slight inconvenience she could easily deal with since she was no longer held to any expectations, no longer had to attend scheduled meetings, and definitely no longer had to be present at appointments.

A smile spread over her face and Fallon took a long, deep, relaxed breath as she stood outside Dutch's Garage near where the young mechanic had parked the Yamaha. He had told her to wait there while he went and brought the rollback around from out back.

She offered to follow him inside to give the secretary her information but he said she could do it when they returned with Agnes.

Well, he didn't call Agnes by her name. He kept calling her a sled.

A sled.

So damn strange but kind of quirky. She wondered how that name came to be since when she heard the word sled, she thought about the kind of sleds kids rode down snowy hills.

In the end, it wasn't important.

Nothing was more important than getting Agnes repaired, getting back on the road and heading to the next destination, wherever the road led her. Hopefully this time in one piece.

She glanced toward the garage and the open bay door Whip disappeared through. He wasn't standing there but some other guys were, including the bushy bearded garage owner she recognized from the picture.

Three other mechanics, all wearing coveralls similar to Whip's, hovered just inside the open doorway, all staring in her direction. She never saw such a handsome crew of mechanics before at the dealership she used to take her vehicles for service.

She turned to face them directly, returned their once-over, shot them a huge smile and gave them an exaggerated wave. Laughter escaped her as they suddenly scattered like roaches when someone flipped on a light, apparently finding something to do.

Were they not used to outsiders around here? When she mapped out today's route last night, she swore she was near the Pennsylvania Grand Canyon and if so, they should be used to hikers, mountain bikers and even tourists who chased the changing autumn leaves.

She shrugged to herself and looked up. The warm sun, clear blue sky and unexpected laughter were so damn soothing to the soul.

Maybe her career didn't turn out quite as she had expected. But, honestly, this was so much better, even with a broken-down bike. She counted herself lucky that she could toss everything else aside and "just be."

Yes, even though today had a slight hiccup, she was still so damn lucky. She was learning to appreciate the little things and not get stuck on the things that didn't matter.

Her attention was drawn to a noisy rollback coming around the corner of the garage. Whip pulled up next to her and yelled over the engine noise and through the open passenger-side window. "Get in."

Get in.

She climbed onto the step, opened the passenger door and, using the vertical metal handle next to the door, hauled herself up and into the cab.

The rig was far from new and the interior stunk like gas and old motor oil. Wrappers and empty cups were strewn along the passenger-side floorboard, as well as clipboards and messy papers covering the dashboard.

She squeaked in surprise when she sat on something hard hidden under a piece of paper and yanked whatever it was from under it. She held it up.

Before she could figure out what it was, Whip snatched it from her fingers.

"What is it?" she asked him.

He fisted it. "Just a mint tin."

"Oh." She snagged it back and opened it. "I could use a…" She lifted her gaze to Whip. "Mint."

He shrugged.

She lifted the tin to her nose. "Is that tobacco?"

"Mmm hmm," he mumbled.

The tin had several hand-rolled cigarettes inside. She didn't know many people who smoked anymore, but she did know those who still did tended to buy tobacco in bulk and hand-roll their own. Never being a smoker herself, she wasn't sure if it had to do with the quality or the cost.

She took another whiff.

No, it wasn't tobacco. It had a different type of pungent odor.

She quickly snapped the lid shut. "Is this yours?"

"Nope."

His baseball cap was now turned forward with the bill pulled low and he wore his sunglasses making it hard to read his expression.

"That's pot, right?"

He ran his fingers down his cheek. "Nah."

His face was baby smooth and wrinkle-free. The only part that wasn't smooth was his tightly trimmed beard. It wasn't a typical beard—something she normally wasn't into —but one that was so short it could be considered a five-o'clock shadow. Or scruff. She wasn't sure of the term. The way he had it, his cheeks were shaved bare and at first glance his facial hair appeared more like a goatee. On closer look, the short wiry hairs followed along his jawline.

He had just enough scruff on his face to make him not look like he was twenty. Though, she wasn't sure how much past twenty he was. Her estimation was he had to be at least twenty-five. But if he was even thirty yet, she'd be surprised.

She shouldn't even be focused on that. She should be focused on getting Agnes back to the shop and then getting back on the road.

A head popping up and into the open driver's side window had her biting back a surprised gasp.

It was the owner of the garage. Now *his* salt-and-pepper beard, heavy on the salt, was long and shaggy, definitely not Fallon's taste. And unlike Whip, the older man had plenty of creases decorating his face to show his age. She guessed he might be in his early sixties. If he was younger than that, he'd lived a hard life.

"Don't you fuck up this rollback, idiot," he growled, "or I'll take it outta your pay."

"Not gonna fuck it up," Whip assured him. He twisted, grabbed the tin still in her fingers and shoved it at the older man. "You forgot this. Good thing she found it instead of one of the pigs when you're towin' one of the pig mobiles."

Pigs? Pig mobiles? Why would a garage haul around pigs?

Dutch took the tin and swatted the air. "Bah. They ain't fuckin' up their contract with us over a little weed. They got it good here and they know it."

"Right," Whip muttered. "Now get off the step before I put it in gear, knock you the fuck off and you break a hip."

The old man's eyes landed on Fallon, stuck for a few seconds, then sliced back to Whip. He pursed his lips, yanked on his beard and smiled.

Even Fallon could see a whole lot of things went unsaid in both his eyes and that smile. Things she didn't want to begin to unpack.

"Get the fuck off the truck, Dutch," Whip said more firmly. "Before I actually go through with it."

"And your ass would be fired."

Whip shrugged. "Trip will hire me for the repo business instead and you'll be missing your best bike mechanic."

Dutch's tightly pressed together lips got lost in the overgrown hair around his mouth. "Don't fuck it up," he said again, tapped his palm on the bottom of the window frame and disappeared.

Whip glanced in the large side mirror, probably to make sure his boss was clear.

"Why is he worried about you screwing up the rollback?"

"I normally don't run it," Whip answered. "Dutch does."

"Then, why are you doing it now?"

"Trust me, you don't wanna ride with him." He shot her another one of those panty-melting smirks.

"Why?"

Whip's smirk disappeared, he scratched the back of his neck, then shook his head. "Just trust me."

"Hard to trust someone I just met," she murmured.

Even though she had to trust him enough to climb on the back of the Yamaha and also into the tow truck with him.

She wasn't getting the crazy psycho stalker vibe from him. Far from that.

He pushed in the clutch, shoved the rollback into gear but kept his feet on the brake and clutch pedals. He glanced over at her. "True."

Hmm.

The way he said that sounded like he might not trust *her* for some reason.

"You never did explain how you knew about that hiding spot," she said, as he released the clutch and the rollback surged forward with a jerk.

"Didn't I?" He kept his eyes on the road.

"No."

"Just a hidin' spot all us locals know."

"Then it's not a hiding spot if everyone knows about it."

His eyes flicked to her and then back to the road, his lips pressed just as tightly as Dutch's had been.

Interesting.

But in the scheme of things, did it really matter how he knew about the spot or why he was avoiding an explanation? No, it didn't.

That was one of the small things she was learning to let go of.

Knowing the whys and hows of where they hid Agnes would not change the outcome of her life.

In less than an hour, they were back at that spot, he had Agnes loaded and strapped down, and then they were back at the garage with not much more conversation between them besides him explaining what he'd do with Agnes once they got back.

Though, she did have to force herself to stare out of the windshield instead of at him, for some reason, as he spoke.

Why was he so damn cute?

Worse, every time he shot her one of his smirks, butter-flies fought to escape her stomach.

What was she? Sixteen all over again?

No, *damn it*, she was thirty-six. *You're way past the point of high school crushes, Fallon.*

Now she sat in the office on the other side of the secretary's desk. It turned out, the young blonde wasn't actually the garage secretary per se but the manager of another business. She only used the office because her boyfriend or husband, or whatever he was, was one of the mechanics in the shop. She also helped out Dutch's business, too.

While Whip put Agnes on a lift and gave her a good examination, Reilly, who was a very sweet but funny smart ass, told her all about Shelter from the Storm with a whole bunch of pride in her voice and eyes. It was nice to see a woman under thirty who was starting off in business with dreams and expectations to build it into a success.

They went down the rabbit hole of discussing marketing and advertising with Fallon giving her tips and suggestions. She couldn't help but get caught up in the woman's excitement.

This was how Fallon was, too, when she first started out. However, it was not how it ended. She hoped Reilly's dreams for building the business came to fruition and she had people around her to support her and not knock her down.

Unlike a lot of others, Fallon loved to see women succeed.

She tried to help other women in her organization on her rise up the ladder, but every time she did, she ended up regretting it. Mostly, because she got tired of pulling knives out of her own back.

But the emergency housing business idea was genius. It turned out Reilly had a business degree and was happy to finally put it to good use.

When her very handsome boyfriend popped into the office, Reilly introduced Rev as her "old man."

Fallon didn't quite get it. Once he left the office again, she mentioned, "He seems very young to be calling him your old man."

Reilly's laughter filled the space around them as she fell back in her chair. "Ol' man. Without the D."

Fallon's brow pulled low. "I don't understand." This area of northern Pennsylvania must have its own language.

Reilly waved a hand toward the open office door. "All those guys out there?"

Fallon shot a glance in that direction. "Yes?"

"They all belong to an MC."

Maybe she needed one of those translation dictionaries to be in this part of Pennsylvania. She was far from dumb but was starting to feel a bit like it. "What's an MC?"

"Motorcycle club."

"Okay?"

"Do you know what a motorcycle club is?"

What was she missing? "A club where people get together to ride motorcycles?"

Reilly snorted. "Yes, that's one part of it."

The twenty-something-year-old went on to tell her about the Blood Fury MC and how the men out in the shop belonged to the Fury brotherhood and how their ol' ladies, including Reilly, belonged to the sisterhood.

"So, it's a riding club, like I said." With motorcycles and members. Probably even dues.

"It's so much more than that." Reilly said.

"How so?"

"We're all family. Not necessarily by blood but by bond."

Interesting how she put that. Fallon actually liked that idea. The saying *blood is thicker than water* wasn't always true. "How big is this club?"

Fallon smiled from the warmth of Reilly's laughter. "I

swear getting bigger by the month. My sister just had a baby back in November. We seem to be multiplying rapidly."

"Oh, congratulations on becoming an aunt. She's part of the club, too?"

Reilly nodded. "Her ol' man is the club treasurer."

"Club treasurer? The MC has an executive board of directors?" Should she know all of this? When she put her nose to the grindstone fresh out of college, did she also bury herself under a rock? She might be missing out on a lot more than she ever realized by putting herself in her career bubble.

Or was her ignorance about MCs to be expected since she never knew anyone who owned a motorcycle? At least that she was aware of.

She had surrounded herself with professional people who pulled into the parking garage in Jaguars, Mercedes, Audis, BMWs, and other over-priced luxury vehicles. If they owned bikes, they most likely only rode them on the weekends.

"Similar to that," Reilly answered.

"So, they have meetings, by-laws, take minutes and all of that?" Why was she so fascinated by this? Maybe it was because she never thought a club of bikers would actually have a structure similar to a professional organization.

She wondered how someone in that club climbed the ladder to take one of the top spots. Did they have to claw their way up to the top, too?

The more Reilly talked, the more captivated Fallon became. It also helped pass the time while she waited for Agnes's diagnosis.

"Kind of. Meetings and by-laws, yes. As for someone taking minutes? I doubt it. I can't see Ozzy, the club secretary, scribbling down notes. Plus, he'd have to pull out his reading glasses to do that and he doesn't want anyone to know he has to wear them." She snorted and rolled her beautiful green eyes. "Men!"

Fallon agreed with that last sentiment. "You're not a part of those meetings?"

Her lips twitched. "No woman is."

Fallon's eyes narrowed. "No woman is, why? Because no woman wants to be a part of it or because the men won't allow women to hold the position of an officer?"

Reilly's answer was interrupted when Whip stepped into the office, using a red rag to wipe off his fingers. "Wanna come out here? Wanna show you some stuff on your girl."

"Agnes."

Whip rolled his blue eyes to the ceiling, held them there for a second, then when they finally dropped back down to her, he repeated, "Agnes," like it took a lot of effort.

Fallon smothered her laugh.

"I love that you named your sled Agnes," Reilly said. "I'm going to have to name Rev's."

Whip's head snapped around to her. "Think you better clear that with your ol' man first."

Reilly tipped her blonde head and raised her eyebrows. "Do you now?"

Oh, Fallon liked her. She was feisty. She guessed Reilly had to be to work with male mechanics. Fallon knew the difficulty.

"Yeah, Lee, I do. Rev ain't gonna like it if you name his sled some grandma name."

Reilly shrugged. "I'll name her something tough, then. Like—"

Before she could finish, Whip stepped back out into the shop, yelling, "Rev, your woman's gonna name your fuckin' sled Pansy or somethin'. Better set her ass straight."

Reilly fell forward over her desk, her whole body shaking and laughter spurting out of her. When she lifted her head, she had tears in her eyes. "They make it way too easy."

Fallon hadn't smiled this much in a long time. In fact, her cheeks were starting to ache, proving those muscles had been neglected for quite a while. "You like busting on them?" She shouldn't even have put a question mark on the end of that. Fallon had no doubt Reilly liked to create a little ruckus just for fun.

"Oh, believe me, they can give it back two-fold. But it's fun and, besides the convenience, it's why I'm in no rush to move my office. I get entertained all day."

If Fallon ever got another job or started a business, she would make sure the next time would be something she found fun. Right now, however, she was in no rush to start a new business venture, and, unless something drastically changed for her financially, she had no reason to.

She could "just be."

Hell, once she was done with her adventure with Agnes, she might just find some hut on a tropical beach, put her feet up, drink Mai Tais and watch the world go by.

A "You comin'?" had her turning her head back toward the office door, where Whip was standing.

The man made greasy coveralls look really damn good.

Focus, Fallon!

A noise from behind the desk had her swinging her gaze back to Reilly, who had her lips rolled under as her eyes ping-ponged back and forth between her and Whip.

Shit. Was it obvious she was a little enamored with the young mechanic?

She frowned and rose from the seat to follow him out into the garage area and over to where he had Agnes up on a lift.

He had the oil pan removed and the oil drained already. He grabbed the pan and held it up. "Needs replaced. Tire, too. But already told you that. Dent we can't do anythin' about, but it's just cosmetic. Dependin' on where you're goin' and how long you're travelin' you might get a few more, so might as well wait 'til your vacation's over and get them all repaired at once. Will save you some scratch that way."

"Scratch?"

He glanced up from the oil pan to her. "Money."

Of course. "I'm not worried about the cost, but that does make a lot of sense." Should she add she wasn't on vacation? That riding across the country was her new normal? At least for now?

No, he didn't need to know that or her life story. And if she told him that he might want to know why and she wasn't ready to spew her personal business to anyone right now. Giving more information than necessary opened her up to questions she wasn't in the mood to answer.

"How soon can you replace both?"

He shrugged. "Gonna have to call around for the pan and that tire. But wanted to make sure it didn't need anythin' else before I did that."

Made perfect sense.

"I'll get an estimate together for you. It'll just take me a bit."

"I don't need an estimate. Just order whatever you need to get her up and running."

His head tilted as he studied her and she could see his wheels turning. She was sure most people wanted to know the financial hit they were about to take so they weren't shocked when they got the final bill. The truth was, she had no choice but to get Agnes fixed. The Scout was all Fallon owned right now besides some personal items in her saddle-bags and luggage pack.

"Yeah, as she sits, she's about useless. We charge a fair price, don't worry."

"I'm not worried," she murmured. "I just need to know when she'll be fixed."

He nodded and set the oil pan down in what looked like

some sort of oil drain funnel on wheels beneath the lift. "Gonna call around, see what I can find and then we can go from there."

Fallon nodded and turned to head back to the office.

"Hey," he called out softly, making her pause.

She glanced over her shoulder at him still standing under Agnes. He should be a model, he was that damn cute.

Men shouldn't be cute, they should be handsome and suave or, on the other end of the spectrum, ruggedly handsome, so why did he make things flutter inside her?

Maybe it had just been that long for her, any man looked good.

She glanced at Dutch who stood in the next bay, staring at her in a very uncomfortable way.

Almost any man.

The garage owner certainly didn't hide his obvious interest, nor was he embarrassed about being caught ogling her. His smile widened as he stroked his beard.

Whip grabbed her upper arm and steered her away from Agnes and Dutch. "Want coffee?"

"Uh... Sure." She could use some caffeine if she was going to end up stuck at this garage for a while longer. She followed him past the office. "Do you think you'll be able to find the tire and oil pan today?"

"Find it? Maybe. Get them delivered? Doubt it. If I can get them locally, maybe by the weekend. If not..."

He stepped into a narrow room behind the office. A counter ran the length of the room and on it was a large coffeemaker with all the fixings needed to make coffee.

"Donut?"

"No."

He frowned, grabbed a donut, asked, "You don't do donuts?" and clamped it between his teeth.

She blinked while she stared at his mouth, then forced

out, "I do donuts, but only occasionally," once she shook herself mentally.

With the donut still between his teeth, he grabbed a disposable coffee cup, filled it and offered it to her. As soon as she took it, he took a bite, chewed and swallowed it down. "Fix it how you like."

She dragged her gaze from his throat after he swallowed, watched him take another bite of the glazed donut and grab a real mug hanging from a rack above the coffeemaker. A worn Harley Davidson emblem decorated it. He checked the inside, probably to make sure it was clean, and poured himself a mugful.

Then he turned and leaned back against the counter, chewing another mouthful of donut.

What the hell was wrong with her?

She made herself move next to him to add some powered creamer since that was the only creamer she spotted and a packet of sweetener to her coffee. After stirring it with one of those tiny straws, she tucked the stirrer between her lips.

When she lifted her gaze, he was staring at her mouth. Their eyes locked as she sucked the stirrer clean and slid it from between her lips.

What was going on?

The donut was forgotten in his fingers and his coffee cooling on the counter, while she was gripping her coffee cup so hard it began to buckle.

She loosened her grip and, after taking a deep breath, she leaned closer and reached up, using her thumb to wipe the dot of glaze clinging to the corner of his mouth.

She stared at her thumb with the glaze on it for far too long, fighting the urge to tuck it into her mouth.

Don't do it, Fallon. Don't. You. Do. It.

It took every effort she had to force her gaze up but

avoided looking at him directly in the eye this time. "Sorry. I…"

Heat licked at her cheeks even though she *never* blushed. Never.

What in the Twilight Zone hell was going on?

She never touched anyone without their permission. Just like she never wanted a stranger to just reach out and touch her.

Personal space and boundaries had always been important. Whether sexual, personal or business.

She glanced down helplessly at the glaze on her thumb again and a napkin suddenly appeared in her line of sight. That was exactly what was needed to snap her out of this unexplainable craziness.

He probably thought she'd lost her damn mind.

She snagged it and wiped her thumb off. "Again, I'm sorry. I invaded your personal space."

He snorted and then that damn boyish smirk tipped his lips up.

That was not helping things.

Act normal! "I… uh… Thank you for the coffee."

"Sure you don't want a glazed donut? Bet you haven't eaten since breakfast."

His blue eyes had both a knowing look in them and a damn sexy sparkle to go with that even sexier smirk. She shook her head as both an answer and to shake herself free of whatever was happening in the tight quarters where they stood shoulder to shoulder.

"I haven't, I…" Maybe that was what was wrong with her. Low blood sugar. Of course!

A donut would solve all this foolishness.

She reached past him, her arm pressing against his since he remained in the way and didn't bother to move as she grabbed one from the open box. She tucked it into the napkin she was still holding and lifted it up. "Thank you."

"Don't thank me, thank Lee. She's the one who gets them every mornin'."

She glanced down at the donut since it was now late in the afternoon. It was probably stale.

It didn't matter. It would knock her blood sugar levels back to normal so she could stop acting like a silly school girl.

"You guys eat donuts *every* morning?"

He shrugged. "Yeah."

She gave him a once-over. "How do you stay... How are you not..." Was there a good way to ask him why he wasn't fat without being offensive?

No, there wasn't.

But he answered her anyway. "Want the truth?"

What kind of question was that? Who wouldn't want the truth? "Of course."

"We fuck a lot."

Fallon blinked.

And here she was worried about offending him. She cleared her throat.

Suddenly she just couldn't hold back any longer.

She burst out laughing.

And she couldn't stop.

She laughed until her stomach ached, her eyes watered, and she couldn't catch her breath. "Oh... I..."

His brow pulled low. "Wasn't supposed to be funny."

She lifted a hand. "I know but..." Then she burst out in a fresh batch of giggles.

Giggles.

She was *giggling*.

No doubt about it.

She had lost her damn mind.

Chapter Four

WHIP SHOVED the last bite of the donut into his mouth, wiped his fingers off on his coveralls and, while he chewed, crossed his arms over his chest, watching her laugh.

And laugh.

And laugh some more.

Did she fucking snap or something?

She was actually crying and almost heaving. She even folded over in half to the point her face was at her knees. All she had to do now was slap her thigh like in some cheesy sitcom.

Only she was no cheesy sitcom, she was far from it.

In fact, after a second, once he realized she wasn't having a complete mental breakdown, her reaction pulled a smile from him. Even though he hadn't meant what he said to be funny.

At least, he didn't find it fucking funny, but apparently, she did. He was okay with that because her laugh did shit to him he didn't expect.

He grabbed his coffee and sucked about half of it down to wash any remains of the half-stale donut into his gut. Then he wiped his arm across his mouth and crossed them again, along with his ankles, as he waited out her laughing jag.

Once she could sort of breathe, she finally tried to speak. "It's just so..." a hiccup-laugh bubbled from her, "refreshing."

"What is?"

"The honesty in which you said that."

He shrugged. "Asked if you wanted the truth. Gave you the truth."

"I was expecting you to say you go to the gym or for a run... I..."

The gym? They had what could be called a "gym" at the farm and sometimes he went in with Easy and some of the other guys to hit the heavy bag or to lift weights, but he didn't do it on the regular. None of them did.

Except for Sig. He used the heavy bag a lot. In fact, almost every day. But he had a good reason for that.

The rest of them wandered in every once in a while when they began to develop beer guts. The only one who didn't give a shit about his gut was Dutch.

Beer gut or not, the Original got more pussy than any of them. To Whip, that was proof women didn't give a fucking shit about six-packs or...

Droopy, gray-haired, wrinkled balls.

Whip snorted at his own thought.

Fallon lifted a palm. "I'm... s-so sorry. I don't mean to laugh." Her cheeks were flushed and her eyes had a sheen to them.

She was gorgeous. Absolutely fucking gorgeous. Enough to make him lose his damn breath.

Some women's laugh were a turn-off. Especially when they brayed like an upset donkey. Or snorted like a pot-bellied pig.

But Fallon's laugh...

Damn.

It definitely got him right in the gut. It made every fucking cell in his body stand up and pay attention to the blonde with the chin-length hair and bright blue eyes.

"You show her your baby gherkin, Sparky?" Dutch grumped from the doorway. "That why she's howlin' with laughter?"

Dutch still occasionally called him Sparky at the garage as if it would bother Whip. It didn't. He'd learned to ignore it since Dutch was always trying to get a rise out of all of them. All it did was make him a target in return.

It had become a sport. He fucked with them. They fucked with him.

Just like the whole Pornhub thing on his phone. He wouldn't be surprised if the site was still bookmarked to the "she-males" category. Maybe Dutch was into that since he loved a damn variety. If they could suck and fuck, that was all that mattered to the old man. He was living his best life and not giving a shit what anyone thought, including his sons.

The most important things to the old man were his business, fucking and now his granddaughter Dyna. Everyone knew deep down he loved his sons, but the Original would never admit it out loud.

"Get that sled off the lift, get her an estimate on the repair and get workin' on the cage you're supposed to be workin' on. That Ford needs to be done before the end of the day. You got that?"

"Yeah, got it," Whip answered even though Dutch had already moved on. He shook his head and glanced at Fallon, who was now quiet and staring at the empty doorway.

"Is he always like that?"

"Every damn day. All right, let me get Reilly to call around for the parts and see what the timeframe's gonna be. Gotta move your Scout from the lift before the boss man has a coronary 'cause I put your sled in front of a customer already on the schedule."

"I appreciate you doing that," she said softly.

Whip stared at her mouth and thought about all the ways she could show him her appreciation.

Because he had more than two brain cells, he kept that list to himself, pushed off the counter and grabbed his coffee mug. He tipped his head toward the door. "Once we figure out how long the parts are gonna take, we... *you* can go from there."

He turned to head out of the break room when she stopped him with a hand planted on his chest. "I just want to thank you for the laugh, even if you didn't mean what you said to be funny. I needed that reminder we shouldn't take life too seriously."

They were inches apart. Inches.

Whip was having a difficult time dragging his eyes from her mouth to the rest of her face.

At least he wasn't staring at her fucking tits. While in the office, she had shed her waterproof windbreaker and he got a good look at them. Her tits being hugged by the short-sleeved cream-colored sweater she wore beneath it didn't hurt, either. Also, with the way her nipples pushed against the thin fabric and how it emphasized her cleavage, her tits were worth a look.

A few looks.

Whip noticed he hadn't been the only one looking.

The sweater not only fit her well, so did the hardly broken-in jeans hugging her hips and thighs. That snug denim also made her ass look very edible.

Smack-able.

Fuckable.

How he ever mistook that she was a man in the first place...

It just proved he hadn't been paying attention as much

as he should've been. Especially near Hillbilly Hill. And that could've been dangerous.

But right now, Fallon had all his attention.

He didn't give one shit that she was older than him. She was still hot as fuck.

Like Dutch, Whip appreciated women in all colors, shapes, sizes and ages. As long as they weren't jailbait or one of his brother's ol' ladies, then he was open to anything and everything.

Billie was proof of that. Especially since she was the exact opposite of Fallon.

Night and day.

Dark and light.

He pulled a slow, deep breath into his lungs as they locked gazes.

If she was stuck in town for a few days waiting on parts, maybe they could get to know each other a little better. He assumed she didn't know anyone in town since it seemed she might've been simply passing through.

Whip wouldn't want her to be lonely. He'd be willing to volunteer to help with that. Yeah, that wouldn't be a sacrifice at all.

Since it was already Thursday, he had no plans for the rest of the week except to show up tomorrow for work and then take part in the club run on Sunday. Other than that he was free.

Available.

Willing to please.

Fuck yeah.

Her clearing her throat yanked him from his fantasy and back to reality. A flush rose from her chest and up her neck but didn't quite reach her cheeks.

Her nipples were pebbled and his fingers itched to brush over them. His mouth actually watered and not because she was squeezing the shit out of that donut.

They were so fucking close that when her lips parted, the warm puff of air that escaped swept across his cheek. She wasn't much shorter than him so it wouldn't take any effort to lean forward and taste her mouth.

"What's going on?" she whispered on a breath.

The fuck if he knew. But what he did know was that he wanted to spin her around, rip down her jeans, toss her bare ass up on the counter and fuck her so hard, she was no longer whispering.

Fuck no. He wanted her screaming his name. Loud and clear.

He blinked, trying to clear that vision from his brain.

His cock was now hard and throbbing in his jeans. Luckily his baggy coveralls hid his reaction. Or at least, he hoped to fuck they did.

She was so out of his fucking league, she'd probably be offended if she knew what his imagination was coming up with.

He was also within kneeing distance and he would like to keep his nuts where they belonged, instead of drilled up into his body cavity.

"Nothin'," he forced out of his mouth.

Just act like you don't got a ragin' hard-on and don't wanna plant your face between her thighs.

Act fuckin' normal, idiot. 'Cause if she gets offended and bitches to Dutch, you're gonna have a Snap-On wrench permanently embedded in your melon.

"I'm gonna… I need to…" He shook his head, trying to reset his brain. "Need to talk to Reilly."

She took a deep breath and nodded. The flush slowly retreated but her nipples remained hard and present.

And definitely distracting.

Damn. He needed to get out of this tight spot. Literally and figuratively.

Because right now? He wanted to lick her glaze. And not the sweet coating on her donut.

"Let's head into the—" His voice cracked like a goddamn fourteen-year-old. He pushed on. "Office."

Fallon only nodded.

Her previous question, *"What's going on?"* circled his brain. Why the fuck was he reverting back to an awkward teenager with raging hormones and lack of skill with women? Just like when he was the only virgin left in his group of high school friends and no matter what he did to change that… failed.

And failed fucking miserably.

At that age, he'd had no game.

It didn't matter that he was on the baseball team. It didn't matter that he'd done pretty decent in school. It didn't matter that he could figure out how to take apart anything and put it back together again. Most of the time even make whatever it was better than the original.

He basically sucked at talking to his female classmates. He didn't know what to say or how to say it. Worse, everything he did say came out awkward and apparently wrong. Most likely because he was never raised by a father who gave a shit and he'd been too young when that drunk, abusive motherfucker died.

And while his grandfather stepped in as his father figure, Whip had been only eight on the day his pap took his last breath. Way too young to be taught how to flirt with girls with any kind of finesse.

His mom wanted him to concentrate on schoolwork and baseball and not high school "hussies." She said they were trouble, could get him in trouble and fuck up his future.

There'd been no point in arguing with her that all the girls in school weren't hussies. In fact, if they were, his damn cherry would've been popped when he was a whole lot younger, instead of at nineteen.

Only ten years ago.

One of the perks of joining the Fury was access to the sweet butts. Once he was fully patched in, he had free access to fuck any of them and none of them could say no. Or they could, but only for certain reasons. Otherwise, they needed to hit the bricks and leave the club.

Not once had any of them said no. In fact, he had to be doing something right since he was in high demand. Most nights he didn't have to find one, they found him.

He was lucky he only had to prospect for the first six months. During those six months, he and Billie had been exclusive and then just like that, the day he was patched over, they decided to do their own thing.

Even though he'd learned a lot from her, after that day he was never with her again. They checked in with each other, but that was about it. Billie realized Whip wasn't enough for her and what she needed, and Whip decided she was way too much.

Whip wasn't into being whipped. And not with whipped cream, either, but with a damn horse crop or a flogger. Or all the rest of the crazy shit she kept in her toy bag.

Instead, he preferred Liz, but so did Ozzy and it was difficult to spend alone time with her. Not unless the Original was there, either watching or participating.

When Liz hooked up with Crash from the Dirty Angels, it sucked, but Whip was nowhere near as bent about it as Ozzy. Whip could understand why. They had a thing. Maybe not a serious thing but definitely a thing.

It was also why the exec committee had been lenient with the older brother and let him get away with some shit no one else might've gotten away with. Like walking out during a committee meeting. Normally, his secretary patch would've been stripped for that.

Honestly, Whip figured Ozzy wouldn't have given a fuck

if it had been. But the problem was, nobody else wanted that spot.

Whip sure didn't.

"Did you crack your head on one of the lifts? Why are you just standing there looking lost?" Reilly's questions dragged him out of his head and into the office where apparently he'd wandered.

He realized Fallon had followed him.

Her question *"What's going on?"* once again echoed through his head.

Apparently, he was losing his goddamn mind, that was what was going on. All because of a customer he'd only met a couple of hours ago.

Reilly's lips pursed and her narrowed gaze zeroed in on his crotch.

Fuck. He guessed the coveralls didn't camouflage his erection as much as he thought. One blonde eyebrow lifted and she flicked a glance to Fallon, then back to him before wiggling both eyebrows.

Shit.

Whip blew a breath out of his nostrils and shook his head slightly, pulling the small scratchpad out of his chest pocket where he'd written down the make, model, year and even VIN of Fallon's Indian. He'd also noted the size and brand of the tire and the OM part number for the oil pan. All Lee had to do was call around for him.

He ripped the top sheet off and dropped it onto her desk. "See what you can do with that."

Reilly glanced up from the spot where the note landed, to him, a slow smirk crossing her face. "Sure you don't want to do it yourself?"

"Got other shit I gotta do," he grumbled.

"Uh huh."

Whip could see she was struggling to bite her tongue. She'd better keep a tight grip on it or he'd make it his personal mission to embarrass the fuck out of her another day.

He narrowed his eyes on her and sent that silent message.

Her lips rolled inward, making him close his eyes and take another deep breath. When he opened them, he said, "Just do it."

"Please."

Jesus fuck. How Rev put the fuck up with her… "Please," he forced out.

She flashed him an over-exaggerated smile that clearly indicated she was up to no good.

"Christ," he said under his breath and turned to Fallon where she had once again settled in the seat across from Reilly.

Of course, watching that whole exchange.

"You need anythin' in the meantime, Reilly can help. Yeah, Lee?"

Reilly winked at him. "Sure, I'll take care of Fallon for you."

"Not for—" He shook his head. It wasn't worth it. "Yell when you find the tire and oil pan."

"I'll do that," Reilly said with a tone everyone in that room could read.

He sighed and walked the fuck out before he embarrassed himself.

———

"No one has the oil pan in stock," Reilly announced after calling him back into the office. "I contacted all the parts stores that I could think of. I swear every damn dealership, too. We can get the tire on Monday but the oil pan is a no-go."

Whip ground his palm against the back of his neck and

glanced at Fallon looking at him like he should be able to snap his damn fingers and create a miracle.

He couldn't.

"No fuckin' dealership had it?" he asked Rev's ol' lady.

"Oh, sure, I found a dealership who had it."

Christ. She was going to make him work for it. "Okay?"

"In Texas."

"What?" That didn't seem right.

Reilly shrugged.

"They gonna overnight it?" he asked.

"As soon as they can find it in their stock."

His brow dropped low. "Whataya mean?"

Reilly shrugged again. "Their computer said they had one. Their parts guy went to pull it from stock and it wasn't where it's supposed to be."

What the actual fuck? "And?"

She bugged her green eyes out at him like he was an idiot. "And they need to find it. Once they do they'll express ship it."

He shot Lee a frown. "So, we have no clue when the fuck it's gonna get here?"

She narrowed her eyes on him and her face became a picture of annoyance. "It'll get here when it gets here. I'm neither a magician or a psychic, Whip."

He snuck a glance at Fallon to see her chewing on her bottom lip. She wasn't liking Reilly's findings, either. He didn't blame her. She probably had somewhere to be. And that place wasn't Manning Grove. Unfortunately, now she'd be stuck here for who knew how long.

He turned back to Lee. "Nowhere else had one?"

"Another dealership I called had one on order but it hadn't come in yet. They said the bike is so damn new they haven't stocked parts for it yet. They'll call me if it comes in soon."

"There's gotta be other dealersh—"

"Do you want to call every damn dealership? I googled it. In case you didn't know, one hundred and ninety five Indian dealerships exist in the States." She pointed at the phone. "Have at it. I called the largest ones and all the ones in the surrounding area."

He rubbed at his forehead. "Christ," he muttered and glanced at Fallon again. "Guessin' you're gonna be stuck in Manning Grove for probably a week. Better call and let anyone waitin' on you know."

"No one is waiting on me."

"No one at all?" Reilly asked with her eyebrows raised and her lips curled up slightly at the very ends. "No boyfriend, husband, kids or anything?"

"No."

What the fuck was Reilly up to?

"How about your job?" she asked next.

"No."

Silence filled the office.

"Won't this fuck up your vacation?" Whip asked. At this point, he was now certain Fallon wasn't a fed. If she was, she was a really damn good actress. But she never did explain why she'd been in the area.

"Not at all since I'm not on vacation." She locked gazes with him. "I'm not expected anywhere anytime soon. No one is waiting for me. My schedule is completely clear. If I have to wait... Well, then I have to wait. I don't have a choice, now do I?"

She was taking this hiccup way too well. Most customers would be screaming and having a tantrum if they didn't live locally. Or if they were local and didn't have another vehicle to get around.

Customers didn't like to be inconvenienced and usually took it out on the people trying to help them. There had been plenty of times one of them had to step in to help Reilly deal with a screaming, entitled customer, even though it wasn't her fault that their vehicle needed repairs. Now Rev usually kept one ear on the office when a customer was in with her, even though Reilly was pretty good at handling irate customers on her own.

Dealing with an abusive ex who almost beat her to death had coated her spine in steel. Whip had seen her pull that spine right out of her back and use it to crack one of those rude customers right upside the head. She knew how to put them in their place without them realizing that was what she was doing until it was already done.

Whip smothered his grin on how hot it was when it came to a badass woman. That shit made his blood run south. Maybe that was why he'd hooked up with Billie. The sweet butt said what she meant and took no shit. In fact, if you gave the woman shit, she'd take it and shove it down your throat until you choked on it.

Billie also didn't give a flying fuck what anyone thought about her. She owned who she was and what she was into. If anyone else had a problem with it, then that was their problem, not hers.

But here and now, he didn't want Fallon thinking he was grinning about her being stuck in town for at least the next few days, if not longer.

Fallon rose from her chair. "Whelp. That settles it. I guess I'll need a rental car. I might as well explore the area while I'm stuck here for a bit. Do you have a hotel you can recommend? I'm sure the hotel concierge can find me a rental."

The hotel concierge? Rental car? Where did she think she was?

He began talking before Reilly did. "Can recommend a good motel. No concierge there, though. You'd be on your own."

She frowned. "I thought I saw a hotel on the square in town when I rode through."

"You did. But it's twice as much as the motel."

The frown that creased her forehead disappeared. "I don't mind paying if it's worth it."

They always tried to steer out-of-town folk toward The Grove Inn. "It ain't. Overpriced. The motel staff is a lot friendlier."

"I don't need friendly, just competent."

Reilly made a sharp noise at the back of her throat like she wanted tagged in and Whip shot her a warning look. She lifted both palms and said, "I lived and worked at that motel for a while. It's more laid-back and much friendlier than the hotel. I mean, it's not fancy five-star accommodations, but it's clean and well maintained."

Fallon frowned. "Are you getting a kickback from recommending the motel?"

Kind of. The fatter the club's coffers, the better. The club being flush benefited them all.

"Not at all. We just know who runs it. It's a locally-owned business versus some faceless corporation," Reilly explained. "We try to support the local businesses and economy first."

Damn, she was fucking good. Like her sister Reese, Reilly was fucking smart, way smarter than Rev or Whip, but he could see she was up to something.

He had a feeling he knew what it was but didn't know why. And, *fuck him*, he couldn't ask her with Fallon standing right there in her office.

"Okay... well... Is there a rental car company around here?"

Reilly answered her before Whip could. "Closest one that I know of is in Williamsport and that's an hour away on a good day."

"Do they deliver?" Fallon asked, pulling her cell phone out of her travel bag that had been on the floor and propped against her seat. "Do you know the name of it?"

Reilly quickly said, "We have a Honda we lend out to our customers at no charge. Unfortunately, another customer has it right now, *buuuuuuut* he's supposed to return it tomorrow when his truck is done. Will that work? That means you'll only go one night without wheels and you'll have something to drive this weekend if you want to *explore*." She grinned.

Whip rolled his eyes.

"What do I do in the meantime?"

"Whip will give you a ride wherever you need to go," Reilly suggested and quickly added, "since the motel is on the west side of town and there aren't too many businesses down there."

"What you're saying is, it would be better to stay at the hotel in the center of town," Fallon concluded like anyone with a lick of sense would.

But Reilly was good. So fucking good. "Let me just look up their number and give them a quick call to see if they have anything available. It's a pretty busy weekend around here."

It was?

She continued, "They get booked up quickly and The Grove Inn usually gets the overflow." Reilly went through the motions of calling the hotel. She was barely on the phone for two minutes before she hung up and announced, "No, they're booked solid through the weekend."

She shot Whip a look that clearly said not to question her.

Oh yeah, she was up to something all right. He wasn't sure if he should like it or if it should pucker his asshole.

With Rev's ol' lady it could go either way.

"Whip can drop you off at the motel and then pick you up tomorrow to grab the Honda once it's returned. Will that work?"

"Do I have a choice?" Fallon asked, sounding resigned.

"Got plenty of choices," Whip mumbled.

Fallon shook her head, her blonde chin-length hair sweeping against her sharp jawline. "Not if there isn't a rental car place close by and the hotel is booked." She turned to Lee. "How do you know the motel isn't booked?"

"I'll give them a call right now," Reilly said, already with the office phone to her ear and her fingers speed-dialing.

"You got your main bag but do you need anythin' out of your saddlebags?" Whip asked while Reilly talked to whoever answered the phone at The Grove Inn.

Fallon sighed softly. "No. This should be okay for now."

"You got those saddlebags locked up?"

Her lips pulled down at the ends. "Yes. Why? Do I need to worry about that around here?"

"No, gonna keep it parked inside at night, but will have to push it back out during the day to make room."

"I appreciate that."

Reilly hung up the phone. "All set. You have a room for the next week. I made sure you got a quiet room on the very end."

"Thank you."

"Not a problem. I'm glad to help." Reilly was staring at Whip when she said that. She added an exaggerated wink on the end while Fallon was busy reaching down to grab her bag.

Son of a bitch.

Chapter Five

"THIS ONE'S YOURS, THEN?"

"Yep," he answered as he strapped her Cordura travel bag onto the back of his '84 Disc Glide.

"It looks like a classic."

"It's older than me."

A soft laugh slipped from her. "Then I guess that makes it a classic."

It might be older but he was proud of it. When he became a prospect a few years ago, he had dug out his uncle's Harley from his aunt's shed. It had needed work but now was a beautiful piece. A classic, just like Fallon said.

He appreciated the fact that she appreciated bikes. Not all women did.

His ride might not be as badass as her Indian Scout, but he couldn't afford a brand new sled and he knew what he had, while not perfect, was rare. Only a limited number of Disc Glides were made that year.

Even with all the work he had to put into it getting it back in running condition after his uncle had abandoned it and disappeared, it hadn't put him in the hole. He had no monthly payments like he would on something new or even a sled only a few years old.

The way things were right now, especially with him living practically rent-free in the bunkhouse, he had zero debt and planned to keep it that way.

When the Dirty Angels came up to Manning Grove for Trip and Stella's wedding, he'd talked to Jag Jamison about getting his Harley customized. Once Jag mentioned some numbers, Whip figured the cost wouldn't be worth it. At least, not now.

Maybe one day.

Or he'd buy something similar to Fallon's Scout Bobber Twenty once he started checking off his sled bucket list. Because her sled was sweet as fuck. He could see himself riding that on the club run. While his sled wasn't the nicest one in the Fury, it wasn't the worst, either, since he kept it in tiptop shape.

His Harley got him from point A to point B. Plus being a bike mechanic, over the last couple of years he'd also put money into tweaking the engine and increasing the horsepower.

He now had a powerful beast between his thighs.

"What's her name?"

He finished securing her bag and straightened. "Who?"

"Your bike."

"Didn't name it." And if he did, it wouldn't be a name like Agnes.

"Reilly said you all belong to a motorcycle club. I would think a biker would be more attached to his ride."

"Don't need a name 'cause I'm not sleepin' with it. I ride it. It don't ride me."

Her lips twitched and crinkles appeared at the corners of her eyes. He was glad she found that amusing and not offensive.

Even though he might have the urge to fuck her, she

was a customer first and foremost. He told Dutch Trip would hire him for the repo business, but Whip didn't want that, he loved tinkering with bikes. He loved making them purr.

Just like he did a woman. Besides the rumble of his straight pipes, no sweeter sound existed.

He straddled his sled and tipped his head. "C'mon. Get on."

She pulled her helmet over her head—hiding her eyes behind the tinted face shield, hiding the hair he wanted to fist while she was on her knees at his feet sucking him off—and tightened the chin strap.

She had spent a healthy chunk of change on that brain bucket, too. It probably had Bluetooth and all the extras.

While some of his brothers wore skullcaps when they rode, he usually wore a five-dollar baseball cap. He bought cheap ones because he'd lost too many in the wind.

When she threw a leg over his bike, instead of pushing herself back against the sissy bar as far as she could to keep a gap between them, she wiggled forward until the V of her legs was smashed against his ass. Her arms snaked around his waist, too.

Damn. He expected her to keep her distance like on the ride this morning to the garage.

He glanced down at where her hands were planted on his gut, studying her long, slender fingers with rounded nails. They weren't super long or painted a crazy color like the sweet butts. Instead, they were painted a neutral color. Only a single, simply designed ring could be found on her right hand. A gold band embedded with blue gems. Sapphires, he guessed.

Classy.

She was too fucking classy for him.

He bet she had no tattoos or piercings other than the two small gold hoop earrings in her ears.

Fallon might be dressed casually, but he could still tell she belonged in a boardroom and not on a bike.

He imagined she looked pretty damn good on her Scout, even though he hadn't seen her straddling it yet. He also figured she looked pretty fucking good as his backpack.

He pressed his hand over top of one of hers, gave it a squeeze and asked, "You good?"

"Yes," came muffled from under her helmet.

He'd tell her to hang on, but she was already doing that without him having to mention it. Between his sissy bar and her baggage, she didn't even need to do that. With his sled's back rest, she could sit back and give each other space.

For some reason she chose not to and he wasn't going to complain. She felt good pressed against his back. Except for that fucking helmet digging into his spine and shoulder.

None of the Fury sisterhood wore brain buckets even though they could choose to. Whip might not be ready for an ol' lady but when he saw the ol' ladies with their cheeks pressed against their ol' man's colors, it was a sight to be seen and something about it pulled at him.

A couple of times before Reilly became Rev's ol' lady, she'd rode with him, but it wasn't the same. Riding together seemed to bring a Fury brother and his ol' lady closer together.

Not one of the Fury sisterhood had their own sled. He wondered what the reaction of his brothers would be if one of them wanted their own. He doubted it would be a huge issue unless they wanted to ride solo on the club run.

Then there'd be a major issue because it just wasn't done.

However, it was difficult to haul around babies and kids on a sled. And a lot of the sisterhood were baking or popping out future Fury members. Because of that, they should stick with their SUVs and crossover vehicles. Except Whip wasn't telling anyone in the Fury sisterhood that.

Not if he valued his balls.

With a twist of the throttle, they shot out of the parking lot and down Main Street. A few minutes later, he pulled in front of the office at The Grove Inn and shut down his sled.

Ozzy was standing out front three rooms down, talking to one of the housekeepers. He gave Whip a chin lift greeting and shouted, "Shay's in the office. She can check her in."

Whip nodded and helped Fallon off his sled before dismounting himself.

After she pulled off her helmet, she once again swung her head around to shake her hair back into place and used her fingers to comb through it, attempting to fluff it back up somewhat.

Even messed up, it was sexy as fuck. Call it bed head or sex hair, either way that was what it reminded him of.

He took her helmet from her so she could dig out her wallet from the front pocket of her travel bag. "Go on and get checked in. I'm gonna get your bag."

"Thanks," she said softly, stared at him for a couple of heartbeats, then turned to go inside.

He watched her until the door closed and cut off his view. And, *for fuck's sake*, it was a *view*. Those jeans were perfect for her ass.

Or her ass was perfect for those jeans, more like it.

Hell, her ass was just perfect, but would be even better without the dark denim covering those cheeks.

He stared at the closed door for a few seconds more, then began to unstrap her travel bag from the back rest. He'd just finished unhooking the last strap when Ozzy sidled up to him. "Since when d'you give rides to Dutch's customers?"

He slipped Fallon's bag off the back rest and set it on the ground at his feet. "Since today, I guess."

Ozzy shot him a knowing look. "Guessin' she's single."

85

"Don't know if she is or ain't." It was only his assumption since that was how she answered Reilly's nosy as fuck question. She could very well have some man somewhere because, in truth, it wasn't Reilly's fucking business. And anyway, not wearing a wedding band didn't mean shit anymore.

As soon as a woman was claimed by a brother at the table, it was just as good as being married. A "property of" cut meant the same as a wedding ring. Commitment.

The same as Dodge collaring Syn.

That was a first in the Fury. As soon as Billie spotted it, she explained to Whip what it meant. He was surprised Sig hadn't had a complete meltdown over his sister being collared, if the VP even knew what it meant.

If he hadn't at first, Whip was pretty damn sure Sig knew what it meant now.

Syn didn't usually wear the black leather collar around the Fury, except for on club runs, but Whip knew she wore it out in public and while on stage.

"She's hot as fuck," Ozzy said, catching Whip's eyes and attention. "Bet if it was some sixty-year-old guy you wouldn't have hauled his fuckin' ass down here. Saw the way she had her arms wrapped around you, too, even though that sled of yours has a sissy bar." His mouth pulled up on one side.

Whip casually lifted one shoulder, refusing to fall for Ozzy's bait.

"Looks like a cougar to me. Since you still got baby fuzz on your nuts, Junior, maybe she's willin' to teach you a thing or two." Of course the Original wasn't going to let it go. He never did. He was an expert at riding someone's ass until it was so damn chapped.

But Whip knew of one way to get Ozzy off his before it needed lotion. "You mean like Liz did?"

The older brother's mouth snapped shut and his lips pressed into a slash.

If Whip had said something like that right after Liz had left, he probably would've found himself on his ass on the pavement with a black eye or split lip. But everyone now recognized the fact that Liz and Ozzy weren't meant to be. The man had found his forever with Shay and Liz finding her forever first had been good for Ozzy.

In the end, they both ended up with the right partners.

"Yeah, just like Liz," Ozzy finally muttered. "Gonna go check on Shay."

He headed inside and not even five minutes later, Fallon was coming back out, her jacket now thrown over her arm. She stepped up to him. "All set."

"Good," he murmured, distracted once again with how well her short-sleeved sweater fit and how perky her tits looked. He was aware it could all be an illusion created by a really good bra.

When she reached for her travel bag at his feet, he stopped her with a hand to her forearm. Her skin was warm and soft under his rough fingertips. "Got it."

"You don't have to. You've already been more than helpful as it is."

"I got it," he insisted, making sure his tone told her that he wasn't leaving any room for an argument.

He reluctantly released her, but he did not miss the goosebumps that followed the trail of his fingers as he slid them along her skin. He also didn't miss when her nipples once again tried to punch through her thin sweater.

He dragged his eyes away and grabbed her bag before he grabbed something else.

Her bag was heavy because it was packed solid. She was probably the type of efficient packer that rolled every- thing so damn tightly, she could fit an entire wardrobe in her bag. Whip had seen someone demo it on a TV show that Reilly was watching in the office one day. He certainly never traveled anywhere in his damn life to need to pack for a trip. Some of their club runs were the farthest he'd traveled.

"Just grab your helmet. Room number?"

When he glanced up, he noticed her lips slightly parted and her eyes dilated. "One," came out a bit breathlessly, too.

Her "*What's going on?*" once again circled his brain. The hell if he knew, but he was interested in finding out.

He mentally shook himself free as he nodded and followed Fallon in the direction of Room One. Reilly said she had booked Fallon a room on the end and she wasn't kidding.

Fallon slid the keycard into the lock. Once it clicked and turned green, she shoved open the door and stepped inside the dark room. After she flipped on the lights, he followed her in, propping her bag against the foot of the bed.

He turned. "Gimme your number, gonna text you tomorrow as soon as the Honda's back so you ain't stuck here." He pulled his cell phone out of the front chest pocket of his coveralls and pressed the side button to take it out of sleep mode.

She didn't hesitate to rattle off her digits. He added them to his phone and immediately sent her a text so she had his number, too. He heard it buzz in the pocket of her windbreaker, now thrown onto one of the two queen-sized beds, but she didn't dig it out.

"'Kay. Gotta get back before Dutch has my fuckin' head for not gettin' that Ford done. Now you got my number, so if you need anythin', just shoot me a text. Or go into the office and ask for Ozzy or Shay. They're aware you don't got wheels right now."

Her brow furrowed. "Ozzy?"

"The manager of the motel and Shay, the woman that checked you in, is his ol' lady."

"Ah, yes. Reilly explained the whole ol' lady thing. So, I guess this Ozzy is a part of your club, too?"

"Yeah."

"You said he's the manager. Who owns the motel, then?"

He paused. There was no point in lying since it was common knowledge. "Our club."

"It seems you and Reilly forgot to mention that part. So, you *do* get a kickback?"

He shook his head. "No kickback. Just a small business tryin' to make do like any other small business. We believe helpin' the local economy's better than handin' scratch over to the big corporations who take it and spend it elsewhere. We prefer to keep things local around here."

"The gentleman inside the office—I'm assuming he was Ozzy—was wearing a leather vest. The patches on the back said Blood Fury MC. That's the club you all belong to, right? Or is there more than one MC in this town?"

"Nope. Just the one. No other MCs would dare try to establish their home base in our territory."

"Why not?"

"'Cause it's ours."

"Yes, you said that. But your club doesn't own the whole town, right?"

"No, we don't own the town, but we own a few businesses in this town, and this is our territory."

She tilted her head as she studied him. "That doesn't explain how that makes it your territory."

The only explanation needed was… "We claimed it."

She sighed at his answer.

He didn't have a better one for her because he just went with the fucking flow. Trip was a good leader, Whip trusted the man, trusted the process, and he'd do whatever Trip needed him to do. That included protecting their territory from other MCs disrespecting the Fury by trying to move in.

Or protecting it from the inbred fucknuts living on that damn mountain.

The Fury protected what was theirs. Plain and simple.

But Fallon was an outsider and he shouldn't go into great detail about the club. She could accept what he said or not. Didn't matter either way. She'd be gone in a few days. As soon as her oil pan arrived.

Until then, he'd like to take advantage of her time in Manning Grove. Maybe tomorrow after the customer returned the loaner cage, he should be the one to come get her. While doing that, he could suggest them heading over to Pete's to watch whatever band was playing instead of her sitting alone in her motel room.

That was, if she was into that type of stuff. Like rock music, beer and a local crowd.

And younger guys.

She might not be. That might not be her thing.

She could have a type and Whip might not even be close. As he suspected, he was most likely totally out of her league. Not that it would hurt to ask. She could only say no.

If she did, no harm, no foul. He'd been shot down plenty of times in the past and wasn't an asshole about it like some men who got bent the fuck out of shape when it came to being rejected.

Whip didn't understand that attitude. If a woman didn't want a man, then the man should move the fuck on, not harass her or try to convince her to change her mind. Doing so wouldn't win the stupid fuck any points. Being an egotistical, pushy dick-for-brains wouldn't change a woman's mind.

Take the fucking loss and get lost.

Simple.

"All right, gotta go before my ass gets fired," he mumbled, turning toward the door.

It surprised him that she had closed the door behind him. Most women probably wouldn't close themselves in a tight space, like a motel room, with a stranger, especially a male one.

It made him think she might be willing to grab that drink with him tomorrow night. By the way she hung onto him tighter than she needed to on the short ride from the garage to the motel, seemed to be a good sign. It appeared she trusted him so far and if so…

"Hey… Um…"

Whip paused with his hand on the door handle and glanced over his shoulder.

"Can you recommend somewhere to grab a decent meal?"

He released the handle and turned to face her. "Decent or fancy?"

She shrugged one shoulder. "Decent will do. No fast food, though."

"Then your best bet's Dino's Diner. Right down from the square. Everything's homemade."

"Is that within walking distance?"

He hesitated. "It is from the garage, but it's a hike from here unless you don't mind walkin'."

"I don't. The town's safe, right?"

He hesitated again. The biggest threat was the Shirleys. He wouldn't put it past those redneck militia wannabes to snag some random woman walking alone after dark. They could probably use some extra breeders that didn't share the same DNA. While it would be stupid for them to snag women off the street in Manning Grove, no one said the Shirleys were smart.

"Same as most small towns. Best to not walk alone after dark." That was the best he could do without spilling details about the hillbilly clan. He wanted her to be cautious but not scared or worried. "Remember what I said about Copperhead Road? Same deal."

She frowned. "Well, then…"

He frowned at the uncertainty on her face. It was the first time he saw it. From the second he met her at the bottom of Hillbilly Hill, she'd exuded self-confidence.

"Do you... uh... have any plans for dinner?"

Shit. Had what he said made her wary? "You don't wanna walk?" Was she asking for a ride, or asking him out to dinner?

"I'm sure I could find an Uber or Lyft, but... It's not that."

For fuck's sake, maybe she wanted dinner, *then* a ride. He had to be misunderstanding the direction she was going. "What is it, then?"

"I wouldn't mind some company."

He blinked and let that sink in. "With me?"

Fallon tilted her head and her gaze circled the room. "Well... I mean... Yes, you. Unless there's a Mrs. Whip? Or a girlfriend? Or someone who might want to gouge my eyes out for asking her man out to dinner?"

"You askin' me out to dinner?" Did his ears need a good cleaning? Because he thought he'd have to pursue her and was not expecting the opposite.

"That was my intent when I asked if you had any plans. Maybe I wasn't clear."

"No, you were clear, I just... I wasn't..." *Don't fuck this up, dummy.*

Her lips curled slightly. "I mean it's only dinner. I've been eating alone a lot lately and it would be nice to have some company. That's all."

Company. That was all, she said.

That wasn't all Whip wanted, but, *hell,* it was a start.

The only time he ate dinner with anyone other than himself or his mother was after the club runs, during a pig roast or one of the club holiday dinners, like their annual Thanksgiving dinner or Christmas Eve party.

His mother insisted he come to dinner once a week and

he did his best to accommodate her. Several times she'd hinted that she'd prefer he come more than once a week. While he loved his mother, there was no damn way he was—

"If you don't want to or if you have someone in your life who'll have a problem with it, I'll understand."

"That ain't an issue. I just need to head back to the shop to get that Ford done. But after I'm finished, I can get cleaned up and come back to get you. Yeah?"

She smiled and echoed, "Yeah."

Not just yeah, but *fuck yeah*. "Gonna text you when I'm on my way."

"That sounds like a plan," she answered with a smile.

That definitely sounded like a plan. He also liked that fucking smile. He liked it a whole hell of a lot. He'd like it even better if that was all she was wearing.

Dinner before dick, he reminded himself. She's probably used to being wined and dined by someone with a fuck-ton more social skills than him.

He opened the door but stopped again when she called out, "Whip."

"Yeah?"

"Thank you for your help. I really appreciate it."

"Ain't nothin'."

No, it was something.

She was something.

He grinned and stepped back outside, closing the door behind him.

Never in his fucking life had he looked forward to dinner this much.

Not fucking ever.

As he headed back to the shop, he couldn't wipe that grin free.

In the end, he didn't even bother to try.

Chapter Six

THE RESTAURANT WHIP took her to was packed with locals so Fallon figured it had to be good. As it turned out, it was better than good. Whip had been spot on.

The food wasn't fancy but it was all freshly made unlike a lot of diners Fallon had stopped at along her trip, where nothing had been homemade and everything simply heated or reheated.

The grilled chicken salad she was eating had a house dressing that, surprisingly, was to die for. The warm rolls were baked on site. And on their way to their booth in the corner, they had passed a dessert case that almost made her sweet tooth ache.

Truthfully, she hadn't felt this excited about a dinner in a long time. Probably because she hadn't eaten with anyone in just as long.

Not that this was a date or anything.

It wasn't.

He was simply kind enough to keep her company. That was all.

He also didn't seem to be an arrogant prick like some of her past dinner dates. Men full of themselves. Their conversation—*hell*, their life—focused on nothing but success, money and appearances.

The same as she had been.

Thinking back about it now made her queasy. She had concentrated on all the wrong things. But then, if she hadn't, right now she wouldn't be free to do what she wanted.

Like travel across the country on Agnes.

She could go where she wanted, when she wanted and take the scenic route as she did so. She could change her mind simply on a whim.

What she had not changed her mind about was having dinner with the very cute, young mechanic sitting across from her, who made her panties a bit damp.

It had to be the sexy smirk.

Even before she'd heard the rumble of his Harley outside her door, she had already decided she'd be buying him dinner tonight. Giving him a proper thank you was the polite thing to do.

It was crazy that fate had dropped a motorcycle mechanic at her feet when she needed him the most. When she and Agnes were stranded along that mountain road.

She was slowly shedding the "step on someone to get ahead" mentality. Not everyone thought like that.

Today reminded her that kind and decent people still existed who weren't all about getting ahead. People simply willing to step up and help out others without stepping on them and trying to only make themselves look good in the process.

Yes, the garage was getting paid to fix Agnes, but still… Whip had stopped to help her when he didn't have to. He also insisted that she ride back with him to the garage instead of leaving her to wait alongside the road, and then Reilly kept her entertained. She also didn't have to call in the reservation for Fallon and Whip didn't need to give her a ride to the motel.

Both had gone out of their way to help.

Not only were those gestures unexpected, Fallon truly appreciated them. Maybe while they were at Dino's Diner, she could grab Reilly a gift card. This way she and her "ol' man" could have a meal on Fallon.

A small payback for her help and kindness. The same reason she was buying Whip dinner.

Even though he didn't know it yet.

When they had walked into the diner, the staff knew him by name, so he must be a regular. Nobody blinked an eye at his leather biker vest, something he called a "cut."

It was basically the same as the one the motel manager wore. Only Ozzy's looked a lot more worn and had an embroidered rectangular patch on the front with the word "Original." Whip's did not.

And of course, like Ozzy, Whip had a patch with his nickname on it. His "road name."

Fallon was quickly learning that bikers had a language of their own.

Not unlike the financial industry. Terms she used to use every day, but now only needed when she logged into her investment accounts, to either check the stock market or make a trade.

Even though she'd been on the road for a couple of months now, she still had enough liquid assets in her bank accounts so she hadn't needed to cash out even one stock or mutual fund. The monthly and quarterly dividends she received as a stockholder for various companies were enough to pay her daily expenses and then some.

She hoped that passive income continued. It should, as long as the market didn't crash. Or she didn't get into any kind of major financial jam where she'd need to liquefy her assets.

Being the former managing director of White Rock Asset Management, Inc., she knew how to diversify her investments and make money work for her instead of the other way around with her working for money.

While at the asset management company she had worked herself to the point of exhaustion because she never thought she had enough. She needed to keep clawing her way up that ladder, she needed to land that next bonus.

It turns out, in the end, she didn't need much. She had proven that to herself in the last two months after she sold all her possessions, including her status quo luxury car and her three-bedroom condo in her high-rise complex. What she didn't sell, she donated to a women's shelter.

Once she was free of all that excess weight, she packed only essentials into her saddlebags and soft-sided travel bag, filled Agnes's gas tank and hit the road.

With every mile she traveled farther away from Chicago and her old life, the more her mind cleared and her narrowed vision widened. She could see the world around her a lot better once she was no longer hyper-focused on her career and making a name for herself.

With every mile she rode, she realized she didn't need the kudos or titles, or even those much sought-after bonuses. She no longer had anything to prove. To herself or anyone else.

With every mile she and Agnes traveled together, she discovered more about who she really was and who she wanted to be instead of who everyone else wanted or expected her to be.

Quite simply, she learned to "just be."

Studying Whip's tattoos—at least the ones she could see —made her contemplate stopping at a tattoo shop some-where along her journey and getting her new but very simple motto tattooed somewhere. This way she'd never forget it. It would be a constant reminder that her mental and physical health were much more important than being named a top executive of an organization that didn't give two shits about her.

The only thing they cared about was the bottom line and appearances. That was it.

Money no longer defined her. Corporate titles no longer defined her.

A brand-new Porsche didn't, either.

She now defined herself.

While, yes, today had been a bump in her road of discovery, she loved her new life and newly-found freedom.

She could do whatever she wanted.

Including having dinner with a younger man with the best damn smile. It could be mesmerizing.

Even though he was a part of an MC, he seemed to be one of the least arrogant men she'd dealt with in a long time.

He was surprisingly sweet.

Definitely sexy.

And while they hadn't talked about anything deep, he'd kept her interested.

He said what he meant and meant what he said. He didn't put on airs and he certainly was far from fake or slick.

So opposite of the kind of people she'd surrounded herself with before.

Refreshing, that was what he was. Just like his honesty in the break room at Dutch's Garage.

Whip popped a loaded fry into his mouth and she couldn't pull her eyes from his lips as he chewed.

"What's your real name?"

The fact that he swallowed his mouthful of food before responding showed that someone had taught him manners. Most men she knew who wore suits and Rolexes didn't have that many. Money did not equal manners or respect.

"Real name?"

"Yes, you know... The one on your birth certificate. You were supposed to tell me it once we got Agnes back to the shop. You never did." She tilted her head and waited.

He cocked one eyebrow. "Don't like the name Whip?"

She jerked up one shoulder. "It's unique but I know that's not what your mother named you." He had already told her it had been his grandfather's nickname for him.

"Gonna make a difference if you know my real name?"

"No, not at all. I'm just... curious." She had this unexplainable urge to dig deeper and learn more about the man sitting across the table from her. It was more than just small talk to fill the silence.

He raised another fry loaded with dripping melted cheese and all kinds of other toppings until it was hovering dangerously near his lips. "Just curious?"

"More than curious," she murmured, distracted by the way his tongue swept over his bottom lip, leaving a shine behind.

She had this strange need to find out every personal detail about him. Why he chose to be a mechanic. Why he belonged to an MC. Who raised him. Even his middle name.

Where he lived. If he ever had his heart broken.

If he had any scars from his childhood from wrecking his bicycle or playing sports.

Instead of shoving the fry into his mouth, he dropped it back onto the plate. "How much more?"

She wiggled one eyebrow, then instantly regretted it, hoping it didn't make her appear like a cougar stalking her prey.

Did her cheeks heat up? *Oh, please, don't be blushing like a silly schoolgirl with a crush. Good lord, woman, get your hormones in line.*

He scrubbed a hand across his forehead and grimaced, like it would be painful to tell her. "Tyler."

"Tyler?" She rolled her lips inward.

"Yep. Tyler Robert Byrne if you wanna know the whole thing."

She didn't want to grin like a damn fool if he didn't like the name, but it had to be said… "You actually look like a Tyler."

The name fit his boy-next-door looks. Well, if he hadn't been wearing his cut, a long-sleeve thermal shirt beneath it with the sleeves pushed up to his elbows, exposing a tattoo covering his forearm, and heavy biker boots. That kind of spoiled the wholesome look.

"No one calls you that?"

"My mother and my aunt."

She considered her forgotten salad and stabbed at a cherry tomato with her fork. She paused with it halfway to her mouth. "What does your father call you?" She popped the tomato into her mouth and chewed.

"He don't."

She swallowed her mouthful. "You don't talk to him?" Whip was young, his parents had to still be young, too.

"Nope. Haven't talked to him since I was eight."

She put her fork down. "Sorry. That has to be difficult."

"Ain't difficult and don't be sorry. The man don't deserve an ounce of sympathy."

"The sympathy was for you."

"I don't need it, either."

The way he said that made her pause. Since she didn't know the circumstances about the break with his father and she didn't know him well enough to dig, she let it go.

Instead, she sat back in her chair and studied him. When he lifted his glass of sweet tea, she zeroed in on the way his Adam's apple traveled up and down his throat as he swallowed.

Why did she suddenly feel like some dirty old lady? She

couldn't be much older than him, could she? Or was she really a cougar? "How old are you?"

"That gonna make a difference just like my real name?"

In reality it might, but she reminded herself for the hundredth time that they were only sharing a dinner. Nothing else. "No."

"Just curious?" His grin caused a reaction deep within her.

She finally realized why. Sweet with an edge was the perfect way to describe him.

Yes, on the outside he looked wholesome and All-American, but he wasn't all of that. Not at all. He was much more.

He had layers.

Layers she'd like to peel away.

This trip was about discovery. Whip was now added to that list of must see and do.

That realization caught her off guard.

So much for only sharing dinner. That just got tossed out of the window while driving one hundred miles an hour.

She had never pursued a man before. Not even back in high school. Mostly because her eyes had always been focused on the prize and men seemed to get in the way.

Had she had relationships? Yes.

Had her drive and determination wrecked those relationships? Absolutely.

At the time she didn't care. Honestly, she still didn't. If any of those short-lived relationships would've been meant to be, the man would've been supportive of her career and not tried to undermine it because he couldn't handle a successful woman.

Cold-hearted, unemotional bitch was the label they liked to put on strong, career-driven women when it usually wasn't true.

Fragile and toxic masculinity made having a long-term relationship impossible.

In her world, successful women were looked at as a threat to successful men. Their misogynistic thought was women were supposed to support successful men, not stand next to them or even in front of them.

Some of the sexist shit she'd heard throughout her career could easily crush a woman who actually put weight behind some of those hurtful words.

Real men supported strong women. Little boys were threatened by them.

The problem was finding the first type instead of the second. They were out there but unfortunately, in her experience, it was like finding a needle in a haystack.

Who the hell had time to dig through hay? Not her.

Well, now she had time but she had no plans to stay anywhere long enough to make the time needed to dig worthwhile. That didn't mean she couldn't find the time to have some much-needed intimacy with someone along the way. Even if it was only for a single night or even a few hours…

"A little more than curious," she finally repeated, realizing he was waiting for an answer.

If he only knew where her thoughts had gone…

That panty-dampening grin widened. "Gonna turn twenty-nine in a coupla weeks."

"Oh, well… Happy birthday." Seven years. That was the difference between them.

He was at that age where he knew where he was going but was still discovering himself along the way.

Not that his age or their age difference mattered since it wasn't a real date. The dinner was supposed to only be a thank you for his help along with some companionship while they ate. She shouldn't have let her thoughts run wild.

He might not even be interested since she was seven years older than him.

"I don't make a big deal outta it. My birthday ain't different than any other day," he continued.

"I'm sure your mom makes a big deal out of it."

"She'd like to." He shoved away the plate that still held a few loaded fries. She was sure they were cold by now. "I don't let her. I ain't twelve anymore."

"But she's still your mom," Fallon reminded him.

"Your mom still throw you a party for your birthday?"

She wished. "No, she stopped once I turned eighteen."

He tipped his head. "There you go."

"But if she was still alive, I'd be thrilled to attend a birthday party just to see her again."

Whip's lips flattened as he sat back and stared at her. "Mom's dead?"

Fallon nodded. "Yes, she…" She sucked in a breath. "She was diagnosed with early onset dementia while in her forties."

"Damn, sorry," he murmured.

"It progressed to where her body didn't even know how to breathe or swallow. Even though it took ten years to get to that point, it was not an easy ten years." Fallon was lucky she could afford quality care for her mother. Even if she hadn't been busy with her career, it would have been difficult to deal with her mother on her own.

Watching a woman go from being her mother to someone she hardly recognized was painful. Seeing her mother disappear like that was devastating, especially when she no longer recognized her own child. Fallon spent a decade of drowning in frustration and heartbreak.

One of Fallon's greatest fears was, because it could be genetic, she could end up the same way or pass it on to her future children, *if* she had any.

"You should appreciate any time you have with your mother."

He ignored that and asked, "Your pop take care of her?"

"No. He wasn't around."

"He ghosted? Before or after she got sick?"

"A couple of years after she was diagnosed, I caught him having an affair."

Whip's brow dropped low. "Damn."

"Well, that wasn't the worst part. The woman he was having an affair with was supposed to be my mom's caregiver. She was definitely a giver and my father was the taker, if you get what I'm saying."

"Damn," he repeated.

"That give and take was happening in my parents' bed."

He whistled softly. "That's fucked up."

"Yes, it is. He forgot the part in his wedding vows where he promised to remain loyal in sickness and in health and all the rest of those uttered words, too."

"What'd you do?"

"I moved her in with me and hired another caregiver for a while until she got to the point where she had to be moved into an around-the-clock care facility."

"What about your pop?"

Fallon shrugged. "Hopefully he's happy with his choices. The last time I saw his ass was when it was bare and he was railing the home health aide while my mother was in the next room."

Fallon tamped down the fury at the memory. She not only was pissed that her father was cheating, but was doing it in the same house, only feet from her vulnerable and confused mother.

Fallon never spoke to him again. She refused to answer his calls or return his messages. She refused to hear his excuses or even an apology. An apology he would spew only because he got caught.

Did she allow him to visit her mother during her last couple of years while in a home? Yes. Fallon decided not to block him from the visitor list. She hoped by him visiting, he would suffer remorse from his decision to mess up their family. She was glad her mother wasn't aware of her father's cheating.

Would Fallon ever forgive him? Probably not.

Was that selfish? No more than her father had been.

Just because someone was related didn't mean you had to blindly accept all their mistakes and faults. You didn't have to forgive them for the pain they put you and others through.

What he did wasn't a mistake because he *knew* it was wrong before he did it. It wasn't an unavoidable accident, it was done with specific intent.

After catching him in the act, it made her wonder if he had cheated on her mother while she was still healthy. All those business trips and late nights at the office became suspect.

She'd seen that same kind of behavior firsthand while working at White Rock. Through the years, she'd overheard some of her coworkers calling their spouses or significant others and blatantly lying about why they needed to work late. The second they disconnected from the call, they rushed out of the office to go do whatever they were about to do.

Or whoever they were about to do.

While that behavior wasn't limited to the men, a lot of them conveniently forgot they were married when their wives weren't around. She had been hit on plenty of times by male coworkers with wedding bands circling their ring fingers. An obvious reminder of the vows they ignored.

After all that, Fallon wasn't sure if she could ever trust a man one hundred percent. She also avoided any kind of committed relationship in which she could be the one cheated on. Especially since she dedicated so much of her time to work and was hardly ever home.

It was simply easier to avoid any serious relationship and

was one less thing to worry about. It also made it easier for her to concentrate on her career.

"Sorry your dad was a dick. So was mine."

His words pulled her from the thoughts that were beginning to make her stomach churn.

That wasn't the only thing that pulled her back to the diner and to the man sitting across from her. Whip brushed his rough fingertips over the back of her knuckles, too. They were there and gone so quickly, for a second she thought she imagined it.

Even that brief touch shot a shiver down her spine and woke up everything inside her. "He cheated on your mother?"

Those same long fingers were now curled around his glass of iced tea. "He did a lot of shit."

The tone of his answer made it clear he didn't want to go down that path. Fallon would respect that. "Did you grow up around here?"

"Liberty. 'Bout a half-hour from here."

"Have you always lived in northern PA?"

"Yeah." His now serious gaze grabbed hers and held her hostage. "So, why were you on Copperhead Road?"

She didn't try to break free from his hold as she answered, "I decided to head north to explore the Finger Lakes area. I figured it would be a beautiful ride since spring's in the air. Maybe find a cabin on one of the lakes and take a breather. Hit some wineries. Explore the local culture up there."

"Local culture?"

She shrugged. "Sure."

"But Copperhead Road ain't gonna get you to the Finger Lakes."

She was aware of that. "Once I decide on a destination, I take the scenic route."

"Most people don't got that kinda time."

"You're right."

"You told Lee that you got nothin' and no one waitin' on you. That true?"

By continuing to ask her questions, he was diverting the attention from himself. "Yes, that's true."

"Why's that?"

"Why what?"

"Why you travelin' alone?"

She shrugged one shoulder. Besides the fact that she didn't have anyone to travel with? "It gives me the freedom to go wherever and whenever I want. That's the nice thing about not having any ties and no one waiting for you at home." Or what used to be home. When she got tired of being on the road, of being a nomad, she would pick somewhere else to settle.

Somewhere without snow. Maybe a place on the ocean or Gulf where she could walk the beach in the morning and watch the sun set in the evening. Feel the warmth of the sun on her skin and the saltiness of the ocean spray on her face.

"Home," he repeated. "Illinois?"

"Right outside of Chicago."

"You born there?"

She shook her head. "Not there. I grew up outside of Indianapolis."

"How'd you end up in Chicago?"

"The company I worked for was based in Chicago."

She had wanted to find out more about him, but here he was firing off questions about her instead. She didn't mind answering them as long as he was willing to do the same.

"So, you don't got a job, either?"

She stared at him. "Don't worry, the garage will get paid."

"Ain't worried about that. Some of the ol' ladies in the Fury's got their own businesses. Like Lee does with Shelter from the Storm. Assumin' you do, too, since you can afford that sweet sled and got the time to take the scenic route."

She tilted her head to the side. She didn't want to talk about her. She wanted to talk about him, so she turned the focus back on Whip. "Do you still live in Liberty?"

"Nah. Here in Manning Grove. Moved closer to work."

"You like what you do." She didn't make it a question, because it was obvious he did.

"Don't not like it. I'm good at it."

His answer wasn't cocky, but honest. She liked that.

She smothered her grin. "Are you saying you're good with your hands?"

He lifted both hands up and studied them, then wiggled his fingers. "Got some skills."

That didn't come off as cocky either, but more in a teasing tone.

It was cute. He was cute.

Damn it. Since when was her mid-thirties ass interested in chasing "cute?"

She snorted softly. "Sounds like a bad pickup line."

He wiggled his eyebrows. "It work?"

She studied him for a long minute. He had removed his baseball cap when they sat down earlier and she could get a much better look at him. "No, because you don't need one."

Were they flirting with each other? Sadly, she didn't even know. She'd never been good with flirting and had always been more of the direct type. She'd always been more attracted to men who were direct, too. Just not the rude, aggressive type.

Whip was not rude or aggressive. He was not slick. He was just… Whip.

Fallon found that very attractive. And, again, refreshing.

Not to mention, tempting.

Very, very tempting.

She reached across the table and took one of his hands

in hers. She turned it over to study the deep lines criss-crossing his palm and the underside of his fingers. Rough. Calloused. Grease in the creases that probably never came out no matter how much he scrubbed them.

A working man's hands. A man who wasn't afraid to get dirt under his fingernails. Or crack the skin on his knuckles.

She turned his hand over so they were palm to palm, his warm and solid against hers. Hers looked so much smaller than his.

She could hear his breathing quicken but she didn't look up. Instead, she kept her eyes on what she held.

The men she used to work with had soft hands, mani-cured fingernails, wore fraternity or signet rings. Like Whip, they belonged to clubs, too. Just a different type. Rotary, Masons, even country or tennis clubs.

"You can tell a lot from a man's hands."

"Yeah?" he murmured. "What can you tell from mine?"

"That you're hardworking, dedicated to your craft and not afraid to get dirty."

"Don't mind gettin' dirty."

She lifted her gaze from the fingers that had curled slightly in hers. That smirk was back but his eyes were heated and focused on hers.

He didn't pull away, even though they were practically holding hands across the table. He didn't seem uncomfort-able with it at all. Maybe she put more weight into the gesture than he did.

She reluctantly released his hand when the waitress came over to ask them if they were finished and if they wanted dessert.

"Dessert?" she asked him, then pressed her lips together. Even so, she didn't bother to hide her interest in a dessert not found in the case with the rotating glass shelves by the cash register.

She swore his timbre was a touch deeper when he answered, "Later."

Fallon fought the shiver that unspoken promise caused. She pulled her attention from him to give it back to the server. "No, just the check, please."

"Sure." The gray-haired woman pulled her pad from her apron, looked it over quickly, then ripped off the top sheet, placing it upside down in the middle of the table.

Fallon snagged it before Whip could even move.

"Did you guys reserve the back room for Sunday?" the waitress asked him.

"Dunno. You know I don't make those plans, Maggie. I just follow the rest of the pack."

"You never know, one day you might be leading that pack." The waitress squeezed Whip's shoulder and gave him a warm smile. "Have a good rest of your evening, Whip. You, too, ma'am."

Fallon thanked her and glanced at the total. So damn cheap. That was probably one of the positives of living in a small town versus a metropolis like Chicago.

But then, when she lived in Chicago she didn't eat at neighborhood diners. She had eaten at restaurants where the bar bill alone was way higher than what both their meals cost tonight.

"You ain't payin'," he grumbled as he pulled out a leather wallet from his back pocket and placed it on the table in front of him, popping open the snaps.

"Yes, I am."

"No, you—"

She cut him off. "It's a thank you for everything you've done."

"Didn't do shit."

"You did more than you realize."

"You ain't payin' for me."

"I asked you to dinner, not the other way around."

His eyes narrowed on her. "Don't matter."

"It does to me."

He stared at her and she stared right back at him. A silent challenge.

"Man pays," he insisted.

"Not in my world."

"Right now, you're in my world."

You're in my world.

Good lord. Something in those words and the way he said it made flames lick at her all the way from the tips of her toes to the top of her head. She had no idea why.

Maybe because his tone hinted that he wasn't really sweet.

He wasn't a boy-next-door at all.

No, he was a man not easily manipulated. A man who held a silent strength.

Suddenly he was no longer only cute, he was much more than that.

"I have an idea…" She uncurled her toes in her boots and steadied her breathing so she could speak normally. "Is there somewhere we can go for a nightcap?"

His eyebrows pinched together. "Nightcap?"

"A drink."

He shook his head. "You ain't buyin' me a drink. Since you're payin' for dinner, I'm buyin' you a drink instead."

Oh, yes, he was taking charge and that made all the nerve endings in her body sit up and take notice. As well as her nipples.

He did a slow roll of his eyes down to them, paused briefly, then took his time lifting his gaze back to her face.

She had made her point. Now he did, too.

"I'm good with that. I'll get dinner, you get drinks? Deal?"

He stuck his hand back across the table. She automatically placed her hand in his, expecting him to shake it for a deal.

Instead he grabbed it, slid to the end of the bench seat and got to his feet, drawing her along with him. Pulling her closer.

Until they were toe to toe.

She tipped her face up while he tipped his down.

His smirk was gone and so was she.

She was so damn gone. As were the diner and its patrons.

Nothing existed but the two of them.

This was so unexpected. So very unexpected.

In this place, in this time, with this man.

Even though none of it made sense to her, she was still tempted to say screw the drinks and suggest they head back to the motel instead.

"Do you…" She cleared her throat and tried again. "Do you know of a decent place to grab a drink?"

"Not sure if you'll think it's decent but it's a place to go."

"Is it a biker bar?"

"You gonna say no if it is?"

She'd never been around bikers so she wasn't sure how a biker bar would be. Her guess, rough and rowdy. "Is it?"

"No, it ain't a biker bar."

"That's fine."

"You sure?"

She was damn sure. But not about the bar.

About what she wanted to happen afterwards.

And whether he'd be open to it.

Chapter Seven

WHIP WANTED to skip the fucking drinks, skip the time that would be wasted at Crazy Pete's and take her directly back to the motel, her room, then her bed.

She wasn't hiding her interest. She didn't seem to give a shit that he was a biker and she was... far from that. She might own that beautiful Indian Scout, but being a casual rider was different. Just because someone owned a sled, it didn't make them a real biker.

What made her even hotter was she didn't act like she was better than him even though there was no doubt that was true.

He still didn't know their age difference but Fallon didn't seem to give a shit about that, either. And that was A-fuck-ing-okay with him.

He only hoped that by the time they were done having a couple of drinks at Pete's, she didn't change her mind and lose interest. Because right now, he couldn't think of anything other than sliding between her thighs. With his fingers, his face and finally his dick.

He couldn't shake the imagery of Fallon on her knees at his feet, taking him all the way to the back of her throat, his fingers wound tightly in her blonde hair and the sounds she'd make as she sucked him off.

He reached down and adjusted his hard-on as he followed her down the dark hallway from Pete's rear entrance into the main bar area.

Once again, even though she didn't have to, she had wrapped her arms around him on the ride over. She had snaked one hand under his cut and planted it on his gut. The other had stayed on his waist, even though he'd hoped she'd plant that somewhere else, too. Like below his belt.

She probably had too much class to do something like that. *Hell*, she had more class in her pinky finger than he had in his whole body.

Did he care? Fuck no.

Did she? He hoped to hell not.

He now had plans and he didn't want anything or anyone fucking those up. But he'd go through the motion of getting drinks since some women preferred to be wined and dined before getting down and dirty. Just like a date, whether it was one or not.

Hell, he hadn't dated since the first night he hooked up with Billie. That was the last official "date" he'd been on and that was years ago.

Here, unlike with dinner, he was covering the tab. Fallon didn't need to know the drinks would be on the house. That was one benefit of the club owning the bar.

Even so, he didn't bring Fallon to Pete's because it would be free, but because there was nowhere else in town to go. In truth, he'd prefer to take her somewhere his club brothers wouldn't be nosy fucks. But besides the fancy pub off the lobby of the hotel on the square, Crazy Pete's was the only drinking hole in town and, more importantly, he didn't want to go too far from home, even if he only drank a couple of beers.

He'd never spent a day in jail and he preferred to keep it

that way. Plus, if he lost his license for being careless and getting popped with a DUI... His whole life would crumble. It would hinder his ability to ride and his ability to work. But more importantly, he'd be hauling precious cargo on the back of his sled after tonight's "date."

Yeah, fuck that. It wasn't worth the risk.

He used to drink here when Pete was alive, at the time not having any fucking clue that Pete had been an Original or that the late bar owner's past and Whip's future would cross because of the Blood Fury.

Too bad Pete was no longer around to see his first grandbaby. Or to see the resurrected club Trip had built back up better than ever.

"Do I hear a live band?" she asked not even a few steps down the hallway.

"Yep," he answered. The farther they walked, the louder it got.

Dodge and Stella normally didn't book bands for any other nights other than Friday and Saturday, but with Dodge's ol' lady being the lead singer of her own band, The Synners tended to play some Thursday nights when their new manager didn't have them booked elsewhere.

It was a good way for them to practice, work on new covers, work on some original songs and, even better, bring in extra scratch for the bar. A win-win all the way around.

It didn't hurt that Syn was fucking good.

Better than good.

Her band could be a thousand times better if she did what her manager suggested and replace them. She refused and, luckily, the Dirty Deeds manager still took them on solely due to Syn's talent and not the rest of them.

Sig's sister was okay with not getting some big recording contract now that she had Dodge as her ol' man and, more importantly, she'd been reunited with her daughter Maya.

Maya needed stability and without a doubt, Syn's nine-year-old was more important to her than making it big.

As they emerged from the hallway into the bar area, Fallon stopped short, her head automatically swiveling toward the low stage in the back corner. "Wow, she's really good. Her voice is... amazing. Impressive." She rubbed her arms. "She's giving me goosebumps."

Yeah, Syn's voice did that to most of them. When she sang, it was like she trapped everyone within hearing distance in a web, making it hard to pull free.

Whip stepped up behind Fallon, rubbed her upper arms for her, and leaned in so he didn't have to yell. "She's got that power."

"Does that band play here often?" She didn't pull away from his touch, but instead, slightly leaned back into him.

Her doing that made him believe she trusted him and that meant more than she'd know.

If he was lucky, maybe she'd only want to stick around for one beer and then they could go somewhere more quiet and private. "Just about every week. Syn's part of the Fury, too."

She glanced over her shoulder at him, her Caribbean blue eyes wide. "She is?"

"Yeah. Her brother's our VP and her ol' man's the dark-haired guy over there behind the bar."

Fallon glanced over toward Dodge, currently hustling to help Dozer and Woody serve customers. The Thursday night crowd was a lot bigger now than it used to be. All due to The Synners.

"I see he's wearing one of those cuts, too."

"Yeah. He's one of my brothers. Can't see him from here, but Scar, the scary-looking dude standing at the door's one of our prospects. Dozer and Woody, the two guys behind the bar helping Dodge, are patched members, too."

"So, wait..." She turned to face him. "You said this wasn't a biker bar."

"It ain't. Stella's father was an Original and ran it forever before he passed. Now she owns half and the club owns the other half but since she's the prez's ol' lady, that pretty much means the club owns the whole thing."

"What's an Original? I saw that patch on the motel manager's cut."

"Someone who belonged to the Fury back in the beginning." That was the easiest way to put it. "Dutch is an Original. He was a part of the Fury since practically day one."

"Ozzy was, too?"

"Ozzy joined later, but was still a part of the original Blood Fury."

"Are there any others?"

"No. That's it."

"Where did the rest of them go?"

He had to tread carefully. "The original club just fell apart and everyone scattered. Trip, the son of the original president, built it back up from scratch. Besides the two Originals, some of the current members are second generation Fury and some are first, like me."

"Interesting," she murmured. "I find all of this fascinating. It's not just some casual club where you guys simply hang out. It's structured like a business organization. Reilly was telling me about the by-laws and executive committee. And while that's fascinating, too, the fact that your club owns businesses to bring in money like an enterprising empire... I'm actually really impressed. So far, what I've seen between the garage, the motel and this bar, they're successful businesses."

"There's more than that, but the garage ain't club-owned. Dutch owns that all on his own. He'll probably pass it on to his sons when he drops over. Or... maybe not.

Knowin' Dutch he might give it to his grandbaby out of spite."

"Well, at least it'll stay in the family, right?"

"Yeah. And I'm damn well sure that family ain't done growin' yet. Cage and Rook both got ol' ladies now. Never know when one of them will get knocked up."

Fallon pressed her lips together.

"What? You gonna bust out laughin' again at somethin' I said?"

She shook her head. "It's the slang you all use. It's a whole other language."

"It bother you?"

"No, not at all. It just takes some getting used to, is all. I spent my whole adult life clawing my way to the top in the business world where every damn thing you say is analyzed and criticized, especially if you're a woman. So, like I said in that break room, I find it very refreshing that you speak your mind and in a way that's all your own."

Whip grinned, glad the way he spoke wasn't going to be an obstacle. He wasn't going to change the way he was for anyone. Even the woman currently standing in front of him, no matter how much he wanted to slide between her thighs. He wouldn't even *pretend* to be someone he wasn't for just one night. "Yeah. We don't really give a fuck what anyone thinks about us or how we talk. Or what we do."

"You just be."

"What?" He tipped his head and leaned closer. Maybe because of the loud music he hadn't heard that right.

"You just live your life. You just be," she explained with a shrug.

"We try to. Sometimes we got people or things tryin' to keep us from doin' that."

"And then what?"

Fuck. He never should've said that. "Then we deal with it."

"How?"

He hesitated. "However we need to."

He needed to get her off this line of conversation. It was going somewhere he couldn't go. Getting into details she didn't need to know.

He tipped his head toward the crowded bar area. "C'mon. Gonna get you a drink. You play pool?"

"No."

Thank fuck because he didn't want to spend more time than necessary at Pete's. He wanted to get to know her better but not through conversation.

Or at least if they were going to have conversation it would be better if they were naked and while taking a breather after their first round of knocking boots.

He settled his hand at the small of her back and steered her toward where Dodge, Dozer and Woody were working.

Halfway there, a whirlwind came out of nowhere and Whip grunted as Maya slammed full force into him, knocking his hand off Fallon's back. The nine-year-old snaked her arms around his waist and squeezed him as hard as she could.

Fuck.

Syn's daughter dug her chin into his gut, tipped her face up to his and yelled, "Hi, Whip!" over the loud music.

He smiled down at her, brushing a lock of dark hair away from her eye. "Hey, Maya, how's it hangin'?"

"Good! How are you hanging?"

He glanced at Fallon to see an amused but confused expression on her face.

Whip was not going to tell Maya how he was hanging right about now. "I'm good, kid."

"I didn't know you were coming tonight." She almost sounded insulted.

"That makes two of us. Fallon here wanted to grab a drink."

"Who's she?"

Whip scratched the back of his neck as he spotted Dodge working his way around some patrons to get to where Whip was being held hostage.

The older brother shot Whip an exasperated look while he shook his head and peeled Maya's arms from around Whip's waist.

"What'd I tell you about tacklin' Whip like that?" Dodge asked her, clamping his hand on her shoulder.

"I was just saying hello."

"That ain't how you say hello to men who ain't Sig or me. We talked about that."

"But—"

"No. Go say goodnight to your mom, then grab your coat and your helmet. Your uncle's on his way to pick you up."

Maya's dark eyebrows pinned together. She looked like a carbon-copy of Syn, but personality-wise she was more outgoing than her mother, which was surprising for a woman who stood on a stage and sang in front of crowds.

Maya squinted up at Dodge. "Which uncle?"

Dodge raised a dark eyebrow at her. "Which one you think?"

"I've got a bunch of uncles," she insisted stubbornly.

She was right, she did. Trip believed in the whole "it takes a village" concept to raise the Fury kids. Luckily, everybody was onboard with that. It not only made sense, it kept the bond within the Fury strong. The kids were their future.

It fell on all of them to protect and teach the kids. Maybe not teach them in a school-type of way, but in a common sense and street smarts type of way.

"Yeah, smart ass, but you know which one."

"But I don't want to go," she whined softly.

Thank fuck she didn't add a Daisy-style stomp to that

complaint. One obstinate Fury kid was enough for all of them. Cassie's daughter was a handful, even for Judge to deal with.

Dodge cocked one eyebrow at Maya. "Yeah, well… You're only nine, baby girl, so you don't get to decide. Anyway, it's gettin' late and you got school tomorrow."

Maya scrunched up her face. "But Whip can help me with my homework."

"No, Whip ain't helpin' you with your homework. First off, you told me it was done already. Was that a lie?"

Maya tucked her bottom lip between her teeth.

Dodge squeezed her shoulder again, dropping his head until he caught her gaze. "You know you ain't supposed to lie to us."

"I'm almost done. Whip can help me with the rest."

"No, he can't. He's gonna be busy with his friend. Autumn can help you when you get home."

"But—"

Dodge raised a palm. "Nope. Stop right there. This ain't a negotiation." He dropped his voice an octave and ordered, "Go say goodnight to your mom and get your stuff. Sig ain't gonna wanna wait. You know how he gets."

Maya sighed dramatically.

"Not one more 'but,'" Dodge warned her.

She sighed again, not so dramatically this time. "Fine. Wake me up when you get home."

"Not gonna wake you up. We'll see you in the mornin'."

Maya stuck her tongue out at Dodge, then giggled.

He shook his head and pointed toward the stage, raising both eyebrows this time. "Go!"

Maya rolled her eyes and dashed toward the stage, her sneakers slapping along the floor as she went.

Since this had become a normal routine for Syn's daughter, she knew enough to wait until her mother finished her song before saying goodnight.

Once Dodge finished watching her go, he turned away from the stage, closed his eyes and shook his head.

The man had never been a dad and now he was suddenly raising a nine-year-old. That had to be tough and Whip was glad it wasn't him.

Did he like kids? They were all right. He liked them better when he didn't have to deal with the drama. But if any of his brothers asked him to step up and do something for their kid, Whip wouldn't hesitate. That was what being a part of a brotherhood and the Fury family was all about.

Dodge turned to Fallon and took his time checking her out from head to toe, then shot Whip a knowing look. Whip was surprised the man didn't give him a thumbs up and a damn wink.

"Dodge, Fallon. Fallon, Dodge."

"Nice to meet you, Dodge." Amusement crinkled the corners of Fallon's eyes.

"Same." Dodge turned to Whip with a grin, "Figure you want a draft," then asked Fallon, "What d'you want to drink?"

"I'll take whatever local IPA you have on tap," she answered.

The bar manager snorted. "Then you're gonna get an empty glass. We got the most popular domestic beers on tap. You want somethin' fancy you need to head over to the hotel bar. But they're gonna charge you the cost of a kidney for that shit, too."

"How about a vodka tonic?"

"Can manage that. Grab a table and I'll get Woody to bring it over to you." Dodge chuckled and whacked Whip on the shoulder before turning and heading back to the bar.

Whip scanned the area and spotted an empty table near the stage. He planted his hand on her back again and encouraged her to head over to it.

As they walked, her eyes weren't on their destination but

on the stage where Syn was talking to Maya. "What does that mean?"

"What does what mean?"

"Maya's wearing a vest similar to yours but in denim with patches on the back that says 'Property of Dodge.'"

Yeah, that. *Shit.*

"Means she belongs to Dodge."

"I don't understand. It means she's his daughter?"

Whip wasn't sure how to answer that. Fallon seemed to be the type of woman who might take offense if he told her that the Fury women and children were property of the club. "Basically. Not biological but he's steppin' in as her dad."

Fallon's gaze sliced back to Dodge who had returned to working behind the bar, though his eyes were glued to that stage where his ol' lady and Syn's daughter were. He always kept a sharp eye on his new family.

For good reason.

Syn's daughter only wore the denim cut while at the bar because Dodge was worried about it making Maya a target for the Shirleys if she wore it out around town.

When they reached the table, he pulled out a chair for Fallon, but she was still staring at the stage.

"Wait. The singer. That's her *mother?* They look like sisters."

"Yeah." With their age difference they could be.

"She can't be old enough to have a child that age."

Whip didn't want to touch that, either. How old Syn was when she had Maya wasn't an outsider's business.

And Fallon *was* an outsider. No matter how curious she was, Whip needed to remember that.

"Maya has a crush on you," Fallon announced with a smirk, finally settling in her seat. "That's really cute."

"She's nine."

"So? Nine-year-olds are probably just discovering boys. And you're really cute. I could see it happening."

You're really cute.

Boys were cute, men were not cute. *Fuck*, did she consider him too young? "Prefer women who are older."

Fallon laughed. "Well, of course. I would hope so. When I was a little girl I had puppy dog crushes on older men, like teachers and coaches."

"Puppy dog crushes?" What the fuck was that?

"Yes, sort of like a mix between puppy love and a crush. A lot of girls have them, I'm sure boys do, too. You never had a crush on one of your teachers?"

"Probably," he murmured.

Fuck yeah, he did. But by the time he hit fourteen, those crushes turned to fantasies that he used to relieve himself of random boners.

Now, if a woman like Chelle had been his school librarian back then...

Because he valued his life, he'd never say that out loud, especially around Shade.

The newly patched-in Woody brought their drinks and dropped off a bowl of pretzels, too.

"Brother," Woody greeted as he set Whip's draft beer in front of him.

"Brother," Whip murmured back.

Woody's gaze stuck on Fallon and stayed there as he put her vodka tonic in front of her. "Need anythin' else?"

He wasn't just looking at her, he was fucking checking her out. Dodge did it out of curiosity. He wouldn't eye-fuck a woman in front of Syn. *Hell*, his eye-fucking days might even be over. But Woody was just being a horny shit.

Worse, Whip had no claim to the blonde sitting across from him.

Whip cleared his throat to catch his attention. "Nope. We're good."

Woody didn't even bother to look at Whip when he said, "Was askin' her."

"And I fuckin' answered you," Whip said sharply. "We need anythin', will let you know. For now, we don't, so get lost." He tipped his head toward the bar.

Woody stepped behind Fallon's chair so she couldn't see him, then made an expression that Whip wanted to wipe off his face. He waited for Fallon to glance toward the stage when Syn started her next song and mouthed, "Fuck off," to his younger brother.

Woody's mouth pulled up on one side and he flipped Whip the bird before heading back to the bar area. The man never would've gotten away with that kind of shit as a prospect, but the man's balls must've dropped as soon as he received his full set of patches.

Whip picked up his beer and sucked down a few swallows to cool off the temptation to go have a few words with Woody. But he wasn't stupid and didn't want to fuck up his chances with her because of teaching the younger biker a lesson.

Fallon picked up her drink and took a sip. "Phew. That's strong." She took one more sip, grimacing a little before saying, "Wow. She's really good. I never would've expected to hear that kind of talent…"

"In this kind of bar?" Whip finished for her.

"Well, yes. In this small of a town, too. She should be on a big stage."

Whip and everyone else who heard Syn agreed with that. "What d'you know about music?"

Fallon shook her head. "I'm just an avid listener, but I know nothing about the actual business end of it. I'm sure, like a lot of businesses, it can be cutthroat."

"Tell me about this business world you were a part of and are now runnin' from."

"I didn't run. I walked away when I realized it wasn't

worth it."

"None of it?" he asked.

"Some things were. For a while. The money was good. The life lessons were valuable, as well. I didn't think so at the time but now that I look back on it, I realize those lessons kicked me in the ass and made me see what was really important to me."

"Which is?"

"Myself. I learned I needed to take care of myself first since no one else would."

"But you got no job now, right?"

"No," she confirmed.

"No business, either."

"Nope."

"Tell me your secret." How could a single woman not even close to retirement age just up and leave everything behind?

"What secret?"

"How you can just buy a sled and travel," he answered. "No business, no job. Gotta cost scratch to do that. Gonna cost a good chunk of change just for that repair. How d'you do all that without goin' broke?"

"You invest wisely."

"You mean like the stock market?" Whip didn't know anything about the market. He had a bank account that he dumped his paycheck into. That was it.

He deposited scratch and when he needed something, he withdrew it. Basics.

He didn't have to spend a lot of dough on anything since the club covered a lot of shit. All he had to do was pay his monthly dues. They were a lot more now than they were when Trip first got the club back up and running, but they were worth every damn penny.

"Yes, the stock market is one place to invest. Stocks, mutual funds, investment bonds, commodities, even real estate. I diversify where I can. Some of my investments are aggressive, some safe."

"Where'd you learn to do all that or d'you have someone doin' it for you?"

She shot him a smile.

"What?" he asked, wondering if that was something too personal and he shouldn't ask.

"I do it myself."

Of fucking course she did. "And you make enough to live off of?"

"Yes, I do now. Enough to keep me and Agnes on the road."

"Damn," he whispered. "How'd you learn to do that?"

"That's the business I walked away from. I worked at an organization that did asset management. It was my life. And when I say it was my life, it was. My. Whole. Damn. Life. Frankly, it consumed me."

"Then you just walked away."

"Yes. I realized it wasn't worth being totally consumed until there was nothing left of me."

That reminded Whip of Reese and how, before Deacon, her life revolved around her law firm. She lived and breathed her business. Now, she lived her life the best way possible. She only put in regular hours and then enjoyed her life outside of those hours. She learned to dial down her intense drive to succeed and discovered there were more important things in life than solely making money. Like Deacon and now Dane.

But it didn't sound like Fallon dialed anything down. Fuck no, she slammed her hand on the "stop" button and got off that ride completely.

"Tell me more," he encouraged. "Wanna hear what led you to here." He tapped his finger on the table.

"You mean to this very moment?"

"Yeah."

"That's a long story. I'll give you the Cliff Notes version."

Whip shrugged and took a sip of his beer. "Whatever you wanna share." *Just keep talkin'.*

"Well..." She inhaled a deep breath as if she had to prepare herself. "I was hired by White Rock Asset Management as an undergrad. I started out as a financial advisor until I finished my MBA, then moved into an asset manager position. Long story short, I clawed my way up the ladder from basically the bottom. I got as far as the managing director while keeping my eye on the CEO position. When it opened up due to the CEO retiring, I was..."

Whip watched her carefully. Her expressions turned from neutral to beginning to twist when she paused. Not because she was upset, but with what might be anger.

"I was skipped over," she finished. She took a much larger sip of her drink before continuing. "I gave my life to that company. I put aside having a family for that company. I gave them everything. And you know what I got in return?"

"A good salary and benefits?" Whip asked.

Her eyes narrowed on him. "Misogyny. I kept hitting my damn head on a ceiling that would never break. I was the most qualified for that position. They skipped over me to hand it to a man who'd been with the company for only two years, didn't have the experience needed and didn't even have his Masters. Even worse, he had two sexual harassment complaints against him."

Whip frowned. "Why the fuck did they choose him?"

"Because I was missing one thing."

"What?"

"A dick. If I had one, I would have been handed that spot. It should've been mine." She slapped a hand against her chest. "I earned that damn position."

Whip could see she was struggling to keep the anger from her voice. Maybe even a whole bunch of hurt.

"I gave fourteen years of my life to that company. The president would've been next in line and I would've understood not getting it if he'd taken it, but he didn't want the CEO spot. He was struggling to balance his home life as it was. He even recommended me, since I was next in line after him. I had everything required to fill that position."

"They didn't deserve you."

"I know that now." She let out a loud sigh. "I probably knew it back then, too, and just ignored the signs, hoping I was wrong."

"So, you just up and quit?"

"Sure did. The minute—no, the very second—I heard who landed the CEO spot, I was done. Luckily, by that time I had invested a good part of my salary and all of my bonuses."

"Sounds like you weren't playin' at all."

"No, I wasn't. I'd had enough. Now I'm living my life on my own terms."

"Lucky."

She circled her fingertip along the rim of her vodka tonic. "It wasn't luck. I sacrificed for a long damn time. With both my mental and physical health, not to mention, my dignity."

"Now you're free."

"Now I'm free," she repeated, sitting back in her chair. "I got rid of everything. Whatever I couldn't pack into my saddlebags and travel bag I sold or gave to a women's shelter."

"Kept those investments, though." He had been in a rush to get her back to the motel, but right now, he found himself too invested in her story.

"Of course, if it wasn't for investing smartly, I wouldn't be able to do what I'm doing. As it stands now, I can live off my investments for a long time. Maybe even forever, if I play my cards right."

That was fucking impressive. Whip couldn't imagine just being able to hop on his bike and take off whenever and go wherever he wanted. No responsibilities, nothing.

He didn't have a lot, but he had family. Not only his Fury family but his mother, too. He wanted to be close by in case she needed him since Whip was her only child.

He was content with the way his life was, he didn't want for anything and he had no desire to be rich, but he did have that bike bucket list. Of course, that would take some scratch.

He began working at Dutch's right out of high school and he figured he'd be working until he couldn't work any longer. He certainly didn't have Fallon's financial knowledge to do anything differently.

"After I rage quit, it took me a while to break out of that rat race habit. My life had always been work, eat, sleep, repeat. A vicious cycle. Then a few days after I quit, it hit me, I no longer *had* to go anywhere. I didn't *have* to answer to anyone except myself. I decided to travel around Europe and Asia for a while, then afterward reevaluate my future."

Manning Grove, Pennsylvania, was far from Europe or Asia. "Why didn't you?"

"Because I bought Agnes."

What the fuck? That answer was too simple. He needed more than that. "You grow up ridin' with your dad or some-thin'? Why'd you decide to travel the States on a sled? Are they in your blood?"

"No."

She swallowed another mouthful of her drink and he watched her long, delicate throat roll. Wanted to put his mouth there, feel her pulse under his lips, taste her skin, feel a moan vibrate against his fingers.

"How it all came about was crazy, really. A couple of

days after deciding to go abroad, I pulled up to a stoplight and happened to look to my right where someone was teaching a motorcycle safety class in a parking lot."

"That's all it took? Seein' someone teachin' people to ride?"

"No, that wasn't it at all. It was the three women I saw standing with their bikes. All three had huge, carefree smiles on their faces. It made me think. When I looked into my rearview mirror and saw my own face, I realized that's what I wanted. I wanted to wear a real smile just like those women, not one that was forced only to make nice with coworkers or clients. I wanted to be truly happy. Of course, I didn't know if riding a motorcycle would put that smile on my face, but I figured it was worth a shot. And I just happened to have time to kill since I no longer had that nine-to-five."

"Damn. So, you learned to ride, got rid of all your shit and hit the road."

She smiled. He wondered if that smile was as big as the smiles of those three ladies.

She tapped her finger on the table in the same spot he had. "And that's the not-so-short version of how I got here. You know the rest."

That he did.

Chapter Eight

FATE.

Fallon chalked it up to fate.

There had to be no other reason.

Sitting at the traffic light, she felt a pull to look to her right. To that parking lot. To those women.

The universe was telling her the way to find happiness.

It seemed so damn cheesy, but it was also true.

She could tour Europe and Asia at any time, but since she was only thirty-six she wanted to do something now that was a little more daring. Traveling the country by herself on a motorcycle of all things.

She wanted to do something different and so unlike her. She wanted to push her own boundaries. This time not for upper management but for herself.

The bar got quiet when the band finished their set. The lead singer stepped off the stage and stopped at their table. She was gorgeous with her dark brown hair and matching eyes, but way too young to have a daughter Maya's age.

Far too young.

Fallon had no doubt there was a story behind that.

However, the two looked so much alike it was uncanny, so Fallon had no doubt they were mother and child.

"Hey, Whip." Not only was her eye makeup smoky, but so was her voice. It did not fit her petite body.

"Syn, this is Fallon."

"Hi, Syn," Fallon greeted.

"Hey. First time I've seen you around here."

"First time I've been around here," Fallon countered with a smile. "I was actually passing through but my… *sled* broke down." *While in Rome…*

Whip snorted and Syn actually smiled at her attempt to fit in. "You have a sled?"

"An Indian Scout Bobber Twenty," Whip answered for her.

Syn's eyebrows rose. "I don't know what that is."

"Badass, that's what it is," he answered.

"What happened to Maya?" Fallon glanced around, not seeing the little girl anywhere. "She's adorable, by the way."

"She left with my brother. You didn't see her leave?" She lifted one dark eyebrow at Whip. "You must've been distracted."

They had been. Whip was easy to talk to and the conversation wasn't only one-sided like the last time she attempted dating men within her professional circle. "Her crush on Whip is very cute."

"Whip probably doesn't think so." Syn released a resigned-sounding sigh. "But we'd rather her crushing on Whip than some man we can't trust."

"I'm sure," Fallon murmured, wondering where that worry came from.

Maybe it was her motherly instinct. Something Fallon didn't have a speck of at this point. But then, her focus had been solely on her career and not having a family. She'd have to revisit that at some point before she got much older. Maybe once she returned from a trip abroad. *If* she returned. If she fell in love with an area somewhere other than in the States, she'd have no problem staying.

In truth, as long as she could afford it, she could move to a different country every year and immerse herself in new languages and cultures.

That might be a great idea.

But that would be later since she was currently sitting in a bar in a small town in Pennsylvania and immersing herself in a *new-to-her* culture with its own language. Bikers and MCs.

One habit she had gotten into during her climb to the top was to compliment other women. There was no benefit in cutting other women down, but even a simple compliment could make their day and lift their spirits. A very simple premise not enough women followed.

The saying "a rising tide lifts all boats" was originally associated with the economy but Fallon found it fitting when it came to women supporting each other.

Fallon pointed to Syn's neck. "Your cat head choker is really cute. I've never seen one like that."

Across from her, Whip choked on his sip of beer. He put the glass down and slapped his chest as he coughed.

"You okay?" Fallon asked him. "Did you inhale instead of swallow?"

He waved a hand around. "I'm good," he managed to get out on another cough.

"I need to grab something to eat," Syn announced unexpectedly. "Nice meeting you, Fallon."

Before Fallon could respond, Syn was gone. She turned to Whip. "Did I say something wrong? I didn't even get a chance to tell her how much I enjoyed her singing."

"Don't worry about it."

"I want to apologize if I've offended her in some way," Fallon insisted. Her comment was meant to be a compliment not an insult.

"You didn't. I don't think she talks about her collar."

Fallon blinked. "Her collar?"

"Ain't a choker. Well, I guess it could be, but it's a collar. With a buckle and a lock you can't see 'cause it's hidden under her hair."

"A lock?" Fallon shook her head. "I'm a little lost here. Is it a new fashion trend that I'm unaware of?" Since landing the job with White Rock right out of college, she never paid attention to fashion or trends except for business attire.

Now she kept her wardrobe of casual clothing simple. Items that didn't wrinkle when rolled tightly for packing in limited space, as well as clothes easily washed and able to withstand riding a bike. She had traded in her business suits and heels for jeans and boots.

"Dodge collared her."

Fallon let that sink in. It took a few seconds but she began to see the light. "So, they're into kink?"

"Can only assume that. Whether they are or they ain't, with them it's more of a commitment thing. Like a weddin' ring. Syn belongs to Dodge. It's one way to show others that she's taken."

While she understood the concept of dominants and submissives—if that was what it was in their case—she wondered if that type of lifestyle was typical for an MC. "Is collaring a normal thing in your club?"

"No. The women usually get a 'property of' cut similar to Maya's when one of us takes a woman as their ol' lady. Kids get denim, while ol' ladies get leather like their ol' man."

She stared across the table at Whip. Suddenly Syn's choker and Maya's vest weren't so cute. "Are you saying that in your club both women and children are considered property of a man?"

As she watched his expression close and become unreadable, she realized that was exactly what he was saying. Especially when he picked up his beer and gulped the remainder down.

Oh yes, he wanted to avoid that answer.

"Tell me, why would a woman want to be property of a man?" Because Fallon certainly didn't understand it. It seemed archaic.

"'Cause she loves him."

That answer wasn't good enough. Not even close. "A woman can love a man and not be a possession."

His lips turned down at the ends. "Ain't like that."

"No? Then explain."

"It's just the way it is."

Fallon shook her head. "That's not an answer. That's a cop-out."

His head jerked back. "You know what? You're right. It ain't a fuckin' answer. I don't need to explain it, and I'm d-done with this fuckin' conversation." His chair scraped along the floor as he shoved it back from the table and surged to his feet. "Let's go."

She stared up at him. His face was stony and his jaw tight. "I only want to understand, Whip."

"You don't need to. You're only here 'cause your damn bike needs repair. That's it. You woulda kept ridin' through if that didn't happen. You're only here for a few days, you're not stayin'."

"While all of that's correct, that doesn't mean I'm not interested. Please, sit down."

"No. We're goin'. You wanna stay, then you find your own way back."

Shit. She could find a way back to the motel on her own. That wasn't the problem. "Whip…"

His jaw shifted and he jabbed a finger in her direction. "You don't gotta like the way we live, but it's our way and we don't need anyone's approval. We got strong fuckin' women in our club. None of them do what they d-don't wanna do. Not fuckin' one. Syn wasn't forced to accept that... that collar, she chose to. She wouldn't have accepted it if she didn't love or trust D—" He grimaced. "Dodge. It's that fuckin' simple."

She met his hard and intense eyes. "You protect your club." The way he defended his club's way of life was hard to ignore. It was hard to ignore his passion on the subject.

"We p—" a muscle in his jaw popped, "protect our family."

"And the Fury is your family."

"Yeah. They are." He swiped his baseball cap off the table and jammed it backwards onto his head. The same way he wore it when he rode his bike. "Know where your mind was headed 'cause of wh—" he blew out a breath, "what happened to you at your job. You mentioned misogyny and this ain't it, whether you believe it or not. My brothers respect their women and will do anythin' to protect them and their kids. It ain't no wishy-washy relationship b-bullshit where a man treats a woman like shit. Like she's less than him. Their relationships are real. Solid. Are they p-possessive? Hell yeah. Are they fuckin' loyal? Fuck yeah they are. It's a commitment that sticks."

Fallon had basically spent all day with the man and never heard him stutter once, but now he'd done it multiple times. Did he have a stutter that only came out when he was angry?

Every time he did it, he seemed to get even angrier. Like it was her fault he was doing it. While she hoped that wasn't true, it very well might be.

Shit.

She finished off the last swallow of her vodka tonic and pushed her chair back. "I don't have to agree with how other people live their lives." Before she could rise, he offered his hand to assist her, surprising her. Did she need it? No. But she planted her hand in his anyway because apparently, men did that in his club. They were the type to be in charge. The "head" of the household. Even the "breadwinner." All of it typical alpha-male mentality.

Did they treat women as second-class citizens? She hoped not.

He said all the Fury women were strong. She saw it in Reilly. She wasn't sure about Syn or Shay because she'd only spent a few minutes with each. But those were the only three she'd met, so she wasn't able to judge.

Truthfully, that was what she'd be doing… Judging. She wasn't here to judge anyone.

She needed to smooth things over with Whip. She wasn't ready for their night to end. She liked him.

Much more than she expected.

Was she planning on inviting him to join her in her room? Yes. But she wasn't sure if she screwed up that opportunity. She sure hoped not.

"If the women are fine with the way things are in your club, then I have to be fine with it, too. It's not my life and I'm just a visitor in yours. I'm sorry if I offended you in any way but I was truly only interested in learning about a lifestyle I've never been around."

He hadn't let go of her hand since she stood, so she squeezed it. In return, he took a visible breath and his jaw loosened, his eyes softened and his fingers relaxed in hers. Basically, his raised hackles had lowered.

He also pulled her closer. To the point where the toes of their boots were touching.

"The women in our club are the strongest women I know. They don't take any shit. Not from their ol' man or from anyone. They only do what they wanna do. No one will ever force them to do otherwise."

"I believe you." Now that his anger was gone, his stutter seemed to be, too.

"Get you're strong, too. Get that you've been in a

powerful spot. Get that you also got fucked over by assholes with dicks. My brothers ain't dicks." He closed his eyes and his chest rose and fell slowly. When he opened them, he said, "No, they can be huge fuckin' dicks. We all can. But not to our women. Ain't nothin' but respect, trust and loyalty between the ones who found their forever."

Fallon tipped her head to the side as she stared up at him. "Their forever?"

"The person they wanna spend forever with."

Holy shit. "I love that. *Their forever,*" she whispered.

Even though a lot of marriages or relationships didn't last forever, it was a great concept. It was something every couple should strive for, but not every couple did. Some marriages were for convenience, some for appearances, some for financial reasons. The list of wrong reasons was long.

Fallon liked the idea of one day finding her own forever. Someone who fit her perfectly. Where their personalities didn't clash and their ideologies were aligned. Someone she could live with in complete harmony.

That had to be a pipe dream, right? Did that really exist?

"You haven't found your forever yet," she murmured.

His nostrils flared the slightest bit. "No. But also ain't lookin'. Figure when it happens, it happens."

"But you do expect it to happen."

He shrugged. "One day."

"You're relying on fate?"

"Just like death, when the time is right, it'll happen. Nothin' I can do about it."

"You could either actively search for it or, contrarily, you could fight fate when you find it."

"I could."

She smiled. "But you won't."

"Didn't say that."

She laughed softly. "Bikers are stubborn, aren't they?"

"As fuck." His sexy smirk was back.

If he could only bottle that, he'd be rich.

Because one thing was for sure, she'd be buying it. By the case.

HE DIDN'T MEAN to be a dick, but when it came to his Fury family, sometimes he couldn't help being overprotective.

It pissed him off that getting ticked off had made him stutter, even though he had fought it. He had stuttered in front of Fallon when he hardly ever did it anymore. It was so rare that he wasn't sure if any of his brothers even knew he had that issue. He had outgrown it for the most part but some instances brought it back to the surface.

One time he did it at the garage when he caught his finger in a damn truck door and he was in so much pain that he stuttered over every curse word he yelled. Most likely the guys at the garage thought it was due to the fact that he almost broke his fucking finger, not because he had an actual stutter. Having a finger smashed would make anyone stumble over their words.

But tonight, he'd shown his vulnerability in front of Fallon.

He knew she'd have a problem with the fact that women and children were considered "property" in an MC. Or at least, they were in the Fury since Whip didn't know how other MCs handled things.

From what he understood, every club was different, had different rules and different values. No universal rule books existed for motorcycle clubs. No national organization existed that governed MCs. They all did their own thing.

Hell, the difference in how women and children were treated between the current Fury and the Originals was night and day. He had heard some real horror stories from Dutch.

Even worse, the old man didn't consider them horror stories because to him, what happened back then wasn't a problem. It had been normal. That might have been the reason Bebe bailed on him and their boys, Rook and Cage.

Luckily, Trip had a different train of thought and steered the club away from that kind of behavior.

Whip hated the way his father had treated his mother. The way he abused her both verbally and physically. He'd have a problem if he saw any of his brothers treat their women the same way.

A huge fucking problem.

To the point he wouldn't hesitate to step in, even if he ended up being the loser in that fight. He wouldn't and couldn't sit back and do nothing.

Real men didn't abuse women. Or children. Flaming pieces of dog shit did.

After crab-walking his Harley backward into the empty spot in front of her room, he shut off the engine.

She was given the room on the end.

Farthest from the office.

Far from the eyes of whoever was currently working the desk.

Far from Ozzy and Shay's eyes, too.

He didn't bother to get off because he wasn't sure if the rest of the night would go the way he hoped it would or if it was now fucked.

Especially after he got bent at Pete's. He shouldn't have since everybody had a right to their own opinion, whether right or wrong. His opinion about the sisterhood and the kids being property of the club, just like the sweet butts, might be different for an outsider.

An outsider like Fallon.

He wasn't only attracted to how the woman looked. It was the way she spoke, her intelligence and confidence, too.

For fuck's sake, how many women were brave enough to travel the fucking country by themselves on a damn sled?

Not very many, if at all.

She had given up on a life full of stability and predictability to start a new one full of unknowns. How many people had the strength and the initiative to do that?

Again, not too many because of those unknowns. Most people were more comfortable sticking with what they already knew. Giving up everything and taking off on a bike to travel the country was far from that.

Just like Fallon ending up with a damaged tire and oil pan. Was it unexpected? Fuck yeah, but she didn't freak out, she calmly dealt with it.

She didn't get bothered when he got pissed, she calmly dealt with it. She didn't seem to be hot tempered but level-headed, and he liked that. It drew him in as much as her blue eyes, her tempting mouth, and everything else about her.

He wanted to join her in her room, but he might have gone and fucked that up. The way she held onto him on the ride from Pete's back to The Grove Inn gave him a little hope, but that didn't mean much.

She used his shoulder for balance as she dismounted. After unbuckling her helmet, she slipped it off. He couldn't peel his eyes from her when she once again shook her head and combed her fingers through her hair in an attempt to get it back in place.

Neat or messy, it was sexy as fuck. Her hairstyle fit her face and her lifestyle perfectly.

"Will text you tomorrow to let you know the Honda's back and what time one of us will come get you. Probably when one of us has a test drive."

She stared at him for a second, tucked the helmet under her arm and stepped closer to his sled. "Will you?"

"Yeah. Got your keycard?"

"I do."

"'Kay then." He was not ready to end the fucking night, but he wasn't going to stay if he wasn't wanted.

"Whip…"

"Yeah."

Putting a hand on his shoulder again, she leaned in and put her mouth to his ear. "Get off the bike."

Her words were soft but firm, and drawn out so slowly they sent his blood rushing south.

Jesus fuck.

As he scrambled off his sled, she stepped back, and as soon as he had both boots on the pavement and his keys shoved deep into his pocket, she fisted his cut and dragged him over to the door, while pulling the keycard out the back pocket of her jeans.

His heart skipped a beat at the same time the light turned green and the lock clicked. Without releasing his cut, she pushed open the door and tugged him inside, slamming the door shut behind them.

Before she even turned on the light, she had him shoved against the door and, in the dark, her warm breath beat against his lips. Their mouths were so damn close it wouldn't take much effort to take hers.

"I'm older than you," she whispered on an exhale.

He inhaled her words. "Yeah."

"Do you have a problem with that?"

"Fuck no."

"Good."

Yeah, it was.

She continued, "I'm assuming you're interested in the same thing I am."

Was that ever in question? "Why the fuck are we still talkin'?"

A husky noise that came from the back of her throat escaped.

Since the drapes were pulled, the room was so goddamn dark he couldn't see shit and could barely even make out her features even though she was standing that close.

But he didn't need to see shit when her mouth found his and he let her tongue explore for a few moments. He'd let her have this moment, this power, for right now, but that was not how tonight would go.

If she thought it was, she'd be wrong.

He'd never been submissive, even with Billie. But his ex-girl-friend—and now sweet butt—had taught him a lot in the short time they were together. One lesson he learned was how he liked sexually aggressive women but not to the point of being dominating. He preferred sexually secure women like Liz, who had a high sex drive but still had a soft and nurturing side.

It was hard to believe he'd only met Fallon this morning. Because of that, he had no idea if she was like that. In the end, it didn't matter if she was or wasn't since this wouldn't be anything more than sex between them.

As soon as "Agnes" was fixed, she'd be hitting the road once again and going back to doing her thing.

But tonight, he would be doing her.

Her hands were fisted in the thermal shirt he wore under his cut, while his fingers had driven into her hair to keep her close when their lips meshed and their tongues clashed.

He was so fucking hard right now, his dick was throbbing. He groaned at the same time her hand released his shirt and slid down to cup him where he ached. His hips twitched at her touch and he wanted her to be touching his bare skin not his denim.

They twitched again when she squeezed him gently.

He twisted his face to the side, breaking their kiss and trying to catch his breath. "Fuck," he whispered.

The only other sound in the dark room was their ragged breathing.

He hadn't been this turned on with a woman since... *hell*, never.

She reached past him and flipped the switch, making him squint when the overhead light hit his eyes. Once they adjusted, he could see the woman before him so much fucking better.

With a glint in her eyes, her cheeks were slightly flushed and her lips shiny from their kiss.

Fucking gorgeous.

"Want you naked."

"I want you naked," she countered, a smile pulling at her lips.

"Easy fix."

He pushed off the door, using his chest to gently bump her back a step, knocking her hand free from where she'd been massaging his balls.

He mourned the loss of her touch, but only for a second because he knew shit was about to get so much better.

So much fucking better.

As she turned away, she stripped herself free from the windbreaker she'd worn on their ride to and from Crazy Pete's. After throwing it on the spare bed, she paused and then pointed to the nightstand between the two beds. "Where did that bowl of condoms come from? It wasn't here when we left earlier."

She wasn't lying. A whole fucking bowl of wraps sat there like a bowl of candy on Halloween. *Jesus fuck.* "Someone's bein' a smart ass."

She turned, not pissed like he would've expected for someone entering her room while they were gone, but amused. "I assume that someone is Ozzy?" Before he could answer that—not that it needed answered—she asked, "How did he know we were going to hook up?"

Because Ozzy was a horny fucker and only thought about sex. "He ain't stupid. But we haven't hooked up yet."

"Then let's solve that right now." She sat on the edge of the second bed and began to unlace her boots.

He sat across from her on the other bed and did the same. Four boots along with their socks went flying across the room and landed in a pile.

He grinned at her and she returned it with an eyebrow wiggle.

Fallon surged to her feet and yanked her sweater over her head tossing that over her shoulder. Whip watched as it landed on the bed before turning his eyes back to her. He didn't want to miss a damn thing.

She wore a black lacy bra that she filled out very well and he had a difficult time pulling his gaze from the creamy flesh swelling out of the cups.

He wanted to bury his face there. He wasn't sure if he wanted to do that before or after he buried it between her thighs.

Her tits couldn't be considered huge or tiny, but, to Whip, were just right.

She popped open the top button on her jeans and unzipped them, the whole time her blue eyes remaining locked with his. "Are you just going to sit there?" Her question came out thick, the look accompanying it heated.

A flush now ran from her cleavage up her neck and into her cheeks. Whip doubted it was from embarrassment but more from anticipation.

After swallowing to loosen his tight throat, he forced out a, "Yeah. Reason for that."

She shimmied out of her jeans and once they hit her ankles, she stepped out, leaned over, giving him a healthy eyeful of those tits, picked up her pants and tossed them behind her, too. Now she stood in only her black lace-front panties and bra.

Holy fuck.

Her body was a thousand times better than he could ever have imagined. His dick thought so, too, when it began to leak in his boxer briefs.

"You're still sitting there."

"Know it. Keep goin'." He ran a thumb down his erection and cupped his balls over his jeans, giving them a slight squeeze. "Likin' this too much."

"But it doesn't do me any good if you're still dressed."

"Don't need to be naked to do some of the shit I'm gonna do to you."

Her mouth opened and a soft breath hissed from her. "That sounds promising but I really want to see you naked."

"C'mere," he said softly, holding out his hand and separating his knees.

When she stepped between them, he put his hands on her hips above her panties and slid them around to her ass. Leaning in, he ran his tongue from the elastic waistband of her underwear up her flat but still soft and feminine stomach. Just how he liked it.

She was in shape but not muscular. Thin but not skinny. A couple of the sweet butts were too stick thin for his taste. Fallon was made up of perfect curves and lines.

Hell, she was more than perfect. She was a fucking wet dream.

He cupped her ass cheeks and squeezed, then ran his palms up along her back until he got to where her bra was fastened. He tipped his head up to see her staring down at him, watching.

He hesitated with his fingers on her bra, but when she slightly nodded her head he took that as encouragement to proceed. As soon as he unhooked it, it fell free.

Fuck yeah.

Her dark pink nipples were perked and the perfect size for his mouth, the tips as hard as diamonds. He took his time taking one, then the other into his mouth.

Her back arched and she planted her hands on his shoulders. He cupped one tit and tweaked her nipple at the same time, while sucking the other as hard and as deeply as he could. Scraping the tightly pebbled tip with his teeth.

Her whimper made his dick flex in his jeans.

She ripped his baseball cap off his head and tossed it over her shoulder, then drove her fingers through his hair, the shortish nails scraping along his scalp and causing a shiver to slip down his spine.

"Whip," she breathed.

Tipping his eyes up toward her face, he watched her expressions change depending on what he did. Through it all, she kept her eyes open and focused on him.

And that was hot as fuck.

She wasn't retreating into some sexual fantasy, but remained right in that room with him.

"I want you naked," she groaned.

"Gonna get there," he said around her nipple.

"Soon," she urged.

"When I'm ready."

Her fingers tightened in his hair, pulling at his scalp, but he wouldn't stop what he was doing. Not yet.

He wanted to worship every part of her and this was only the beginning. This wasn't going to be a quickie and he refused to rush. He planned on taking his damn time and making this last for as long as she allowed.

He took her other nipple in his mouth, nipping the tip and causing her muscles to tighten beneath his fingers. He tucked his fingers into the waistband of her panties and slowly... so fucking slowly slid them down over her ass cheeks and down her thighs until they dropped to her feet.

"Whip," she moaned. "Hurry."

"Ain't hurryin'. Warnin' you now, more you push, the slower I'm gonna go."

She shook against him and when he glanced up, he saw she was silently laughing.

He grinned but then went back to work, dragging his tongue around each areola, and over each puckered tip while his fingers kneaded her ass cheeks. When he separated them, he dragged his thumb through her crease, finding another spot that was puckered, circling it a couple of times before moving on.

Tucking his hand between her thighs, he stroked the soft, warm and plump flesh between them. She was already slick and ready for him, but he was nowhere near ready to hit that. Fuck no. As much as he wanted to throw out his plan of taking his time to just fuck the shit out of her, he forced himself to remain on his slow course.

In the end, it would be worth it.

If he rushed to shoot his load, she could very well kick him out of her room once they were done and the night would be over.

He wasn't ready for that.

Again, if they only had tonight, he didn't want to rush it.

Using his mouth, he tugged on her nipple at the same time he slipped his middle finger inside her. She immediately clamped around it, making his dick flex in his jeans.

Fuck yeah, she was wet.

So fucking ready.

Damn.

He released her tit so he could grit his teeth to fight the urge to throw her on the bed and just sink deep inside that warm cocoon. He managed it, but barely.

Slipping his finger from her, he used his foot to encourage her to widen her stance, to give him more room, and she did. This time, instead of coming in from the rear, he cupped her pussy, squeezed it, then buried his thumb against her clit and two fingers in her cunt.

His breath rushed from him as he worked them in and out, her unrestrained whimpers filling his ears, her hips rolling with the same rhythm of his hand and her fingers now almost ripping his hair out.

"Want to come." Her voice was husky and thick and sounded even better than Syn's singing. "Make me come."

She released his hair and cupped his cheeks, forcing his face up as she leaned down and took his mouth.

He plunged his fingers in and out of her, capturing her cries in his mouth, grabbing her tit with his free hand and squeezing it to the point she gasped. She didn't try to pull away, instead, she pushed it deeper into his hand.

Their tongues twisted together, clashing, tasting, playing a power game. He fought to keep control of the kiss with the same intensity she fought to take it.

It wasn't going to happen.

Just because she was older than him, didn't mean she'd be the one in control. But the current struggle was over just as soon as it began when she tensed and exploded around him, soaking his fingers and releasing his mouth as she cried out.

Her thighs trembled and she dropped her head forward, breathing quickly as the intense ripples around his fingers slowly faded away.

"Get naked," she demanded when she finally lifted her head and locked gazes with him again.

"You don't call the shots tonight," he told her. "You might be used to bein' in a powerful position but that was business. This is pleasure. This ain't work, this is play."

A smile slowly spread across her face and her eyes narrowed. "You think so?"

He smirked. "Know so."

"All right, I'm game."

She wasn't the only one.

But before he could move to get up and undressed, she slammed her palms into his chest, knocking him backwards. She quickly followed him, crawling onto the bed and onto her hands and knees, working her way up his body. "You never had dessert earlier."

Well, damn. Great minds and all that shit... "Nothin' in Dino's dessert case is as sweet as what I'm about to eat."

Chapter Nine

EXCEPT FOR HIS boots and socks, he was still fully clothed as he laid on his back, watching a completely naked Fallon move to straddle his face.

He couldn't wait to dive into that sweet pie.

But instead of facing him, she began to turn. With his hands on her bare hips, he helped her readjust until both knees sandwiched his head and she faced his feet.

It surprised the fuck out of him when his mouth watered the second he picked up her aroused scent and saw her shiny, wet pussy.

Perfect.

Definitely better than any fucking pie at Dino's.

He slid his finger through her crease again, through her folds, gathering her wetness. "Goddamn beautiful."

She glanced over her shoulder at him. "Pussies aren't beautiful."

Some were, some weren't. They were all unique. "Then you haven't taken a good look at yours."

"I'm glad I shaved earlier since you're getting so up close and personal."

"Wouldn't have cared if you didn't. If no man's told you

this before, I'm tellin' you now, women worry about it 'cause they think we care. News flash, we don't. As long as it's edible, we're gonna eat it. We also don't mind a little road rash on our face."

She dropped her voice a few octaves and mimicked him from earlier. "Why the fuck are we still talkin'?"

He snorted. "Then sit on my fuckin' face and shut me the fuck up. Smother me with—"

Before he could finish, she did. She glanced back at him with amusement while grinding her pussy against his mouth and nose, effectively shutting him the fuck up.

She planted her hands on his thighs and leaned forward to make sure he didn't suffocate. But the way her pussy tasted, he wouldn't mind one bit if he died that way. His brothers would probably put a memorial picture up at The Barn of him dead with a smile and pussy juices coating his face.

He sucked each fold into his mouth, savoring the tang, then licked down the center just like licking down the side of an ice cream sandwich.

Reaching around, he played with her clit as he concentrated on eating her pussy. But his concentration was broken when she began undoing his buckle.

What was she doing? Was she...

Fuck yeah, she was.

She had his belt undone, his jeans unfastened and shoved off his hips and halfway down his thighs in record time. He grunted when she dug his dick out of his briefs and without even a *hello, how ya doin'?* she sucked him all the way to the back of her throat.

Fuuuuuuuuck.

He not only forgot to breathe, but had stopped licking her pussy because he became so distracted.

How the fuck could he not?

Her warm, wet tongue traveled down the underside and

she sucked his sac into her mouth for a few seconds before licking her way back up the thick ridge to the crown and circling it.

Then she went so damn deep he was surprised she didn't gag. The hot, wet suction pulled a long, low groan from him. Was she trying to suck his brains out through his dick?

Yeah, she was.

Holy fuck.

Shoving his brains back into his head, he did his best to focus on the luscious pussy pressed to his mouth.

He upped his game by licking her, sucking her, fucking her with his tongue, while he thumbed her clit and she ground circles in his face.

He never ate out the sweet butts because he never knew if they had just done one of his brothers. Even though all of them wrapped it tight, he mentally struggled with putting his mouth where one of his brother's dicks might have been.

In fact, after he and Billie had decided to go their separate ways, he'd only went down on one other woman who had been invited to party with the club one night. She had been hot, about his age and wasn't a patch whore trying to bang every Fury member that night. That was a fucking plus.

But he shouldn't be thinking about any other woman than Fallon right now. She was so fucking different from any other woman he'd been with and it would be wrong to compare her to anyone else.

He reached under her and cupped her tits, using the rough pads of his thumbs to brush over tightly budded tips as he squeezed and kneaded.

Her groan vibrated around his dick, making it flex in her mouth.

Pulling her nipples, he stretched them as far as he could, making Fallon grind down even harder to the point he was now struggling to breathe. But fuck if he was going to stop her.

Goddamn heaven. That was what this was.

This woman got *wet*. She was so into it, he didn't want to discourage her in any way. If she wanted to smother him to death... He was ready to order a headstone.

Here lies Tyler "Whip" Byrne. Died with a shiny smile.

He released one of her tits and threaded his fingers through her hair. His fantasy had been to have her on her knees at his feet while he fisted her hair and she sucked his dick, but this was just as good. Maybe even better.

He gripped her hair even tighter when she scraped her nails lightly along his balls and up his throbbing length while she circled the head with her tongue and sucked the tip.

Jesus fuck.

His balls were tight. The urge to come strong. And as much as he wanted to blow in her mouth, he couldn't let that happen.

Not this time.

He hoped to fuck there was a next time. She'd probably be in town for a week. While she was, he wanted more time with her than only tonight. That meant his game and his techniques had to be on point. And shooting his load down her throat first thing might not leave a good impression.

He tipped his head back enough so he could suck in much-needed air and ask, "Gonna come soon?"

For fuck's sake, say yes.

Her mouth paused. "Are you?"

"Yeah, but don't wanna come yet. Wanna be inside you when I do."

Just the thought of coming deep inside her took him closer to that edge. He needed to think about something else. Like... Punctured oil pans and flat tires.

"Me, too."

When he tugged on her hair, she sat up, once again

planting her hands on his thighs and taking some of her weight off his face.

"But also want you to come all over my tongue, so…"

"I can do that," she breathed.

He liked her team mindset.

He nipped her ass cheek, making her jerk. "Then get on it."

She glanced over her shoulder again. "You get on it. I'm sitting on your face, which means I'm just the rider and you're the ride operator."

"Then make sure to listen to my safety instructions so we can get this ride movin'."

Amusement filled her eyes. "I'm all ears."

He released her hair and slipped his hand from the front of her, grabbed her hand and put it where his had been. "Touch yourself."

He left her hand there, used his to separate her cheeks again and he dove in face first. Giving her pussy no mercy, he drove his tongue deep, scraped his teeth along her swollen flesh and sucked her to the point she cried out.

He did not let up.

He circled her puckered hole with his tongue twice, then gave it a flick before returning to her sweet spot. Within a minute, she was riding his face the same way she would a runaway horse while playing with her own clit, filling up the room with her hot as fuck noises, smothering him to the point he had to slap her ass when he needed to take a breath.

He thanked the orgasm gods when she finally got *there*. Coming all over his tongue and his lips, driving herself down even more as a climax ripped through her.

When it was over, she rose onto her knees enough to let him breathe but didn't pull away. Her legs trembled, her fingertips dug into his thighs and her panting filled the room.

Fuck yeah.

He lifted his head so he could lick her lazily and collect her sweet tang on his tongue as she continued to quiver from her climax.

As much as he wanted to flip her over and drive his dick deep to chase that same result, he had to give himself a few moments since he was ready to lose his shit. His dick was a rocket primed for launch. If he came as soon as he slid into her, he would throw his own ass out the door and never come back.

So yeah... Deep breaths, thoughts of shit other than the woman still straddling him, and trying to ignore the perfect, dark pink pussy hovering over his face.

Im-fucking-possible.

He slapped her ass again. "Need to move."

"You or me?"

"Both. Unless you don't mind me starin' at your gorgeous glory and don't want fucked."

She let out a soft laugh and shifted until her ass was out of his face, then collapsed to the side and off him.

"I want fucked," she said with no hesitation and plenty of amusement.

"That's good 'cause I wanna do the fuckin'."

"You're not fucking me with your clothes on."

Whip sat up and wiped a hand over his mouth. "Nope. You're gonna see all my glory, too."

"I'm sure it's 'gorgeous glory.'"

"You can let me know." He rolled away and to the edge of the bed since his jeans were pushed down far enough to hobble him. "Grab a wrap."

She shot him a confused look. "A wrap?"

He tipped his head toward the nightstand. "In the bowl." He worked his jeans down the rest of the way and yanked them off.

"Ah." The mattress shifted as she moved off the bed and went to the bowl.

Thank fuck she wasn't shy about her body. He liked a woman who didn't have any hang-ups. Everyone had scars and faults, nobody was truly perfect.

The ones who looked perfect were usually Photoshopped.

Reilly had gone off on a tangent one day about a calendar Dutch hung up in the shop. It was full of women in bikinis straddling Harleys. It went up next to the yellowed and worn 1996 calendar of naked women spread across the hoods of restored muscle cars.

She bitched about how fake those photos were and how they gave girls and women unrealistic expectations of themselves. Dutch had flapped a hand in her direction and grumbled. The rest of them just shrugged.

"See? You all expect us to look like that. We don't!" she had shouted, stomped into the office and slammed the door behind her.

They all shared a "what the fuck" look and shrugged again.

"Who's gonna buy a calendar full of ugly bitches with tiny tits?" Dutch had shouted at the closed door.

"Might wanna quit while you're ahead and still breathin', old man," Cage had warned his father.

"I'm gonna go take cover. It'd be smart if the rest of you do, too." Rook paused on his way to his work bay at the far end of the shop. *"Wait, none of you fuckers are smart. Never fuckin' mind."*

But staring at Fallon naked in her room and her not giving a flying fuck if any of her "faults" were hanging out, made him appreciate her all the more.

He was no fucking magazine model, either. He rarely worked out, he ate and drank whatever the fuck he wanted and he certainly had marks left behind from the last twenty-eight years. He was sure as fuck before he was buried six feet under he'd have plenty more.

He surged to his feet, his erection hard and heavy, and shrugged out of his cut, folding it up and placing it on the spare bed. Before he could remove his thermal, Fallon stopped him.

"Let me."

He shrugged and raised his arms enough for her to tug his shirt up his gut. Her fingers dragged along his heated skin, tracing his chest piece along the way. After playfully tweaking each of his nipples, she pulled it up and over his head, then tossed it over her shoulder. Whether it made the other bed or not, he wasn't sure because he had a difficult time pulling his eyes from hers.

"I said you were cute, but I was wrong," she murmured.

Damn. "I ain't cute?"

"No." She shook her head and let her gaze rake down his body. From his tattooed chest all the way down to his bare knees. "You're smoking hot. And, I never thought I'd ever utter these words, but those tattoos only add fuel to the fire."

One side of his mouth pulled up.

Like earlier, she planted her palms on his chest and shoved him. He let himself fall onto the bed. Before he could scramble backward to give her room to join him, she was climbing on the mattress and over him, a wrap tucked between her teeth. She straddled his waist, her hot pussy pressed to his gut, let the wrap fall onto his chest, and stared down at him. With both hands planted on the bed on either side of his head, she leaned forward and took his mouth.

She had to be tasting herself on his lips and tongue. Thank fuck she didn't mind since she deepened the kiss and practically tickled his tonsils with her tongue.

He drove his fingers into her hair and took control of

the kiss, shoving her tongue back into her own mouth. He ended it pretty damn quickly to demand, "Wrap."

She plucked it from his chest, tore it open, took the latex disc within her fingers and reached behind her to roll it down his dick, causing his hips to jump since she took her time doing it.

When she was done, she looked at him again with cheeks once again flushed and her eyes hooded. "Ready?"

Instead of answering her, he twisted his body, knocking her off him and before he could settle between her thighs, she had them wrapped around his waist and within seconds he was sliding into her snug, wet heat.

FALLON TILTED her hips and accepted every inch of him inside her. Once he was fully seated, he paused balls deep. It had been a while since she had sex so, even as wet as she was, her body took a minute to adjust to him.

But, *damn*, it felt good.

He felt good.

It had been long enough for her to forget how much she needed the connection achieved by intimacy. How important another person's *welcomed* touch was.

With his forehead pressed to hers, they simply breathed as their bodies synced with each other. His mouth hovered just above hers. His beautiful blue eyes held hers.

Warmth slithered through her from her scalp all the way to her toes.

"Whip," she whispered.

"Yeah?" he breathed.

"I want you to move but I also really like where you're at."

"Yeah," he murmured, his warm breath kissing her lips. "But if you want the truth, tryin' not to bust a nut in thirty seconds flat."

She shouldn't laugh at that but again, his honesty was refreshing, and she couldn't help it. The only problem was, when she did so, it shook her enough for him to shift slightly inside her.

She hissed out a soft breath and clenched around him, pulling a grunt from him in response.

"Also, don't wanna disappoint you," he admitted.

"How would you do that?" When he didn't answer, she continued, "I've been disappointed plenty of times in the past. Believe me, it can't be any worse than some of those awful experiences." A couple of them had been so bad, she wished she could forget them.

Keeping her knees bent, she dropped her feet to the mattress and hugged his hips with her thighs.

"Don't wanna be on that list."

"Then don't." She grabbed his bare ass and dug her fingers into the muscular cheeks, giving them a squeeze. "No pressure. I promise not to rate your performance too harshly," she teased. "But if you don't start moving, there won't even be one to rate."

He dropped his head and pressed his cheek to hers, digging his knees more firmly into the bed. "Just gonna go for it and hope for the best."

She grinned at his subtle sense of humor. She liked it as much as his honesty. "That sounds like a good plan of attack."

She liked him. *Really* liked him. He wasn't overly loud, aggressive or obnoxious. Everything she detested in a man.

She didn't know much about *real* bikers—not just people who rode motorcycles but people who actually lived the lifestyle. However, if she had to guess, she figured he wasn't a typical one.

Even in the brief time she spent with Ozzy, Dodge and the guys at the garage, she could see Whip wasn't quite the same. She assumed that most bikers were loud, outspoken and "in your face." Especially if you disagreed with them.

While at Crazy Pete's earlier, Whip had a moment but it wasn't overblown. He got defensive because he was simply protecting what belonged to him. His family.

She couldn't fault him for that.

Even if she could, there'd be no point. Tonight was all about the sex and a little bit of companionship. Nothing more. Manning Grove was nothing but a stop on her latest journey and Whip simply happened to be a part of this experience.

An unforeseen but pleasantly surprising detour.

Never in her wildest dreams could she have imagined hooking up with a biker in a *motorcycle club* for a one-night-stand.

But here she was.

His body hiccuped against her and then began to do an age-old dance. With a smooth and steady pace, he drove in and out of her using long, full strokes. In, until he couldn't go any further. Out, until they almost parted.

He dug his elbows into the mattress on either side of her head and stared down at her, trying to catch her gaze. Her eyes fluttered shut to avoid it, but his firm, "No," had them flashing open again.

No?

He shook his head slightly. "No. Eyes on me."

She'd never stared into anyone's eyes while having sex before because it had always felt awkward when anyone tried it. To her it seemed way too intimate for casual sex.

For two people deeply in love, making that visual connection while having sex made sense, but not for two people who were practically strangers and had only met earlier in the day.

Even so, she got sucked into his blue eyes that held things she didn't understand and maybe he didn't, either.

She certainly didn't want to explore whatever it was. Not with a man she'd never see again after Agnes was repaired.

Things between them needed to stay surface level and not go any deeper than that. If he was in agreement, they could have fun together while she was stuck in town.

Maybe they could check in with each other with an occasional text or two in the future, this way if she was ever in the area again…

No, she'd have to make a conscious effort to be in this neck of the woods and it would have to be for a very good reason.

A younger biker couldn't be it.

Their life experiences were on opposite ends of the scale.

And she was sure women, much younger than her, threw themselves at him regularly. Because of that, it had surprised her that he agreed to have dinner with her.

Pleased, but certainly surprised.

"Where you at?"

She dragged herself out of her head and back into the room. "Right here."

He paused mid-stroke. "No, you weren't. You were gone. Want you with me."

The demanding way he said that made her heart pump a little faster, a little harder, and her breath catch. "I'm with you."

"Stay there."

"Whip."

"Stay with me," he repeated more firmly. "We're in this together, right?"

"You're right."

His brow dropped low. "Unless you're plannin' on ratin' me less than a five on a scale of one to ten, then I might need to rethink some shit."

"I have you at about a—I don't know—solid eight point

five right now, teetering on a nine. But I might take a point away for all this talking instead of doing."

"Hang on. I'm the one doin' the doin' while you're off somewhere else."

She did her best not to laugh at his fake outrage. "I'm right here in this bed with you."

He tucked his chin into his neck, shook his head and snorted. When he lifted it again that sexy as hell smirk was back. "Gonna carry on, then."

She smiled up at him. "You have to work on that last one and a half points to make it a perfect ten."

"Fuckin' pressure," he muttered. "Gonna give me performance anxiety."

"I doubt that." She slapped his ass like he did earlier with her. "You still have time to score that perfect ten. Let's do this."

He laughed but managed to pull off a performance that would not be forgettable any time soon. In fact, it would stick with her for a long time.

With his age, he still had plenty of energy, enthusiasm and even better, flexibility. His hips were definitely limber. He did not just stiffly pump in and out of her—Fallon had been with a few men like that—he added a little extra *oomph* at the end of each stroke.

He'd continued to pull out until he was almost free, pause for a heartbeat, then do his smooth move again. If there was a name for it, she didn't know it, but if it was up to her she'd call it "awesome."

It was that and then some.

He didn't seem to be in a rush to get to the end, since he kept his pace smooth and steady. Dropping his head and also breaking that eye contact, he pulled a nipple deep into his mouth. Her back arched and she dug her fingers deeper into his ass, encouraging him to pick up the pace a little.

He did.

With a lift of her hips, she met him stroke for stroke, clenching and unclenching around him, tilting her head back, squeezing his ass again, a silent encouragement for him to take her where they both wanted to go.

He moved to her other nipple, sucking it hard enough she almost had to tell him to ease up. After taking her right to that very edge of discomfort, he'd back down just a hair. Then do it all over again.

He might be on the younger side but he knew what the hell he was doing.

It was when he began to roll his hips, hitting the right angle for her G-spot while somehow still grinding himself against her clit, that she realized at some point, some woman somewhere had taught this man how to move and hit all the right spots.

Maybe it was more than one. But whoever it was, she'd love to thank her. Because Fallon truly appreciated that he wasn't a selfish lover and everything he was doing was for her benefit. Truthfully, he very well could've done a few stiff pumps and finished quickly.

Like her trip around the country on Agnes, this was quickly becoming a journey, too. A rediscovery of how great and satisfying sex could be with the right partner. She was unexpectedly pleased that was Whip. She only hoped she was pleasing him just as well.

She wasn't one who put a lot of weight in the concept of "fate." But maybe fate had a hand in where Agnes had become damaged.

Maybe it happened at the right time and place.

Maybe it was simply meant to be.

Now was not the time to analyze it since she had more important things to accomplish.

Like her second orgasm.

And Whip's first.

If he stuck around, she'd make it up to him later by

doing what she really wanted to do earlier… Give him head until he came. She couldn't imagine he'd pass on that opportunity. She had always enjoyed giving it and most men enjoyed being on the receiving end.

He released her nipple with a wet pop and went nose to nose with her. "Gettin' really fuckin' close. Hope to fuck you're close, too." The strain in his voice was apparent.

Luckily for him, she *was* very close. "Keep going," she whispered.

"Wasn't plannin' on stoppin'."

"I meant keep doing exactly what you're doing. That hip action is…"

That hip action paused.

She feigned a frustrated scream. "Whip!"

He chuckled and went back to business.

It was great business.

The best.

He definitely deserved a "ten" and some repeat business, too.

He drove his fingers into her hair, using his grip to tip her head back. He licked up the side of her neck, along her jawline, and took her mouth.

Yessss. He was a good kisser, too. He wasn't sloppy and his lips were firm. He took possession of her mouth, almost as if he owned it. Or at least, claiming it for himself.

A groan got caught between them as he powered in and up into her over and over, his pace no longer slow or steady but determined.

His determination paid off. Not even a minute later, the fire he'd been stoking flared up and sparks exploded through her, within her, burning her skin, blinding her, making her gasp.

He kept going, kissing her, fucking her. Riding the waves of her orgasm. He ended their kiss with a groan, shoved his face against her throat and grunted as he thrust one last time before going completely still, once again balls deep.

Even as her orgasm began to subside, she could feel his cock pulsating deep inside her as he came, his warm, damp breath sweeping over her throat, along her neck.

They stayed like that for what seemed like forever and a day.

His weight on her was heavy, but bearable, and she surprisingly liked it.

This whole night had been full of good surprises.

Releasing a groan, he lifted his head, gave her a quick kiss on the lips and rolled off her. The bed jiggled as he removed the condom, tied it shut and did who knew what with it. She wasn't sure she wanted to know since he certainly didn't get up to throw it out.

She laid on her back, panting, her forehead damp with sweat as she smiled up at the ceiling.

He was still out of breath, too, when he asked, "My final ratin'?"

She turned her head on the pillow to see him turned toward her, as well. "Hmm." She rolled onto her side to face him. "I'd rate that a nine and a half."

His eyebrows pinned together. "Only a nine and a half?"

"Well, that gives you something to work toward." She did her damnedest to keep from grinning ear to ear.

"Damn, woman."

Finally, she relented and let him see it. The one side of his mouth pulled up into his signature smirk.

"So... Mr. Tyler 'Whip' Byrne, do you have any plans for the next few nights?"

"Fuck yeah. To earn that fuckin' ten."

Chapter Ten

FALLON GLANCED at the bowl of condoms next to the bed. If she had to guess, there were at least two dozen left. Maybe more. That would last them the rest of her stay in Manning Grove as long as they didn't stay in bed twenty-four-seven. Whoever left them had high hopes for Whip scoring tonight.

She heard the toilet flush and the sink run. He had waited for her to do her thing in there before taking his turn and also getting rid of the used condom.

Watching him walk naked out of the bathroom, she not only felt like a cougar, but a sex-starved one. She knew even before he had rolled out of bed to use the bathroom that one time with him would not be enough.

Her eyes tracked him walking through the room. She wasn't lying to him when she told him he was smoking hot. While he had muscles, they weren't overdone and he had enough flesh covering them making him a perfect cuddle candidate.

Cuddle.

That was a strange and unexpected direction of her thoughts. She hadn't been interested in cuddling with a man for quite a while. Again, like the staring into each other's eyes, cuddling was more of an intimate act usually not involved with casual sex.

All the encounters she'd had in the last few years ended up being no more than similar to a business transaction.

Some worthwhile, others not.

Those encounters had their purpose and that was it.

Just like her encounter with Whip.

Whip rounded the bed and he immediately went to where his jeans were discarded on the floor. She couldn't help but be disappointed that he was ready to bolt.

But if he came back tomorrow night...

He slipped his cell phone from the back pocket of his jeans and checked it. She assumed for any missed calls or texts. But instead of pulling on his boxer briefs and jeans, he set his phone down on the nightstand and turned to toss his jeans onto the spare bed.

That was when she saw it.

His back.

A huge tattoo that matched the back of his cut exactly. The patches, the skull, even down to the dripping blood.

"Holy shit. How did I miss that?" Had she been so distracted by his good looks that she missed it somehow? Or was this the first time his back had been turned toward her?

It had to be the latter.

"What?" He glanced over his shoulder at her.

"Your tattoo. It's..." *Large.* "It, uh... shows your..." *Dedication?* Were MCs like a cult? Was having their patches inked into their skin normal? "Loyalty," she finished weakly. "Was that required?"

He dug into his cut and pulled out a tin and what looked like a lighter from an inside pocket. "In our club? No. In other clubs? Not sure."

He turned and came over to the bed she was sitting on. The covers had been shoved to the floor and the top sheet was a balled-up mess from their very satisfying sexcapades. "Move over."

With that order, she guessed he wasn't rushing out the door. Relieved, she shifted over, giving him enough space to climb on and sit next to her. He leaned against the headboard attached to the wall, stretched his lightly hair-dusted legs out in front of him, crossed his bare ankles and placed the tin and lighter on the nightstand next to him.

The man had a very nice cock, even when it was soft, so she had to drag her eyes away from it to ask, "It wasn't required but you did it anyway? What if you decide to no longer be a member?"

He huffed, reached over and popped open the tin, similar to the one she had sat on in the tow truck, pulling out what looked like a hand-rolled cigarette. "Ain't gonna happen."

She hated smoking. She was also damn sure that motels no longer allowed smoking in rooms. "There's a saying and I'm pretty sure you know it, but... Shit happens."

"I'm Fury through and through."

The fortitude he said that with... "But what if—"

"Ain't worried about it," he stated with conviction.

"I guess it's just like any other tattoo, you hope you don't regret it later in life."

"Ain't gonna regret it."

"I like your confidence."

"Like yours, too." He tucked the cigarette between his lips and grabbed the lighter.

"You can smoke in here?"

"Our motel, our rules."

"I hate cigarettes." She didn't know too many people who smoked anymore. It was so damn expensive. More people seemed to be into vaping than smoking. She wasn't sure if that was any cheaper. Or any healthier.

She had no desire to do either.

"Ain't tobacco. Don't smoke cigarettes."

She wasn't sure if that made it better or worse. It could be a clove cigarette but she doubted it since those were illegal in the States and she also couldn't see the biker in her bed smoking one of those. Again, it had to be pot like in the container he had handed to Dutch. "Marijuana?"

He pulled the joint from his lips and nodded. "Yeah? You mind?"

"I've heard of wanting a cigarette after sex, but pot?"

"Ever try it?"

"Yes. A few times," she admitted. "Mostly in high school and college when at parties."

"You like it?"

"If I didn't want to be productive, yes. It was a good way to relieve my stress from pushing myself so hard."

"Tryin' to get those good grades."

"Yes. And keep my scholarships. Plus, land a good position in an organization."

"Paid off."

"Yes, it did."

"Don't gotta smoke it if it's gonna bother you."

She really liked that he took her into consideration. Just like during sex.

"We have no place to go and no plans to do anything productive, so..." She shrugged. "Your motel, your rules."

"Won't do it if you don't want me to. Your room, your rules."

"I appreciate that. Go ahead. If it bothers me, I'll let you know."

"Deal." He wrapped his hand behind her head and pulled her closer. With a tip of his head, he indicated she should put hers in his lap.

This man was full of surprises. So far, all good ones.

She shifted to her back and dropped her head in his lap,

staring up at him as he stared down at her. Once she was settled comfortably, he tucked the joint between his lips again, flicked the Bic and lit the end.

The crackle and pop of the dried bud igniting and burning filled the silence.

She wrinkled her nose. The scent of whatever strain he was smoking was *strong*.

After his first deep inhale, he held it for a few seconds, then tipped his head back and to the side to release the smoke.

He relaxed even more, his muscles loosening, and he began to rake his fingers gently through her chin-length hair.

She had cut it that short years ago thinking it would be easier to maintain than when it was longer. It wasn't but she really liked the style and the way it framed her face. She could wear it up or leave it down, depending on her mood. Even better, it was the perfect length to keep tucked under her helmet so her hair didn't end up in a knotted mess while riding Agnes.

It actually looked better when it was mussed versus neatly brushed.

"Saw the tat you got on the back of your shoulder. Truthfully, didn't expect you to have any ink." He took another long draw on the joint, holding the smoke deep.

"Some people have a problem with tattoos. I'm not one of them. However, I do prefer them not to be on the face or neck. I find that a bit distracting."

"Think my mom would still try to tan my hide if I got them on my neck or face."

Fallon laughed. "I'd pay to see her try. But I agree with her. You're way too cute to mark up your face."

"Not out to be cute."

"Handsome, then." If he kept combing his fingers

through her hair, she might very well fall asleep, but she was loving every second of the unexpected tenderness.

Again, he kept surprising her.

He was so not what she expected.

He was so much more.

"Not handsome. You said smokin' hot. Too late to take it back now."

"Well, that, too, of course."

"Prefer to be smokin' hot over cute or handsome."

"Can't you be all three?"

He shrugged. "You tell me."

"Then, yes, you can."

"Speakin' of smokin'..." He held the joint in front of her face. "Want a hit?"

She stared at it for a couple of heartbeats. Should she?

No, the question should be: Why shouldn't she? It was late and they weren't going anywhere. They were just relaxing after a good night together of dinner, drinks and sex. So, why not "chill" in the best way possible?

She didn't answer to anyone but herself. She could do... Whatever. The. Hell. She. Wanted.

That made her smile.

"Guessin' that smile means yeah?"

"Yes. Just one little puff, though. It's been a long time."

He snorted and shook his head, put the joint to his lips and took a deep inhale, making the end glow brightly.

She lifted her hand, expecting him to pass it to her next, but instead, he leaned over and pressed his lips against hers. He waited until she opened her mouth and then he let the smoke gently roll from his into hers.

She quickly inhaled the smoke but blew it out just as fast since she wasn't used to the burn in her lungs. She released a little cough and he chuckled.

That damn smirk was back.

"I told you I'm out of practice."

"Let's try it again." He took another hit, leaned down and sealed their lips together once more. This time she had a better idea of what to do and slowly stole the smoke from his mouth but this time he never separated their lips. When she pushed the smoke back out of her lungs, he inhaled it, sat back and blew it out of his nostrils.

It reminded her of a cartoon bull pissed off to the point smoke was bellowing out of its nostrils.

"Now you're definitely the definition of smoking hot."

"One more before I put it out?" he asked.

She nodded and he shared another hit with her, once again doing it mouth to mouth. She held it longer this time, trying her best not to cough.

When she blew it out, she felt a calm begin to descend over her. She stared up at the man whose lap she laid in as he took one more hit for himself, then pinched the end and tucked the remainder back into his tin.

His fingers went from brushing through her hair, to stroking it and now he was basically massaging her head.

If there was a heaven, this could very well be it.

Every bone in her body turned to liquid and her eyelids became heavy. His began to droop, as well, as they quietly stared at each other.

No words needed. Simply companionship.

She'd been alone for the last couple of months, only speaking to motel staff, waitstaff and retail workers wherever she stopped.

No deep conversations, no real connections. Just passing words.

As crazy as it appeared to be, she seemed to have a real connection with Whip. One more surprise in the long list of them this day had brought.

In truth, it had been a *long* day. She was ready to curl up with the man and sleep. A man she only met along the side of the road this morning. Hard to believe.

She wanted her new life to be spontaneous and it couldn't get any more spontaneous than today.

He sounded tired when he said, "Tell me about that tat on your shoulder. That's the only one you got, right? Or do I need to do a search for more?"

Both of them were too exhausted for any kind of thorough "search."

"Yes. I actually got it my first year at White Rock. You know the saying 'bright-eyed and bushy-tailed?' That was me. I started out all eager to be a success and to make a good impression. But always kept my eye on the ultimate prize. I got the tattoo to remind myself to stay focused and not let anyone knock me off that path."

He tucked a hand under her shoulder and rolled her enough so he could see the powerful statement. She decided to put it there to make it easy to hide. She had picked a really feminine script for the motto she lived by for over a decade.

But no longer. She had a completely new outlook on life.

He leaned down and pressed his lips to the tattoo. "*Non desistas, non exieris*. I say it right?"

"Close enough."

"Don't know what that means. Don't even know what language that is."

"It's Latin. It means 'never give up, never surrender.'"

He released her shoulder and she rolled back into place to continue using his lap as a pillow.

"Good words to live by."

She shook her head. "It doesn't fit any more. I gave up *and* surrendered."

He placed his hand on her sternum and left it there, a connection that seemed as if his touch was grounding her. Surprise number one thousand and one. "The fuck you did.

You mighta gave up on a shitty-ass job but you didn't give up on yourself."

"I gave up on my goal of being a top executive of a large organization." Being a managing director might have been one of the top three spots, but it wasn't number one.

Should she have been happy with it? Maybe. But she'd always been goal-driven.

She'd been told on the first day she walked into White Rock that no woman had ever been CEO. Hearing that made her more determined than ever. She wanted to be the one to break that glass ceiling. When they bypassed her to promote a man instead, she couldn't smack her head on that ceiling anymore. She knew it was bulletproof glass.

"Find a new goal. No, fuck that, you already got one. Doin' whatever the fuck you wanna do while livin' off the spoils of that war. Right?"

"True. It's not really a goal, though."

"Were you happy in your managin' director spot?"

He remembered what her former position was? Impressive. He had actually paid attention. Surprise number one thousand and two.

She thought about his question. "I thought so. But… Now? I don't know. I did what was expected, I did what I needed to do to get ahead. But was I truly happy?"

"If you're askin' yourself that, then my guess is no."

By riding Agnes around the country, was she chasing happiness? Was it even achievable? She felt peace, for sure. But true happiness? She wasn't so sure.

"If you had to get a tat now, what would you get?" he asked.

That was easy. "One that says 'Just be.' A short but simple message with a much deeper meaning."

"And that deeper meanin'?"

"Live your life how you want to live it. Just be. Honestly, life's too short to concentrate on the wrong things. Or, in my case, to give it to a company that, in the end, only sees you as nothing more than a commodity. I wasn't a person. I was an asset."

"Simple and to the point. I like it."

"Do you?"

"Yeah, you should get it."

"Where should I put it?" Was she really considering getting a second tattoo?

Why the hell not? She was allowed to be impulsive and spontaneous. She reminded herself that she answered to no one. Not one person.

She didn't need to explain herself or even make excuses to anyone.

"Somewhere you can see it. You can't see the one on your back."

"I can in the mirror."

"Yeah, but it's ass backwards in the mirror. Supposed to be a reminder for you and not anyone else, right?"

"Yes, but it was easy to hide there," she explained.

"Shouldn't have to hide shit."

"Women have to hide a lot of shit while working in a man's world. For a long time I thought I was the same person who I was at work, outside of work, too. It turns out I didn't like her very much."

"Like yourself a lot better now?"

She nodded against his thigh. "Yes."

"I like her, too."

"She likes you, too." She reached up and cupped his cheek. "You're really sweet, do you know that?"

The way he twisted his face made her huff out a soft laugh.

He removed her hand from his cheek and kissed the inside of her left wrist. "Put it here. This way you can see it and so can everyone else. Fuck anyone who don't like it."

That was a perfect place to put it. Now she just needed to find a good tattoo artist along her journey.

The pot was beginning to make her head fuzzy and she was quickly losing focus as sleep pulled at her.

"Are you staying the night?" Her question came out a bit slurred.

"Want me to?"

"Yes."

"Warnin' you now, leavin' if you call me sweet again."

"Okay. I won't call you sweet again."

He leaned over and growled, "Ever."

She grinned. "Ever." She crossed her fingers and drew an X over her heart. "I promise. I'm going to remove that word from my vocabulary when it comes to you."

———

"FALLON," he whispered.

He hated to have to wake her but he didn't want to simply ghost without telling her. Especially if he wanted to return to her bed tonight—which he sure as fuck did—that wouldn't be smart. Women tended to get pissed about shit like that.

"Fallon," he repeated, a little louder this time. He was trying not to startle her.

She stirred and slowly rolled over, blinking open her eyes. She let her gaze glide down his body. She was half asleep until she noticed he was fully clothed. "You're leaving?" Her voice was husky from lack of use.

The rough in his own voice was more from lack of sleep, since they'd woken up in the middle of the night and used another wrap in the bowl Ozzy had so generously left in Fallon's room.

But every second of missed sleep had been worth it. In

fact, he struggled to unwrap himself from around her to get up and get dressed.

The last time he stayed all night with a woman was with Billie, back when they were together. So, it had been a couple of years.

"Yeah. Gotta go. Need to head back to my place and get ready for work." He purposely worded it the way he did because he didn't want to tell her that he lived in a room in a bunkhouse full of men. Like a damn college dorm.

Ry said that the bunkhouse was a bit better than his dorm because of the access to the kitchen with plenty of food and free booze in The Barn. Judge's son usually stayed in the bunkhouse whenever he had a break from school since it made him feel more independent than staying with his dad and Cassie. And then, there was their daughter Daisy. Most of the guys could only take her in small doses.

Whip pitied the man who tried to tame her. If anyone even attempted to try.

Fallon released a yawn as she stretched her arms over her head and her legs toward the foot of the bed. She was totally fucking naked and her doing that shifted the sheet down enough to expose her awesome as fuck tits. That was enough to tempt him to climb back in bed with her and call in sick. But Dutch would kick his ass and know exactly what he was up to. The man might sometimes act dumb but he was shrewd and far from fucking stupid.

"What time is it?" she asked on another yawn.

"Around five."

She groaned and pushed her hair out of her face. "Five? Why so early?"

"Need to head back to my place to shower, change, eat. You know, all the shit needed done when someone still has to do the whole J. O. B. thing."

"I can't say I miss that." She covered a third yawn with her hand.

"All right... They usually got coffee in the lobby and if you need breakfast just ask whoever's workin' the front desk to arrange somethin'. Or shoot me a text once you get up. I can get Lee to drop off stuff from Coffee and Cream. Their shit's the bomb. Once you have a ride, promise you'll be headin' there every damn mornin' while you're in town."

"That good, huh?"

"Yeah. Way better than those fuckin' big chains."

Her tousled hair was spread over the pillow and she blinked her blue eyes up at him. He wondered what the fuck she was thinking. When she reached out to him without a word, he stared at her hand for a split second before taking it.

She gave it a squeeze. "Thanks for last night."

He interlocked their fingers, lifted her hand to his mouth and brushed his lips over the back of her knuckles. "Should be thankin' you." He settled a knee on the mattress and it sank when he leaned down far enough to take her mouth.

Fuck. He didn't want to leave. Kissing her was only going to make it harder to walk out the door.

He reluctantly ended it, pressed the side of his nose against hers and closed his eyes.

They might be nothing alike but he liked her. A lot. And for as long as she was in Manning Grove he planned on landing in her bed every night.

"Sorry, I probably have morning breath," she whispered.

"Don't give a fuck," he whispered back. He probably did, too. It wasn't like he kept a toothbrush tucked in his fucking cut.

He straightened and stood next to the bed, their hands still clasped together like neither wanted to let go.

"Last night was... fun."

"Yeah, it was."

She wiggled her eyebrows and shot him a smile. "Repeat tonight?"

He only had one answer for that… Fuck yes. "We can do that. Gonna text you later when the Honda's back. One of us will come get you."

"Okay. I appreciate it. Once I have the Honda, maybe I can find a salon for a haircut while I'm stuck in town."

"Got the perfect place for you."

Her eyes went wide, probably shocked he'd know of any salons. "Really? Can you text it to me?"

"Yeah. I'll do that. Don't go anywhere else, yeah?"

She blinked up at him. "Sure. She's that good?"

"He. Yeah, Teddy's that good. All the ol' ladies go to him. He'll hunt me the fuck down and lob glitter bombs at me if I don't send you his way."

She released a soft laugh. "He sounds dangerous."

"He's a complete pussy cat. You end up knowin' more than you need to about this town in the short amount of time you sit in his chair."

"Are you saying he'll keep me entertained?"

"Hell yeah."

"Okay, that sounds like fun."

"Hopefully you still believe that afterward."

Her laughter filled the room.

So far nothing had stressed this woman. Not her sled breaking down, not being stuck in a small town in Bumfuck, Pennsylvania. Nothing. It was like she was coated in Teflon and she let everything roll off her.

But with what she'd said about her career, he was damn sure she wasn't like this before telling her organization they could take their job and fucking shove it.

He reluctantly released her hand, letting his fingers drag slowly over hers as they separated.

"Are you sure you need to go?" she asked with a tempting as fuck smile and a wiggle of her eyebrows.

He blew out a breath and grabbed his crotch. "Don't make it harder than it already is."

"Leaving or your cock?"

"Both."

"Well, since I don't have wheels and you're not coming back to bed, I'm going back to sleep."

"Not 'til you lock the door behind me."

She nodded and sat up, not bothering to pull up the sheet to cover herself.

Fuck yeah, loads of confidence. Smart. Easy-going. And hot as fuck.

The complete package.

Her tits were icing on that edible cake. He was fucking them later, that was for damn sure.

He shook himself mentally and forced himself to move to the door. Every step he took was like fighting against a thick elastic band hooked around his waist trying to snap him back to the bed.

He slid the chain off the door and flipped the deadbolt.

As he pulled the door open, he said, "Lock the door," one more time and stepped outside into the dark late-March morning. It was cold as fuck and he wished he'd had more than his thermal and cut to wear. Good thing the farm wasn't too far of a ride.

He took two steps toward his sled before he heard a deep clearing of a throat to his left.

He shot a glance toward the office and—*What the fuck?*—Ozzy was slouched in one of the Adirondack chairs out front. A wool beanie was pulled over his ears and down to his eyebrows, his boots were planted on the ground and his knees spread wide. He was also smoking a hand-rolled.

He shot Whip his typical Ozhole grin.

Whip groaned under his breath and braced for dealing with Ozzy this early in the morning.

"What are you doin', Junior? Playin' with the adults?" the club secretary called out.

Whip quickly glanced over his shoulder at the closed door when he heard the lock click behind him.

He was tempted to ignore the man but he would get shit either way, now or later, so he might as well get it over with. He moved away from Fallon's door so she wouldn't overhear their conversation. Last thing he wanted was to lose out on hooking up with her again because of Ozzy fucking that all up by being a dickhead.

He strode over to where the older biker was sitting. "You're an asshole."

The Original took another hit off his cigarette and, when he laughed, the smoke shot out of his nose. "You make it sound like it's somethin' new."

"Thought goin' into her room and leavin' a whole bowl of wraps was funny?"

"Guessin' since you're sneakin' out before sun up, you used them, so maybe you should be thankin' me."

"Ain't sneakin' out."

"It's dark and early as fuck. What would you call it?"

"Havin' a damn job."

Ozzy took another long drag on his hand-rolled and blew it in his direction. "Shoulda known you were into older women as much as you sniffed around Liz."

"Fallon's not much older."

"She's got a few years on you. Sure she can teach you some stuff."

"I know enough. Just ask Liz." Using Liz as a slap back against Ozzy wasn't as effective now as it used to be. Which sucked. Now Whip needed better ammo.

"Think you're gonna get me riled up with that shit?"

"Dunno. Are you?"

Ozzy sat up and took one more hit on his cigarette before grinding the end out on the chair's arm. "Nope. More than happy with my ol' lady."

Yep, Oz had made his peace with Liz leaving his

ass. He was lucky that he found Shay. She had the patience of a fucking saint to deal with the man sitting before Whip. "Shouldn't you be in bed with her right now?"

"Had to pull an all-nighter. My midnight clerk called off last minute."

"That sucks. Thought you had that buzzer to wake you up."

"Yeah. But don't want it to wake up Shay. She's gonna relieve me in a coupla hours."

"What's goin' on with Josie?"

"She got class. Soon as she's done with this semester, she's comin' back full time."

"What about Maddie?"

"She's working this evenin'. Can't wait for Ry to get his ass back for summer break so he can take these fuckin' midnight shifts. Wanna be upstairs warm in bed with my woman."

"Hear that."

Ozzy jerked his chin toward the end of the motel, where Fallon's room was. "She good."

"With what?"

Ozzy chuckled. "You fuckin' know what."

"How's Shay in the sack?"

Oz's chuckle quickly faded away.

"Yeah, thought so. How she is or ain't, ain't your business."

"If you gave her a glowin' recommendation, was thinkin' I could ask Shay if she's up for a third."

"The fuck you will."

Ozzy shrugged as he flicked the remainder of his hand-rolled out into the dark. "She ain't against it."

Whip shook his head. "But I am."

"Ain't askin' *you* to join us."

"You ain't askin' Fallon, either."

Ozzy smirked. "Pussy must be sweet then, if you're bein' all possessive."

Whip sighed. Ozzy got what he wanted, to get a rise out of Whip and Whip fell right into it.

"Gonna end this conversation the same way it began. You're an asshole." He spun on his boot heels and strode over to his bike.

"Tell me somethin' I don't know," Ozzy called out.

Chapter Eleven

WHIP DIDN'T BOTHER to park his sled in the shed, instead he pulled it around to the back of the bunkhouse since he would be hitting the road again soon, anyway.

His first stop would be his room to shower and change, then he'd try to dig up something to eat in the kitchen. After last night he needed to refuel his body. With food *and* caffeine to make sure he stayed awake.

He dismounted and rubbed his numb hands together to get his circulation moving. At the end of March the weather could go either way and at night it tended to still be bone-chilling cold. *Hell*, a snow storm could blow in at any time, too. They'd had some nasty ones even in late April and early May.

He hoped to fuck it warmed up for Sunday's club run.

Jerking the rear bunkhouse door open, he stepped inside and—

Slammed directly into someone in the dark, making him grunt at the impact and the woman he ran into gasp.

"What the fuck?" he growled. Who the fuck was rushing out of the back door at this time of the morning?

Was it a sweet butt sneaking out since they weren't supposed to spend the night?

He grabbed the arm of the person trying to escape and dragged her with him over to the light switch.

In a flash, the corridor lit up and so did Tessa.

What. The. Fuck.

"What the fuck are you doin' in here?" he practically yelled.

"Keep your damn voice down!" The dark-haired woman quickly glanced around and then frowned at him. "I needed to grab something from the kitchen."

Bullshit. She lived in a house with a stocked kitchen. She had zero reason to be sneaking out the back door this early. "At five in the fucking mornin'?"

She shrugged. "Yes. And why is it any of your business?"

Whip stared at Trip's sister and she stared back. One of his eyebrows lifted slowly when it dawned on him why the fuck she wouldn't want to be seen. And no doubt why she wouldn't want to be caught. "Who you doin'?"

Her dark brown eyes went wide for a second before she quickly hid her worry. But he didn't miss it.

He was right.

She answered, "Nobody," way too calmly.

"Then why are you sneakin' out the back door?"

"I'm not sneaking anywhere. I was trying not to wake anyone."

"Bullshit, Tess."

"Whip, don't read any more into it than what it is."

"Don't see food in your fuckin' hands."

She glanced down at her empty hands and when she glanced up he could read it all over her face that she fucked up. "I need to get back before Dyna wakes up."

She tried to push past him, but he blocked her with his body and grabbed her arm to stop her. "Nope."

"You can't keep me here," she hissed, trying to tug her arm free from his grasp.

Oh yeah, that guilt was rising again. She was fucking busted.

"Who you doin'?" he asked again. He glanced down the corridor. The only fully-patched members who didn't have an ol' lady and still lived in the bunkhouse was him, Easy, Dozer and Woody. He glanced at the bunkroom where Scar, Castle and Bones slept. "You ain't doin' one of the prospects."

He didn't make it a question because there was only one right answer.

"If I am, it's none of your business."

"Tess, Trip will fuckin' kill whoever the fuck it is." When she pinned her lips closed, he continued, "You know he has to approach the prez first. And if it's a fuckin' prospect..." Whip shook his head. "You just fucked that fucker's chance of gettin' patched in. A prospect ain't gonna get away with fuckin' the prez's sister behind his back."

"Half-sister," she corrected him.

That deflection was not only weak, that wasn't how the Fury prez saw it. Half-siblings didn't exist in his world. Family was family. No halves about it. *Hell*, he even considered Syn his sister even though they didn't share a drop of blood. "Sister."

"And I'm not fucking any of the prospects."

Whip looked down the corridor again and his gaze landed on the room on the right at the end of the hallway closest to The Barn. His eyes cut back to her, then back to that door. "He needs to approach Trip."

"Nobody needs to do shit."

"You're' playin' with fire, Tess."

"How about you mind your own business?"

"You are my fuckin' business. Just 'cause you don't like it, don't make it not true."

Tessa closed her eyes and inhaled deeply. Once she released it, she opened her eyes and asked, "So, where are you sneaking in from?"

"Fuck that. You ain't turnin' this around on me. And I ain't sneakin' in." He cocked an eyebrow at her. "Unlike you sneakin' out."

They stared at each other for far too long before Tessa said, "I have to go."

"Yeah, so your ass don't get caught where it shouldn't be. And with someone it shouldn't be with, either."

She shook her head and stepped around him.

"You're gonna cause a fuckin' problem, Tess."

"I'm not," she threw over her shoulder. "Don't worry about it." She stepped outside and quietly closed the door behind her.

Whip stared down the long hallway again and at that closed door at the very end. "Ain't you I'm worried about."

———

Whip pulled the Honda into the empty spot in front of Fallon's room. He had texted her to tell her he was on his way and was surprised when she wasn't waiting out front. He needed her to drop him back off at the garage.

He shoved the shifter into Park and stared at the closed door. He could text her, he could beep like an impatient motherfucker or he could get his ass out and go knock on her door.

Or, for the hell of it, all three.

If it was up to him he wouldn't rush back, but Dutch was already on the warpath today and it wouldn't take much for the garage owner to begin throwing wrenches at anything that moved.

Stepping in Cujo's shit and getting it stuck in the treads of his boot did not make for a happy old fuck.

He scratched the back of his neck and climbed out of the old four-door sedan, the door screeching loud enough to be cringeworthy as he slammed it shut. As soon as they got back to the garage, he'd hit the hinges with a squirt of grease so Fallon wouldn't have to deal with it.

Within three long strides, he was pounding on her door with the side of his fist. "Fallon!"

He put his ear to the door and almost tumbled inside when it was flung open. But she wasn't standing there ready to go.

The doorway was empty. Where the fuck was she?

A hand came out of nowhere, grabbing at his coveralls and yanking him inside.

Once the door slammed shut, he found himself pinned to the inside of the door with the woman's mouth on his. Fallon was taking it like she fucking owned it.

Whip was not mad about this turn of events. Not at fucking all.

He let her have her way with him for a few minutes, when she finally ended the kiss, they were both panting and Whip was rock hard.

Yeah, he should've called in sick today.

"How soon do you have to go back?" she murmured against his lips.

"Like now," he answered.

"No time for a quickie?"

Hold on. "That what you want?"

"I wouldn't ask if I didn't."

His dick reminded him it was ready, willing and able. "Might be able to oblige."

"Might or will?"

"Hate to see all those wraps go to waste."

"That would be a real shame," she practically purred.

Fuuuuuck.

How the fuck did he get so damn lucky all of a sudden? "Did it hurt?"

She shook her head. "Did what hurt?"

"When you fell from Heaven."

Laughter burst from her. "That's the worst pickup line ever."

He grinned. "Yeah, but it's fuckin' true."

"And you don't need it to get lucky." She was already unzipping his coveralls and shoving them off his shoulders.

"It's gotta be quick otherwise I'll have a wrench permanently imbedded in my noggin. Then gonna have a hard time findin' a hat to fit."

She snorted softly. "We can take our time later."

He stared at her. She stared back at him with raised eyebrows.

Then just as if someone had pushed their "start" buttons, they both scrambled.

He dropped his coveralls just far enough to get to his jeans, unbuckled his belt, and unzipped his jeans, shoving them down enough to get out his hard-on.

Before he could even tell her that he needed to grab a wrap, either from his wallet or the bowl, one was in front of his face.

The woman was prepared. She knew he was a sure thing.

"Thinkin' I'm easy." He pretended to be insulted. "Just gonna use and abuse me?"

Her lips twitched in amusement. "Do you mind?"

"Fuck no." He snagged the wrap from her fingers. "Get those off."

She peeled the leggings or yoga pants, or whatever the fuck they were, along with her panties down her legs and over her bare feet, tossing them to the side.

"Bed?" she suggested, starting to head in that direction, her lower half naked, her top half in a sweatshirt.

He grabbed her arm and yanked her back to him. "Nope." He spun her around and pinned her back to the door just like she'd done to him when she kissed him. "Right here." He handed the wrap back to her. "Put that on me."

She kept eye contact with him while she ripped open the foil package, removed the wrap and grabbed his hard as fuck dick to roll the latex down its length. When she was done, she smiled.

He smiled. Then he wrapped his hand around her thigh and pulled it up high to his hip height. "Ready?"

"It's all I've been thinking about since you left early this morning."

Damn. "You wet?"

"I'll give you one guess."

"Don't need to guess." He reached between their sandwiched bodies and drew a finger through her folds. Wet wasn't even a good word to describe it.

Soaked. She was fucking drenched even though they hadn't done anything for foreplay except a single kiss.

Like him, she must have been thinking all morning about what they had done last night. Maybe she'd been thinking about what would happen tonight, too. Just like he had.

"Keep your leg there." He bent his knees, tucked his dick where it needed to be and surged up and into her in one thrust.

Once he was deep inside her, he paused and they both simply breathed for a moment.

Yeah, the whole falling from Heaven thing was cheesy as fuck, but, *fuck him*, it was true. Being inside her was pure fucking heaven.

"Keep your leg there," he ordered again, "and give me your hands."

After she hooked her leg around him, he interlocked

their fingers, stretched her hands over her head and pinned them to the back of the door.

Then began to move.

He usually liked to make good things last, but he didn't have the time right now. She had also confirmed them hooking up later, so right now he could give her what she wanted.

Hard and fast.

This was no leisurely fuck. He kept it direct and to the point with one goal in mind.

Powering up and into her, he drove his tongue deep into her mouth while pinning her to the door with his hands, with his chest, with his hips.

With every answering tilt of her hips, with every gasp caught in his mouth, he quickly raced toward the end.

"Need to slow down," he groaned after pulling his lips off hers and planting them against her neck.

"No. Keep going." Her words came out breathless. "Just... keep going." Her fingers tightened within his.

"Ain't gonna stop, but..." He blew out a breath against her soft skin.

"Keep going," she insisted again. "Tell me when you're going to come. I'll be right there with you."

"But—"

"Just do it. I'll be ready."

Her pussy squeezed his dick just as tightly as her fingers squeezed his. He was trying to hold off a little longer but she was making it impossible. *Christ*, her pussy was a hot, tight, very fucking wet fist.

He didn't want to blow in a couple of minutes, he wanted to stay inside her. *Hell*, for the rest of the day, since there was no better place to be, but that would be impossible.

"Fallon," he groaned against her throat. "Don't wanna disappoint you."

"You won't. Promise," she whispered. "I'm right there with you. Just…"

He didn't wait for the rest, he *"just…"*

"Comin'," he warned her. With a grunt he drove up harder and deeper, pulling a cry from her.

Even as he came, he could feel her orgasm exploding around him.

When they both came back to Earth, he realized it was the best goddamn quickie he ever had, and he'd had plenty.

The reason it was great wasn't only due to the sex but because who it was with. Sometimes people simply seemed to fit. He'd seen it time and time again with his brothers who found their ol' ladies. Whether they were similar, like Trip and Stella, or opposite, like Reese and Deacon, there was an unbreakable bond between them.

That bond had to make the sex even better than just grabbing the nearest sweet butt and getting off.

He fought the shiver that threatened to slither down his spine.

That wasn't what was happening here. No fucking way.

A bond couldn't exist. They'd only known each other for about twenty-four hours. So, anything more was impossible.

The sex they'd had wasn't some secret sauce. It was only that… sex.

Get the fuck outta your head, idiot, before you say or do somethin' stupid and you freak her the fuck out and then you won't be gettin' any of this later because you fucked up.

He needed to get back to the garage and that was the last thing he wanted to do right now. He reluctantly pulled out and she dropped her leg until both feet were on the floor.

"Let me clean up quick and get dressed, then we can go," she said, still slightly out of breath.

She slipped from between him and the door but instead of heading directly to the bathroom, she paused. He was in the middle of sliding off the full wrap when her hand cupped his cheek and lifted his face.

"Thank you." Her blue eyes were full of warmth and said a lot more than those two words.

Again, he had to be imagining shit. "Once again, should be thankin' you."

"No thanks needed."

"Same here."

She rose on her tiptoes and pressed her lips to his for a quick kiss. He stared at her as she marched her naked, edible ass into the bathroom.

Yeah, he truly was beginning to believe she fell from Heaven and landed in his path on Copperhead Road.

And that was just fucking crazy.

———

"WANTED to do this before the run and before your ol' ladies join us. That's why I told you to send them up to the farmhouse with Stella. Need to give you all an update and really don't need to hear their opinions on our plan. 'Cause guaran-fuckin'-teed they're gonna have them."

Next to Whip, Rook snorted. A few other grumbles rose up at the last part. Nobody was going to argue with the prez on that point.

"Anyone knows about opinionated women, it's you," Whip said under his breath.

"Jet ain't the only one. Stella's the fuckin' queen of opinions," Rook murmured, not loud enough for Trip to hear.

Whip couldn't argue that, either, and he doubted Trip would disagree.

Trip would be riding solo on the club run today since Stella popped out their son just a couple of weeks ago and was still recovering in places Whip didn't want to think about on the prez's ol' lady.

Trip had stated she'd join them later at Dino's for their meal since they weren't doing a pig roast today. As soon as the weather was a bit warmer, they'd start up again instead of heading to Dino's afterward.

Whip wondered how Crystal was working out as their new house mouse. She had lost her job at the convenience store on the other side of town and it happened to be perfect timing since Rush had just been born. Trip and Stella wanted help they could trust. Crys had proven to be trustworthy and reliable. Even better, she had helped take care of her baby sister, so knew all about newborns and toddlers. A plus in Trip's book.

While he hoped to increase the Fury numbers, until that happened, the four remaining sweet butts—Billie, Amber, Angel and Brandy—were more than enough to go around. Truthfully, there weren't enough patched members to keep them busy or satisfied. Even so, Trip didn't want to lose any more. Especially like they did with Liz, Stella's sister.

Whip was surprised Liz and her ol' man weren't up from Shadow Valley this weekend. When they were, they joined the Fury on their bi-monthly runs. Of course, with Crash and Liz wearing their Dirty Angels MC cuts.

"You all know I've stressed to death the importance of allies. With both the Dark Knights and the Dirty Angels." Trip's gaze landed on Ozzy and hung there for a minute. "Allies are always good to have. Especially right now. We got a relationship with the Angels that will now pay the fuck off. This was somethin' we talked about a while back but back then we couldn't swing it… and I vetoed it for other obvious reasons." He took an audible breath and his gaze sliced through the club. "Kept this from you all 'til me and Judge got the plan organized and cemented. Plus, it wasn't anythin' the people involved wanted to be known to anyone other than the two of us. Mostly because of how things are gonna go down."

Trip removed his signature black baseball cap and squeezed the bill between his hands. Usually, the only time the man removed it was when his temper was flaring or he was frustrated. It was clear this wasn't either of those things. This was something else Whip hadn't seen before.

For a second, his heart skipped a beat. Was the prez giving up? Was he throwing in the towel when it came to the Shirleys? Because that clan was what this meeting had to be about.

Those hillbilly motherfuckers.

The constant thorn in their sides.

Their only goddamn enemy.

At this point they were down to two options... Kill or be killed. And nobody standing in The Barn wanted the second one. That left the first option and Whip was damn sure Trip would prefer to avoid it, even though it wasn't possible.

"Here's the thing. None of us standin' in this barn right now has the fuckin' know-how to finish this war. Even me. Willin' to admit it since to be a good leader I have to recognize my... hell, *our* weaknesses. My time in the Marines was fightin' foreign enemies, not domestic. But right now," he pointed to the floor, "I'm standin' on American soil. Ain't the same. Also, I got so much more to fuckin' lose now. We all do." He tipped his head toward the club enforcer, standing to his left. "When the Angels came up here when Stel and I got hitched, Judge had a long convo with the Angels' enforcer to spitball some options. Their man Diesel runs a security team—"

"Security?" Dutch barked out. "We don't need fuckin' security. What are we? A bunch of pussies? The Originals—"

Trip held up a hand to cut the old man off. "We ain't the Originals."

Judge picked up from there. "Ain't the kinda security you see at a public event or even for a celebrity. Though, they will be bodyguards for people who got enough scratch to pay them to keep them safe. Let's just say they're more like mercenaries than bodyguards."

"Yeah, so… We discussed using them when Dyna was taken, but they ain't cheap and there's a good reason for that."

When Trip hesitated, Whip realized he was right. Whatever the prez was about to propose was his last option. The man didn't like it, but he was going to have to live with it.

"They're good. They're ghosts. They know what the fuck they're doin' and get it done. They get in and get out before anyone knows what the fuck hit them. Most of us got some kinda skill but not *that* kinda skill and not at that level. They live for this kinda shit. But, again, it's costly as fuck, one reason why I was avoidin' it. But now? We got no choice. Can't put a price on our families. If we gotta pay for this for the next coupla decades, then we do, but want it so we don't have to keep lookin' over our fuckin' shoulders for those decades. Also don't wanna leave this war for the next Fury generation." He glanced at Judge. "For Ry." He found Shade in the group. "For Jude. Hell, even for Dane and Rush. We're growin' somethin' good here and the fuck if I'm lettin' those inbred goat fuckers destroy it. Also tired of worryin' about our women and kids."

"Like the prez said," Judge started, "what we got planned will wipe out every fuckin' dime this club has saved. Every fuckin' penny. And we're still gonna owe a big chunka change. We're gonna be payin' for a while. But we'd rather go into debt than go to a fuckin' funeral. You get what I'm sayin'?"

Grumbles moved around Whip, but those grumbles all sounded like they were in agreement.

"What's the plan?" Cage asked their president.

"We're gonna do what we talked about but I didn't think was possible. We're gonna blow up that fuckin' mountain."

Chapter Twelve

"WE'RE gonna blow up that fuckin' mountain."

Silence engulfed them all for a long moment after Trip's announcement.

Until Sig exploded with, "Fuck yeah," at the top of his lungs. "About fuckin' time."

Trip raised his hand, trying to settle down all the conversation now swirling around The Barn, jump-started from Sig's outburst. Some of it surprise, some of it eagerness. While some might not agree with the method, all were onboard with the fact they needed to end the Shirleys once and for all.

Warnings hadn't worked. Picking the Shirley men off one at a time hadn't worked, either. Even the feds coming in and clearing that mountain hadn't done shit.

The clan was truly made up of redneck roaches.

They needed to do something drastic. Blowing up that fucking mountain was certainly that. If that didn't finish off the Shirleys, nothing would.

"Like I said, gonna cost us scratch we don't got. We're gonna be hurtin' for a while 'cause we'll be runnin' on empty," Trip emphasized. "Personally, don't like that. Hate not havin' reserves available for emergencies. All of us in this room have done a lot to build up the club's account, we've done a lot to build our businesses and it's gonna feel like we're goin' back to square one. But our safety, the safety of our women and especially our kids, is always gonna come first. Our kids are priceless."

A wave of *fuck yeahs* swept through the room.

"So, we're gonna have to bite the bullet and pay. No other way around it. Otherwise, this shit will never be over and we'll never live in peace. Think we can all agree on that. But here's the thing… This ain't a decision I can fully make on my own or even the exec committee. It's gotta be all of us. This is somethin' once we decide to move forward with, we all have to be able to live with the results, if you get what I'm sayin'. Diesel's crew, the Shadows, might also need help. They normally don't but this is a huge job. Of course, it's also a dangerous job. My Marine buddy Slade might even come up with them. He steps in and helps them out when necessary, but the rest of it might fall on us. They're gonna come up, do their thing and then they're gonna disappear like, just what I said, ghosts. We'll be the one dealin' with any aftermath. Guess what I'm sayin' is this ain't gonna be a social call. It's gonna be all business. And, just so you know, it took a lot of convincin' from Judge for Diesel to agree to take this job for those very fuckin' reasons."

"Ain't easy gatherin' that kinda explosive power," Judge added. "Gonna take time for the Shadows to accumulate the items needed for such a big job. They have to be careful about it so it doesn't set off any red flags. They don't want the job to end before it even begins. Especially with the kinda scratch they're gonna be makin' on it."

"Holy fuck, are they blowin' up that whole fuckin' mountain?" Whip asked, unsure how the fuck that would even happen. It was a *mountain* not a dirt hill. That was going to take some major explosives for massive detonations.

"It ain't gonna be that simple. Wish it was," Trip answered. He tugged his baseball cap back on his head. "The plan as it stands without them actually surveyin' the clan's compound is to take out every fuckin' buildin' on Hill-billy Hill and fuck up the terrain enough that they won't be able to rebuild easily, if at all. That is, *if* there's any in the mountain clan left to rebuild. They need to use enough explosives to not only deter them from livin' up there, but from ever comin' back. The goal is it needs to be a message they can't ignore."

"That'll be a huge kick in their fuckin' asses," Easy said with a grin.

"Won't the feds and the locals be crawlin' all over that?" Rev asked.

"No doubt," Judge answered. "But we're gonna have an event planned that night so we all have alibis. *All* of us. We're gonna make sure we're seen in public, so we'll probably hold this 'event' at Crazy Pete's where we're not only gonna be seen, but will also have privacy to deal with whatever we gotta deal with, like communication between us and the Shadows, shit like that. Still workin' out those details but it should all be in place before they get up here."

"Don't you think the pigs are gonna set their sights on us?" Rook asked. "Nobody wants the Shirleys gone more than us."

"You better believe they're gonna be up our asses. 'Specially the Brysons. But Diesel's team's gonna make it look like the Shirleys were makin' their own explosives for revenge against the government and, just like the meth they were makin', they're gonna make it look like the clan was makin' it and storin' it the half-assed hillbilly way, so…" Trip shrugged. "You know how that goes… shit happens."

"Ka-fuckin'-boom!" Sig shouted, then rubbed his hands together, a fucked-up gleam in his eyes.

Whip never saw the man look this excited over anything.

"What about the rest of them?" Deacon asked, looking the exact opposite of Sig.

"Rest of who?" Judge asked his cousin.

"The kids. The women. The reasons we never did anythin' this drastic before."

"Yeah," Trip mumbled, then ripped his hat back off his head and raked his fingers through his hair. "Still workin' out those details."

"That cunt and her man are goin' down. Don't give a fuck what's between her legs," Sig announced. "Anyone who can do that to her own blood needs to lose every drop of that blood in that traitorous body 'til there's nothin' left."

He had to be talking about Red's mom and stepfather since they were the ones who had traded Red to the Shirleys in exchange for another female for their Ohio clan. They were the ones who put Red in the nightmarish spot she'd been in. To be abused and assaulted. Pregnant and desperate to escape. Ultimately, carrying the baby of one of her rapists.

What Red's mother did to her own daughter was the whole reason Sig found his ol' lady. It was also the reason the tension between the Fury and the Guardians of Freedom began.

As well as the whole reason Levi was brought into this world. Before Jet hooked up with Rook, that baby was the only connection between the Fury and the Brysons.

"Can tell you the Shadows prefer that the women and children be cleared from the mountain before they come up," Judge said.

"And how the fuck's that gonna happen? We have a fuckin' party for them and invite their breeders and snot monkeys?" Dutch grumped. "Maybe we can invite all those dumb motherfuckers to Cassie's baby shower." The old man shook his head and tugged on his bushy salt-and-pepper beard.

In truth, he only said out loud what the rest of them were thinking. How the fuck did they remove the women and children without instantly getting into a war with the Shirleys or putting those fuckers on notice that something was about to go down?

"Even if we can get them off the mountain, what the fuck we doin' with them?" Rook bitched. "They ain't fuckin' stray cats we can drop off at the shelter."

"Workin' on a plan. Had Castle do a count the last time he was up there, which was two nights ago. Right now there are more men up there than women and kids," Trip announced.

"But that can change quickly with the way they're movin' on rebuildin'," Dodge spoke up. "We don't got anyone sittin' on that mountain twenty-four-seven. They can be bringin' in more vans full of women and children than just the one that brought in Red's mother."

The Shirleys were out to rebuild their mountain clan the same way Trip had worked on rebuilding the Fury. Of course, without the incest.

"Grabbin' those fuckin' kids," Sig muttered.

"Sig," Trip barked in a warning tone.

"What kids?" Ozzy asked with his thick brows pulled together.

Whip wanted to know, as well.

"Red's siblin's."

Oh fuck.

Hell, he guessed something had to be done with them if the VP planned on taking out their parents. They'd end up orphans and, like it or not, they were Red's blood.

Did *Sig* want to take them? That couldn't be fucking right. But then, the man wasn't quite in his right mind.

Red dealt with severe PTSD from her ordeal up on that mountain, could she even deal with raising three young kids at this point? They might be constant reminders of how her own mother betrayed her.

"And what the fuck you gonna do with them?" Trip yelled, beginning to unravel. The stress of coordinating this whole thing, plus doing his best to keep everyone safe, along with having a newborn, had to be wearing on him. His temper was touchy on a good day. When he was overwhelmed and exhausted, it flared much more quickly.

Stella was usually his calming force. However, she wasn't anywhere within reach right now.

"Not subject them to being raised by fuckin' inbred goat fuckers. She don't want them growin' up thinkin' fuckin' their sisters, cousins or anythin' else is goddamn normal. The point of that fuckin' clan is to procreate, they just don't give a fuck who it's with. She can't fuckin' sleep knowin' they're up on that mountain. And if she can't sleep, I can't fuckin' sleep." He squared off with his own brother. "We're grabbin' those kids. Whatever we do with the rest of them, don't give a fuck, but those kids I do."

"Again, what the fuck are you gonna do with three kids under five?" Judge asked, dragging a hand down his long beard.

"Same as you and Daisy. Same as Jemma and Dyna. Same as Shade with Maddie and Josie or Chelle with Jude. Cassie with Ry. Dodge with Maya. Fuckin' raise them like they're our own. Bring them into the Fury family and make them ours." Sig with his fingers curled tightly into fists, those fists pressed to the sides of his thighs, turned his attention back to Trip. "Brother, you constantly spout about how family's family, no matter what. We're holdin' you to that. You spout off about how it 'takes a fuckin' village.' Red and I both belong to that fuckin' village. We're takin' them and gonna do what we need to do. We don't, she'll never be able to live with herself. And I ain't standin' by and watchin' that eat away at her. You get me?"

The Barn was completely quiet as the two brothers stared each other down for what had to be at least a minute. No one dared say a fucking word during their intense but silent conversation.

Trip sucked in a deep breath and scrubbed a hand over his mouth. Finally, he nodded. "We can grab them but not so sure you should take them on, brother."

"You sayin' I'm too fucked up to raise those kids? You think I wouldn't have taken Levi as my own if Red kept him? That what you're sayin'?"

Whip decided to wade in. "Sig raisin' those kids can't be as bad as those hillbilly inbreds raisin' them." He didn't say it loud but he didn't have to. His point was made and also heard.

"Whip's right," Shade said in his slow, careful manner. "Those kids will have all of us to help. Seen Red with Maya. Seen her with Rush, Dane and Dyna. Got no doubt she'll be okay. If I can help raise three kids, so can he."

"Josie and Maddie were already raised," Judge reminded him. "Jude's a teen. Ain't the same as three young kids like that."

"We all got each other's backs, right?" Dodge asked. "Never planned on havin' any crotch goblins, now I'm raisin' a nine-year-old. It easy? No. Can it be done? Fuck yeah. Doin' it for Syn. Sig will do what he needs to do for Red."

When Sig and Dodge locked gazes, the VP gave the bar manager a chin lift.

"Five of you can't live in that apartment."

Sig acknowledged Trip's statement. "Yeah."

But the prez wasn't finished. "Also got to come up with an explanation how those kids got into your possession."

Sig glanced at Shade. "No different than Jude. We'll make somethin' up."

Shade just stared back at Sig, not confirming or denying

if Jude was really his son by blood. They all suspected he wasn't. But in the end, it didn't matter as long as however he came to join Shade and Chelle didn't bring any heat on the club.

If Shade claimed Jude was his son, then everyone accepted it as truth. The man had a lot of secrets, where Jude came from was just one more.

"You know once this plan starts movin' it's gonna be done at a fast pace, right? That means we gotta get those women and children out of there and you gotta deal with Red's mom however you wanna deal with her. All before the Shadows detonate the explosives." Trip shot Sig a look.

Even Whip could read the prez's look which clearly said Red would have to live with what Sig planned on doing to her mother. Whip assumed Sig had already worked that out with his ol' lady.

"Then we're gonna separate those three from the rest quickly and quietly. Once we do, we need somewhere to house them, Sig. You can't be havin' those kids sleepin' on the floor."

"Yeah," Sig said again. "Know it. Figure we can set up one of Reilly's emergency trailers temporarily 'til we figure everythin' out."

"Dodge, Syn and your niece are already livin' in one 'til their place is built. That leaves two available. You take one, that leaves one. Lee's got one more on order but not sure when it'll be delivered. Even so, we need them available to financially recover after this whole damn thing."

"What the fuck do you want me to do then?" Sig asked his brother, the tone sharp. "Let 'em stay with that cunt? Let that bitch live after her selfish motherfuckin' actions damaged her daughter beyond repair? Ain't gonna happen."

Trip's eyes narrowed on his brother. "How 'bout we discuss it later."

"If you're only gonna say no, no point in talkin' about it."

"Ain't sayin' no, Sig. Only sayin' we need to have a fuckin' plan. It's just one more thing in a long list we need to coordinate. This has to go down as smoothly and neatly as possible. Shouldn't have to explain why for the hundredth time. You get that?"

Sig's nostrils flared when he took a deep inhale. A second later, his fingers uncurled and his shoulders relaxed a bit.

"We'll figure it out, brother," Judge assured Sig. "We ain't gonna abandon those kids."

Sig nodded.

The tension in The Barn lessened a little and everyone breathed a little easier.

"All right," Trip started, his gaze slicing through all of them. "Like I said, this ain't a decision that should only be made by me or the officers. That means if anyone's got any issues with hirin' the Shadows to take care of this Shirley business once and for all, speak the fuck up now. 'Cause once we give them the go-ahead, the ball's gonna start rollin'."

Silence descended the group.

Judge's eyes scanned them all. "Anyone? Last chance to say your piece."

"Burn the bitch to the ground!" Cage yelled. "They used my daughter as bait. No tellin' what else they'll do."

"Blow those motherfuckers to smithereens!" Easy shouted near Whip.

"Put them on the fast track to hell," Dozer added enthusiastically.

"No mercy for them touchin' my Duchess," Dutch bellowed from the other side of the group.

"I guess that means we're a 'go,'" Judge said.

A chorus of stomping boots and hoots were the enforcer's answer.

Trip raised a hand and called out, "Hey, pay attention for a sec. Got one more thing, and this is *really* fuckin' important. No one says a word to the women 'til I tell you. Not one fuckin' word." He turned to Rook. "Even Jet. Hell, especially Jet. If we need her, we'll catch her up to speed. We don't want her tippin' off her family."

"She ain't gonna snitch," Rook said. "She ain't riskin' me goin' back inside."

"Brother, she might not do it on purpose, but we don't wanna put that extra pressure on her. She still got a shitload of loyalty to her family, as well as her former profession. You get what I'm sayin'?" Trip asked. "Jet might be Fury but her last name's also Bryson. Let's not forget that."

"You could change that last name if you wanted," Cage said, elbowing his brother in the ribs.

Rook shoved him, but addressed Trip. "You know she's gonna kick my ass afterward for not cluin' her in ahead of time. Just sayin'."

"Would pay to see that," Cage muttered.

"Bet you would," Rook said to his brother.

"You know the sayin'… easier to ask for forgiveness than permission," Deacon said with a smirk.

"You got that down pat," Judge told him.

Deacon grinned. "I ain't stupid. And make-up sex is the best fuckin' sex. Am I right?"

Fuck yeahs rose up from the brothers with ol' ladies.

Whip wouldn't know. He never gave a woman a reason to have make-up sex with him.

But, like hate sex, he bet it was hot as fuck.

"All right, enough jawin', " Trip said. "Get your ol' ladies and let's get rollin'. But first, you know what we need to do…"

They all started stomping their boots on the floor again.

This time they added the pounding of their fists on their chests as Trip yelled out, "From the ashes we rise…"

In unison, everyone shouted, "For our brothers we live and die!"

Fuck, with that proposed plan, that actually might happen.

———

"Where's Fallon?" Reilly asked after Rev pulled his sled next to Whip.

"Who's Fallon?" her ol' man asked.

"The blonde who owns that Scout, remember? You know, the sled you guys keep jerking off all over." She made a jerking motion with her fist.

"Why the fuck would she be here?" Rev asked, ignoring his woman's second comment.

"'Cause Whip has a thing for her."

"What are you up to, woman?" Rev shot her an annoyed frown over his shoulder.

"I'm not up to anything," Lee exclaimed, working way too hard at sounding innocent. "Ozzy said you never left the motel until Friday morning. You also returned Friday night and didn't leave until this morning. Are you heading over there tonight, too?" She wiggled her damn eyebrows at Whip.

"Stop your fuckin' meddlin'," Rev ordered.

"I'm not meddling. I'm just encouraging. There's a difference."

"Not when it comes to you," Rev muttered.

Reilly leaned into her man's back and whispered loudly, "She gave him a boner the other day at the shop."

"Yeah, and? So what? Lots of women gave me a boner and they never came along on a run. That ain't how it's done, Lee. You know that."

She shrugged and smiled.

"Christ," Whip muttered. "You both done talkin' about me and my fuckin' boner?"

Rev's head spun toward him. "She really gave you a fuckin' boner?"

Reilly rolled her eyes. "They fucked, Rev. So, what do you think?"

Rev's blue eyes widened. "You fucked her?"

She whacked his arm. "Were you not paying attention when I mentioned the motel?"

"Damn, she's hot." Rev grinned. "And older. Ripe for the pickin'."

"Right? I think she's perfect—"

Whip sighed and tuned out whatever Reilly was now going on about.

Fuck these two. He took enough shit from them during work, he didn't need their abuse on a Sunday, too. Especially when it came to someone he had sex with.

Whip shook his head, started his Harley and began to twist the throttle to drown them out.

"Gonna take tail today," he shouted with another twist of the throttle and got out of line. He did a U-turn and went to the back of the pack where the single members usually rode. He pulled up next to Easy and let his sled idle while everyone else got in formation.

Cage, being road captain, and Jemma always took the lead.

Behind them were usually Trip and Judge. The prez was flying solo for the run, but Cassie, now at over six months pregnant and with a decent sized baby belly, was joining her ol' man.

In the third row were Deacon and Ozzy. Reese was actually glad to hand their son, Dane, over to Saylor, so she could finally come along on a run. Shay clung to Ozzy, the club secretary.

Sig, Red, Dodge and Syn made up the fourth row.

Rook and Jet were in the fifth row with Shade and Chelle.

Rev and Reilly made up the sixth row, and since Dozer was one of the last to join the formation, he filled the spot Whip left open with his departure.

Dutch, riding solo of course, was in the seventh row next to Woody.

Easy and Whip made up the last row. Now with the two newest members, the formation was getting longer.

Whip shoved his sunglasses to the top of his head and pulled down the bandana he tied around his nose and mouth. He leaned closer to Easy and whispered, "What the fuck you doin', man?"

Easy frowned. "What're you talkin' about? I'm waitin' for Cage to pull out. What the fuck are you doin'?"

"Meant about Friday mornin'."

Easy's eyebrows pinned together and the creases on his forehead became deeper. "What about Friday mornin'?"

Whip glanced around to make sure no one was paying attention to their conversation. "With Tessa."

"Got no idea what the fuck you're talkin' about, brother."

"Easy. You're playin' with fire if you don't approach Trip. You know that."

"Approach him about what?"

"About what the fuck you're doin'."

"What the fuck am I doin'?"

Jesus fuck.

"If she ain't doin' you, who the fuck is she doin'?"

"How the fuck would I know?" Easy asked. "What'd you see?"

"Tessa sneakin' out of the bunkhouse. Like early, too. Tryin' not to get caught."

Easy stared at him. "She probably needed somethin' from the kitchen."

"You tellin' me Cage and Jem don't keep their fuckin' kitchen stocked?" Of course, they did. That was a bullshit excuse, especially since Tessa left empty-handed. And why would Easy use the same excuse Tessa used?

Obviously, the women raided the bunkhouse kitchen since Trip stocked it with fresh foods from the Amish, but not at five in the fucking morning.

"How the fuck would I know what's in their fuckin' kitchen? They don't invite me over for goddamn dinner."

"You think she's doin' a prospect?" That question left a bad taste in Whip's mouth.

"She better not be," Easy growled.

"What about the other two?"

Whip's brother shook his head. "She better not be."

"Well, she's doin' someone. If it ain't you, then it's one of them."

"Tessa's gotta have better taste than Dozer or Woody," E muttered.

"Ry ain't home yet, so I know it ain't him."

Easy narrowed his eyes on him. "Why the fuck do you care, anyway?"

Why the fuck *did* he care?

Whip sighed. "You're right. Why the fuck should I care? It ain't me who's gonna get the shit beat outta me with The Punisher."

Easy stared at him, his brown eyes a little wider than they should be for someone supposedly so damn innocent. "You think that's what'll happen? It didn't with Rev."

Whip shrugged. "Don't matter. Ain't my problem, right? I just know it ain't my dick stickin' her, so it ain't gonna be me havin' a blanket party." He shot Easy a smirk and twisted his throttle, revving the engine. "Great day for a ride, ain't it, brother?"

Chapter Thirteen

THANK FUCK the warm weather was returning because he'd missed the club runs. He missed the bonding with his brothers on Sunday between the ride and dinner at Dino's or the spread the sisterhood and the sweet butts set up at The Barn afterward.

Those rides were necessary because they actually settled their souls. Every last one of them. Because of that, Cage purposely never led the formation past Hillbilly Hill. Their runs were a time to forget any shit clawing at them or disturbing their peace.

The kids were left at home. The prospects remained behind. It was just the fully-patched members and their ol' ladies.

The Fury foundation.

The runs were a good way to keep that core both committed and connected. It was one reason Trip required every patched member to go. Otherwise, they needed a damn good excuse.

But during the whole ride, Whip's mind had been elsewhere. Back at The Grove Inn. In room number one.

Even though he hadn't answered Reilly, he was definitely heading over there after they dispersed later.

Did he want to go there instead of being on the run? Hell yeah, there was a first time for everything.

Was he stupid enough to break formation to do that? Fuck no. Not unless he wanted his ass ridden so hard it would be raw.

While he didn't need to keep Fallon a secret, he also didn't want what they were doing in the spotlight. It was bad enough Ozzy knew. The older biker took any opportunity he could to bust Whip's balls.

Even so, for the whole fucking three-plus-hour run through the back roads of northern Pennsylvania, Whip had been in auto-drive since he couldn't think of anything but *her*.

The confidence Fallon had about her body, with her life, with fucking everything… That shit oozed from her pores.

But it wasn't only that. It was also the way she sounded while they had sex. Her expressions while she came. The softening of her facial features after she orgasmed, knowing *he* caused that satisfaction, *he* took her there.

The way she looked at him when she thought he didn't notice.

He'd seen it.

Whip figured he had surprised her by not being who she had expected. Realizing he was more than just a dick to ride while waiting for her real ride to be fixed.

She probably never imagined she'd end up knocking boots with a biker younger than her from a small town in a mostly rural area.

Fallon had been an executive in a big city. A professional. A woman who had complete control of her life. Whip was so damn far from that. The only real thing they had in common was their bikes. And the fact they were good in bed together.

But that was it.

Not that it needed to be anything more. She'd be continuing on her journey as soon as her "Agnes" was repaired. Unfortunately, by fixing her sled, he would be the one sending her on her way and out of his life.

He scrubbed a hand down his cheek, not even hearing the conversation surrounding him where he sat at the table.

The staff at Dino's always set up the back banquet room for their group whenever they came in. Their numbers had increased so much over the last few years with adding new members and ol' ladies that they now had to push enough tables together to form a U. The room wasn't big enough to set them up end to end anymore.

This morning, he had to force himself to leave Fallon's motel room to head back to the farm to get cleaned up, changed and ready for the ride. They had remained locked in her room since Friday night, never leaving once. The only time either one of them dressed was when he pulled on his jeans long enough to answer the door for food deliveries.

They had made a pretty good dent in that bowl full of wraps. His goal was to use every damn one of them before she rolled back out of Manning Grove. Fallon had also taken that as a challenge and thank fuck she was onboard with it.

She must be trying to get her fill of dick while she had someone ready, willing and able. He had no problem being that dick for her. It wasn't a sacrifice on his part whatsoever.

Whip stared at his half-eaten bowl of now cold homemade chicken and dumplings. A heavily-ringed hand waved in front of his face and he lifted his eyes to the asshole it was attached to.

"Damn, Junior, you got it bad. It's pussy. There's plenty of it out there," Ozzy said. "No need to be obsessin' over one."

"Ozzy," Shay scolded him softly. "Leave him alone."

The club secretary shrugged. "The woman musta fucked his brains out. He's sittin' there like a fuckin' zombie. Or a teen boy after his first wet dream."

"Maybe he's tired," Shay suggested.

"Yeah, from all that fuckin'," Ozzy said with a grin. "That cougar have claws?"

"Shoulda told her to stay at the hotel instead of the motel since you're nosy as fuck," Whip told him.

"Hard not to notice with your sled parked out in front of her room all fuckin' weekend. And you texted me to have the housekeeper skip that room. Pussy must be sweet as fuck."

"Ozzy," Shay said a little more sharply this time.

He turned toward his ol' lady. "What?"

Shay bugged her eyes out at him and shook her head.

Whip didn't need a woman fighting his battles. "We wanna discuss your sex life?" He lifted an eyebrow. He was pretty damn sure Shay didn't know all the shit Ozzy had done in the past and also with whom.

The list was long on both accounts.

"Problem over there?" Judge asked from the other side of the U. Leaning back in his chair and finished eating, the sergeant at arms had an arm thrown over Cassie's shoulders and one massive hand planted on her protruding belly.

"Nope," Oz answered the club's sergeant at arms. "No fuckin' problem at all. Just bustin' on Junior here." He grabbed Whip's shoulder and shook him. "Right?"

"Fuck off," Whip said under his breath, jerking up his shoulder to shed Ozzy's hand.

Ozzy laughed and removed it, then patted Whip's chest over his cut. "Just havin' a bit of fun."

"And that's what Whip is having with Fallon, so leave him alone," Shay said quietly but loud enough to make a point with her ol' man, especially when she added a raised eyebrow.

Ozzy ginned, grabbed her chin, leaned over and planted a kiss on her lips. "Anythin' for you, baby."

A whole bunch of mocking kissing noises rounded the group of tables.

"*Anythin' for you, baby,*" Deacon mimicked with a laugh. "Never thought anyone would be able to bring you down a peg, asshole."

"Look who's talkin'," Ozzy said. "If anyone's got their nuts in a vice, it's you."

"That vice gave me a son," Deke answered, not taking offense at all. "I was in that fuckin' delivery room. After witnessin' that, I can tell you whatever this woman wants, this woman gets. 'Cause fuck if I'd survive pushin' a head this size," he made a circle with both hands, "outta a hole this size." He made a much smaller circle with his thumb and forefinger.

"Can we not talk about that part of my life ever again, please?" Reese asked on a sigh. "Especially at the dinner table."

"Yes, can we get off this subject because it's too damn fresh for me, too," Stella said with a grimace.

Cassie planted a hand over Judge's on her belly. "And that's the part I'm not looking forward to."

"Okay," Trip said with a single clap of his hands to get everyone's attention. "Some of us are still eatin' and yeah, it's fresh in my mind, too."

"Lookin' a little green there, prez," Dutch said on a chuckle.

"He almost passed out," Stella stage whispered. "Especially when—"

"Woman!" Trip shouted. "We're done with this fuckin' conversation."

"I'm so glad I'm done. Three kids are enough," Chelle said from down the table. "I can't imagine raising an infant at this age. Especially with having two in college." Her fingers were interlaced with Shade's and their clasped hands sat on the table between their plates.

Two servers came in and began clearing the table and refilling waters, checking if anyone needed anything more before they hit the road and headed back to The Barn to do a little partying.

Share a bong. Share a sweet butt. Play a few games of pool or darts. Drink and enjoy each other's company.

It was a tradition after a run and most of Whip's brothers stuck around for that. He'd split as soon as he could and head over to the motel to join Fallon.

"Everybody ready to head out?" Trip asked, getting to his feet and pulling out his chained wallet from his back pocket. He removed a few Benjamins and dropped them onto the table. "Might not be doin' this again for a while."

Stella stood, too, wearing a frown. "Why?"

Whip saw the second Trip realized he fucked up, but the man recovered like a pro.

"'Cause weather's gettin' nice and we can party back on the farm after the runs. With this size group, eatin' here costs a shitload of scratch."

"We have the money," Stella reminded him. "And we don't do it that often."

"Yeah, but wanna watch our spendin'."

"Trip," she began.

"All right, let's head out. I could use a fuckin' beer."

Everyone still sitting rose and began to file out of the back room and through the plastic accordion door that separated it from the main dining area. Whip was one of the last ones in line. He was in front of Trip and Judge who usually took the rear whenever the large group was on foot and on the move. Shade and Sig usually took the front. It reminded him of the formation they rode in but with the ol' ladies in the middle. If the kids were with them, they were kept in the center of the group, too.

They had a system set in place for safety and it worked. It never had actually been discussed, but had come about naturally.

It was their job to protect the sisterhood and the kids and they all took that seriously. The Shirleys could be anywhere at any time. Jemma had been attacked and Dyna taken in the middle of the day in the public parking lot at the center of town. That proved no one was safe and everyone should stay vigilant.

When the group came to an abrupt and complete halt, Whip peered around Easy to see why everyone had stopped. He closed his eyes and groaned when he realized who brought the group to a complete fucking standstill.

Reilly and Shay. Two of the ol' ladies who would recognize the woman sitting at the counter eating dinner by herself.

Fuck.

He'd been anxious to see her, but in private, not in front of all of his brothers and their women.

Fuck!

Even his brothers who'd been walking ahead stopped and turned back to see what the fuck was going on.

Fallon sat frozen with her fork halfway to her lips as she glanced over her shoulder at the huge group of bikers behind her. She probably didn't notice him standing behind Easy and Dozer.

"What's goin' on?" Trip asked, plowing past them. "There a problem?"

"No problem," Reilly told him. "Just stopping to say hello."

Fuck. He needed to get up there, too, before Rev's ol' lady said something stupid. Because knowing Reilly, she would say something totally fucking stupid. He followed quickly in Trip's wake.

Fallon placed her fork on her plate and, once she spotted

Whip, shot him a smile that was a hell of a lot more than just a friendly greeting.

Fuck.

Trip glanced from her to Whip and back. "What's goin' on?"

"Woman, mind your biz," Rev ordered his ol' lady. "Keep movin'."

"I don't want to be rude, Rev. She's one of our *customers*. And she's eating *alone*."

"I'm used to eating alone," Fallon answered with obvious confusion on why that was a big deal.

"But there wasn't any reason for you to eat alone *tonight*," Reilly continued, "If Wh—"

Rev dragged his ol' ladies' ass past Fallon and toward the front entrance. "Rev!"

"Woman, get the fuck outside," was the only thing Whip's coworker and club brother said, pushing his ol' lady out the door with a shake of his head.

"Let's go," Judge ordered. "Everyone outside. We're blockin' the waitresses." He put his hand on Cassie's back and steered her through the group. "Outside now!"

Thank fuck for Judge. Otherwise, all of them would remain crowding around Fallon and rubbernecking.

"Maybe we want to meet her," Red whispered. But of course, it was loud enough so almost everyone heard it.

"You heard Lee, she's just one of Dutch's customers," Easy said and pushed past Whip.

"Hello, Fallon," Shay, one of the few who hadn't moved, greeted with Ozzy standing next to her.

For fuck's sake.

"Hi, Shay, did you have a good weekend?"

"Bet *you* did," Ozzy said slyly.

"Hello, Ozzy."

"Well, damn, you remember my name. Ain't brainless like Whip after all that—"

"Your name's on the front of your cut," Fallon quickly reminded him with a lift of her eyebrows.

He chuckled. "Oh yeah."

"But even if it wasn't, it's hard to forget you," Fallon said dryly.

"Damn," Reese whispered. "I think I like her already." She held her hand out to Deacon. "Come on. Let's clear out and give the servers space to move."

Deacon hesitated only for a few seconds as he checked Fallon out and then turned to Whip, cocking an eyebrow and giving him a nod. Reese yanked on his hand, tugging him forward, hissing something under her breath at him.

Jet herded any stragglers out, dragging Rook with her, until the only people remaining were Whip, Trip and Stella.

Trip jutted out his hand. "I'm Trip, this is my ol' l— wife, Stella."

Fallon shook his hand. "Reilly took the time to explain what an ol' lady was. Nice to meet you, Stella. You, too, Trip."

"He's the president of our club," Whip said.

"Yes, I can see that on his cut."

Trip's eyebrows rose. "Reilly explain what a cut was, too?"

"No," Fallon murmured, locking gazes with Whip.

Trip's own gaze sliced back and forth between Whip and Fallon. "You stayin' in our motel?"

"I sure am."

"How long are you in town for?" Trip asked, giving Whip's shoulder a squeeze.

"Just until my sled is fixed."

Trip stared at her for far too long. When the prez turned to him, probably wondering why the fuck she was using those terms, Whip shrugged. "She's got a badass Scout Bobber."

"Didn't see it out front when we came in."

Of course he didn't. Even if it hadn't been in the garage for repairs, she hadn't been sitting out in the dining room when they came in. Whip would've noticed.

The prez was digging.

"It got some damage," Whip explained. "The reason she's in town. Broke down at the bottom of Hillbilly Hill."

"Hillbilly Hill?" Fallon asked, her eyebrows knitted together.

"What we call the mountain along Copperhead Road," Trip quickly explained. He turned to glance at Whip. "Apparently where you broke down."

"Yeah. That's where I came across her."

"Like a knight in shining coveralls," Fallon added with amusement in her voice.

Stella snorted and Trip directed a cocked brow to Whip with his lips pressed tightly together.

Jesus fuck, Fallon wasn't helping. "Just did what anyone would do comin' across someone stranded."

"Not true," she murmured. "You went above and beyond."

"Well, um…" Stella covered her laugh with a cough. "That's our Whip. Going above and beyond."

Whip stifled a groan.

"If we'd have known you were sitting out here alone, we would've invited you to join us in the back," Stella went on to say.

"I'm used to it," Fallon answered. "I'm doing a little soul searching as I travel the country on Agnes."

Trip frowned. "Agnes?"

"My sled."

Trip stared at her. "Wait… Your sled's named Agnes?"

"We should let her finish eatin'," Whip said quickly.

"I'm interested in the story behind it," Trip said. "Should invite her out to The Barn so we can hear the rest of it." Trip nudged him and slapped a smartass grin on his face.

That was the last thing Whip expected since Trip didn't like strangers out at The Barn.

"What's The Barn?" Fallon asked, her eyebrows pinned together.

"Our clubhouse," Trip explained, his arm now around Stella's waist.

"For?"

Trip pointed to Whip's cut. "The MC."

She blinked. "Oh. MCs have a clubhouse?"

"Guess Lee or Whip didn't divulge that info, then," Trip said dryly. "We're gonna be hangin' out for a while, so if you wanna spend more time with our boy here, you're welcome to join us out at the farm. It can get a little rowdy but it's all in good fun. As long as you're not easily offended."

What the fuck was Trip doing?

"Our sisterhood would love for you to come hang out with us," Stella added. "We don't bite."

Fallon gave Stella a half-smile. Whip was sure she had no idea what the fuck was going on.

"She's only here for a few days," Whips muttered.

"A lot can happen in a few days," Stella answered. "Whip can give you directions, just stop out when you're done with dinner. The ladies would love to hear more about this soul-searching cross-country trip."

"You wanna come to the farm?" Whip asked Fallon.

She shrugged. "Do I have anything else to do?"

Yeah, me.

She continued, "I would love to hang out for a little bit. Whip, why don't you follow me back to the motel and I can ride with you from there? Since you're planning on—"

"Yep," Whip said, cutting her off before she spilled their plans for later. "Can do that."

"All right," Trip said, not bothering to fight his grin.

"We'll see you in a little bit." He whacked Whip on the back and steered Stella to the door.

What the fuck just happened?

He watched the prez and his ol' lady exit Dino's, leaving Whip alone with Fallon. "Don't gotta come."

She tipped her head toward the empty stool next to her, inviting him to sit down. "You don't want me to?"

He straddled it and sighed. "Ain't that... It's just..."

"They're going to be asking questions, right? Is that what you're worried about? I'm good at deflecting questions that are no one's business. I worked in the corporate world remember? So, don't worry."

If only it was that damn simple. Those women could draw blood from a damn stone.

———

"THIS PLACE IS SOMETHING ELSE," Fallon said, once Whip tore her free of the sisterhood's claws. "The building is not only amazing, I love that you all are so close. Those women are great. It's hard to find a group of women that are warm and welcoming without even a hint of cattiness."

"Yeah? What'd they ask you?" His asshole definitely loosened a bit after he got her away from the women, especially when they drove him away so he couldn't eavesdrop.

"Just about my trip, that was all."

There was no fucking way that was all they asked about. "Nothin' else?"

"Well, they mentioned a few times how sweet and cute you are."

"The fuck they did," he growled.

Fallon laughed at his reaction. "They did. They're very protective of you."

"Don't need their protection."

"You're like their little brother."

He closed his eyes and groaned, making her smother another laugh.

"It's fine," she said, her amused tone making him open his eyes. He shot a quick glance to over where the women were gathered and Reilly gave him a thumbs up and a huge smile.

He turned his back on them, grabbed Fallon's arm and guided her over to the bar. "Want another drink?" He grabbed the empty glass she was holding.

"Sure."

Crystal was behind the bar and Rush was in one of those baby carrier things sitting on top of the bar as she poured herself a draft.

"You want the same?" Whip asked Fallon.

"Sure."

"Crys, get her another Jack and Coke."

"I can get it, Whip," Fallon insisted. "She has the baby to take care of."

"The kid's knocked out." And he was, Trip and Stella's baby was passed out cold.

"And that's why I'm finally getting a beer," Crys informed him. "He fell asleep after Stella nursed him."

He noticed but tried not to notice whenever the prez's ol' lady pulled out a damn tit to feed their kid. She didn't give a fuck who was looking. Reese was a little more stealth about it and avoided the nip slips.

"And that's stoppin' you from gettin' Fallon a drink?"

Crystal set her draft beer down and stared at him across the bar separating them. "Did you forget I'm no longer a sweet butt and not at your beck and call? Get it yourself."

"A what?" Fallon asked, a deep crease wrinkling her brow. "Is this another term I need to learn?"

Crys raised both eyebrows at Whip, grabbed her beer and the handle of the carrier and, with a smile, said, "You're welcome," before she and the baby wandered away.

Of course, leaving Whip to explain the bomb she just dropped.

He risked a glance at Fallon. Just what he thought, she was staring at him, waiting for an answer.

Was she one of those crazy feminists that would have a huge issue when it came to the sweet butts just like the women being considered "property" of their ol' man?

Of course she would.

She owned her own damn sled, *for fuck's sake*. She'd be the type of woman who would insist on riding her own Scout in formation instead of on the back of Whip's sled.

That would never fly with his brothers. Especially Trip and the rest who were around during the original Fury or who *were* Originals, like Ozzy and Dutch.

They wouldn't need explosives to destroy Hillbilly Hill, their reaction for an ol' lady riding on her own during a club run would be enough to destroy, not only that mountain but the whole damn county.

"What's a sweet butt?"

"Jack and Coke?" he asked, rounding the end of the bar and going behind it to find the whiskey.

"You already asked me that," she stated.

"What's goin' on?" Easy asked when he sidled up next to Fallon, not hiding the fact he was checking her out.

"Just gettin' her another drink." Whip busied himself doing just that. He needed another beer himself. Or two.

"What's a sweet butt?"

He glanced up and noticed Fallon was no longer asking him but Easy.

Christ almighty.

If she gets bent about that answer, the only reason he'd be headed back to The Grove Inn would be to drop her off.

He tried to catch Easy's attention, but as if in slow-motion, he watched the man open his mouth. Whip almost launched himself across the bar to stop him.

"They help out around here."

Oh, thank fuck.

"Like employees?"

"Uh… More of a volunteer type of thing," E answered.

"What do they do?"

Whip coughed loudly and beat on his chest. "Damn, that went down the wrong pipe."

"What did? Air?" Fallon asked with a tilt of her blonde head. She turned back to Easy.

Easy's eyes cut from Fallon back to him. Whip hoped his silent message was heard.

E shrugged. "Brother, she's gonna figure it out eventually."

Whip mentally groaned. The woman was only going to be in town a few days, she didn't need to know what a fucking sweet butt was.

"What's the big deal?" Fallon asked, glancing back and forth from Easy to Whip.

"Ain't a big deal," Whip quickly answered before Easy could. "E, Billie's over there lookin' for you."

Easy rolled his eyes. "I ain't lookin' for her."

Fallon glanced over her shoulder in the direction Whip had jerked his chin. She turned back. "She's already talking to a gentleman."

Did she just call Scar a gentleman?

Easy just about fell over when he burst out laughing. As soon as he could catch his breath, he said, "That fucker ain't no gentleman and she can't do him. Though, she's chompin' at the damn bit to take him to his knees and beg for mercy."

Whip would pay to watch that.

"Why can't she be with him?"

"'Cause she's a sweet butt and he's a prospect," Easy answered her, oh-so-fucking helpfully.

"E, is that Tessa over there talkin' to Castle?" Whip asked.

Easy spun around. "Where?"

"Just saw them head into the bunkhouse together. Trip ain't gonna like that." He wouldn't if it was true. But it wasn't. "Better check and warn him about fuckin' with the prez's sister. We don't wanna lose him as a prospect."

Before he could say anything else, Easy was gone.

When he turned back to Fallon, she was doing something on her phone. He finished making her the Jack and Coke, also pouring himself a beer, and when he placed the drink in front of her, she raised her eyes to his.

"According to the Urban Dictionary—"

He groaned.

She read verbatim from her phone, "'In motorcycle club culture, sweet butts are women who hang around the club and make themselves available for sex.'"

Fucking Google. "That ain't all they do."

She lifted her blue eyes again. "You mean that's not enough? So, tell me, what else do they do?"

"Stuff."

"Like?"

"Like... Cookin', cleanin', whatever needs done."

"Whatever needs done?"

"Whatever needs done," he repeated, not liking where this conversation was headed. He had a feeling that destination was about to fuck up his night.

"No matter what it is?"

He scratched the back of his neck. "For the most part."

"And what do they get out of this arrangement?"

Ah, fuck.

Chapter Fourteen

FALLON WATCHED WHIP CLOSELY. "That's not a difficult question."

Clearly he wanted to avoid the conversation but if it was a big part of the MC culture, she was curious. Were some of the women in the club's "sisterhood" sweet butts, too? Or were they not included in that close-knit group?

Were they respected or disrespected by the ol' ladies? Used or abused by Whip's club brothers?

Whip's mouth opened and nothing but air escaped before it snapped shut again.

"What do they get out of it, Whip?" she repeated. Since he was reluctant to answer, she could pretty much guess.

"They get to hang out here."

"Okay…" That couldn't be all.

Fallon believed every woman had a right to do whatever she wanted to with her body. If they were into having sex with or doing "chores" for bikers, that was on them. She had to assume they weren't being forced and, like Easy said, it was similar to a "volunteer position." They were hanging out with an MC because that was what they wanted and had the right to say no, or could leave, at any time.

"And protection," he added.

"Protection from what?"

He shrugged. "Whatever they need protected from."

That was a non-answer. "Between that mountain and your answer, I'm beginning to wonder just how unsafe this small town is."

"Every town's got its problems."

That also was a non-answer. For someone who had been refreshingly honest about everything else, those vague answers made her wonder. "Should I be worried?"

"Nope."

"I'm going to go out on a limb here and—"

"Don't need to. Whatever you're thinkin', you're probably right."

She finished anyway. "That the women are like groupies for a band or a celebrity. Or maybe badge bunnies for cops?"

"It's a way to be a part of our club without bein' an ol' lady."

While she had noticed the women wearing leather cuts like their significant others at Dino's, when she and Whip arrived at The Barn, none of them were wearing them anymore. When asked, the ladies had explained they only wore them on a club run or when other MCs were visiting.

An easy way to identify who they belonged to.

That would be a good explanation, except when she asked why the patches on the back were different from the men, specifically that their top patch said, "Property of" and their bottom one had the name of their ol' man, they gave murky answers.

Then they acted as if they only wore them to satisfy their husband, boyfriend, or whatever they considered their significant other.

However, a woman being property of not only a club, but a man... Did the club members truly believe that they "owned" their women? Was it possible in this day and age? Or was there no real meaning behind it and she was over-thinking it?

Either way, it was one more piece of the MC lifestyle she was eager to learn about and planned on asking Whip for more details later. If he refused to answer, she'd look it up herself online.

In the end, if she wasn't overthinking it, she had no say to how those ladies lived their lives. It didn't affect her in any way and, truthfully, all the women appeared happy, with both their men and their way of life.

On the surface, none appeared downtrodden, abused or even coerced.

"Do the sweet butts want to be an ol' lady?"

He tilted his head. "Guessin' so."

"Do they ever get that chance?"

"They could. Nothin' is stoppin' one of my brothers takin' a sweet butt as their ol' lady."

His answer made her believe that in the club, the status of an ol' lady was much higher than a sweet butt. If true, it would make sense. "Would you?"

She didn't miss when he glanced over her shoulder at something—or someone—behind her. "Depends."

She slowly turned on the stool and noticed who he was looking at. A woman with short black hair dressed in a black leather mini-skirt, fishnet stockings with rips in them, shin-high black lace-up combat boots, an off-the-shoulder tight black top that showed off her many tattoos, a thick black leather collar circling her neck, and wearing very dark, heavy makeup, along with black lipstick. She was short and stocky.

Goth, that was what it reminded Fallon of. Or Emo. She wasn't sure what the correct term for that look was anymore. Did Whip have a crush on her or something? Was Fallon stepping on another woman's toes? Because she was not there to do that. Up to this point, she had enjoyed the time she had spent with the younger man and had more than enjoyed the sex. But none of that was worth causing issues between him and another woman. "On?"

"She'd have to be the right one."

She turned back to him and watched his face carefully when she asked, "Is she the right one?"

His blue eyes hit hers and he frowned. "Not even close."

"Is she a sweet butt?"

"She is now."

Five thousand more questions popped in her head at that. She wasn't sure how many he'd answer, but she'd ask some of them and see. "She wasn't always?"

"Not in the beginnin'."

"You were dating?"

"Not... quite datin'," he answered, but also didn't volunteer any further information.

If he didn't like her line of questioning, he could shut it down, but until he did... "Then what?"

"Just experimentin' for a time."

Experimenting? "I don't understand."

He shrugged again. "At the time, I didn't, either."

He was a man, he wasn't going to have a cozy little chit-chat with her about a previous relationship or whatever it was, without her dragging every answer from him. "And now you do?"

"Know what I want."

He put a lot of conviction behind that answer. "And what *do* you want?"

"Not her and not what she's into."

Fallon asked, "What's she into?"

"Hardcore shit."

Once she processed his answer, Fallon lifted an eyebrow. "Like BDSM?"

"Yeah, like that."

"And your club brothers still sleep with her." She didn't have to make it a question, Fallon figured since she was a sweet butt it was true.

"What they do with her don't got anythin' to do with sleep."

"I was being tactful."

"Don't gotta be tactful. Just call it what it is. Slick words don't cut it around here. Go ahead and say what you mean since you like me doin' the same."

"Okay. Your club brothers have sex with her and that doesn't bother you?"

"Nope."

"Why?"

"'Cause it was what it was for how long it lasted. We hooked up, then after a bit decided to do our own thing 'cause it wasn't workin'."

"For her or you?"

"Both. Mutual decision."

"So… You're not into that."

"Again, say what you mean, Fallon."

"You're not into whips and chains and all of that."

"Turns out I ain't."

Her lips twitched when she tried to imagine the process he went through to discover that.

"How 'bout you?"

She hadn't expected that turnabout, but it was only fair that she answer. "Umm…" She shrugged. "I can't say I haven't tried a few things but it usually didn't go past a man's necktie being wrapped around my wrists." And then tied to the headboard.

His sexy smirk appeared. "Did you like it?"

"Not with who I was with."

That smirk quickly disappeared again. "Why?"

"I didn't trust him." She didn't know much about kink or BDSM lifestyle, but she did know enough that trusting the person restraining you was important. So was communication.

But that was important with any partner, vanilla or not.

The man was back to not mincing words when he said, "You trusted him enough to fuck him."

That was all it ended up being, a fuck.

No matter how smart one thought they were, it was hard to avoid an occasional bad decision. No one was immune. Ideally, one would learn from it for the future. Fallon did in this case. It was one reason why after that night she hadn't dated much. And when she did, she was much more cautious. When first meeting someone, that person seemed to put on a "good face" to impress. But it was what was under that surface that counted.

You could coat shit with sugar, but once you bit through that sweetness, you could still taste the shit.

"Once I was restrained, I realized I had put myself in a bad spot."

Before her eyes, he went solid, every muscle locking. "He hurt you?"

She shook her head. No, but she'd never been so uncomfortable before. "Let's just say I was glad when it was over."

He grabbed her chin and held it, dipping his head enough to catch and hold her eyes. "He hurt you?"

"No. Even if he did, what could you do about it?" It was years ago and back in Chicago—

"Fuckin' hunt him down and—" He pressed his lips together and a muscle jumped in his cheek.

The intensity in his eyes was unexpected. Especially since it was over something in the past and had not affected him. This man kept catching her off guard. "And?"

"Teach him a lesson 'bout hurtin' women."

"That wasn't what you were going to say."

"Close enough."

Maybe the man before her wasn't so sweet at his core

after all. Even though his unnecessary protectiveness was flattering. "While I appreciate the sentiment, I don't need you to teach anyone a 'lesson.' I got myself into that situation and I got myself out. Luckily, with no damage done."

"Not every woman's as lucky as you."

"That we can agree on," she said softly. "But these women... these sweet butts... They're here by choice and could leave at any time without any repercussion?"

"Yeah."

"Do all your club brothers take them up on what they offer?"

"Not the ones with ol' ladies."

She stared at him. "So, only the members without ol' ladies. Like you."

He tipped his head slightly. At least he didn't deny it because she knew that would've been an outright lie and would've lost some respect for him if he lied to her like that.

She wasn't stupid and Whip didn't treat her as if she was. Unlike some "professional" men who liked to talk down to women.

Misogynistic pigs.

Every time someone of that breed opened their mouth, she heard the silent, patronizing, "little lady" added on to whatever bullshit they were spewing from their mouth. She would grind her teeth and do her best to refrain from kicking them in the nuts before calling them "little boy" in return.

But, of course, then she would be labeled as "overly emotional" or "on her period."

She mentally rolled her eyes and focused her attention on the man who did not give her that vibe at all. "Now that she's a sweet butt, do you still hook up?"

"You mean with Billie?"

"If that's her name, yes. Do you two get along?"

"Yeah. Like I said, it was mutual. We both realized it

was better for both of us. I didn't give her what she needed, she didn't give me the same."

"That was a very mature decision." When Fallon was in her twenties, she didn't remember men her age being so mature. "How many sweet butts does the club keep around?"

He took a long sip of his beer. "It matter?"

"I'm fascinated with this MC culture. It's... unique."

He snorted softly. "Yeah, ain't a country club. Guess you're more used to that kinda atmosphere."

"Actually, no. I didn't come from money. Everything I have, I earned myself. And I never got into the country club scene. Tennis, golf, swollen egos and non-stop bullshitting never did anything for me. Well, maybe it did. Some of it turned me off."

"Never dated anyone like that?"

She lifted one shoulder. "Sure. But as you see, I'm single and sitting on this stool right now in an MC's clubhouse, so that should tell you how those dates ended." Unlike the time she'd spent with Whip so far. Besides him going to work on Friday and the time between when he left her room earlier this morning until dinner, they'd spent a lot of time together.

So far, every minute had been worthwhile.

Traveling alone, even though it was her choice, sometimes got lonely. So, she appreciated his companionship and conversation.

And of course, the sex.

After the last few days, though, she was starting to worry that she was falling for him.

But that couldn't be right. They were so wrong for each other, weren't they?

He was younger, living his life the way he wanted to live it and right now, she was living as a nomad, doing what she wanted when she wanted it.

"Weren't into any of them." Instead of a question, he made it a statement.

"I don't like fake. I don't like slick. I don't like people who don't say what they mean. I also don't like liars." She had been surrounded by people like that for years.

"You like people who speak their mind."

"Yes, as long as it's appropriate, of course. I mean, I don't want to hear people screaming racial or ethnic slurs. I don't want someone to insult others because they're being an asshole."

He grinned, lifted his pint glass and also his chin.

She understood the gesture, raised her drink and tapped her glass with his.

"Agree with you on the slurs, but as for the rest... just a warnin' there ain't a lotta 'appropriate' around here. And there are plenty of assholes."

She finally took a sip of her drink and did her best not to cough as the drink hit the back of her throat. He'd made it strong. Luckily, she wasn't driving. "We all have a little bit of asshole in us. We wouldn't survive if we didn't."

His grin widened and he stared at her for a few heartbeats with his bottom lip caught in this teeth. He might not have meant that gesture to be a thirst trap, but, to her, it damn well was and made her heartbeat quicken. She wanted to grab his face and plant a kiss on those skilled lips.

She wondered if she had the sweet butt Billie to thank for that skill. She looked like she had no problem teaching someone a lesson.

"You ready to go?"

"Now?" She didn't even have to look around to know the 'party' was only getting started. Behind her, she could hear the conversation, the laughter, the good-natured joking, the clack of the pool balls and, of course, the rock music playing from hidden speakers throughout their clubhouse. Loud enough to hear it, but not loud enough to drown out the socializing. "Things are only getting into full swing. And we haven't finished our drinks yet."

"No reason to rush out of here, Junior," Ozzy said, stepping behind the bar and whacking Whip on the back.

She was tempted to tell the motel manager to stop calling Whip Junior, but it seemed that they all busted on each other similar to siblings. Or best friends. If it bothered Whip, he was quite capable of telling the older biker himself.

Fallon wasn't Whip's sister, girlfriend or wife. She needed to stay out of it. If she said anything, Ozzy might bust on Whip even more and, in turn, that might cause some tension between the two. She didn't want to be the cause of that.

Even so, it was difficult to keep her mouth shut. She could make her feelings known in a roundabout way, instead. "I've been wanting to thank you for the bowl of condoms," she told Ozzy instead. "They've come in handy. We might need you to refill it soon. You know, since it's clear you like being generous."

While Ozzy filled his glass under the beer tap, he glanced up at her. "You've been teachin' him a thing or two?"

"Well, actually, he's been teaching me a thing or two."

Ozzy stopped filling his glass and cocked an eyebrow at her. "Yeah?"

"I'm always up for learning something new. Nothing wrong with expanding my horizons. That's what this whole cross-country trip is about."

Ozzy shot a quick glance at Whip before turning back to Fallon.

She shot him a smile.

That earned her a stare before deep laughter burst from him. "Damn, Junior, she fits right in." He finished filling his glass and pounded him on the back again. "Maybe she should stick around a little longer."

Fallon answered before Whip could since she wasn't done with the salt-and-pepper bearded man. "I'm not going anywhere until Whip repairs Agnes."

"Women around here don't ride their own sleds."

"Well then, it's a good thing I'm only passing through."

Ozzy laughed again, shaking his head. "Good thing. I'd be concerned with you cuttin' Junior off at the knees if you weren't. His balls only dropped a coupla years ago."

"He's done nothing to warrant being cut off at the knees, as you put it. I would never demasculinize a man unless he gave me a reason." She raised both eyebrows at him.

Ozzy stared at her for longer than he should. "Careful with that one, Junior. Seems like this cougar bites."

She bared her teeth, then snapped them together. "*Whip* hasn't complained about my biting yet."

"Oz, what are you doing?" a woman's soft voice came from behind Fallon. She didn't have to look to know who it was. From her conversations with Shay in the motel's office and also with talking to her earlier while with the sisterhood, the woman seemed to be the exact opposite of the man whose cut she wore.

With the little Fallon had dealt with Ozzy, it was easy to see he needed someone like her to balance him out. Shay was super nice and introverted versus her ol' man who was outspoken and rough around the edges.

"Gettin' a beer."

"You're doing more than that," came the accusatory tone. It didn't come off as bitchy or bossy, but the undertone screamed disappointment.

One thing Fallon was picking up very quickly with this MC was that the men did not like disappointing their women. So, that undertone could be very effective instead of outright scolding.

Smart.

Her respect for Shay bumped up another notch.

"Huh," Fallon said loud enough for Ozzy to hear. She made a sideways cutting motion with her hand.

Whip turned away and pretended to look for something behind the bar.

Ozzy shot her one last grin and worked his way around the bar, shaking his head and chuckling under his breath.

She was also learning that these bikers didn't take offense to a good smackdown. If they could dish it, they could take it in return. No wonder why they busted on each other so much. It was almost like a sport.

When Ozzy was finally out of earshot, Whip turned back around, his blue eyes full of amusement. "Told you there were plenty of assholes."

"For all the years I spent in the corporate world, I'm quite proficient in sniffing them out on my own. The world's full of them, from billionaires down to the destitute." She picked up her Jack and Coke to finish it. "Why don't we swing by your place on the way back and grab whatever you're going to need for work tomorrow?"

He directed one of his sexy grins at her that, if she was being honest with herself, heated her core and curled her toes. "Want me to stay all night?"

That wasn't even in question. "Do you?"

"Ain't gonna say no."

"Well, that's good because neither am I."

He finished his beer, then came around the end of the bar to where she sat and planted his hand on her back. Just that touch did things to her, once again, that she wasn't expecting.

A simple touch creating a more complex reaction than it should.

It was possessive and protective, especially when coupled with his words. "You gonna be okay here for a few while I go to my room and grab a few things? The sisterhood dispersed but I see Lee over there. I can send her over to keep you company."

She didn't need anyone to keep her company, but it was sweet that he thought so. "You live here?"

"Yeah. In the bunkhouse."

"Bunkhouse? Like something similar to where ranch hands sleep?"

"Kinda."

Just when she thought she couldn't be surprised any more. "Where is this bunkhouse?"

He jerked a thumb over his shoulder. "Right behind that door."

"So, you live here?" She pointed to the floor.

"Yeah. Well, back there."

"I need to see this. I've never been in a bunkhouse." It wasn't the bunkhouse she wanted to see, it was where Whip lived. Where and how a man lived could tell a lot about him.

It didn't have to be big or fancy, but she was curious to see if it was clean and organized.

"Ain't nothin' but a room and a shitter."

"Like my motel room."

"Yeah. Without the daily service."

And most likely, the big bowl of condoms. "You just don't stop surprising me."

"What d'you mean?"

She shook her head. "My whole life I've had certain expectations and that's why this trip was and is important to me. To change my way of thinking that things were only black and white, or even different shades of gray. I thought I had to be a specific way to be accepted, speak a certain way, act a certain way. Work and dress to succeed. I actually got stuck in a rut without realizing it. My goal when I started on this trip was to break that old mold of me and become the new me, but organically this time. No expectations."

"To 'just be.'"

She finished the last swallow of her drink and smiled at him because he seemed to "get" her more than any other man she'd ever been with. She appreciated that. "Yes, to just be. I never could've imagined stepping into this new world, but, honestly, Agnes getting damaged might've been the best thing to happen on this trip so far."

"Your sled gettin' fucked up was good?"

"Sounds crazy, right? But look what I'm discovering." She stood up and turned toward the center of The Barn and swept her hand out in front of her. "A way of life so different from my former one. New people, new friends, new world," she reached up and cupped his cheek, "even a new lover."

"Glad you kept that last one singular." He leaned in and put his mouth to her ear. "All right, so you wanna see my room, huh? That all you wanna see?"

She shivered, reached down, interlaced their fingers and tugged on his hand. "I'm game for an in-depth tour."

"Then I'm gonna give you one."

"Are your sheets clean?"

He snorted. "Don't gotta use the bed."

She laughed as he tugged her across The Barn's floor to the closed door that led to the bunkhouse.

Were heads turning as they went?

Damn right they were and neither of them cared one little bit.

Chapter Fifteen

WHIP STARED up into Fallon's hooded eyes as she rose and fell on his hard as fuck dick. Her blonde chin-length hair, still messy from sleeping, swept back and forth along her jawline. Her throat was arched a bit, her mouth slightly parted. The little noises she made was music to his fucking ears.

He brushed one thumb across a tightly budded nipple. The other pressed and circled her clit.

She moved up and down lazily, taking her time, not rushing their morning fuck, even though he needed to get up and get ready for work. This had become their routine every morning he woke up in her bed. It happened every night before they fell asleep. And sometimes even in between.

This woman loved sex and lots of it. Luckily, it was something they had in common.

While she slept, he'd wrap himself around her and hold her close, listening to her soft, steady breathing until he eventually followed her into slumber.

Tomorrow would be a week since he came across her at the bottom of the mountain. He had no idea at the time a broken down motorcyclist would, or even could, quickly become a habit. One, he had a feeling, that would be hard to break when the time came.

Fuck that, it was more than a feeling, he knew it would.

But she had places to go and things to see. Manning Grove had only been an unexpected stop along the way.

It would fucking suck when they said goodbye but he would deal with it the same as anything else.

People came, people went.

Life went on.

But while she was here, while he was in her bed, he would enjoy every fucking second.

He would enjoy her weight pressed into the palms planted on his chest while she used her arms to leverage herself. The warm, wet cocoon of her pussy squeezing his dick. Her mouth brushing over his. Her encouraging whispers in his ear. Her unrestrained cries when she came.

His name on her lips.

Her companionship when they watched TV in the dark late at night, or ate dinner together. Laughed at a stupid joke. Or shared a story about when they were younger.

But, yeah, soon she'd be on her way again.

She wasn't for him.

Or more like it, he wasn't for her.

A simple mechanic with only a high school diploma, who belonged to a motorcycle club that occasionally did very questionable things. Things she would not want to be involved with.

Like blowing up a fucking mountain. Or taking people out, even when it was to protect their own.

Or "kidnapping" children for their own good.

Fallon was smart, successful, classy and had done so much already in her thirty-six years that she could now afford to quit the rat race every adult was expected to take part in.

Of course, she hadn't told him how much money she had in her portfolio. She checked her investment accounts and did any trades during the day while he was at the garage, but he could assume the amount of scratch she had was substantial.

The woman was not financially hurting. While his sorry ass lived in a fucking small box in a bunkhouse.

On one hand, he didn't wish her life to be any different, because he wouldn't want to take away any of her accomplishments. On the other, he selfishly did so he wasn't so fucking far out of her league.

He'd been with Billie for months and hadn't felt anything toward her like he already did with Fallon in only a few days.

At that thought, his chest tightened and his heart began to thump heavily.

Some of his brothers had mentioned fate when it came to finding their ol' ladies. Coming across Fallon the way he did made him wonder if it had been meant to be.

And if so, what did that mean to them, if anything?

Or would it end up being no more than what they currently had? A week of great sex and even better company.

Seeing his brothers, one by one, finding their ol' ladies hadn't made him want to look for himself. He would be turning twenty-nine in a couple of weeks, so he wasn't in a rush and figured when the time was right, he'd find the right one. In the meantime, he wanted to avoid getting stuck with the wrong one.

His parents' relationship had been rotten to the core. It was a marriage that never should have been and Whip preferred not to make that same mistake. He'd seen how his father destroyed their family, long before it turned deadly.

But that was then and this was now. He needed to get out of his own head and come back to the room and Fallon.

Unfortunately, Wednesdays tended to do this to him. He looked forward to them, but always dreaded them, too.

"Hey."

He blinked.

"You okay?"

Her question dragged him from his thoughts and he realized she had stopped moving. "Yeah."

"Am I going too slow for you?"

"No."

"Then, what is it?" she asked, her brow now furrowed with worry.

"Nothin'."

"It has to be something. I've never seen you check out like that before."

"Got a lot of shit on my plate today, that's all."

"With work?"

No. "Yeah."

She stared at him and his pulse raced when, for a split moment, he thought she could see the thoughts in his head he was trying to beat back.

"If something's wrong, I need you to tell me."

"Nothin's wrong, Fallon. With you naked and ridin' my cock, everythin's good."

Her lips twitched. "Only good?"

"Well, it'd be better if you kept ridin' me... Or not." He quickly knocked her off balance and rolled the two of them until it was Fallon now on her back. He settled between her spread thighs.

She patted his ass, then dug her nails into his cheeks. "You biker boys like to be in charge, don't you?"

"Coulda left off the 'boys' part since we're far from boys."

"I can't argue that. Does that mean you don't want to be called bad boys, either?"

He smirked. "More like bad asses."

"Well, you do have a great ass. I've admired it quite a few times as you've trekked naked to the bathroom." She squeezed his while digging her nails in even deeper, causing his muscles to flex there.

"So do you. In fact…"

He lifted his weight from her and flipped her over, settling his knees between hers. He nipped each ass cheek once, making her muscles twitch, then worked his way up her spine, tasting her skin with his lips and tongue as he went.

Who needed breakfast when Fallon was naked? She was a more than satisfying meal.

He swept her hair off the back of her neck and pressed his lips there. He ordered, "Ass up," against her skin.

When her hips rose slightly and her thighs widened to give him more room, he tucked his hand between them, slid his dick through her wetness to find exactly where he belonged—in more ways than one—and slowly sank inside her until he couldn't go any further.

Yeah, waking up to this every fucking morning… It would be difficult to give up.

A couple of times he'd woken up to her mouth on him. A couple of times, he'd returned the favor. There was nothing better than waking up Fallon with his mouth on her sweet pussy. It was a great way to start the day. For both of them.

But this morning, he was done taking it slow. If he was late to work, he'd never hear the end of it, so it was time to get serious.

He slid his palms up her sides, over her shoulders and down her arms until his fingers interlaced with hers. He pinned their clasped hands to the mattress, anchored his knees into the bed, and took them on a journey that only had one destination.

Her fingers tightened within his as she slammed her ass

back and against him, driving him even deeper with each thrust.

She fit him perfectly.

He didn't give a fuck who she was or that their lives were so fucking different.

He didn't give a fuck that he was seven years younger than her.

None of that mattered. Not in that room. Not in that bed.

He gave a fuck that she would be gone soon. He gave a fuck about *her*.

No, it was more than one fuck. He gave a lot of fucks.

More than he expected.

"C'mon, babe, give me everythin' you got," he murmured into her ear as he tilted his hips and powered into her, while giving her as much of his weight as he could without crushing her.

She moaned into the pillow and her pussy tightened around him, clenching and unclenching, driving him even quicker to that final destination.

"Come with me," she moaned.

"Ready?" He sure as fuck was.

"Almost. Clit."

He released one of her hands and snaked his beneath her. Once again using his calloused fingers against her sensitive nub, her hips jumping against him before falling back into their rhythm.

"Whip…" she groaned, fisting her free hand in the sheet. "Whip…"

"Right here, babe. Got you."

"Don't stop."

No fucking way he was stopping.

"Oh… don't stop."

"Not gonna. Give me you. Give me everythin'."

"Take it. Oh God, take it from me. Take it all."

She said shit like that when she was ready to come. She didn't when they first hooked up but now that they were completely comfortable with each other and had discovered a lot about each other along the way, she had begun to open up even more.

He fucking loved every second of it, every word that slipped from her.

She could call him a "stupid motherfucking asshole," but as long as she did it in the same way she did when she was about to explode around him, he wouldn't give a fuck.

"It's all yours."

Jesus. That wasn't helping. It only made him want to pound her pussy harder. "C'mon, babe," he growled the encouragement in her ear. "Soak my fuckin' dick."

Wearing a wrap sucked because he couldn't feel it. He couldn't feel when she gushed around him. That warm honey coating him. The proof of how good they were together.

How they simply clicked.

"I'm coming," was screamed into the pillow, followed by a muffled cry.

Thank fuck, since she wasn't the only one.

He slammed into her twice more, stayed deep the second thrust and grunted into her ear as he spilled inside her. Once again, making him wish he wasn't wearing a goddamn wrap.

He wanted to fuck her without one. He wanted to feel every fucking tiny pulse, every ripple, every drop of goodness. He wanted "it all." He couldn't feel it all with latex covering his fucking dick.

If she planned on staying in town, he'd ask for that, because he had seen she was on the Pill. She left her pack sitting on the counter in the bathroom in plain view.

Since she wasn't staying, he didn't ask.

After learning about the sweet butts, he doubted she'd

ever agree to him raw-dogging it with her, even though he always wrapped it tight whenever he was with a woman. He always took precautions, even with Billie when they were exclusive.

He never fooled himself with the idea that Billie wasn't seeing other guys and not telling him. He knew he hadn't been enough for her, that she needed certain shit that he couldn't give her. He couldn't fault her if she had been finding that elsewhere.

He didn't ask and she didn't volunteer that info. But she seemed to be much happier once she became a sweet butt than when she was his "girlfriend."

Some people weren't meant to be monogamous. He had no doubt Billie was one of them. At least at this point in her life.

To each his own.

He released their clasped hands, planted his palms on the bed, and relieved some of his weight off Fallon. He asked what he always did before pulling out, "You good?"

Because if she wasn't, he'd do his best to get her there. There was no fucking way he was leaving her unsatisfied.

He was not going to be a selfish prick in bed. If he was, he'd probably find himself outside looking in with a fuck-load of regrets. And if he was like that, she'd most likely regret letting him in her bed.

He'd seen his brothers be selfish with women, not with their ol' ladies but with others—sweet butts, hang-arounds, whoever—and Whip wouldn't want that shit done to him. So, he didn't do it to the women he was with. Not fucking ever.

He made sure the woman got what she needed before going their separate ways, even if he had to grit his teeth to get it done.

Dutch was a good example of who he didn't want to become. Though, the man got more pussy than any of them. The Original had some sort of skill no one could put a finger on.

Fallon's answer of, "Perfect," drew him back to the bed.

"Gonna pull out," he warned her, grabbing the wrap at the root of his dick and slipping from her.

He rolled away, removed the wrap, tied it off and tossed it into the small trash can they now kept near the bed. Fallon had come up with that solution since she quickly got sick of full wraps being found where they shouldn't be. But Whip was never in a rush to leave the bed to dispose of them.

The compromise meant he didn't have to rush to get up, and she didn't have to step barefoot on a full wrap in the dark. Once was all it took for the trash can to appear on his side of the bed.

He leaned back against the headboard, grabbed his tin from the nightstand and tucked a joint between his lips. Right before he lit it, he asked, "Whatcha gonna do today?"

She rolled over so she was no longer on her stomach and sat up. Her nose wrinkled when she saw what he was about to light. "This early?"

"Gotta deal with Dutch all day." That wasn't the real reason, but it was an easy excuse. Even though some days it was best to deal with Dutch while slightly stoned.

He flicked the Bic, put the flame to the tip and took a long draw on the joint to get it burning evenly. Once it was, he blew the smoke up and away from her.

"Well," she started. "I managed to snag an appointment this afternoon at the salon you recommended. I may head down to the store to pick up a few needed items before getting my hair done."

"Teddy's gonna love you."

"I'm sure I'll love him, too, since the women spoke highly of him the other night when I asked."

"Should be good. Whatcha gettin' done?"

She raked her fingers through her messy hair. "Just a

trim and highlights. I'm overdue. I hesitate to walk into any salon without a recommendation first. Not only because of hearing other women's horror stories but I've had a few of my own." She faked a shudder.

She spun around and settled her head in his lap, like she always did when he sat up in bed to burn a fatty.

"Like your hair," he murmured, taking another hit and combing through her medium-length locks with his fingers.

She grinned up at him, captured his hand with hers, interlaced their fingers and pressed their joined hands to her chest. "Me, too."

She was always linking their hands together and, *fuck him*, he didn't mind one fucking bit. It seemed to ground her and if he was being honest with himself, it did the same for him.

It reminded him of how touching Stella calmed Trip down when he was losing his temper or how having Red touch Sig helped keep the VP from spiraling out of control.

Whip didn't have a temper and so far, he hadn't seen Fallon lose her shit over anything, but still... Fallon tended to touch him whenever they were near each other. She cupped his cheek often, held his hand constantly, played with his hair while they watched TV, settled her hand on his arm when they were walking. Sometimes she hugged him for no good reason.

Of course, since he wasn't a stupid fuck, he didn't deny her any of that.

If he was forced to admit it, he kind of liked it and quickly got used to the constant contact, something he never had before. He'd miss it when she was gone.

He took another long toke on the joint, filling his mouth with the smoke, and leaned over to put his lips against hers.

That was the only way she would share a joint with him. He wasn't mad about the method, either. Like her touching him, he used any excuse to put his mouth on her.

She willingly stole the smoke from his mouth, held it deep and then turned her head to blow it out. He took one last drag and did the same before pinching out the end. He never took more than a few hits before going to work since he found it helped him focus.

Especially on Wednesdays.

"Know we've been doin' dinner every night, but tonight…" What he had to say next might disappoint her but he needed to tell her. He didn't want to just blow her off.

"Tonight?" she prodded, sliding the fingers from her free hand up his ankle to his bare thigh and back down. Her light, playful touch made the hairs on his legs stand at attention.

"You keep doin' that, I'm gonna slide between your thighs again," he warned.

She wiggled her eyebrows at him. "And I'd hate that, why?"

He shook his head. He could recover quickly, but not that quickly. And as tempting as that was, he'd really be late for work.

The good thing about crashing with Fallon in her room was he didn't have to get up so early to go back to the bunkhouse before heading over to the garage.

"So, are you about to tell me that you can't keep me company for dinner tonight? Got a date?"

"Actually, I do. Every Wednesday night."

She moved until she was sitting crossed-legged on the mattress, facing him.

Fuck, the woman was goddamn gorgeous, especially freshly fucked.

Correction, especially freshly fucked by him.

"You really have a date?"

Damn. "Ain't a date like what you're thinkin'."

"Is it with a woman?"

Was she jealous? Or was she just being her normal curious self?

"Yeah, but… Ain't like that. It's…" *Christ.* "It's with my mom."

He never talked about his weekly dinner with his club brothers because it would only give them more fuel to fuck with him.

Did they know? Most of them, yeah.

Did he talk about it? Fuck no.

Of course, they were all about family when family life was good. But he still didn't want to remind them that he spent every Wednesday night with his mother. He'd been doing it ever since he became a prospect, moved out of her house and into the bunkhouse.

His mother claimed she had nobody but him. Even though he knew that was a lie—she had a younger sister who lived in the Midwest, as well as a few local friends—but she had guilted him anyway into coming by once a week.

Truthfully, it wasn't a hardship.

The only problem was after he moved out, she moved back into his pap's house. Unfortunately, that house held not-so-great memories for them both.

He didn't understand why she wanted to do that. But she explained that his grandfather's house was paid for, while the house they had moved to after his pap died was rented. However, every week he went to his pap's house for dinner, he begged her to sell it, take the money and move somewhere better.

She told him the house wasn't worth enough to buy something decent and she didn't want to be strapped with a mortgage payment.

If he could buy her a house, he would. If he could give her the damn world, he would.

But he couldn't.

He was just a mechanic living in a room in a bunkhouse.

He really had no lofty goals or dreams. He didn't give a fuck about being rich or traveling the world or impressing anyone. Like Fallon, he was content to "just be."

He had a solid job. He loved his mother, his brotherhood and his Fury Family.

He might not have a lot, but what he had was more than enough.

But because his mother currently lived in that house, he gritted his teeth and went back to sit with her while she made dinner and caught him up on her life. After dinner, they watched Jeopardy together and then he left.

It made her happy. And he wanted nothing more than for her to be happy. She more than deserved that after all the shit his father put her through.

"That's so sweet."

He groaned. "Gotta stop sayin' that shit." It killed him every time she did.

"Why? I think it's sweet that you make time for your mother."

"She gets lonely."

"Whip, you don't need an excuse to do it."

"Ain't makin' an excuse, just sayin'."

She shot him a smile and whispered, "It's sweet and you're being a good son."

He grabbed her face and took her mouth.

When he was done, she said, "Just so you know, I don't mind you shutting me up that way. It'll only encourage me to tell you just how sweet you are even more."

He shook his head. "You don't gotta say that shit if you want my mouth on you. Just tell me where you want my mouth and I'm gonna oblige. No hardship on my end."

"If no one's told you yet, then I want to be the first... You're a really good kisser," she teased, poking him in the gut.

With a snort and a shake of his head, he got up. "Gotta get ready for work."

"While you're there, can you ask Reilly to get an update on my parts?"

He paused while rounding the bed to glance over at her.

Fuck, she looked too damn tempting sitting naked in bed. It was one reason why he struggled to walk out that door every morning.

Plus, no one at the garage looked as good as Fallon. And he'd seen their bare asses more than he could count. Reilly maybe, but even if she hadn't been already claimed by Rev, she was too much like a sister to him, so fuck that.

Again, to each his own. Rev and Reilly were perfect for each other.

"You in a rush?" he asked.

He'd already replaced her tire yesterday but her oil pan should be coming in any day now.

A harsh reminder that time was running out.

"I'm not in a rush, but I'd like to get her back sometime soon."

Once that happened, she'd be good to leave. "Gonna have her check for you, then."

He heard the clock counting down in his head, and each tick made the tightness in his chest increase. *Shit.*

"How 'bout you come to my mom's tonight for dinner?" *Goddamnit.* He hadn't meant to ask her that.

Fuck. He closed his eyes and mentally groaned at that slip-up.

Did he want to have dinner with Fallon? Fuck yeah.

Did he want Fallon to meet his mother? Fuck no!

Not because he didn't think they'd like each other. His mother would love her. *Hell*, she'd love any decent woman he brought home to her.

Well, except Billie. She never quite understood Billie or why Whip was with her. Luckily, Billie had tough skin and never took offense to that. She found it more amusing than anything.

But damn...

Maybe Fallon would decline the offer because she might think meeting his mother meant—

"I'd love that. I can't wait to meet her."

For fuck's sake.

"Since I'm stopping at the store, ask her if she wants me to bring anything."

He would not be doing that. If he did, his mom would be up his ass all day asking five thousand questions, wanting to know every damn detail about Fallon.

Yeah, no. Wasn't going to happen.

He'd already fucked up once. And once was more than enough, fuck you very much.

Chapter Sixteen

"Sooo, girlfriend, you said one of those hunky leather-clad gorillas sent you my way?"

Fallon settled into the chair and was quickly spun around to face the large mirror at the hair station. Teddy, owner of Manes on Main, fluffed up her hair with his fingers and eyed it critically with one perfectly-plucked eyebrow pulled high.

Why did she suddenly feel like she had sat in an interrogation chair? "Yes. You came highly recommended. Which is great, since, as you see, I'm overdue."

"*Oooo*. Who was it so I can thank him with a big fat kiss next time I see him?"

She laughed, wondering if Whip would mind receiving a kiss from a man. "Whip. He's working on my Agnes."

Teddy's fingers froze in her hair. "He's working on your Agnes? I know I've been off the market for a while now, but am I that out of touch with *hoo-hah* terms? Not that I was ever in *that* particular market."

"Agnes is my Indian."

Teddy frowned into the mirror over her head and shook his own. "Still confused."

"My motorcycle."

Teddy's confusion quickly cleared. "Oh! Oh, yes, that cutie-pie is very good with his hands."

"Yes, he is."

"*Oooh,*" Teddy purred and began fluffing her hair again, still giving it a critical eye. "You like them young, then?"

"Not normally."

"But I detect a bit of interest in your tone. You can tell little ol' me if there is."

She lifted and dropped one shoulder, not hiding her grin. "Maybe."

"No maybes about it. He's super-duper adorbs."

She gave him an over-exaggerated scowl and shook a finger at him in a teasing manner. "He's made it very clear that he doesn't like being called cute. He'd probably hate being called 'adorbs.'"

Teddy released a little squeak, threw up his palms in surrender and laughed. "So, what can I do you for?"

"I need my highlights touched up and a trim."

"You came to the right person." He tilted his head and made eye contact with her in the mirror. "I've never seen you around here before and I know *evvvvverybody.* Did you just move to town? And if you did, what the hell were you thinking?"

"You don't like it here?"

"Oh, I love it because my family is here, but some people around here don't love me. I'm too open, I'm too loud, I'm too," he sighed, "extra. *Whatever.* But I will never step back into that closet again. They can kiss my sweet ass." He made a kissing sound, popped a hip to the side and smacked his own ass sharply.

She hated hearing stories like that. "I'm sorry you have to deal with people being closed-minded. But, actually, I'm only passing through. Or I was when Agnes got damaged."

"It's fab that you call your," he dropped his voice a

couple octaves and growled, "*sled,*" then returned his voice to normal, "Agnes."

"Well, she's my travel partner so she deserved a name."

His hands paused again and his head tilted. "You're traveling alone?"

"I am."

His perfectly-shaped eyebrows rose again. "Interesting."

"It has been so far." This unexpected stop along the way had been the most interesting one on her trip so far. "Just so you know, the Fury ladies also sang your praises."

He took a step back from the chair, wiggled his ass and snapped his fingers on both hands, quickly following all that with a single clap. "Love those ladies. I swear they are my best clients. They're all very lucky to land those sexy hunks of man-meat. Who doesn't like all that alpha growly deliciousness?" He clawed the air with his fingers. "*Rawr!*"

"I'd have to agree, most of them are pretty damn sexy."

"Mmm hmm. It makes my day whenever I can get their tushes in my chair and clean them up a bit." He made a snipping motion with his fingers. "Okay, so… Do you want the same color highlights?"

"Yes, or something close." She wasn't going to be picky about it.

The whole time he mixed the color, applied it to her hair with the foils and while they waited for the timer to ding, he chatted non-stop. Not only was Fallon having a hard time keeping up, most of the stuff he rattled on about—in his very animated, entertaining way—she had no idea what he was talking about. Especially when it came to the local gossip.

But no matter what he was rambling about, his antics made Fallon smile and laugh so much that her cheeks were beginning to ache. If she lived in this town, she would definitely be sitting in his salon chair on a regular basis simply for the entertainment factor alone.

Teddy clicked his tongue. "It's a damn shame about those Shirleys, too. For some reason, that clan is a thorn in those gorillas' sides. Not sure what those hillbillies ever did to the Fury for them to be such enemies."

Her smile fell in confusion. Clan? Hillbillies? Enemies?

This info was much more interesting than his previous diatribe about Helen's sister's cousin's nephew getting caught messing around with Margaret's neighbor's daughter and now they were expecting twins.

"Who are the Shirleys?"

He flapped a hand around in the air. "Oh, that group of crazies who lives up on the mountain."

She blinked. The mountain? "On Copperhead Road?" Where she broke down?

"Oh yes! It sounds like they're infesting that mountain again after the feds came in and cleared them out once already. I haven't seen them around town yet, but it's just a matter of time if they're repopulating that damn place. Just like roaches." He did an exaggerated shudder. "*Guuurl*, I only heard about their return because my very handsome hubby is a cop in this town." He cupped a hand around the side of his mouth and whispered, "He's a scrumptious cake in uniform, I have to add."

"Are they trouble?" Didn't Whip say the town was no different than most small towns when it came to safety?

Teddy paused and his head tilted again. "Who? The cops? No, my whole family is part of the force, well except for Jet and—"

"The Shirleys."

Wait... Was Teddy related to Jet, Rook's ol' lady?

Now her mind was definitely spinning. While she was interested in learning more about Jet and Teddy's connection, she wanted the 411 about the mountain clan first.

It might explain why Whip was a bit cautious when she broke down along Copperhead Road and why he didn't want to leave her waiting alone with Agnes. It might also explain the look on his face when he glanced up the very same mountain that morning.

Could she have been in danger if he hadn't come along? "Are these Shirleys dangerous?"

He leaned in close and lowered his voice dramatically. "Honey, any group of people sharing the same DNA, one tooth and two brain cells are dangerous. That clan doesn't follow the same laws as you and me. They were also making moonshine, meth and had a huge stash of illegal weapons up there. It was a *huuuuuge* kerfuffle around here when the feds came in to clear them out and dismantle their production. We all sighed in relief when the clan was gone. They're a threat to any government official, including my hubby. Now, word is, they're back."

"Feds?"

"Oh yes, FBI and the ATF were swarming the area for a while. Good thing I'm already taken or I would have been a very, *very* busy boy opening those closed closet doors and peeking inside." He wiggled his eyebrows. "Some of them had some very big... guns."

"But if the feds removed them once, won't they come back and remove them again?" If they had violated federal laws, wouldn't the FBI be monitoring them?

Teddy shrugged. "As long as they're not doing anything illegal, I'm not sure if they can. I'll have to ask the hubby to see if he knows."

A bell over the door rang when it opened.

"Speak of the handsome devil..."

A very good-looking, very fit man walked into Manes on Main wearing perfectly-fitting jeans and a snug dark gray Henley over his broad shoulders, making Fallon's mouth drop a little. She snapped it shut since she might be ogling a gay man's husband. If she was, he was not only taken but played on the wrong team.

Though, that didn't mean she couldn't appreciate him from afar.

"He's yours?" Fallon asked under her breath, still checking out the man carrying an infant.

If that didn't make her ovaries tap her on the shoulder and remind her that her clock was ticking, nothing would.

She silently told her ovaries to shut up and sit down.

"Oh yes, girl. That man there is *all* mine. Every last inch of him."

Teddy was not lying when he said the dark-haired, crystal blue-eyed man was handsome. "You're very lucky," she whispered.

"Well, Whip's a hot one, too. Mine just has a little more seasoning."

"You know I can hear you, right?" the man said as he stopped next to the chair, leaning in to give Teddy a quick peck.

Teddy's husband adjusted the baby in his arms, and glanced down at Fallon.

Teddy whispered loudly, "He's wondering why he doesn't know who you are since, like me, he knows everyone in this one traffic light town."

"I'm Adam."

Fallon smiled up at him through the mirror. "Hi, Adam. I'm Fallon."

"Young Whip's new squeeze," Teddy whispered with a grin.

One of Adam's dark eyebrow lifted. "Whip."

"You know, from—"

Adam rolled his eyes. "I know who Whip is, T. Hello, Fallon. Nice to meet you."

"Same. So, you're a police officer?"

His eyes sliced to his hairdresser husband. "Yes."

"He's Jet's brother, too," Teddy added with a flip of his hand.

So, *that* was the connection between the female bounty hunter and Teddy. Jet was Teddy's sister-in-law.

The police department and the MC must have a good relationship with each other.

Adam tipped his head down at the baby in his arms. "This is our little stinker, Mira. Sorry, Fallon, but I need to leave her here because I have to go work second shift. I hope you don't mind babies."

"I don't—"

Teddy slapped a hand against his chest. "I wanted to name our precious bundle of joy Miracle since that's what she is to us. But this one," he rolled his green eyes and tipped his head toward Adam, "who is much more boring than *moi*, decided it was way too *extra*. We ended up compromising with Mira."

"Well, the name is beautiful just like her."

"Do you have any?" Adam asked.

"No," Fallon answered with a little shake of her head.

"Do you want any?" Teddy asked with a sly smile. "Mmm. My ovaries explode just thinking about having that boy's babies. I'm sure yours do, too."

"Theodore!" Adam barked.

Teddy pressed his fingers to his mouth. "Oops. Did I say that out loud? Silly me."

Adam sighed. "Good thing I love you."

"Good thing." Teddy winked. "And you know the only baby batter I—"

"Okay!" Adam said sharply, cutting Teddy off. "Well, I need to get to work." Adam handed the baby over to Teddy and set the diaper bag that was over one shoulder onto the empty salon chair at the next station over. "I'll grab the bouncer and put it next to you so you can keep an eye on her while you work."

Teddy pressed a kiss to the awake but quiet baby's forehead. "You do that, Daddy." The baby gurgled and turned big eyes up to Teddy.

Adam headed to the other side of the salon where some baby stuff sat in the corner. Fallon had been so busy with Teddy's chatter she hadn't even noticed it until now.

"She just ate and probably will need changed soon," Adam warned when he returned.

"Thanks for the warning, Daddy."

"I know how much you enjoy changing her diaper," Adam said dryly.

Teddy shrugged. "Meh. Comes with the territory."

Adam smiled. "That it does." He leaned in, they shared a longer kiss this time, then the cop planted a noisy one on Mira's cheek, making the baby's little arms and legs jerk in response. "Try not to make your daddy cry again, baby girl."

Teddy gasped. "Of course I cry when she cries. How can I not?"

Adam cocked a brow at him. "Do you really want me to answer that?"

Teddy clicked his tongue. "Sorry if not everyone is as stoic as you, lover."

"It has nothing to do with being stoic. Okay, gotta go. Nice meeting you, Fallon. And I'm going to apologize in advance if they both start crying in stereo."

Fallon laughed. "Are you saying I need tissues and earplugs to get my hair done?"

"It wouldn't hurt to be prepared," Adam said with all seriousness. "Okay, see you tonight, T-bear."

"Hold up, hun bun." Teddy grabbed his arm to stop him. "We're both dying to know why the feds are allowing the Shirleys to move up on that mountain again."

Adam stared at him for the longest time before his gaze sliced to Fallon and back to him. Fallon could see the guarded look in his crystal blue eyes. "Who says they are?"

"So, they *are* keeping an eye on that crazy clan?"

"Teddy," he warned. "You know I can't talk about what's going on with the Guardians of Freedom."

Guardians of Freedom. That kind of sounded like some militia-type group. The kind who believed taxation was theft and the government was the enemy. It made sense then, if they were stockpiling weapons and making meth among other things, that federal agents had gotten involved.

She would have to search online when she got back to her room later to learn more about them and maybe find some news articles about the bust. This cozy little town might have some deep dark secrets. "Are they a threat to the Blood Fury?"

"They're more of a threat to anyone wearing a badge than that MC, unless the Fury gives them a reason to be a threat. But as long as that club stays in their own lane, no."

As long as that club stays in their own lane...

Hmm. No one mentioned any mountain clan at The Barn the other night and besides Whip being overly cautious when she and Agnes were stuck along that road, he hadn't mentioned them by name, either.

She had to assume the Fury was "staying in their own lane" and wondered what it would take for them to swerve out of it to get involved with what sounded like a dangerous group of people.

They were a motorcycle club, not a brotherhood of vigilantes. Right?

But wait... Whip had mentioned protection. Were the Shirleys why?

"Okay, I really have to go before I'm late and Max hands me my ass on a platter."

"Yum," Teddy purred. "I'll take a platter full of that ass with a side of—"

"T," Adam growled shaking his head.

Right before his husband walked out the door, Teddy called out, "Love you, lover."

Adam paused and glanced over his shoulder. "Love you more."

"Impossible."

Adam shot him a warm smile and the door shut behind him.

Teddy turned back to Fallon, once again catching her gaze in the mirror and sighed. "I'm the luckiest bastard in the world."

"He loves you very much."

He grabbed a comb and a pair of scissors for the trim. "I'm not sure why he puts up with me, but I'm damn glad he does."

"That's the sweetest."

"Mmm hmm." Teddy began to snip off the ends of her hair. "So, tell me more about you and the cutie-patootie Whip... I want to hear *eeeeeeverything!*"

"There's really not much to say. He found me broken down on Copperhead Road, pulled over to help me and—"

Teddy gasped loudly and slapped a long-fingered hand to his chest. "He rode in and saved you like a knight in shining armor! *Awwwww.* How fabulous!"

"Yes, well..."

"And he swept you off your feet and look at you now... You have your tush in my chair, you two will get married, have pretty babies and live happily ever after. And so will I because you'll become one of my regulars." He clapped his hands together and bounced on his toes. "A real life fairy tale!"

Mira gurgled in her bouncer nearby. Though, she probably wasn't old enough to bounce in it yet. Fallon wasn't sure. She didn't know much about babies since she had been an only child herself.

"See? Even my angel agrees with her tada."

"Tada?"

"Oh yes. Like Dada but it starts with a T and ends with flair." He kicked out a heel and threw an arm up in the air. "*Taaaadaaaaa!*"

The man was too much. "Too cute. As for Whip, I only met him a week ago."

"The universe knows when a match is made in Heaven."

They were nothing like that. It was simply chance that Whip came along when he did, wasn't it? It had nothing to do with fate. Right? No, it couldn't. They got along, yes. Had great sex, yes. Had easy and great conversation, yes... Did she enjoy spending time with him? Very much so.

Shit.

No, it was nothing like... "Like you and Adam?"

"We definitely had an instant spark." He wiggled his fingers in the air simulating little explosions. "The second I saw him across that parking lot, I knew I finally found a Bryson Buck of my very own. It was like he fell from the puffy clouds above. The angels were singing and a bright rainbow appeared like a halo around his handsome head. My gay prayers had been answered." He pressed his palms together, dipped his head and murmured, "*Aaaaah men.*"

"Wow." The man was quite the storyteller.

"Yes, it was quite a wow moment. Then he ripped my cigarette from my mouth, smashed it on the ground and told me he doesn't kiss smokers."

Fallon grinned. "I guess he was enough motivation to quit?"

"*Giiiirl*, that night I smashed the rest of the pack myself. I've screwed up a lot in my life but that man," he sighed, "and the whole Bryson family..." He sniffled loudly and flapped a hand in front of his face. "Look at me getting the vapors." He took a deep inhale. "And now we're married and have our very own munchkin."

"Will you have any more?"

His hands moved efficiently and expertly as he continued to trim the ends of her hair, turning her this way and that to make sure everything was even. "We haven't decided yet. We struggled to find the right surrogate who would accept our combined baby batter."

It took her a second to figure out what he meant. She wasn't sure whether to laugh or gag at the term. "Do you want to know whose batter made the cake?"

She couldn't believe she was calling sperm baby batter. She'd never be able to scrape that out of her head again. She hoped like hell that wouldn't pop into her head whenever a man came.

"I'm sure we'll figure it out once Mira's eye color changes. If they turn green, one of my swimmers was the winner. And if not, then…" He shrugged. "Though, I'm pretty sure Adam's swimmers were more determined to cross the finish line first, while mine… Well, they probably paused to do some synchronized swimming along the way."

Fallon chuckled. "Do you care whose was the winner?"

Teddy didn't even hesitate to answer. "No. If we did, there would've only been one of us providing the ingredients for that recipe. But enough about me and my handsome lover, tell me more, more, more about you and our young virile Whip. I want to hear *all* the juicy details."

Should she mention it? Maybe she could get his opinion on the surprising invitation Whip blurted out this morning. "I'm meeting his mother tonight. He invited me to have dinner with them."

Fallon almost got whiplash as Teddy spun the chair around, stopped it abruptly with his foot, almost flinging her from her seat. His eyes, the color of jade, were wide and a hand covered his gaping mouth. "He did? You are?"

Fallon winced at his squealed questions.

"My goodness, girlfriend! That's a huge step already. Now I'm doing your makeup and nails, too. All on the house! You never get a second chance to make a first impression. You have to dazzle the potential momma-in-law."

"I don't need to impress her. It's only dinner. She's not going to be my—"

Teddy did a "shut it" motion with his fingers to stop her from speaking. "It's never 'only dinner' when the momma gets to meet the lover. Don't kid yourself. Take it from me. The first time I met my future in-laws, I was sweating so badly, you could wring me out like a soggy dish cloth." He slapped the back of his hand against his forehead in an overly dramatic gesture. "Adam thought I was so sick that I needed to go to the ER."

That couldn't be why Whip invited her. Teddy was making a bigger deal out of tonight's dinner than he should be. "I'm not staying in town, Teddy. Once Agnes is fixed—"

"Uh huh. Once one of those possessive gorillas sets his sights in your direction, you're not going anywhere. Trust me. I've seen it with my own two eyeballs."

"Not this time."

"Sure, girlfriend, you keep telling yourself that. When we're done here, I'll set up your next appointment and we'll see if I'm wrong."

Chapter Seventeen

"Tyler, is this an April Fool's joke? Please tell me it isn't. Did you actually bring home a *girl?*" Fallon was hardly a "girl" and Whip's mother was whispering much too loudly with her eyes lit up like someone just handed her a tax-free million dollar check.

He groaned under his breath. Maybe this wasn't the greatest idea, but his mom would be upset if he missed their weekly dinner. He also didn't want Fallon to spend dinner alone, even though she was used to it.

She was traveling the country by herself. She ate alone most nights and was fine with it.

He wasn't.

Maybe his invitation was more for him than her.

Though, he did notice that her excitement to come to dinner with him had sort of waned when he picked her up at the motel.

Was it nerves?

He kept his voice down since Fallon was sitting in the living room just off the kitchen. "It's not like that, Mom. And why would you think it's an April Fool's joke?"

His mother stared at him like he was an idiot.

Maybe he was.

He closed his eyes and whispered, "Christ." Today was April first. "It's not a joke, Mom. Fallon's in town by herself and we've…"

His mother's smile got as big as her eyes.

He ignored that and pushed on. "We've been eatin' dinner together out…" *every night*, "a lot and figured she could use a good home-cooked meal. Told her you're a great cook."

His mother ran a hand over her hair and tugged at her shirt. "But you should have warned me. I don't have on any makeup and…" She glanced down at the Justice Bail Bonds T-shirt she was sporting. "Look at me. I'm a complete mess! I spilled coffee on my T-shirt earlier! I should go fix myself up."

"You don't gotta do that. She don't care."

"I don't *have to do* that and she *won't* care," she corrected him.

He groaned.

"You're not going to find and keep a woman if you keep speaking so sloppily like that."

"Mom…"

"Don't you dare 'Mom' me. I'm your mother."

He strained his eyes trying not to roll them. "No shit. It's why I call you 'Mom,'" he muttered under his breath. "And, news flash, she don't give a fuck how I talk."

"You don't know that!" his mom hissed at him. "You should always put your best foot forward so you can find yourself a nice wife."

For fuck's sake, there she went. Same old, same old. "Don't need a wife, Mom. I'm good."

"All your *friends* are getting them."

He sighed. Loudly. "They're not my *friends*. They're family. And the women are their ol' ladies."

She grabbed a pot holder from the counter and moved

over to the oven. "I'm your family. And ol' lady is such a horrible term. As is sweet butt, by the way."

"Can you stop? This is my life and I like it the way it is."

"It could be better."

"It could be worse," he countered.

She pulled the pan of bubbling homemade mac and cheese out of the oven. It had the perfectly browned bread crumb topping. Just how he liked it.

"It would've been worse if you'd married that Billie."

Whip closed his eyes and ground his teeth. "Nothin' wrong with Billie."

"If there wasn't—"

"Enough!" he barked. He quickly glanced over his shoulder toward the living room and dropped his voice. "We're not talking about Billie. We're not talkin' about marriage. Or grandkids. Or anythin' like that. We're gonna sit at the table and enjoy the food you made. Yeah?"

His mother turned to face him with her hands on her hips. "I only want what's best for you. And, by the way, that club is not it."

"You got your opinion. I got mine. Let's leave it at that."

"I worry about you. I don't want you falling into the same trap as I did. You saw how that turned out."

No fucking shit. He certainly would never forget that fucking day. He actually considered sleeping in the bunkhouse tonight just in case he relived it again as he slept.

Normally he kept that shit under control but it was the main reason he hated coming home. It brought the shit he buried deep back up to the surface. He didn't understand how she could live in that house and not constantly be haunted by it.

Maybe she had buried it even deeper than he had.

"No need to worry and I won't. And we ain't discussin' that tonight, either."

"That club is bad news. Just like your father."

Of course she had to fucking mention him anyway. "It ain't."

"It *isn't!*" she shouted, making him wince. Her face fell. "What happened to my good boy?"

"He grew the fuck up," Whip growled.

They stared at each other. His mother's mouth got tight and her blue eyes narrowed. "Fine."

Thank fuck. "Thank you," he said more softly, attempting to reduce the tension between them. "Now—"

"Is everything all right in here?" came from the doorway that separated the kitchen and the dining room.

Shit.

He turned and Fallon's eyes met Whip's. He pushed a breath out of his nostrils, trying to unclench his jaws. If anyone could take his mind off what happened out front twenty years ago, it was the woman leaning one hip against the archway.

To him, she looked just as sexy in her black jeans, button-down cream-colored blouse with just a hint of cleavage and heeled boots than if she was wearing a see-through negligee.

He didn't need to see her in a negligee. He knew every inch of what was under those clothes.

"Everythin's good. Food's done if you wanna grab a seat at the table."

Fallon turned eyes to his mother. "Do you need any help, Tonya?"

"That's sweet, but no. You're our guest. Please have a seat and we'll have dinner out shortly. I hope you're hungry!" she finished in a sing-song voice.

Fallon turned her gaze back to him and stared at him a little longer, then nodded before disappearing from the doorway.

His mother whispered, "How old is she?"

"Mom," he warned.

"I'm just curious is all."

Sure she was. "It matter?"

"I only want to make sure she's not taking advantage of you, Tyler."

"Mom, she ain't takin' advantage of me. You know I don't got a goddamn pot to piss in. While she could quit her job and still afford to travel wherever she damn well pleases."

"How?"

"That's somethin' you can talk to her about over dinner. Yeah?"

His mother rolled her eyes. "Talking about money is rude. Especially at the dinner table."

Jesus fuck. "She ain't gonna care."

As soon as his mother opened her mouth to correct his language, he lifted a palm to stop her. "Don't. Just don't. Not tonight, for fuck's sake."

A slow smile spread across her face. "You like her."

"Yeah, Mom, wouldn't have brought her along if I didn't."

"I'm just concerned about her age."

"Don't be."

"Well, she looks like her biological clock might be ticking. You don't want to saddle yourself with someone who might not be able to give you babies."

Christ. "Babies ain't even on my radar." He lifted his hand again to stop what normally came next. "They're on *your* radar. Enough talk about babies and that's another subject you won't be bringin' up at the table. Along with marriage. Billie. No bitchin' about the club, either. Got me?"

She rolled her eyes.

He grabbed his mother's shoulders and dipped his head until they were almost nose to nose to make sure she heard him clearly. "Mom, she's only in town for like a week. She don't need to know about any deep, dirty secrets when it comes to Manning Grove, the club or this family. Just talk about stupid shit like the weather." He pressed a kiss to her forehead. "Please."

She sighed and patted his cheek when he straightened. "I just want you to be happy."

"Wanna make me happy? Avoid talkin' about that bullshit."

"Fine."

He grinned. "Fine. Now, what d'you need me to carry out to the table?"

———

Down the hallway, where he sat just a few feet away from the bathroom, Whip had his back pressed to the wall. He had his teeth clenched together tightly and whatever was happening inside the closet-sized bathroom could be heard past the hands clamped over his ears.

His father had come stumbling into the house only a few minutes before while his mother was cleaning up the kitchen after she and Whip had eaten.

His father had been very, very angry that they hadn't waited for him to come home to eat or that a plate wasn't waiting for him on the table. He had been over an hour late, so Whip's mother decided to put away the leftovers and clean up.

That had been a mistake.

Now she was paying for it.

His mom always told him that at four years old he was now a "big boy" and he needed to be brave.

He wasn't feeling so brave right now. He wished he was bigger and stronger so he could stop his father from hurting his mother when he'd been drinking the stuff that made him mean.

But he'd tried that before by jumping on his father's

back, by pounding his fists on his father's head, by kicking his father to try to make him stop. Whip ended up thrown across the room, breaking both the wall he crashed into and his arm.

His father blamed his mother for Whip's injuries, even though she had nothing to do with it.

Bobby Byrne said she had "made" him do it. He insisted it was all her fault for not listening. That night after they got back from the emergency room with Whip's arm in a cast and a made-up excuse to tell everyone how it happened, she ended up with broken ribs and bruises in places where no one would be able to see them.

The story was that his arm had broken when he fell off the swing hanging from the big oak out front. If Whip told anyone the truth, his father would break his other arm.

But that was then, this was now. Despite covering his ears, he could hear her crying and begging.

For him to stop.

For him to leave her alone.

To wait until Whip was asleep.

Promising she'd never not keep a plate warm for him again.

Promising she'd keep supper on the table for him.

Promising, promising, promising.

Anything to get him to stop.

Promises never did any good. His father ignored them all and his yelling continued to fill Whip's ears.

Whip winced with every thump.

Cringed with every cry.

Then he jumped out of his skin when the bathroom door banged open so hard that the door stopper twanged loudly.

His father stepped out of the bathroom, his mother's hair in his fist as he dragged her down the hallway toward their bedroom.

Tears streaked her red and swollen face, blood trickled from the corner of her lip, and her eyes widened when she spotted him sitting on the floor with his knees pulled to his chest and his hands covering his ears.

"Get the fuck in your room and don't come out!" his father bellowed at him with spittle flying from his mouth. His face was red, too, but for a different reason than his mother's. His eyes were bloodshot. The stench of whatever he'd been drinking so strong it made Whip's nose wrinkle and his stomach hurt. "Pickled" was what his grandfather called it.

Whip hated pickles.

He hated his father.

He wished the man was dead. Then he couldn't hurt his mom any more.

Whip helplessly reached his hand out to his mother. He wanted to save her. "M-m-mom!"

"Tyler, go to bed!" she ordered on a sob.

"You don't get to your room right now, boy, I'm gonna beat you bloody. Do you hear me?" his father yelled.

He wanted to yell back.

He wanted to hit his father.

He wished his father would leave and never come back.

He wanted him dead.

Dead.

Dead.

Dead like the squirrels his pap shot.

He was too small to pick up his pap's shotgun. It was too heavy. Too big.

And his pap forbid him to touch it.

One day when he was visiting his grandfather he got caught doing that. His pap swatted him so hard he couldn't sit down for an hour. He was told to never touch it again.

Ever.

He sat frozen in the hallway as his father finished dragging his mother by her hair to the end of the hallway, her hands gripping his wrist, her tears continuing. Her body dragging along the carpet because Whip's father wouldn't wait for her to get onto her feet.

She didn't fight it. If she did, it would only make it worse.

"Go to bed, Tyler!" his mother cried one last time before they disappeared into the bedroom and his father slammed the door shut.

His heart was pounding in his chest. His bottom lip was trembling. His muscles ached and shook. His eyes burned. His cheeks were wet.

His room was right across from theirs.

He'd hear everything.

Everything.

All of it.

Every second of it.

Until it ended.

He forced himself to rise from the floor, to get to his feet.

He should run away. Right now. Just run as fast and far as he could.

But he couldn't leave her.

He couldn't leave her with him.

He couldn't.

He couldn't.

Who would protect her?

He would tell his pap. Pap would have to protect her until Whip was big enough to do it himself.

He felt the weight in his hands. He glanced down and saw the shotgun. The one he was forbidden to touch.

Not caring, he strode to their bedroom and grabbed the door knob. But the hand wasn't a four-year-old's. Fuck no, it was a man's hand. Calloused. Permanent stains under the nails. Mechanic's hands. Working hands.

Hands that held that shotgun easily.

Hands that could turn a door knob.

Only the door was locked.

Whip took a step back, got a better grip on the shotgun, lifted his boot and kicked the door next to the knob. Once the jamb splintered with the force, he shoved open the door the rest of the way to find his mother still crying.

She was now naked from the waist down but Whip couldn't see anything he shouldn't because his father was blocking that view. The bastard had his jeans pulled down far enough that Whip could see his naked ass pumping but that was it.

He was grunting with each forceful thrust. Non-stop bullshit spewed from his mouth. Telling her that she was his wife, that he could do anything he wanted to her and she couldn't do shit about it.

He called her a whore. A slut. A stupid bitch.

She was useless. Good for nothing.

She sucked at being a wife. She sucked at being a mother.

"I shoulda k-killed you, you m-motherfucker. Not P-pap. M-me!" Whip shouted, raising the double-barreled shotgun and pointing it dead center at his back. "G-get off her, you worthless p-piece of fuckin' shit. Nothin' but a d-deadbeat drunk."

His father acted like he couldn't hear Whip and just kept pounding his mother, squeezing her throat, fisting her hair. His mother's hands tightly gripped the wrist of the hand cutting off her air. Her mouth was open, her eyes wide, her face turning colors from the lack of oxygen.

That drunk motherfucker was going to kill her.

He was going to snuff the life right out of her.

Whip wasn't going to let that happen. He wouldn't let the wrong person die.

He slipped his finger through the trigger guard, the pad

of his index finger sliding over the cool smooth metal of the front trigger.

But he didn't pull just that one, he pulled them both at the same time.

The deafening blast rattled his brain and the recoil knocked him backwards, making him lose his balance and begin to…

Fall.

Fall.

Fall.

He jerked awake and the air rushed from his lungs as he landed hard.

Not in his parents' room, but in a bed.

Not his own, but still familiar.

Fuck.

He blinked once, twice.

Sucking in oxygen, his heart raced, sweat beaded on his forehead.

For fuck's sake, this happened almost every goddamn week.

Not the same nightmare, but always one similar. Always a memory he wished didn't exist.

He hated that fucking house. He was putting his fucking boot down and getting her to move if it was the last goddamn thing he did. If she refused, he wasn't going over there for dinner anymore. They'd meet at some restaurant halfway between Liberty and Manning Grove.

Would he miss her home-cooked meals? Fuck yes, but he was done reliving that nightmare. Homemade meatloaf with smashed potatoes and gravy was not worth the shit he dealt with afterward.

He scrubbed his hand over his eyes and stared up at the ceiling through the dark.

He should've killed that motherfucker instead of his pap.

It should've been him.

Maybe his pap would still be alive if he had. Still planting his ass in front of the TV every night at seven. Still heading to bed at eleven.

Early to bed and early to rise makes a man healthy, wealthy, and wise. His pap repeated that Ben Franklin quote every night when he rose from his recliner with a groan.

Like clockwork.

Whip missed his fucking pap every goddamn day.

That goddamn abusive, drunk motherfucker destroyed Whip's family.

If he could go back… *For fuck's sake*, if he could do it all over again…

"You okay?"

Fuck.

He cleared the thick from his throat and took a breath to make sure he didn't stutter. "Yeah."

He should have followed his first instinct to sleep in his bunkhouse rack tonight. He tried to roll out after he and Fallon fucked earlier but found it impossible to tear himself from her side. He didn't want to miss one fucking second with her while she was in town.

She'd be gone soon enough.

And his bastard father had already done enough damage. He wasn't going to chase Whip away from Fallon.

"What was that about?"

He took another deep breath, calming his thoughts before he spoke. "Nothin'. Just a fucked-up dream."

She rose onto her elbow, propping her head in her hand. "You yelled about killing a motherfucker."

Shit. He had been talking in his sleep. He wondered if he had stuttered, too. "Did I? Don't remember."

"Whip…"

"Just a dream, Fallon. Nothin' more."

She rolled against him, wiped the sweat from his brow and planted her chin on his chest. His fingers automatically combed through her hair, that soothing action helping slow his pounding heart and racing pulse.

He always woke up before he could see the damage done to his father by him pulling those triggers.

Every damn time.

Just once he'd like the satisfaction of being the one to kill that rat fucking bastard. Just once.

Women complained often that they'd like to see other men step up to intervene when a man was either mentally or physically abusing a woman. If Whip saw it, he'd get involved in a goddamn second.

Even if it was one of his brothers.

"I've noticed something…"

Whip mentally groaned. He didn't want to talk about his fucking nightmare, about his asshole father or losing his pap. He clenched his jaws and waited.

"You only call me 'babe' when we're being intimate. Every other time you use my name."

"Yeah?" That wasn't what he was expecting. Was she trying to distract him from his nightmare?

"You're not aware of that?"

Of fucking course he was. "Figured you bein' a strong, independent woman, you wouldn't like bein' called babe. Didn't want you to see it as me bein' disrespectful and not appreciatin' you for bein' you."

He tried to avoid calling her by any kind of pet name but it slipped out when they were having sex because he got lost in her.

Totally fucking lost.

She didn't say anything for the longest time.

"I wrong?" he finally asked.

"Normally, I'd say you're not wrong."

"But?"

After a slight hesitation, she continued, "I've had men call me babe when they shouldn't. It was clearly an attempt to degrade me in a professional setting. Sometimes even in a social setting. I wasn't their 'babe.' I wasn't anything to them and in their eyes it was an attempt to knock me down a notch. Time and time again I've seen men threatened by strong, independent women. They think we should need them, that we shouldn't be able to function without a man's help. When we don't need them and we can function perfectly without them, they don't like it. So, they find a way to disrespect us. Using honey, sweetheart and babe are just examples to try to put us in our 'place.' Trying to put us where *they* think we belong."

"Yeah. Figured you wouldn't like it."

She shifted more of her weight onto him until their faces were only inches apart. "But truth be told, I like it coming from you."

He blinked. "Say again?"

"I like it when you call me babe. It…" She blew out a breath. He tucked a thumb under her chin and lifted her face so he could see it. At least, as best as he could in the dark room.

"Tell me," he encouraged her softly. Did she get just as lost in him as he did her?

"Honestly, it feels right when you use it. It…" She blew out another soft breath and the warm air rushed over his skin. "Okay, I'll just say it… It warms my soul."

Did he hear that right? "Just to be clear, 'cause I'd like to keep my nuts where they currently hang… You *want* me to call you babe?"

"You don't use it to demean or belittle me."

"How do I use it?"

She cupped his cheek and whispered, "Like you care. It has a whole different tone and feel. You're using it organically and with affection. When *they* use it it's in the same tone they would order me to get into the kitchen and make them a sandwich."

His pulse sped up again. *Jesus fuck.* What was going on here? Was he still asleep and he was dreaming this conversation in the middle of the night?

"A motherfucker ordered you to make him a sandwich?" Every muscle on his body turned to stone.

"Not just one. Again, when men feel like they're losing their power over a woman, or to a woman, they say some really ignorant shit."

"And you fuckin' knee them in the nuts, right?"

"No, we grin and bear that treatment when we have to. We laugh it off even though we find it far from funny. Then we *fantasize* about kicking them in the nuts. Or doing even worse."

"I ever hear a fuckin' asshole tell you to go make him a fuckin' sandwich, gonna rearrange his nuts myself. Then gonna knock out every fuckin' tooth in his head."

"That's sweet, but—"

"Babe," he cut her off, "it ain't sweet, it's a fuckin' promise."

"I doubt you'll be around to do that the next time it happens."

He sighed softly. Yeah, that. He couldn't protect her because she'd be gone.

"Earlier you said that Reilly's tracking my oil pan with the shipper and it should be in on Monday, right?"

"Yeah." He was hoping the damn thing would get lost in transit, but that would be selfish of him. He continued to stroke her hair, occasionally pausing to rub the silky strands between his fingertips.

"Your mom reminded me that your birthday is in two weeks—"

He froze. "She did what? When?"

"When I was in the kitchen helping her clean up, she—"

"Fuckin' Christ."

"She was simply making small talk, Whip."

He sucked in a long breath through flared nostrils.

"Don't give her grief for mentioning it. From what I saw, she seems to be a wonderful woman and she loves you. That much is clear."

He grunted.

"She's also worried about your involvement with the Fury."

He groaned.

"And since I'm spilling all the tea… She asked me how old I am."

"Fuckin' Christ!" he repeated. "You tell her?"

"It's not a big deal."

"Yeah it is, 'cause I told her to let it go."

"She's your mother. She's going to look out for your best interest."

"Old enough to do that myself."

"You're her only child, Whip. Of course, she wants to be involved in every aspect of your life."

"Stop defendin' her."

Fallon planted her face into his chest and her body shook. "Ain't funny."

When she lifted her head, her smile was so damn bright he could see it in the dark.

"Ain't funny," he grumbled again. "Treats me like I'm still fuckin' ten."

"She's going to treat you like that your whole life, just so you know. It's the sign of a loving mother."

"Smotherin' mother."

Fallon shook her head and drew a finger across his chest from one nipple to the other. "So, anyway, the reason I brought up your birthday is, I want to spend it with you."

She wanted to do what? "It's a coupla weeks away. Oil pan's supposed to be here Monday. You really wanna stick around that long?"

"I'm in no rush and I don't mind staying to celebrate your birthday." She paused. "Unless you do?"

Fuck no, he didn't. That just gave him more time with her. Though, he didn't say that since he didn't want to sound like a desperate dick. "Don't want you to feel obligated."

"I don't. I won't."

Did she really want to spend the next two weeks in Manning Grove just for him? "Wanna live in this damn room for the next coupla weeks?" He wished he had a better place for her to stay. He never hated living in the bunkhouse more than right now.

"I've been living in hotels and motels since I started on this trip. It's nothing new."

"You ain't gonna get bored?" With the motel, with Manning Grove, with him?

"If I do, I'll go find something to do."

"Got me to do."

"You're busy with work and your club. I can't take up all of your time." She moved until she was lying on top of him. "And as much as I'd like to keep you naked in my bed twenty-four-seven, I know that's not possible."

"Wish it was."

"If you're okay with it, I'd like to stay to celebrate your twenty-ninth birthday."

He was more than okay with it, but... "Ain't a big thing."

She shrugged. "It doesn't have to be. We can have a quiet celebration if you'd like."

That sounded good, but her staying for another two weeks sounded even better.

He rolled until she was under him and he was settled between her thighs. "Ain't gonna say no."

"I mean, I don't want to force you," she teased.

"Ain't forcin' me. Wanna spend my birthday with you. You'll be the best birthday present I ever got."

"I doubt that," she huffed.

"It's true." He pressed his hard-on against her. "You too tired?"

"You're not, apparently."

"Never too tired to be inside you, babe."

"Call me that again," she breathed.

"You like that?"

"Yes," she hissed as he slid his hard dick along the soft, warm folds of her pussy.

She was made for him. She was where he belonged.

"Babe."

She moaned when he tilted his hips again.

"Know what I want for my birthday?" he murmured around her nipple as he pulled it into his mouth.

Her fingernails scraped his scalp, making his dick flex against her. "What's that?" she breathed.

"To fuck you without a wrap." He wanted nothing between them. No barrier. Just the two of them.

She was on birth control. If it would make her more comfortable, he'd get tested first.

"I'm willing to get tested if you are." She moaned again as he sucked her nipple deep into his mouth.

Fuck yeah. He'd make the appointment tomorrow.

This was going to be his best birthday yet.

Happy fucking birthday to him.

Chapter Eighteen

"THE TEXT SAID NINE SHARP," Cage grumbled. "Anyone know what the fuck's goin' on?"

Whip glanced around the group. The only Fury members missing, besides the prez and sergeant at arms, were Dozer and Woody since they had to run Crazy Pete's. Dodge, the bar manager, was currently standing with the rest of them in the back of Tioga Pet Services in the furnace area.

It had to be big news since even the three prospects had been included. And big news only meant one thing...

Still, Whip had no idea why they were told to meet at the crematorium instead of The Barn. He trusted Trip had a good reason.

"Don't get your fuckin' panties in a bunch," Sig told Cage. "All of you. You know the prez called us here for a reason. Have a little fuckin' patience."

Easy snorted next to Whip and said under his breath, "He should fuckin' talk about patience."

"Heard that," Sig growled, his brown eyes narrowed on E.

"Ain't a lie," Easy challenged.

The VP squared off with E. "How 'bout you just keep your fuckin' trap shut?"

"Brother, let it go," Whip whispered to Easy when he felt the man tense next to him. E's reaction surprised him since he had the road name Easy for a reason. The two men were as opposite temperament-wise as they could get.

Luckily, E did let it go, but it had more to do with the steel door next to the loading dock opening.

Jesus fuckin' Christ.

He had to make a conscious effort to keep his jaw from hitting the floor as he watched six men follow Trip and Judge inside.

What the actual fuck? They had to be the "Shadows" Judge had talked about. The "security" team who worked for the Dirty Angels' enforcer.

They weren't in suits with earpieces like bodyguards. They were dressed in full tactical gear. Neither their knives or guns were concealed and Whip had no doubt they had more weapons hidden on their person.

They were dressed as if they were going to war.

Trip and Judge both said when "it" happened it would happen without a lot of warning. "It" being blowing up that fucking mountain. Putting an end once and for all to the Shirleys.

Problem was, they never had a final discussion on what to do with the women and children up there or who would assist these guys.

No, not guys. Mercenaries. Killers. Take-no-prisoners type of badass motherfuckers.

They were no Gravy Meal Team Six. They were the real deal. No doubt they'd dealt with some real shit. Probably shit they wished they never had.

Their eyes were laser focused and their heads on swivels. They put the hillbilly militia, Guardians of Freedumb, to shame.

Fuck, they put the Fury to shame. Whip did not want to be on their bad side. Not one of them and certainly not all six.

Trip did his sharp single clap to catch everyone's attention as he stepped in front of the intimidating line of Shadows while Judge moved off to the side.

"All right, everybody here?" Trip asked Sig.

His brother nodded. "Everybody accounted for 'cept for Dozer and Woody."

"Yeah. They're doin' their part by runnin' Pete's."

He turned to the side and began to introduce the men behind him. He pointed to the huge guy on the end with a very noticeable scar running diagonally across his face that made him appear even more menacing. Especially with the way one corner of his lip pulled up into almost a sneer.

"That's Mercy. He's gonna be in charge. He gives you an order, you listen. Don't want to hear any fuckin' backtalk, yeah? Hell, any of them tell you to do somethin' they got a good reason, so fuckin' do it. I hear otherwise…" Trip shook his head. He pointed to the man standing next to him. "Brick." The prez went down the rest of the line. "Steel. Hunter. Ryder. Walker." He turned back to the Fury members and said, "Remember those fuckin' names and faces. They're gonna get done what we can't on our own."

It had to bug the fuck out of Trip that they couldn't handle the Shirleys on their own. He knew it bothered them all that they had to call in outsiders. And, worse, those outsiders weren't cheap. The club would be financially hurting for a while but seeing the Shadows in person, he knew it was the right choice.

The shit with the Shirleys had to end and those six men appeared more than capable of ending it.

Trip continued, "They're gonna stay at the motel 'til this whole thing's done. But you see them, you pretend they're strangers. Want no ties between them and us. One reason we ain't holdin' this meetin' on the farm." He turned to Ozzy. "You brought the keycards with you?"

"Yeah, six like you said," the motel manager answered with a nod and patting his cut.

Hunter spoke up. "Stayed in that fucking motel before when my wife and oldest boy lived in this town. It was a fucking dump back then. Tell me it's no longer like that or we're gonna need other accommodations."

What the fuck? Whip guessed if they were as good as they were supposed to be, they could make demands.

"Yeah, it's no longer the roach motel it used to be," Trip assured him. "Anythin' you need, you let Oz know and he'll get you squared away."

"Gonna give you my number so you can get ahold of me directly," Ozzy told the men. "Unless you don't want my number in your phones."

"We got burners," the Shadow named Steel spoke up. "Once this job's done, there isn't gonna be anything left to tie us to this job."

"That's one thing we need to do yet, is grab a few burners. We don't want our phones pingin' our location on that mountain when we head up there," Judge announced.

Mercy nodded. "Yeah, get that done. You don't want anything tying this club to what's going to happen on that mountain. You told us they're a sovereign nation and they were stockpiling weapons, right?"

"Yeah. Buyin' parts and building the guns themselves. Reloadin' ammo, too," Trip answered.

"Good. They already have a beef with the government. And since the feds came and cleaned them out, they're going to be out for revenge," the big man named Walker said. "We're going to make it look like they were gearing up for a war against the government. Building and stockpiling more than just illegal handguns and long guns."

"You told us they were sloppy with their weapons, their

moonshine stills and their meth labs," Ryder added. "That'll make it easy to look like they were sloppy making home-made bombs, too."

"Explosives are fucking dangerous and should only be handled by professionals," Mercy finished dryly.

"And when you don't know what the fuck you're doing… *Kaboom*," Brick said with a sly grin.

"You got enough explosives to flatten that place to the ground?" Dutch asked to Whip's right. The old man was standing just on the other side of Easy.

"Don't you worry about that shit," Mercy answered. "That's our job."

"What the fuck! Of course, we're gonna be worried," Dutch growled. "Need to know if you're worth the fuckin' scratch we're payin' you."

"Worth every fucking dime," Steel reassured him with a smirk. "Best pest control operation out there."

The Shirleys certainly fit the description of pests.

"Right now the plan is," Mercy explained to Trip, "we're heading up there tonight to do some recon and, once we get the lay of the land, we'll start setting the explosives. This won't be done all in one night. In fact, it's going to take a few. We have to be cautious, not only with the handling of the material, but with not being spotted. From the map and photos you provided, looks like a pretty big compound with buildings scattered throughout the woods and clearings. That right?"

"Yeah, that's right," Trip answered. "You need any of us to go with you?"

Mercy stared at him. "Any of you got experience with explosives? Slade said you were a Marine."

"Yeah, we served together, but I ain't got that kinda experience."

Mercy gave a single nod. "Yeah, figured. Then no, we don't need help for this part. My team will go up later, do our thing and see how much we get done. You got alibis set up for the night of?"

"Yeah," Judge spoke up, tugging on his beard. "One of our brothers got a birthday comin' up. Good excuse to gather for a party at our bar in town. It's open to the public, so we'll have eyes on us other than our own."

Birthday? Party? What the fuck was Judge talking about? *Jesus fuck*, was the sergeant at arms talking about Whip's birthday? If so, that would mean Fallon would want to be there.

He was damn sure he didn't want Fallon anywhere near this whole plan. Or being a part of the "alibi." She wanted to hang around to celebrate his birthday, so if she got wind of this party…

"Don't all arrive at the same time," Mercy continued. "Once you're done up there clearin' out the women and children, don't walk in as one group. Trickle into the bar. Different times, different directions."

Judge nodded in agreement.

"What *are* you doing with the women and children?" the Shadow named Brick asked.

"Had a long discussion over that," Trip started. "We got a plan."

"Wanna share it?" Ryder asked next.

Trip yanked his ball cap off and ran his fingers through his hair. "Figure once you get all the explosives into place, we're gonna go up and gather the women and their spawn. We already stole a set of keys to one of their vans. Gonna load them all up, and two of our prospects will take them to Ohio to drop them off with another branch of the Guardians."

Mercy scowled. "Not expecting blowback from that?"

"It could, but we're gonna make sure it don't," Trip assured him, slapping his cap back on his head.

"The only way to ensure that is to dispatch them all," Brick informed the Fury prez.

Mercy quickly followed with, "Yeah, well, we don't want any part in taking out women and children. Not unless it's in self-defense. Even then we try to disable and not kill."

"Understood," the Fury prez said. "We got a plan set. Scar and Castle know what they need to do and how to do it but, if needed, all of us are gonna be gatherin' the women and children."

"Okay then." Mercy took a quick glance down his line of men. "While you all are doing that, we're going to quietly take out the men. Depending how many there are—and will get that count during the next couple of days—we'll drag them into the buildings where we'll set it up to look like they were building and storing pipe bombs and other homemade explosives. This way there's nothing left of them after the detonation. All evidence will be scattered."

"What little's left of them will be scattered and splattered," Hunter said without an ounce of humor.

"Yeah, there isn't going to be much left once we're done," Steel added. "Which is why we're doing it the way we are."

Mercy slowly scanned the room again, his piercing gray eyes touching on each one of them. "Once you all clear the mountain and we detonate the explosives, we'll ghost. You won't see us again. This is one and done. Any of you get caught up there when you should've been clear, that's on you. That means make sure you stick to the timeline. There won't be a lot of wiggle room."

"Rest in fucking pieces," Hunter muttered.

"Ain't a way you want to die," Steel added. "There won't be enough of you left to scrape together for a funeral."

"We'll meet up again one last time early Saturday." Mercy shot Trip a look. "In a different location. Then once it's dark, it'll be go time. Just want to be clear… Once it's go time, there won't be any stopping it because we're going to make sure there isn't any evidence left that we were ever up that mountain. And there's only one way to do that."

Whip just needed to be sure to be off that mountain before it went *kaboom*.

They all did.

———

"ARE you sure I'm dressed okay? You never said where your mom's taking us."

"Just a casual place in Mansfield. She knows we're comin' on my sled so expects us to be dressed for that." He didn't need an excuse to check out Fallon, so he did so. "You look gorgeous, babe. I'd rather eat you than dinner." No lie.

Her lips curved into a smile before he shut her motel room door behind them and ensured it was locked.

"Your sled or mine?" she asked. When he turned back to her, she had her key fob hanging in the air from her fingertip.

"You know if we take that, you're my backpack, right? I ain't yours."

She rolled her eyes teasingly and sighed. "I figured that. Can't have a woman driving around a big, bad biker."

He wasn't sure how big and bad he was, but he'd take that as a compliment. "Yeah, ain't gonna happen."

She shrugged. "I'm fine with you driving. Agnes is more comfortable than your ride."

Because it was practically brand new. Even better, it had all the fucking bells and whistles, while his Harley was older and basic.

"Think we need to do a threesome with Agnes," he said as he leaned in, planted his lips on Fallon's and snagged the fob from her fingers at the same time.

When he went to straighten, she snaked a hand into the

opening of his cut and grabbed his T-shirt, holding him there while deepening the kiss. When she finally pulled back slightly, she murmured against his lips. "Is it crazy that I can't get enough of you?"

He grinned against her lips. "Same, babe." It was so damn true and he wasn't afraid to admit it.

His birthday was tomorrow and he figured she'd leave afterward on Friday morning, even though she hadn't mentioned it yet. He was expecting her announcement after tonight's dinner with his mother.

Or maybe after they fucked later.

The second they got their negative results from the lab, they'd ditched the wraps and gone hog wild. It could be a mental thing but, not only did it feel a thousand times better, it seemed to strengthen the connection between them.

Maybe it was because Fallon was the first woman he'd ever fucked without a wrap and yeah… He'd miss it once she checked out and hit the road again.

Fuck, in truth, he'd miss her.

If he had to, he'd admit that out loud, too.

A noise at the other end of the motel had them separating and glancing that way. Two of the Shadows came out of a room at the far end of the motel and were climbing into some non-descript four-door cage. Whip had no fucking clue where they were going and pretended he didn't know them as was instructed.

Hell, they could be going out to grab food, to go shopping, or slice some throats for shits and giggles.

He glanced down at Fallon to see her staring at them. "Have you *seen* those guys?" she whispered, the awe unmistakable in her voice.

For fuck's sake.

"There are six of them."

He decided to play dumb. "What guys?"

"Really, Whip? How can you not notice them? They

remind me of action figures. After you left this morning, I went out to grab breakfast and they were out here eyeing up Agnes."

They were doing what? "They exchange words with you?"

"The pretty one said she was a really sweet ride, that's it. The one with the scar just stared at me with empty eyes like a serial killer."

Mercy could very well be a serial killer. But hold the fuck on... Which one was the *pretty one*?

It didn't fucking matter.

Did it?

No.

Were they hitting on Fallon?

They'd better not be.

Like he could do anything about it. He'd end up wearing his tongue as a tie and dismembered in probably five seconds flat if he tried.

"How 'bout you just stay away from them," he muttered.

"Why? Do you think they're dangerous?"

"Don't know them, Fallon. Got no clue if they're dangerous. That's why I'm tellin' you to stay away from them." He handed over her helmet. "If you're wearin' this, put it on so we ain't late."

She smiled up at him.

He shook his head. "You don't know her. The second we're late, she'll start blowin' up my phone."

Fallon laughed softly and patted his chest. "She loves you. And I say that with confidence since I learned a lot about her in the past three weeks."

It wasn't quite three weeks, Fallon had come along to two of their weekly dinners. Tonight would be the third and probably the last.

His mom would be disappointed.

So would Whip.

He straddled her Scout and held out his hand to help her climb on behind him. This wasn't the first time they'd taken her sled. It was such a sweet ride, he had moved the one he had on his bucket list up a few spots.

Less than a half-hour later, and after they pulled into the lot of the restaurant that Reese had recommended, he shut down the Scout and scanned the lot. His mother's SUV wasn't anywhere to be found.

He slipped his phone from the inside pocket of his cut and checked his texts. His mother's was waiting for him. She would be about ten minutes late.

"Mom's runnin' late. Wanna hang out here or grab a table?"

Fallon climbed off the back of her sled and pulled off her helmet, shaking out her hair. Like always, he watched her do it. Something about the way she did it always turned him the fuck on.

Christ. If they had more time and a private spot, he'd be pushing for that threesome with Agnes.

"We can wait out here for her since it's beautiful out tonight."

That it was, and it had nothing to do with the weather.

Instead of getting off the sled, he shoved the key fob deep into the front pocket of his jeans, spun around until his ass was perched sideways on the seat and both boots were planted spread apart on the blacktop. He grabbed her hips and pulled her to him, sandwiching her tightly between his thighs.

Since they had ten minutes to waste, he was dying to know, "What's your plans after tonight?"

"Your birthday isn't until tomorrow."

"After tomorrow night, then."

"I wasn't planning on leaving until after the party."

He froze and his fingers dug deeper into her hips. "What party?"

Fallon's head tipped to the side and she stared at him for a few seconds with her eyebrows pinned together. "The party your brothers are having for you at Crazy Pete's Saturday night. Why didn't you tell me about it?"

Holy fuck. "Who told you that?" He was going to strangle whoever it was. Probably Reilly and her big fucking mouth. Rev's ol' lady was always fucking meddling.

Just like she did with the delay of the damn oil pan.

It turns out, *she* had been the reason Fallon had to stay in town longer, not because an oil pan wasn't available. When Dutch had found it hidden in the back room, Rev had yelled at her. *"Why the fuck would you do that?"*

Of course, she bugged her eyes out at her ol' man like she hadn't done anything wrong. *"Because I saw the way they looked at each other. And I—"*

"She was playin' fuckin' matchmaker. For fuck's sake!" Whip screamed. *"Why you women gotta be a busy body like that?"*

Reilly had the fucking nerve to shrug it off. *"I was just helping."*

"Lee!" Rev shouted.

"What? I want Whip to be happy."

"He don't need a woman to be happy," Rev told her. *"In fact, men are happier without one."*

Suddenly, the garage went silent. Most likely more than one asshole puckered.

Reilly's head had cocked. If she'd been holding a gun, that would've been cocked, too.

"'Cept for me," Rev had backpedaled quickly. *"Much happier havin' you as my ol' lady."*

"Nice save, but yeah. That head you wanted later? You can kiss that goodbye."

"Jesus Christ," Rev muttered, scrubbing a hand over his head.

"Hate to tell you but he's not helping you. You screwed the pooch on that one, bub," Reilly had announced. Loudly.

306

"How about anal instead?" Rev asked hopefully, following her as she strode back toward the office.

Reilly had laughed. Not a *funny, ha-ha* laugh, but a *get-bent* one. *"Yeah, no."*

"Fuck!" Rev had punched the air, spun on his heels and strode away.

Whip had not told Fallon any part of that conversation from almost two weeks ago. But Fallon's answer to who told her about the party brought him back to theirs.

"Shay. I went into the office earlier to spend some time with her like I normally do when I'm bored. She asked if I was sticking around long enough to attend." Her eyes went wide and she slapped a hand over her mouth. "Oh… shit… Was it supposed to be a surprise party? Did I blow it?" She squeezed her eyes shut. "I'm so sorry! Shay didn't mention that it was a—"

"Ain't a surprise party, babe. Didn't mention it 'cause it ain't a big deal. Thought it was a joke at first since that ain't somethin' we normally do. It turns out they were just lookin' for an excuse to party, that's all." Lies. Lies. And more fucking lies.

He ground his teeth together.

Fallon frowned. "She said specifically that the party was for your birthday. She was a little confused on *why* they were making such a big deal out of your twenty-ninth birthday and treating it like it's some sort of milestone. Do they think you're turning thirty by mistake?"

He shrugged. "No idea. Like I said, I don't normally give a fuck about that kind of shit. Not sure why they decided to throw a party at Pete's."

Fallon shrugged and cupped his cheek the way she always did. "Because you're family to them. No different than you are to your mother. My plan is to go to the party and then head out Sunday morning."

Fuck. "We're celebratin' tonight with my mother and we can celebrate tomorrow by ourselves."

She continued to stare at him.

It was not a good stare. It was one that made him want to end this conversation as quickly as possible. It also pretty much guaranteed he wouldn't be getting head or anal, either.

Where the fuck was his mother? She could pull into the parking lot at any time now and distract Fallon from this whole thing.

Her voice was flat and he could hear the disappointment in it when Fallon said, "You don't want me there."

Goddamnit, not for the reason you think. "Ain't that."

"Then what? Why not tell me?"

He could say he forgot about the party Saturday night but if he did, she'd still want to go. He needed to come up with an excuse for why she shouldn't be there. "It might get rowdy."

"In a public bar? Worse than how it got at The Barn last weekend?"

He grimaced. *Shit,* that was true. Last Sunday she had come along on the club's run and they'd taken her sled. But once the kids disappeared for the night, things got a little wild. Not over the top crazy, but crazier than what Fallon was probably used to.

The Barn was no damn classy martini bar.

"Fallon…"

She lifted her hand. "Listen, you don't have to make excuses. If you don't want me there, just say so."

Christ. Just the way she said that told him he needed to come up with a damn good excuse or she'd get bent out of shape. They only had a couple more days together, if that, and he wanted that time to be good. Un-fucking-forgettable.

This whole birthday party shit was pissing him the fuck

off. Trip could've used any other fucking reason to get them to gather at Pete's.

Problem was, he didn't have a damn good excuse to give her. Because, in truth, if it *was* only a stupid birthday party, he'd want her there. He also wanted her to extend her stay in Manning Grove as long as possible.

But he didn't want her there due to the real reason they were having that party and why they were having it at Pete's instead of The Barn.

He'd be gone for hours beforehand doing what he needed to do up on that mountain with the rest of his brothers. His disappearance would raise her suspicions. She'd want to know where he'd been and what he'd been doing during that time. Especially since every Saturday she'd been in town, they'd spent it all day in bed doing nothing but each other.

Even worse, he sucked at making up believable excuses. His pap had said his lies were always like Swiss cheese. Full of fucking holes big enough to see through.

Some people had the gift of lying. However, Santa never left that gift under the tree for Whip.

What made it more difficult was Fallon being too damn smart to pull one over on her. Way smarter than him.

The plan was to let the ol' ladies know what was going down but not until after the Fury met up with the Shadows Saturday morning. This way the sisterhood knew the deal and how to act that night, but not to give them enough time to freak out too badly or try to put a stop to the plan.

If any of them actually tried. Trip decided not to take that risk since, while every damn one of the sisterhood wanted the Shirleys gone, they might not approve of the way the club was going about it.

However, it wasn't up to them. It was up to the men to protect the Fury family.

The other problem was, Fallon wasn't an ol' lady. She was an outsider.

He couldn't tell her the truth but he also didn't want to lie to her more than he had to.

The whole thing was fucked.

And so was he because he didn't want to hurt her.

For fuck's sake, that was what he was about to do.

"You said you didn't mind me sticking around until your birthday."

"Yeah, babe. Birthday's tomorrow. Just said that. No reason to go to the party."

"Why?"

She wasn't going to let this fucking go so he needed to finish it. "Want the truth, Fallon?"

"Of course I do. Why would you even ask that?"

Because it wasn't going to be the truth and the lie was going to hurt like fuck. He braced. "Ain't gonna lie then… Don't want you fuckin' there."

Her mouth opened just slightly but nothing came out for far too long.

He waited with his heart pounding in his throat and dread twisting his gut. He did everything he could to keep his expression from showing it.

"Shay said all the ol' ladies are going."

Fuck! "You ain't an ol' lady."

She stared at him, unblinking, her face a complete mask. But he could fucking see it. Right in her eyes. She hadn't been expecting that comeback from him. Normally that wouldn't have been his damn response, but he was trying to keep her out of the mess that was about to happen.

Unfortunately, if he told her the real reason, it would just open a box of worms. One he wouldn't be able to close the lid on.

He wanted her safe. He wanted her hands clean. Since

she wasn't an ol' lady, he didn't want any of this Shirley bull-shit splashing back on her.

That could very well happen.

It could happen to any of them. *Hell*, all of them. Even the sisterhood. If any Fury members ended up dead or in prison, it would affect their ol' ladies, too. Their future, their family. It could be, *would* be, devastating.

One reason why Trip was so big on protecting, not only the women and children, but his brothers. As far as Whip knew, every one of his brothers, except for Deacon, had come from a broken home. The prez did not want that happening to the next generation.

"You're right, Whip. I'm not an ol' lady."

Fuck.

"I guess I overstayed my welcome," she finished. "I didn't mean to intrude or push my way into your life like that. I figured... I thought..." She shook her head and took a step back so they were no longer touching.

He closed his eyes and inhaled, slowly filling his lungs, then pushing it back out just as slowly.

He was fighting the instinct to fix this. To invite her to Pete's, anyway. But he had to remember the risk.

What if she got wind of what was going on?

What if she saw the truth of what his club was capable of?

What if she saw what *he* was capable of? She might not ever look at him the same way again.

Wouldn't it be better if she continued on her trip before she learned any of that? Clueless of the deep, dark secrets not only in Manning Grove, but his MC?

It would be safer for her to have zero knowledge of what was going down. But if she had decided to stay in town... To stay with him...

Then things might be different. His approach on this whole thing would be different.

But she never once hinted about staying. Not once.

The fact was, she couldn't leave knowing their plan and the secrets behind it, the secrets because of it. It wouldn't be smart for her or the Fury.

The less people who knew about the plan, the better.

She wasn't staying so, no matter what he said, no matter what he did, he was losing her anyway.

Fuck me upside down and sideways.

"That's the problem, Fallon, you think too much. You're too goddamn independent. In my world, to be an ol' lady you'd be my property. That means when I tell you I don't want you goin' somewhere, you'd listen. When you don't listen, you make me look weak and less than a fuckin' man. I can't fuckin' have that. I'd lose all goddamn respect from my brothers."

All of that was probably the worst thing he could say to her—especially since it aligned with the bullshit she had to deal with at her former organization—but that was the reason why he said it.

He knew how she felt about women not being treated as an equal, so he used that as the sharp knife to cut the ties cleanly instead of continuing to hack at it like he'd been doing.

At this point, he pretty much guaranteed his birthday dinner with his mother was fucked. If possible, he'd try to make it up to Fallon later but he wasn't sure they'd ever recover from this moment.

She was leaving sooner or later, anyway, he told himself one more fucking time.

So, it didn't matter.

It didn't fuckin' matter.

Protecting and taking care of her was what mattered and this was the best way for him to do so. Whether she knew it or not.

Whether if felt wrong as fuck or not.

He just needed to stay strong and not let her expression, not let the hurt in her eyes, not let anything she could say sway him to tell her the truth.

He needed to get her away from the club. Away from Manning Grove. Away from the Shirleys and away from the mess that was about to go down.

He knew her well enough now to know she would be horrified if she discovered what the club had planned.

But that didn't make this any easier.

Her lips were pressed together when she slid her hands up his thighs. Before he could stop her, she had her hand dug deep into his front pocket. When she pulled it free he didn't have to see what she held.

He knew.

This was it.

What he'd been dreading.

It was finally here.

The end.

But he asked it anyway. To continue with this fucking bullshit. "What're you doin'?"

"Get off of Agnes." Her tone was flat. Cold.

She was done. Right then. Right there. She wasn't even going to wait until after dinner. She wasn't going to bother to pretend everything was okay with his mother sitting across the table from them.

"Get off my bike." This time she said it a little louder, a little stronger, with her spine straight, stiff. Her chin held high.

This was no weak woman, she was powerful in her own right.

He'd been a dick and she wouldn't stand for it.

Exactly what he'd hoped. But exactly what he feared.

He'd done the unthinkable to her and did not treat her as an equal. A mortal fucking sin in her eyes.

But she'd be clean and clear of the mess that was

coming. Especially if shit went sideways and there was no guarantee that it wouldn't.

She grabbed her helmet and right before she pulled it on, she said, "Have your mother take you back. I'll drop anything you left in my room at the office when I check out."

Jesus fuck. "Fallon."

She pulled her brain bucket on and secured the strap before throwing a leg over the seat and settling on it. She hit the starter, then flipped up her visor. "I don't beg and I don't like lies. And my internal bullshit detector is going off. I'm more disturbed by that than the fact you didn't tell me about the party. If you were honest about it, it would've stung but that's all. However, the lying cut me deep." She leaned in and whispered just loud enough to be heard over her exhaust. "Please tell your mother I'm sorry and goodbye for me. Happy birthday, Whip."

She smacked the visor down, heeled the kickstand up and twisted the throttle.

He remained standing in the now empty parking spot, in the dark, trying not to fall to his goddamn knees while watching Fallon ride away.

You knew this was coming, idiot. If not now, then later. She wasn't even supposed to stay as long as she did. You had more time with her than you were supposed to.

This was for the best.

This was for the best.

For fuck's sake, this was for the best.

Eventually he could no longer see her back, see her tail-lights, or hear her exhaust.

He pressed his fingers to his chest, over his heart, trying to relieve the stabbing pain.

He must have nicked himself with that knife when he was making that cut.

And, *fuck him,* did that wound sting.

Chapter Nineteen

WITH ONE KNEE bent and a boot propped against the vehicle lift's post, Whip stood amongst his brothers. He had been the first one to arrive at Dutch's Garage and unlock the doors since he hadn't been able to sleep.

He'd slept like shit since Wednesday night.

The first night he'd slept alone in weeks. The first night he'd slept in his own bed for weeks.

The first night he hadn't fallen asleep wrapped around Fallon. For fucking weeks.

He glanced around the garage trying to shake those thoughts free.

His brothers now gathered around the middle bay after staggering their arrivals on purpose. Those employed at the garage had parked out front like normal. The majority of the group parked around back in the fenced junkyard area so no one driving by would think some sort of meeting was going on. The less red flags flapping in the wind, the better.

Normally the garage was closed on Saturdays unless they were working on their own shit. Or on the rare occasion Dutch had enough work to pay overtime. So, them being seen there wasn't out of the ordinary. But what *was* out of the ordinary were the six Shadows.

This morning they weren't dressed in tactical gear, but kind of… normal.

Not that there was anything normal about them. Even dressed in jeans, T-shirts and light jackets—probably to conceal their weapons—they stood out.

The Shadows had entered through the rear door along with Trip and Judge.

Even with the whole MC there, including the prospects, it was fucking crazy how small that garage felt as soon as those six men stepped inside.

Whip had no doubt the six-man team could take down a small hostile government on their own.

Hell, he wouldn't be surprised if they had.

Why did he even fucking care? He didn't. He just wanted to get this whole thing over with and wake up Sunday morning with the Shirleys in the Fury's rearview and everyone else intact and ready for a safe future ahead.

Though, it might take him awhile to become whole again himself. Waking up alone in his bunkhouse rack for the last three mornings sucked motherfucking ass.

He hadn't tried to call or text Fallon. She hadn't done the same, either.

Not that he expected otherwise.

But at least he could live with the fact that she was safe and away from the fuckery that was about to go down later that night.

How he felt didn't matter. The goddamn hole in his chest didn't matter, either.

Nothing mattered except keeping the Fury in one piece and all the women and children safe. That included Fallon. She might not be an ol' lady but, in his book, she still counted.

To keep everyone out of danger, the cancer threatening

them had to be eradicated. And that malignant tumor was the Shirleys.

Even if he wanted a future with Fallon and, for some reason, she wanted the same...

Didn't matter anymore. It was too late.

Dinner with his mother hadn't gone well. The ride back to Manning Grove went even worse.

Then a text from Ozzy drove that last nail into his coffin.

Fallon hadn't wasted any damn time. The motel manager told him to come get his shit as soon as he could. Or if he had a chance, Ozzy would drop it off at the garage.

Whip texted him back and told him not to take it there. Otherwise, he'd have to explain what happened with Fallon to more than just the Original.

He hadn't wanted to deal with that. Not yet. That time would come soon enough.

He preferred to suffer in silence for a while. Let that cut heal and scab over before everyone tried to poke their finger in it.

Because, *fuck him*, his club brothers couldn't resist prodding at each other's wounds.

Trip glanced around, his gaze landed on his half-brother Sig. "Everybody here?"

Sig had taken a head count prior to the president and sergeant at arms walking in the back door. "Yeah."

Even Woody and Dozer were included this time since the bar was closed this early in the morning. Trip wanted everyone aware of the plan and what was going down. He warned them all that they needed to stay on their toes.

None of them needed that reminder.

Dodge had already gotten the orders for him, Dozer and Woody to prepare Crazy Pete's for the party tonight. He also made sure to have Micah working the bar since the bartender had no ties to the club—besides working at Pete's —and could be used as an alibi.

The Synners would be playing on stage tonight, too. That meant Syn's bandmates would make witnesses if needed, though they weren't aware of why the party was being held at Pete's.

Syn wasn't, either. Yet. Dodge's ol' lady only thought her band was playing for Whip's birthday.

Trip had already spread the word that all the Fury kids would be taken to Shade and Chelle's house in town for the night since it now had a good security system. Josie, along with one of her girlfriends, would entertain them with movies, games, pizza and loads of junk food.

Jude would be there, too. Even at only fourteen, Shade had taught his son how to be proficient with knives and the boy was damn impressive with his skills. Shade had a lot of confidence in the kid to keep the next generation of Fury safe if he had to.

Everyone hoped he never got that opportunity.

Maddie was asked to stay at the house, too, but insisted on going to Pete's since she was now old enough to drink and party with the club. Shade didn't like it but said it wasn't worth the argument or raising suspicions since, of course, he couldn't tell Chelle's oldest daughter the truth.

Without a word, the Shadow named Brick moved to the stack of weapons Shade and Easy had gathered from their hiding spots. Every single weapon piled on the concrete in the next bay over had been taken from the Shirleys. The man squatted next to the stack, picking them up one by one. He racked shotguns, checked bolt actions, peered down barrels and tested triggers. The entire time shaking his head.

When he was done he rose to his feet. "This is all fucking shit. More dangerous than not having a weapon at all."

Shade, standing nearby, shrugged. "Besides some personal weapons, this is what we got."

"We don't run guns, so don't have access to anythin'

else," Trip informed the Shadow. "Best we can do if you want an army at your back."

The six Shadows glanced at each other and Whip swore amusement filled their eyes, even though none of them smiled.

Since Trip didn't want the Fury to be in constant battles and most of them were ex-felons, they didn't have their own stockpile, only what they stole from the Shirleys knowing they would never report the guns missing.

Brick shook his head again and toed one of the rifles at his feet. "This shit ties you back to them. Get rid of it all after tonight. Whatever you take up there, leave there once all the targets are secure. This way anything you got from them will get blasted into oblivion and nothing but scrap metal will be left."

Anything you got from them.

Those guns weren't the only thing they got from the Shirleys. They got Red, too.

She was the main reason the conflict between the clan and the Fury started.

Was she worth the war? Ask any of them, and they'd all say yes. She was family, she was Fury.

Mercy stepped in front of his line of men, his icy gray gaze sweeping over the group and finally landing back on Trip. "Did our final recon last night and finished planting the remainder of the explosives in and under the unoccupied buildings. Figured you wanted every standing structure destroyed, even down to the outhouses, right?"

"Yeah," Trip answered. "Don't wanna make it easy for them to return. The more debris, the better, too. To the point they'd have to bring in some major heavy equipment to rebuild."

Mercy nodded. "Yeah, that's how we have it set up. Going to flatten that compound and fuck up the ground enough so that it would take a crazy amount of scratch to go in there and make it right. The point is to make it easier for that clan to walk away from the property and start fresh elsewhere."

"Nobody's walkin' away anywhere," Sig muttered. "None of their fuckin' legs should be attached by the time you're done."

The Shadow named Walker jerked in a way that drew everyone's attention.

Whip wondered what that reaction was about.

Mercy continued as if nothing happened, ignoring both Walker and Sig. "An explosion that size will make a clear statement of your future intentions if they do try to come back and settle up there."

"You got numbers for us?" Judge asked, also pushing on.

"Numbers were lower than we expected. Makes me wonder if they're holding off on bringing in more and, if so, why," Mercy continued. "Especially with the way you described their cult."

Ryder picked up from there. "Ten was the head count we got on the men. But from what we could see, only six women and thirteen kids. That includes a couple of older teenagers. We counted each time we went up there to get that number as accurate as possible. A miscount could be a misstep."

Those numbers seemed manageable. Whip had no doubt that if they waited any longer the amount of women and children would double or triple. In the past, they had outnumbered the men since the men liked to take multiple wives and breed like fucking rabbits.

Trip nodded. "My guess is that they're bringin' them in slowly as they're rebuildin'. By doin' that, they're also testin' to see if the feds will storm in and remove them again. But since they're confident enough now to begin increasin' their numbers and the feds seemed to have ghosted, it's another reason to make it difficult as fuck for them to return after tonight."

"Was there a redheaded slit up there?" Sig's question pulled all eyes to him.

Hunter answered after an awkward pause. "Yeah. Saw a redhead in one of the habitable cabins deep in the woods about a half click north of the main compound. A man and another woman seemed to be sharing the place with her. Five kids in total between them."

"The redhead's mine," Sig stated loudly and in a tone that said he didn't want any argument. "Three of those kids we're separatin' from the rest."

Judge spoke up next. "Sig, the plan is that you're gonna grab those kids while the rest of us deal with the remainder."

"Fuck that. Someone else needs to grab them for me. I gotta handle the redhead."

Mercy stared at the VP, his face reminding Whip of cracked concrete. "If you're talking about dispatching one of the women, it isn't smart."

Sig's head tilted to the side as he faced Mercy. "Don't give a fuck how smart it is. She's fuckin' mine."

"Then you do what you have to do with her on that fucking mountain and you leave her there for the detonation. You get me?" Mercy growled.

With his jaw popping, Sig stared back with his eyes narrowed on the much bigger man. After a few tense moments, he nodded.

Whip would've agreed, too. It made sense. Leaving her up there with the men when the explosives went off would leave no evidence behind of whatever he planned to do to Red's mother.

But what Sig was planning on doing with three kids, Whip had no fucking clue. He wasn't sure if the VP should be raising a damn puppy, forget three young children.

"How old are her kids?" Hunter asked, with his brow furrowed and hands on his hips.

"All three under five," Sig answered.

"You separating them for a reason?" the Shadow asked next.

"Yeah," Trip answered before Sig could. "They're comin' with us. They're family."

The six Shadows shared a glance between them, then Mercy, wearing a scowl, nodded. "Don't care what you do with the kids. That's on all of you. As long as you aren't dispatching them."

"That ain't the plan," Trip assured him.

"Here's how it's going to go, then... We'll all go up together and my team will take control of the men while your crew handles the women and children. You said you have keys to one of their vans. If you're using that to transport them elsewhere, make sure to cover the windows so no one can see your cargo. Best if you restrain the women and the older teens while transporting them to wherever you're taking them. For your safety and theirs. Your guys get busted hauling kidnapped women and children, it'll blow this operation wide open. We won't feel the heat but you will. Your club will be decimated worse than that mountain.

"But this is important, so pay attention. I'm only going to say this once... No matter what fucking happens up there, that compound's getting a facelift. Stay on schedule and get the fuck out of there before detonation time. You remain behind, nothing's going to be left of you to scrape together for a funeral. You all get that?"

A chorus of *yeahs* rose around Whip.

Mercy turned to Trip. "Bottom line is, don't expect us to come save your asses. I'm responsible for my men. You're responsible for yours."

Trip nodded. "That's the plan." The prez turned toward Whip's brothers and his gaze swept over all of them. "Will go over the timeline with you. We got it down to the second. We gotta be organized, efficient and work as a team. Anyone havin' second thoughts?" The prez waited for a few seconds and when none were voiced, he continued, "Great time for a reminder…" He pounded his fist twice over his heart and yelled out, "From the ashes we rise…"

A loud stomping of boots and chest beating filled the garage, causing goosebumps to rise along Whip's skin.

His voice rose in unison with the rest of his brothers as they yelled, "For our brothers we live and die!"

"Hell hath no fury like the Blood Fury!" Sig continued yelling at the top of his lungs. "Boom! Welcome to hell, motherfuckers!"

THANK FUCK FOR THE MOON. Unlike the Shadows, the Fury didn't have access to night vision goggles. If it had been a cloudy night, working their way up the heavily wooded mountain would've been more treacherous than it already was.

They needed to stay out of sight until they had all the Shirleys—or whoever was now a part of the Pennsylvania branch of the Guardians of Freedom—restrained or dispatched. They didn't want any of them warning the rest so it turned into a gun fight. If it did, their plan would go down the shitter and who knew who would survive that.

The odds were better if they hit the clan by surprise.

While the group hoofed it up Hillbilly Hill, they also had to make sure they didn't get caught in any booby traps. They had no idea if any still existed or even if they ever existed in the first place. But to make sure they didn't set any off, the Shadows kept them off any obvious human paths and stuck to the tighter, less obvious wildlife trails.

However, several times in their climb to the main

clearing of the Shirley compound, too many of them stepped in holes, tripped over downed branches and stumbled over rocks. Smothered curses and bitching rose around Whip as they attempted to move as a unit.

The Shadows, none who fucking tripped, probably thought they were a group of bumbling biker idiots who couldn't kill a fucking fly with an oversized swatter.

Every once in a while, the lead Shadow, Mercy, would lift a fist into the air, stopping the procession. They'd all freeze in place and hold their breath to just listen.

After a few moments, the big scarred man would give them the hand signal to move forward again.

The Shadows were dressed in all-black tactical gear, wore camo face paint, had some wicked looking military-grade rifles strapped across their backs and were armed to the teeth.

The Fury were also dressed in dark clothes, all had knives on their hips or strapped to their calves and carried the weapons they'd pilfered from the Shirleys. Judge had decided it was best that no one carry their own personal gun. That way there was no risk of it getting left behind. And, more importantly, no risk for it to be on their person once they cleared the mountain in case they ran into five-o.

To keep on top of the pigs, Jet, now reluctantly in on the details, went to the station to "visit" with her brother, Adam, and her cousin-in-law Leah Bryson, both who happened to be working second shift. The timing of the explosion was about halfway through their shift and by being there she'd hear any call come in so she could warn Rook if it happened to be about the area around the mountain.

No doubt calls would come in since they expected the blasts to rock the whole area, but they hoped to be clear by the time that happened.

Trip and Judge tried to have all bases covered. While they didn't want to do it this early since darkness had only blanketed the mountain, they had no choice since the party was scheduled to start at nine. Any later than that might raise suspicions.

The women were heading over early to help set up the bar for the party. They were told to remain there where Dozer and Woody would watch over them.

At the edge of the main clearing, the group would go their separate ways and break off into teams of two. The Shadows targeting the ten men. The Fury targeting the six women and thirteen children.

If any of Whip's brothers ran across a male Shirley that a Shadow had not gotten to yet, they were told to take them down—preferably in a quiet manner, like slicing a throat or strangulation—and drag them into the closest building.

Whip had no idea how the Shadows set up the explosives to make it look like an accident, but, *hey*, he wasn't the pro and they were. That was why they were earning the big bucks. He didn't need to know the exact details since he hoped like fuck they'd never have to do anything like this again.

Castle remained hidden at the bottom of the mountain as lookout. Once they were done and the clan was all secured, he and Scar were taking the van full of women and children to Ohio. The prospects were instructed not to stop once they left the mountain until they reached their destination. They were also warned to obey every damn traffic law along the way so they wouldn't get pulled over.

If they got pulled over, shit would go sideways.

Mercy stopped the group again just before the edge of the main clearing. Lights were on in the biggest house in the compound, the one where Vernon Shirley, all his wives and his kids used to live.

Whip had no fucking clue who lived there now or even who was their current cult leader. He also didn't fucking care. After tonight, if everything went as planned, it wouldn't matter.

If everything went as planned. It *had* to go as planned. If not, they were fucked in more ways than one.

Mercy glanced over his shoulder toward Trip and gave him a chin lift. The prez returned the signal. The Shadow raised his hand high enough for everyone to see it and tapped his watch.

Stay on schedule. *Right.* That gave them about forty-five minutes to find everyone, get the women and children to the main clearing and loaded in the van. They'd have fifteen minutes to spare to get the fuck out of Dodge before the whole Shirley compound went *boom.*

The problem with going up the mountain this early was the clan would still be awake and possibly moving about doing whatever inbred hillbillies did at night.

Most likely breeding a new wannabe army.

If they were, it would make it easier to sneak up on them with their pants down around their ankles. They could be dead before their next hip thrust.

Since he'd been paired up with Cage, Whip turned to him and whispered, "You ready?"

"Ready as I'm gonna be," Cage answered under his breath.

The Shadows, along with Trip, disappeared into the dark first. Then like Noah's fucking Ark, two by two his brothers headed out.

"Let's go," Cage murmured, nudging Whip in the ribs with his elbow.

After checking for the hundredth time to make sure his knife was still where it should be—sheathed on his belt—and the pistol he had snagged from the pile in the garage was still securely tucked in his waistband at the small of his back, he followed his older club brother and coworker through the woods, keeping to the outside perimeter of the main clearing.

Sig and Shade, along with Rev and Rook, were ahead of them since they were heading to the cabin highest up Hillbilly Hill. The residence where, supposedly, Red's mom, her sister-wife and Red's stepfather were living in. Rev and Rook were to deal with getting the five kids and the sister-wife down to the van where Easy was hiding nearby with the stolen key, while Shade "dealt" with the husband.

Cage and Whip were to head northeast of the main house to a pair of small cabins tucked deep in the woods. One occupied, one supposedly not. To be safe, they weren't going to stupidly assume the second one was truly empty.

Cage let out a hiss when the road captain stumbled beside him and Whip caught his arm. "You okay, brother?"

"Fuckin' doin' this in the fuckin' dark with nothin' but the goddamn spotty moonlight. Gonna be surprised if we all survive this. Don't wanna leave my baby girl an orphan."

"She ain't gonna be an orphan. Dyna's got Jemma."

Cage stopped and, even in the dark, Whip could see his glare. "Okay, fatherless, then. Jesus fuck."

"Let's concentrate on what the fuck we're supposed to be doin' then so that doesn't happen. And keep your fuckin' voice down."

After Cage huffed out a breath, they kept moving, skirting bushes, trees and boulders. Fortunately—or unfortunately—they'd been up Hillbilly Hill enough to know the area where they were headed. It also helped that the Shadows had drawn some damn good maps. Much better than the crude one Shade drew a couple of years ago.

It was hard to believe it had been about three years since Sig found Red running naked and pregnant down the mountain.

Three fucking years of dealing with these goat fuckers.

Tonight that would end.

After this, if the Fury ever came up this mountain again it better be for a damn good reason. And by good, he meant something they wanted to do and wasn't forced to do.

Somehow they managed to reach their assigned destination without any broken bones or spilled blood. Two cabins sat alone in a very small but overgrown clearing. Whip peered around the big tree he had ducked behind.

The lit-up cabin had a piece of shit, rusty four-door cage sitting in front of it. The other cabin behind it was completely dark. But there was no way he would assume it was empty. Or not booby-trapped. At least with something other than the explosives the Shadows planted.

The thought of entering any structure knowing that they were rigged to explode soon made every fucking hair on his body rise. But they had a job to do and, *goddamn it,* they were going to get it done. And afterward they were all going to get off that mountain in one damn piece.

"We know most of these half-assed cabins only got one way in and one way out, so how do we wanna handle it?" Cage asked while scanning the area.

"Quickly," Whip answered. The fucking timebomb was ticking.

"No fuckin' shit," Cage muttered. "Think we should make a noise outside the cabin to draw the fucker out. Then we take him down and slice his fuckin' throat. Once we got him under control, we'll go in and assess how many women and children are in there."

Whip shook his head. "How about we look in the fuckin' window and do a head count before drawin' the fucker out so we don't go in blind?"

"That could work, too."

No shit.

"How many flex-cuffs you grab?" Cage asked.

"Two."

"Same. Fuck it, let's do this."

They both pulled out their knives since they were told not to use guns, if possible. One, because a gunshot echoing through the woods would blow their cover, and two, when the explosion was investigated and the dead were found—or whatever was left of them—they didn't want any ammo found in those bodies. Proof that the goat fuckers died before the explosions.

The guns were a last resort and would only be used in case of self-defense. Kill or be killed scenarios.

"Stay here for a sec. I'll go look in the window."

Cage warned, "Watch for skunks and snakes and other shit in those weeds."

Whip stared at him for a second. "Like we don't have enough shit to fuckin' worry about already."

Cage shrugged. "I'm gonna check the cabin in the back while you check this one. Meet back here."

Whip nodded and kept low as they separated and approached the cabins. He crouched down under the dirty as fuck window and slowly rose until he could see inside.

He spotted one woman in a rocking chair sewing what looked like one of those prairie dresses by hand. Her uncle-cousin-husband was sitting at a crudely made table, cleaning what looked like a hunting rifle.

Thank fuck that gun was in pieces.

Two kids, maybe four and six years old, were sitting on the floor playing marbles.

Marbles.

No tablets, no TV, no comics, nothing from outside the Shirley bubble. Simply entertaining themselves by rolling small colorful balls of glass in a hand-drawn circle drawn in chalk on the wood floor.

Whip took one more quick glance throughout the cabin —thank fuck it was a basic open floor plan and nowhere for anyone to hide—and didn't spot anyone else. He ducked down again and almost crawled back to Cage.

When he got there, Whip whispered, "Two adults, male and female, two boys. My guess four and six. Though, I suck at judgin' that kind of shit. The important part is they're small enough for us to handle."

"The other place seems to be abandoned. This should be a piece of cake, then."

"Let's not fuckin' jinx it," Whip warned Cage. He focused on the rust bucket parked near the front door. "Gonna check to see if that piece of shit's locked. If it ain't, you hide inside it, and I'll hide behind it after I slam the door," Whip instructed Cage as they worked their way around the outer edge of the overgrown clearing.

Cage paused and glanced back at him over his shoulder. "My old man's right. You *are* an idiotic savage."

"Fuck you," Whip muttered under his breath.

The Fury road captain snorted and Whip shoved him to remind him to keep it down so they weren't caught before they even got started.

They approached the passenger side of the car and, after taking another quick glance at the door to the occupied cabin to make sure it was still closed and no one was peering out of the window, Whip slowly and carefully opened the rear passenger door, worried that the hinges would squeal like a stuck pig. "Lie on the back seat. When that fucker comes out to check the noise, you get him from the front, I'll take him from the back. Just gotta keep our eyes open to make sure that Shirley bitch don't start pluggin' buckshot at us 'cause I swear they're all fuckin' crazy."

"Gotta be to wanna fuck your uncle-cousin-brother. Can't trust those damn snot monkeys, either."

No truer words.

Cage shook his head as he considered the sedan. "Damn fuckin' shame the rust bucket's too old to have an alarm. Settin' that off would get that toothless inbred out here quick-like."

"Yeah right, asshole. A car alarm would echo just as loudly through the damn woods as a gunshot. It would put everyone on notice and could fuck up the plan."

Cage shrugged and climbed into the back seat, scrunching up his face. "Fuck. This thing smells like month-old road kill in July."

"That's just you. Should shower more often than on Saturdays. No wonder that Amish chick was attracted to you. You probably smelled like a fuckin' manure pile and it turned her on."

"Fuck off."

"You fuck off."

"You're just jealous you can't keep a fuckin' woman."

Now was not the time to get bent about Cage's insult, that arrow hitting him directly in his chest. "Jemma only puts up with your miserable ass 'cause of Dyna."

"Nah, she worships my big dick."

"Yeah? Gonna ask her that at the party later." They were wasting valuable time. "Okay, we gonna do this before we also get blown to fuckin' bits?"

"Leave the door cracked open," Cage grumbled before stretching out on the back seat, a flex-cuff by his hip and a knife in hand. Luckily, the overhead light in the old Chevy was burned out and he could leave the door just open enough so it wasn't latched. Cage would be able to kick it open quickly if he had to.

With a last glance at Cage lying in wait, Whip moved around the rear of the Chevy to the driver's side, yanked opened the door and then used his boot to slam it shut. As he hoped, the rusty hinges screamed in protest, the glass rattled and the slam was loud enough to draw attention from anyone nearby.

He just hoped there weren't more Shirleys in the area. He wanted to concentrate on the ones they were tasked to deal with first.

He hurried around to the rear of the cage and squatted behind it. He hoped to fuck they could hear the noise inside, then he hoped to fuck the goat fucker wasn't too damn lazy to check out the noise.

He *really* hoped to fuck the Shirley didn't have any other weapon except the one he had in pieces on the table. But he knew that last one would be a pipe dream since the clan was a wannabe militia organization.

So, his last, and most important, hope was that the man didn't storm out of the cabin with a fifty-caliber cannon in his hand.

When he heard the door to the cabin open, he rose just enough to see the Shirley standing in the doorway and, of fucking course, he was holding some kind of handgun.

Fuck.

Chapter Twenty

"WHO THE FUCK'S OUT THERE?" the man bellowed into the dark. "Jimmy Dean, that you out there?"

A noise came from inside the Chevy. Fucking Cage. He probably thought it was fucking hilarious someone was named after a breakfast sausage.

Whip held his breath as he heard the man come down the two wood steps. "Don't make me put my fuckin' boots on!"

Whip rolled his eyes and whispered, "C'mon, fucker, come check out the noise, we don't got all night."

He heard a female voice from inside the cabin.

"You just stay inside, Birdie. I'm gonna check it out. JD might be tryin' to sneak off with the car again. If he is, I'm pluggin' a bullet in his ass this time."

The woman inside kept squawking but Whip couldn't make out what she was bitching about.

"Shut up, woman. Don't give a fuck if he's your kin. We're all kin and he can't be takin' what ain't his. Includin' you. Warned him once. He ain't gettin' another one."

Even with his heart pounding in his ears, Whip heard

heavy footsteps approaching. His adrenaline was spiking as much as his damn pulse.

Cage better be ready.

"You hidin' in there, Jimmy Dean?" The driver's door squealed as it was yanked open.

Whip peeked his head up and saw the man leaning into the car and waving the gun around the interior.

"Get up so I can see you when I plug a bullet 'tween your eyes."

Holy hell, had the fucker spotted Cage?

Whip crept around the back of the Chevy and quietly stepped behind the man, raising his knife in preparation of slicing the fucker's throat. But before he could do that, Cage surged up from the rear seat and plunged his knife directly into the man's heart.

Complete fucking bullseye.

Whip didn't have time to appreciate his brother's accuracy. He jumped forward, yanking the gun from the Shirley's hand as the man slowly crumbled to the ground next to the sedan.

As the Shirley gripped the knife sticking out of his chest, his mouth opened and, before he could shout a warning to the woman inside, Whip crushed the fucker's face with his boot to keep him quiet.

Cage jumped out of the Chevy and rushed around the car, pulling his imbedded knife free and wiping it clean on the man's flannel shirt as he continued to bleed out.

"Gotta drag him back inside as soon as we get his woman secured," Cage said.

Whip put his finger to his lips because the door to the cabin was still wide open and he didn't want to tip off Birdie. "Let's go stand on either side of the door and see if she comes out to check on him. If she does, we can grab her and pull her out. Guaranteed there are more weapons inside," he warned in a whisper. "Need to get her away from those."

Cage nodded. They moved quietly to either side of the door and pressed their backs to the front of the shitty cabin. Whip took a quick glance at his cell phone to check the time. He had set up a timer on his burner phone to make sure they were done with their part and off that fucking mountain well before detonation. He turned the phone toward Cage to show him how much time they had left.

They were thirty-five minutes in. They had ten more minutes to finish up, get the woman and her kids to the van, and about another fifteen to get clear from Hillbilly Hill.

His asshole was starting to pucker with how close it might be. Glancing at Cage across the open doorway, he had a feeling his brother's was puckering, too.

Cage barked out a loud cough.

Whip mouthed, "What are you doin'?"

Cage lifted a *just-wait* finger and coughed again.

"Elvin, that you? You find JD?" The questions were accompanied by quick footsteps heading toward the door.

Cage lifted three fingers, then counted them down. When no fingers were left, the woman stepped out of the doorway, peering into the dark. "Elvin!"

Cage lunged, grabbed the woman by her hair, using it to fling her off the steps and to the ground.

She shrieked like a bobcat caught in a trap and Cage fell on her, straddling her and using his weight to hold her down. He covered her mouth with both hands to keep her quiet. "Shut up! You want your kids to keep breathin', you shut the fuck up, you hear me? Nod."

The woman, whose eyes were at first wide but now narrowed on Cage with hatred, nodded.

"We need to gag her. She ain't gonna stay quiet. I'll keep her mouth shut while you secure her hands behind her back. You better not bite me, bitch. You do, you'll never see those two spawn again. I'll sell them off to the highest bidder and they'll still have a better life than with you."

Whip ignored his brother's empty threats and Cage turned her enough so Whip could bind her wrists with a flex-cuff. Once her hands were secured, he sliced off a piece of fabric from the bottom of her dress and handed it to Cage, who quickly gagged her, despite her struggling against him.

"I'll hold her here while you get the kids," Cage said.

After another quick glance at the burner phone, Whip entered the cabin to see both kids standing in the center of the cabin, their arms wrapped around each other, their eyes wide as they stared at him.

They probably hadn't had a bath in a while since their skin was dirty as were their clothes and their hair was a complete mess. The older boy even had a bruise on his cheek that appeared to be a handprint.

Fuckers.

Whip hoped to fuck that they saved those boys from future abuse by taking out Elvin.

"It's gonna be okay," he assured them, holding his empty palms up. "Not gonna hurt you."

"That's not what you told our momma," the older one said, his bottom lip quivering and his eyes shiny. "You touch us, I'll kill you."

"No you won't. We're takin' you and your momma away from here and to a better place. C'mon."

Both kids stared at his outstretched hand suspiciously.

"Your momma's right outside and waitin' for you so we can all leave."

"Get the brats and let's go!" Cage yelled into the cabin. "Tick fuckin' tock."

Whip grabbed the youngest kid and pulled him from his brother's arms. He picked up the crying boy and told him to hang on. He turned back to the older brother. "Let's go, kid.

You don't gotta choice. You're comin' with us whether you wanna or not."

"My daddy's gonna kill you."

His daddy wasn't going to do shit besides soon be splattered matter. "Let's go, kid." He got a better grip on the boy he was carrying and put a hand on the older boy's back, nudging him toward the door. "We don't got time to waste."

"Where's my daddy?"

"Go outside."

"I don't like you," the kid yelled.

I don't fuckin' care, Whip answered in his head.

"You're mean."

"You're welcome to your opinion," Whip told the oldest boy. "Now, come with me."

"My daddy's gonna be real mad."

"I'm sure he will be. But he told me he'll be even more mad if you don't go with your momma."

The kid wiped his palms down the side of his homemade pants as he shifted from dirty bare foot to dirty bare foot, then he began to wring his hands together. "Like get the strap kinda mad?"

Oh fuck.

"Yeah, kid. He told me to tell you that you need to listen, yeah? Then no strap."

Without taking this boy away from the Guardians of Freedom he wouldn't have a great future, but Whip still felt like he was fucking with the poor kid's head by lying to him.

Even so, he had no choice because they needed to get moving five minutes ago.

He finally said, "Your momma's leavin' and your daddy already left. You wanna stay up here alone with the bears and coyotes? 'Cause I'm takin' your little brother with us. Stay or go. Don't care," Whip lied and left the cabin carrying the four-year-old.

Cage had the mother up on her feet with one hand on

her arm to keep her from running off. "Where's the other snot monkey?"

"Inside," Whip answered loud enough to be heard in the cabin. "He wants to live up here by himself. It won't be long 'til the coyotes come and eat him as a snack."

The kid appeared at the doorway, pulling boots on over his bare feet. "I'm goin' with my momma."

"Good choice, kid," Whip said. He turned to Cage. "What about..." He tipped his head toward the car. They were supposed to leave all male Shirleys in the buildings by dragging them inside or dropping them right there on the spot.

"Fuck it. Once this place goes, that cage is gonna go with it, takin' out anythin' around it. Plus, shit's gonna burn. It'll take a while for these woods to recover from that fire."

The whole side of the mountain going up in flames was a real possibility. Actually, more like a reality. What the explosives didn't take out, the fire would. At least until the surrounding area fire departments could respond to get it under control.

That wasn't his problem right now. Right now, he and Cage had to get the five of them to the van.

Still hauling the four-year-old on his hip, Whip took the gun Cage had on him as well as the one he himself had tucked in his waistband and went back into the cabin, hiding them in a cabinet. Now they'd only have their damn knives for protection.

He rushed back out and told the six-year-old, "Hold onto your momma's dress as my buddy helps her down the lane. It's gonna be dark and you could trip."

By the time they reached the main level of the compound, it looked like it had been cleared of anyone still breathing.

The Shadows were nowhere to be seen, of course. They

had warned that they would ghost as soon as the men were dealt with and prior to detonation.

Trip was waiting outside what looked like a packed van. Were he and Cage the last ones back? That couldn't be possible.

"Thought we were gonna have to send a search party for you," Trip called out as they approached.

Because of the six-year-old's short legs and also the mother being barefoot, they had moved much slower down the dirt lanes and paths than Whip wanted. He knew time was getting extremely tight, even though he hadn't had a chance to check the timer on his phone or for any texts. He needed both hands to carry the four-year-old so he didn't drop him in case Whip tripped or slid in mud or wet leaves. The boy might be on the small side but he got really fucking heavy, really quickly.

It didn't help that he was far from in shape, unlike the Shadows.

"How much time we got?" Cage called out, pulling the mother toward the van's open side door.

"Not much. We need to jet," Trip answered.

"We hitchin' a ride down the mountain in the van or we hoofin' it?" Cage asked.

Trip shook his head. "Not enough room in the van for all of us and we're still missin' Scar. He ain't back yet."

Whip frowned. "Thought he was with Bones."

"He was, but they got separated somehow."

Trip did not look happy about that fact. The teams were supposed to stick together.

Beside him, Cage asked Trip, "Where's Bones?"

"Already sent him down the mountain to grab our van and drive it up here. He's gonna pick us up so we can get the fuck out of here."

Whip glanced around. "Who else we missin'?"

"No one. Dutch and Sig already left with Red's brother

Ezrah and his two younger siblin's. Once they drop off the kids, they're headed over to Pete's."

The plan was to drop off Red's half-siblings with her and Saylor. The women were to be waiting in a vehicle behind Dutch's Garage. Whip had no idea what would happen with those kids from there, but he was sure it was all figured out.

"Where the fuck is that asshole?" Rook yelled, pacing next to the van.

"Texted him a few times already. No answer," Judge growled. "You sponsored him, he's your fuckin' responsibility."

"And I regret every fuckin' second of it," Rook growled back.

"He's supposed to be drivin' the van to Ohio with Castle," Trip said.

"If I gotta go find him, I'm droppin' him right where he stands," Rook threatened.

"Then you ain't findin' him." Trip shook his head. "For fuck's sake."

"We got all the women and children in the van?" Shade asked. "Anyone do a head count yet?"

"Supposed to be six women and thirteen kids," Judge reminded them.

Even in the dark, Whip could see the windows had been blacked out. Someone had come prepared. Most likely Easy had done it while he waited for the first of the "cargo" to arrive.

"Someone do a quick head count while we wait for the prospect. We gotta make sure all the women and children are accounted for before we head out, anyway," Trip said. "We ain't leavin' anyone still breathin' behind."

"I got it," Deacon yelled, moving to the other side of the van where the sliding door was still hanging open.

"Can't tell who's uglier, that Mercy guy or Scar. They'd be in a fuckin' run-off," Cage grumbled next to him.

"Wouldn't say that too loud, brother," Whip warned him. "You never know if he's hidin' in the shadows."

"Who? That dumb fuck Scar?"

"No, Mercy."

Cage's head swiveled around as he searched the area. "Shit."

"They're probably called Shadows for a reason," Whip warned him. "They lurk in the fuckin' shadows and you don't know what hit you 'til it's too late." He drew his finger over his throat in a slicing motion.

"Scar's much uglier," Cage said a little too loudly. "Much fuckin' uglier. That scar Mercy has is badass."

Whip smothered his snort. "You see your life flash before your eyes?"

"Saw my life *and* my fuckin' afterlife flash before my eyes."

Deacon came around the front of the van to where the rest of them had gathered. "Six women, nine kids."

"Supposed to be ten in the van," Judge informed his cousin.

"Counted the rug rats twice to be sure."

"Fuck," Trip muttered, scrubbing at his beard.

Deke shrugged. "Scar's probably bringin' down the last one."

"He better hurry the fuck up," Judge growled.

"If he didn't have one of the kids with him, I wouldn't give a fuck about leavin' him behind. He can take care of himself and knows the deal. 'Cause he might have one of the kids, I do. Jesus fuckin' Christ." Trip flipped off his baseball cap and ripped his fingers through his hair. "For fuckin' once, I'd like somethin' to go smoothly." He slapped his hat back on and squeezed the bill so tightly it creased.

The prez's agitation was building with every damn

second that passed. He could explode at any minute just like Hillbilly Hill.

"All right," he continued. "We need someone to go look for that asshole and report back. If we don't find him in the time we got left, then fuck it. He never shoulda separated from Bones in the first place."

"I'll do it," Judge muttered. "I'll take Deke with me."

"Fuck that," Trip said to his enforcer. "You got two kids and another on the way. Deke just had a baby. You two ain't goin' back up. It's too risky."

"The only two standin' here without an ol' lady or kids are Easy and Whip," Rev reminded them.

Great, another fucking reminder that he had nothing and no one. And, apparently, because of that he was dispensable.

"We're wastin' precious time here," Trip barked. "Easy and Whip, you willin'? Ain't gonna force you."

"I'll go," Whip volunteered. He already lost Fallon, what else did he have to lose?

In truth, Trip was right. Why risk someone who had an ol' lady or a family?

"Keep an eye on the time," Judge warned them. "Don't got much left. You don't find him in the next ten, then you bail and whatever happens, happens. He knew about the timeline like everyone else. He was supposed to stick with Bones, he didn't. Best you split up to cover as much ground as possible."

"In the meantime, we'll keep callin' and textin' him," Trip said. "Wherever he's at, he might not have coverage. If he responds or shows up, we'll call you to get your asses back down here."

"Ten minutes," Judge reminded him and E. "No more. Even that's gonna cut it too fuckin' close."

Whip nodded and glanced over at Easy, who was also nodding.

"Fuck it, let's do this," Whip muttered. "Text me if you find him. I'll do the same."

Easy nodded again as they set out.

At the far end of the clearing, they separated. They'd only have time to check a few places not far off the dirt lane, it was impossible to check them all. Whip took the left fork and jogged up the road, hoping like fuck he didn't twist a fucking ankle in a rut. Ten minutes wouldn't be enough time to hobble back down with a fucked-up ankle.

Just ahead was one of the larger cabins in the clan's compound and he could see a light on inside through one of the windows. Whip assumed the Shadows had already cleared it of any Shirley men.

Still, he approached with caution. The door was hanging wide open and as he carefully crept up the rotting wood steps he couldn't see or hear anything.

Unlike the crude cabin he and Cage entered earlier, this one had a bathroom inside instead of an outhouse, as well as a few rooms that could be bedrooms. It wasn't as big as the clan leader's house since it was only a single floor, but it was bigger than the majority of structures up there.

He saw a muddy boot peeking out from behind a dingy couch and he headed that way to make sure the body was a Shirley and not Scar.

It turned out to be more than one body. Two men were stacked on top of each other with eyes wide open, both bearded throats slashed, and dark blood pooling around the gray, lifeless bodies.

Whip took another quick glance around the interior. He didn't see any more bodies in the main portion of the cabin, but he'd check the bedrooms before moving on. With his knife in hand he quietly crossed through the messy kitchen and stopped at the entrance to a short hallway.

That was where he heard it.

A muffled, rhythmic sound. Maybe even something—or

someone—getting knocked around. What also might be a few deep grunts.

Did one of the Shirleys manage to take Scar as a hostage? Maybe the prospect was bound, gagged and struggling to free himself.

The clock was ticking in his head as he slowly approached the room where the noise was coming from. It could be a Shirley the Shadows left for dead but somehow managed to survive.

It could be the missing kid.

Or it could be that asshole Scar.

No matter who it was, he didn't want it to be his ass getting slingshotted to kingdom come when that clock ticked down to zero, so he needed to hurry.

He pressed his back next to the room's open door and quickly peered around the door frame. He jerked his head back and froze, trying to process what he saw.

What the fuck *did* he just see? There was no fucking way it was what he thought it was. That motherfucker wouldn't dare, would he?

Whip peeked around again.

Fuckin' motherfucker.

Just what he thought, Scar wasn't alone and he wasn't tied up. Or struggling.

But the person he was with was.

Whip stepped into the open doorway and saw Scar had his jeans pulled down just enough to…

Jesus fuckin' Christ!

Scar's hand was gripping the throat of a female, her face turning an ugly shade of purple at the lack of oxygen. Her mouth opening and closing in a struggle to breathe.

Was this the thirteenth *kid* they were looking for?

His chest tightened painfully and his stomach dropped.

It better not be.

It fucking better not be.

Scar had her pinned against the wall, her dress pulled up to her waist. Blood clung to the corner of her swollen bottom lip. Her left eye was twice the size it should be and starting to bloom into an ugly bruise. Tears streamed down her cheeks.

Fuck. Fuck. Fuck!

"What the fuck you d-doin'?" Whip screamed as he rushed over to them, yanking on the prospect's arm, trying to pull him off.

"She was fightin' me," the prospect growled, flinging off Whip's hand but not backing off from what he was doing to the girl.

"Fightin' you from t-takin' her or fightin' to k-keep you from fuckin' her?"

"Don't matter."

"Scar! That ain't the p-plan. You were s-s-" *god-fuckin'-damnit,* "supposed to take her to the van. Get the f-fuck off of her, now! Trip will f-fuckin' kill you for this."

Scar turned his attention back to the girl. "Teachin' this bitch a lesson. She clawed my fuckin' face."

"Don't give a fuck if she kneed you in the g-goddamn nuts. You ain't t-teachin' her a damn lesson. She ain't one of the women, she's a fuckin' k-kid, you sick f-fuck."

"Fuck off, you pussy. She ain't no kid. I'm treatin' her like they would. Old enough to bleed, old enough to breed. I wasn't the first, just gonna be the last."

Just gonna be the last?

"G-get off her right f-fuckin' now," he ordered, trying to pull the man free.

"Fuck off."

"You dis-disobeyin' my order?"

Scar finally twisted his head enough so Whip could see his sneer. "You d-don't got the f-fuckin' b-balls b-big enough to g-give orders. Or to stop me, you st-st-stutterin' bitch."

Scar was bigger than him. Not by much but the man

was a soulless killer. He wouldn't think twice about taking Whip out.

But Whip didn't care. The girl's eyes were on him, and he read the pain and pleading in them.

That made him lose his fucking shit. Totally fucking lose it. Enough to give him the strength to pull Scar off the girl and knock the prospect off his feet. The larger man stumbled back but caught himself.

Whip turned and met him head on with his feet spread apart for balance and prepared for a fight.

He never got the satisfaction of stealing his father's last breath from him, but he *would* get it by taking Scar's.

The prospect yanked up his jeans and, with a snarl, rushed him, his face full of fury, his hands clenched into fists. Whip braced for the impact.

It was like getting hit by a charging bull. Whip fell backwards, all the air rushing from his lungs as he hit the floor. Before he could take a breath, Scar was on him, his sledgehammer fists hitting Whip's face one after the other.

He didn't fight it, he let the man hit him. That allowed Scar to concentrate on striking him while Whip concentrated on what he needed to do... Pull his knife from the sheath where he had tucked it before pulling the prospect off the girl.

Whip's head was ringing, his jaw on fire, his vision getting dark around the edges and he swore stars were circling his head. But as soon as his fingers touched the hilt of his knife, he curled them tightly around it and pulled it free.

As Scar cocked his arm back for another powerful punch, Whip punched him first. Right in the throat with the blade.

The prospect's eyes widened and his raised fist dropped. His mouth opened but only a trickle of blood escaped. With all his weight behind it, Whip shoved him and Scar fell to the side, clawing at the embedded knife.

As soon as the prospect yanked it free, blood spurted from the hole in his neck like a fountain. Whip quickly twisted away from the ex-con since he didn't want that fucker's blood on him. He had enough of his own running from his mouth and nose.

He rolled enough to get to his knees. Once he did, he glanced over and was surprised the girl was still there.

She had slid to the floor and onto her ass, her knees pulled to her chest, her eyes squeezed shut and her hands covering her ears, taking him back for a second to his own nightmare.

Her dress had been pulled back into place but next to her on the ground was her shredded underwear.

Goddamn bastard.

He always had a feeling Scar wouldn't make it through his prospect period. Only Whip had no fucking clue how it would end.

Or that he would be the one to end it.

Rook would be pissed it wasn't him that took the bastard out.

But none of that shit mattered right now. They had to get clear of the cabin before it shot into orbit, taking them along with it.

He didn't have time to check the timer on his phone. He just had to fucking run as fast and as far as he could while taking the girl with him.

It seemed an impossible task.

Like Scar, he could very well die on Hillbilly Hill.

Without telling the people he loved that he loved them.

Like his mother.

Like…

Fallon.

Fuck.

He surged to his feet and, as soon as the vertigo slowed, he approached the girl. "We gotta go! Now!" He grabbed her arm to help her up but she flinched, cried out and tried to jerk free. "We don't got time for this shit. This place is gonna blow at any minute."

He didn't have time to reassure her that she'd be okay.

He didn't have time to get her to trust him.

He didn't have time to explain.

He didn't have time.

They didn't have time.

They needed to move.

Now.

He pulled her to her feet. "There's a van waitin' on us. It's goin' to Ohio where you're all gettin' dropped off." Thank fuck his stutter was gone. He didn't have time for that, either.

But instead of walking, she pulled back, using her free hand to swipe the tears off her cheek. "I don't want to go there. Please don't make me go there." Her plea was thick with tears and as soon as she wiped one away, another escaped and rolled down her face.

"What are you talkin' about? You ain't a Shirley?"

She shook her head.

For fuck's sake, they didn't have time for this conversation. "You ain't part of the G-Guardians of Freedom?"

Damn it, he thought it was gone. He needed to calm the fuck down.

"No! I've been trying to get free. I don't belong with them," she pleaded, her voice raspy, most likely from Scar crushing her windpipe.

What the fuck? "Where's your family?"

As he waited for her answer, he quickly texted Easy: *Found Scar. Head back.*

"I... I..."

"Fuck this. We'll figure it out later." He shoved his phone

back into his back pocket, still not checking the countdown timer. He didn't want to go into panic mode. He needed to concentrate. "We need to go. This cabin's wired to explode."

Her red-rimmed eyes widened and she finally stopped resisting. He pulled her along as he ran out of the cabin and outside.

He decided to take a shortcut that might shave off some time and put more distance more quickly between them and the cabin. Ducking and weaving, he dragged her through the woods until they made it out farther down the dirt lane. He knew the lane had deep ruts and holes and he could easily break a fucking leg if he took a misstep.

The hair on the back of his neck stood as an imaginary timer ticked in his head. His lungs were on fire and his face throbbing. The faster his heart pumped, the faster the blood trickled down his face.

He ignored all that as he dragged the girl down the lane, both of them almost eating dirt several times. But not once did he slow down.

"F-faster!" he yelled.

At this point if he fell, he was just going to keep rolling forward. Because no matter what, he couldn't stop.

If he did, they were dead.

Then he heard it.

The first blast.

And what was the beginning of the end.

Chapter Twenty-One

THE SECOND BLAST, even though not close, was powerful enough to throw him forward and to his knees. Then debris began falling around them like a hail storm. Only some of the hail was on fire.

Christ, if the explosives didn't kill them, the raining hellfire might.

He covered his head with one arm and yanked the girl to her feet with the other.

"Jesus fuck, that only s-sounded like one or two. We g-gotta get the hell outta here."

The detonations must be timed to start at the top of the mountain and work their way down, giving them extra time to escape.

Thank fucking fuck for that. That was the only thing that might save Whip's ass.

He realized at that very second those Shadows were worth every damn penny. Even the last tarnished one they had to dig out from under a couch cushion.

With a hiccup-sob, the nameless teenager fisted her long dress and pulled it up enough so she could sprint alongside him.

For fuck's sake, he wanted to kill that motherfucking prospect all over again.

Former prospect.

Dead prospect.

Hell, he didn't even deserve to be called a prospect anymore. He'd been a shit stain on the Fury.

A third blast came northeast of the direction they were running. The ground fucking shook on that one, too. He wondered if it was the two cabins he and Cage had been assigned.

Then he saw it. Just ahead.

The main compound. When that blew, it would be a major hit to the mountain. Most likely only leaving deep craters behind.

That clearing had the largest and the most number of structures, especially with the barn and the main house and all the smaller outbuildings. Including what was left of the shack that Red had been kept in like breeding livestock.

Fuckers.

Was that the van? Was it still there, waiting?

No, that wasn't the Shirley van, it was the new crematorium van. The one they used when they needed to go incognito.

"Get the fuck in this van now!" Trip shouted, standing next to the open passenger door.

He yanked on the girl's hand, since he still had a firm grip on it, and continued to run. Thank fuck she realized how much danger they were in and didn't fight his forward motion.

Another distant blast shook the ground under their moving feet.

"Where the fuck is Scar?" Trip asked as he jumped into the passenger seat.

"We don't got time for this. Let's get the fuck outta here!" Judge yelled out the driver's side window.

"Hurry up and get her in the van," Trip ordered.

Whip pulled her around to the open side door. Since their van didn't have seats in the rear like the Shirleys', some of his brothers were sitting on the floor in the back.

From the interior, Shade reached out and grabbed the girl's arm, helping her inside.

"Dead," Whip answered as he climbed in, gulping down air, his lungs searing, his heart pounding a hole through his chest. Even though his muscles were cramping, he managed to drag himself inside the van without assistance.

"What the fuck you talkin' about?" Judge asked, throwing the shifter into drive and stomping on the accelerator.

Dirt and stones kicked out from the rear wheels and Shade slammed the side door shut as Judge barreled down the rutted lane.

Whip raised a finger and shook his head, trying to catch his breath enough to speak easier and make sure he didn't stutter. But before he could talk or get settled on the floor, Judge hit a hole so large, he was thrown across the van into Rev, who caught him. They both muttered a "Fuck!"

"A Shirley took him out? How?" Judge asked, glancing at him from the rearview mirror, not giving a fuck that Whip almost slammed his head into the side of the van.

Once he planted his ass on the floor, he held on as the van continued to bounce down the lane. He wouldn't be surprised if they broke a damn axle. But if they did, they were screwed.

"What the fuck happened to your face?" Easy asked, staring at him. "It wasn't like that when you went lookin' for the prospect."

Whip considered lying but what was the point? Scar was dead, he did it and he might as well own up to it. He swallowed and concentrated on his answer, hoping like fuck his stutter was finally gone. "The prospect happened."

Trip spun around in the passenger seat. "Scar did that to you?"

"That and more." What he wasn't going to say right now in that van full of men was that Scar raped the girl. An underaged girl.

She'd already been through enough.

"Why the fuck would that motherfucker do that to you?" Rook asked. "He's done."

Whip shot Rook a loaded look, since he must have missed the part when Whip said the prospect was dead. "He's done."

Rook's eyebrows rose. "You took him out?"

Whip nodded.

Shade's dark eyes sliced from him to the girl and back. His nostrils flared but he said nothing.

The man knew. Shade could pick up on shit others couldn't. The man's jaw shifted and he gave Whip a slight nod. A silent way to let Whip know he had done the right thing.

Another blast rocked the van and Judge slammed on the brakes, almost throwing everyone in the back toward the front seats.

Suddenly the sliding side door was flung open by someone outside the van. Cage appeared. "You find number thirteen?"

"Yeah, she's in here," Trip told him. "Load her up so we can get the fuck outta here before the main compound blows. That's gonna be so fuckin' big it'll be heard and seen in New York. We need to be long gone before then. If not, we might not be goin' anywhere except for wherever our pieces land."

"All right," Cage said, leaning inside the cargo area and locating the girl. "Let's go. The rest of your clan's waitin' for you."

The girl grabbed Whip's arm tightly. "I don't want to go

with them," she said in a shaky whisper, her short nails digging painfully into his skin. He could also hear the panic in her words. "Please don't make me go with them."

"Get her in the van," Trip ordered as he hopped out of the passenger seat. He appeared at the side door.

Whip stared at the girl's pale face. Bloodless except for the bruises. No surprise she was scared as fuck, and she couldn't be more than fourteen or fifteen. Scar's actions would leave a lifetime scar of her own.

And who knew what the inbred goat fuckers had already done to her in their effort to increase their numbers.

Worse, here she was surrounded by a bunch of strange men who held her future in their hands.

Christ.

He wouldn't blame her if she hated or distrusted men for the rest of her life. Someone had to step up and protect her, to be on her side. "She ain't goin' with them."

Trip's eyebrows shot up in surprise. "Why the fuck not?"

"Red," he answered.

"What the fuck d'you mean Red?" Trip asked, his brow pulled low.

"Think they got her as a breeder."

"Fuck," Trip muttered. He poked his head into the van. "We don't got time for this. You a Shirley?"

Her hand squeezed Whip's forearm even tighter as she shook her head.

"You related to the Shirleys?"

She shook her head again.

"Were you bein' held against your will?"

She nodded, more silent tears rolling down her face.

"Your family know you're here?"

She shook her head again.

"You got anyone lookin' for you? Family? Someone?"

"We don't got time for this, Trip," Judge warned sharply

as the van shook violently again from another blast. The detonations were getting closer.

Another huge blast immediately followed and it was so strong that Trip had to hang onto the van to remain on his feet.

When debris started raining down on the van, Trip ducked and covered his head. "Fuck! Gave this kinda shit up when I left the fuckin' Marines!"

"We gotta go," Judge urged. "Prez, get back in the van. Cage, go with Castle and tell him to follow us down the road a bit. We'll regroup there where the fiery depths of hell ain't rainin' down on us."

Trip slammed the side door shut and jumped back into the passenger seat. "I'm sure the pigs are gettin' plenty of calls by now, so head in the opposite direction of the farm. Pull into one of the fields off County Line Road."

With a nod, Judge hit the gas and the van shot forward.

Whip couldn't see shit since the back of the crematorium van didn't have windows. But within five minutes, he could feel it go off road and Judge turned off the lights as soon as it did. Within a few more feet, he stopped, shoved the shifter into Park and shut off the engine.

Easy opened the side door from the inside and they all climbed out between the two vans to regroup and take a fucking breath.

"Change of plan, Castle," Trip told the prospect. "Bones is goin' with you instead of Scar."

"Not a problem, prez." Castle nodded. "We'll get the job done." He glanced around. "Where is Scar?"

"Not here," was Trip's abrupt answer.

Castle didn't question that like the valuable prospect he was. "Want us to head out now?"

"In a minute, I gotta address the occupants first and then you can go. Like we said, no stoppin'. Drive the speed limit. Don't draw attention to yourselves. You get stopped, you're fucked. You got six women restrained in there. And let's not mention transportin' kids across the state line."

Federal offenses right there. Castle and Bones might not see the light of day ever again if they got caught. But they couldn't say no to the job, not if they wanted to remain prospects.

"What about the missin' kid?"

"We got her and we're gonna deal with her. She don't belong with them."

Once again, Castle didn't question his president. They needed more prospects like him and less like Scar.

They thought Scar would be an asset. He turned out to be a liability. A hard lesson to learn, but one that wouldn't be forgotten any time soon.

Trip opened the side door of the clan's van and leaned in. His voice was loud, clear and left no room for negotiation as he addressed the six gagged and bound women. "Pay careful attention... None of what I'm gonna say's a sugges-tion. It's a fuckin' warnin' you best heed. You come back here, we'll hit that mountain again and not save any of you or your kids. You got me? You tell your leaders we'll not only take out that mountain again, we'll start hittin' every branch of the Guardians of Freedom. So, you tell whoever is the Grand Poohbah of your little cult that Pennsylvania's now and forever off limits. Without exceptions. This state's closed to the Shirleys and any member of the Guardians of Freedom. If I even get the slightest whiff that any of you stepped over the Pennsylvania border, we're comin' for you all with no mercy. *All* of you. Not just the men. Every fuckin' one of you and the offspring you produced. You're all headed to the compound in Ohio. Don't care where the fuck you go from there, just not back here. Nod if you understand."

Silence surrounded them for a few moments.

357

"They nod?" Whip impatiently asked Shade, who stood in a spot where he could see inside the van.

"Yeah," he murmured.

Trip slammed the door shut as two back-to-back blasts came from the direction of the mountain formerly known as Hillbilly Hill.

Whip glanced in that direction and saw a red glow lighting up the night sky. What might be first thought of as clouds were actually billows of smoke. The fire had started. What the explosives didn't destroy, the fire would.

Once the smoke cleared, this shit with the Shirleys would finally be over.

For fucking good.

He only hoped to fuck that was true.

———

MORE EXPLOSIONS ROCKED the van as they sped through town and back to the crematorium where most of them had parked their sleds near the loading dock.

The street lights were flickering and every type of alarm system—car, business and home—was going off. Judge stuck to the side streets and stayed off Main Street to avoid being spotted.

Main Street was busy with emergency responders, anyway.

Just as Judge turned the van into Tioga Pet Services, it happened.

Like the finale at a fireworks show, but on major steroids.

Powerful booms came in quick succession and the ground actually rocked and rolled under the van as he pulled it around back and parked it.

"Jesus Christ," Judge grumbled, jerking on his long, bushy beard. "And that right there is why this club's now fuckin' broke."

"Had to be the big house, the barn and all the outbuildin's on the main level," Shade said. "That should be the last of them."

Sitting next to Whip, Cage said, "Worth every damn penny."

"Sure as fuck hope so," Dodge said. "Otherwise, we spent all of that for fuckin' nothin'."

Ozzy was the first to climb out of the van. "Gonna head back to the motel and check on shit before I head over to Pete's."

"Yeah, good idea to stagger our arrivals like Mercy said," Trip told him. "I'm gonna guess Sig and Dutch are already there."

The Original disappeared and his 883's exhaust could barely be heard over the sirens and alarms going off through town. Including the pet crematorium's.

Shade climbed out next. "Gonna go home and check on the kids before headin' over."

"Red and Saylor should be there by now with the three little ones. If not, you get ahold of me or Judge right away. Dutch and Sig were supposed to accompany them and then head directly over to Pete's."

Shade nodded in answer to Trip and disappeared into the dark.

Everyone else took their time climbing out of the van, talking amongst themselves about who was heading over to Pete's next.

"You can go in pairs," Judge told them. "That ain't gonna be a problem. Let's just all get there ASAP." He turned to Whip. "'Cept you. Need you to clean up your damn face before showin' it anywhere. You look like you ran into a fuckin' brick wall."

He didn't doubt it looked as bad as it felt. His face throbbed with every damn heartbeat, he was forced to breathe from his mouth and he needed to rinse out the metallic taste of his own blood. He was just thankful as fuck his jaw wasn't broken or dislocated.

"Got the keys for the crematorium. You can clean up in there while I shut that fuckin' alarm off," Easy offered, pulling the keys from his front pocket and waving them in the air. "Also got a spare shirt inside you can change into. It's got the business name on it, but fuck it, better than nothin'."

Whip glanced down. No surprise his shirt was stained with his own blood.

"We're forgettin' one thing." Whip tipped his head toward the van.

All eyes turned that way.

"Fuck," Deacon muttered. "What are we gonna do with her?"

"Trip…" Whip murmured, not really wanting to go into details at that moment but a warning needed to be given.

Trip blew out a breath. "Yeah, don't gotta say it. Figured you had a good reason to take that motherfucker out. We fucked up. This is on us." He pulled his baseball cap off and whipped it out into the dark parking lot in frustration. "What happened to her is on us."

"We don't know what the Shirleys did before—" Rev started.

The prez cut him off. "Don't fuckin' matter what those assholes did. We know their intent. The problem is we made it fuckin' worse by turnin' that goddamn psycho loose up there."

"You couldn't have known," Deke assured him. "No one expected him to do somethin' like that."

"We should've known," Trip said in a tone that told everyone not to bother arguing with him. "We couldn't control what the Shirleys did but we should've been able to control one of our own. It's on us."

"It's on me," Rook corrected him. "I brought him in. I fuckin' sponsored him. I fucked up."

"The committee had to approve him and we did. Ain't all on you," Judge said. "It's on all of us. We knew he was bad, but hoped he'd be an asset. Turns out he wasn't."

"We gave him too many chances," Rook said. "One too fuckin' many."

"Nobody's gonna disagree with that fuckin' fact. But now what? What do we do with her?" Trip asked.

Dodge spoke up. "Why don't we get through what's currently going on and afterward we can figure it out. Ain't nothin' gonna be done tonight. We just gotta cover our asses for the next day or so. Once we're on the other side of this, we can help her. Whether that's findin' her family or whatever needs to be done. But think it's smart to keep her hidden 'til then." He turned to Whip. "She got family?"

Whip shrugged. "Don't know. Didn't have a shitload of time to get too many details."

Dodge nodded. "Why don't we take her over to Pete's, let her clean up and rest upstairs 'til the party's over."

"And then what?" Rev asked.

The bar manager shrugged. "Don't know. But at least it'll give us a little time to get more answers from her and think about our next step."

"We could drop her off at the pig pen," Rook suggested. "Have Jet drop her off with some kind of story."

Judge snorted. "Yeah, right. We take her to five-o, or whoever, questions are gonna be asked. Lots of them. And all of those fuckin' answers will lead back to us bein' the cause for what happened up on that fuckin' mountain. She's a witness to everythin' that happened up there, too. Includin' what Whip did to Scar. She saw almost every one of our faces."

In the silent pause, a soft but shaky voice came from the van. "I won't say anything. I promise."

They all stared at her perched in the open van door,

unsure if she was telling the truth or only telling them what they'd want to hear.

"You got family lookin' for you?" Trip asked the girl.

She shook her head and gave the same answer as earlier. "No."

Whip didn't know if that was good or bad. Or even a lie. But what the fuck were they going to do with her?

Easy knocked his arm. "Let Judge and Trip figure it out. Ain't on us. Let's head in and get you cleaned up. Don't need the pigs showin' up here for whatever reason and seein' your face. Questions will be asked since it's fresh."

"Yeah," he breathed, mentally and physically drained.

He wanted to know the girl's story but E was right. It was best they weren't all standing outside in a group, even if it was behind the building. People were nosy in that town, plus, with the explosions, they'd all be on edge.

By the time he and Easy rolled into Pete's, the girl was already upstairs in the apartment with Stella and Chelle.

It turns out the girl's name was Gabrielle and she was only fourteen.

Fucking fourteen! Practically still a baby.

It also turned out she was not a virgin before Scar assaulted her but she had been before the Shirley clan took her from a group home in upstate New York where she'd been living.

Whether it was true or not, she kept insisting she had nothing and no one.

That was the word Whip got when he and Easy were the last to arrive at his own "birthday party."

He was sure he'd hear more about her later once things settled down.

Whip kept kicking himself for not finding Scar sooner. He also hoped Gabrielle, or Gabi as she preferred, wasn't already pregnant by one of the Shirleys. He had no idea when they had taken her. She could've been their captive for days, months or even years.

As he glanced around a packed Pete's, it wasn't only full of Fury members and their ol' ladies, it also included all the sweet butts, as well as Pete's regulars who were invited to stay and drink on the house.

Because of that, it was packed as fuck and pretty much standing room only between the free drinks and Syn's band, The Synners, rocking out on stage. The whole bar was overdone with birthday decorations, the sweet butts and ol' ladies had arranged for tons of food to be set out like a buffet and the Fury members weren't to stay in one spot too long but to keep moving through the crowd so more people saw them at the party.

The only Fury family missing were Red and Saylor since they were staying with Red's siblings at Shade and Chelle's until the sham "party" was over.

Wait… He hadn't seen one other person. Jet.

Whip moved over to Rook busy pounding down a beer at the bar. "You seen your woman, yet?"

Rook finished swallowing and before he could speak, Dozer set a full pint glass in front of Whip.

He'd need more than a beer tonight. As soon as enough people saw him at the party, he was going to step out back, light a joint and get lit himself. Maybe it would get rid of the nauseous feeling he couldn't shake.

He winced when the glass pressed against his swollen and split lip, but the cold beer went down smoothly. It would hopefully dull the pain soon enough and maybe settle his stomach.

"Nope," Rook finally answered after emptying his glass and slamming it on the bar. He belched loudly, wiped his hand across his mouth and waved Dozer back over to get him another. "But she texted me and said she should be here any fuckin' minute."

"Guess she stayed long enough at the pig pen to get a good read on what their response was."

"She already said as soon as they heard the first blast the pigs were scramblin' and the head oinker was callin' everyone in, along with getting ahold of the staties."

"You fuckin' call Max that to his face?"

Rook smirked. "Yeah, why not? The fucker *accidentally* calls me Crook."

Whip snorted and instantly regretted it as pain shot through his busted-up face. "Bet that makes for a fun family gatherin'."

"Try to avoid them, but when I can't, by the end of the night they usually regret invitin' me. Eventually they'll stop."

Whip shook his head and carefully took another sip of beer.

Rook rapped on the bar with his knuckles. "Won't they shit a fuckin' brick when I recruit those Bryson boys into the Fury instead of them goin' into the pig academy. Time to break that cycle."

"That'll never happen."

Rook's eyebrows shot up. "Gonna do my best."

"You do that, you're gonna make Jet's family our enemy."

"Ain't gonna cry about that. Are you?"

"No, but Trip might make you cry about it. You know he's tryin' to stay off their radar and remain civil with them."

"Yeah, well, the second I stole Jet from them, we landed on their radar."

His ol' lady would probably disagree that Rook "stole" her from anyone. She was a strong woman who made her own decisions. And not necessarily ones Rook approved of.

"You're single-handedly tryin' to undo the good that was done by allowin' them to adopt Levi." Whip took a another sip of beer.

"Nah, they know they're fuckin' lucky they got that kid."

Whip sighed.

Out of nowhere, Jet was standing behind them, surprising the shit out of Whip. He was off his game, for sure.

"You better have a cold beer ready for me."

As soon as Dozer brought Rook's next beer, her ol' man turned and offered it to her.

She took it and gulped down half of it. When she finished she didn't let out an obnoxious belch like her ol' man, but instead released a weary sigh. After wedging herself between Whip and Rook, she dropped her voice down so no one else nearby could overhear her. "There's practically an army headed up there going code three." She looked at her ol' man. "I don't like being a part of this, Rook."

His jaw tensed and he growled, "Already heard you every other fuckin' time you said that. They didn't leave us any fuckin' choice. Think we wanted to spend this kind of scratch to end this fuckin' shit? Think I wanted to get you involved? You knew what the fuck you were gettin' into when you decided to be with me. You walked away from the job and into this life with your eyes fuckin' wide open."

Oh fuck. This whole plan must have been an issue in their household. Especially with giving Jet the task of spying on her own family.

They both turned until they faced each other with only a couple of inches separating them. Their expressions were stone hard as they stared at each other. Whip didn't like being in the middle of their fight, or whatever was happening.

Now was probably not the best time or place for this type of disagreement, anyway. This party was supposed to be their alibi, not the reason they got busted.

After a few tense moments, Jet whispered harshly, "I don't like lying to my family."

"You ain't lyin'. You just ain't bein' a snitch. If they out and out ask you if the Fury was to blame, then when you say no, which is the only right answer, that might be considered a lie."

"*Might?*" she hissed.

Whip waded in, hoping to end this before anyone overheard them. "Depends how they ask it. She can honestly say none of us set off those explosives since the Shadows did."

"Semantics," Jet muttered. "I still don't like it."

"I don't like worryin' about my fuckin' niece every damn day, either. Neither does my pop or my brother. You'd do whatever you gotta do to protect your family, we're doin' the same. You're part of this family as much as that one. Don't forget that."

Whip understood Jet's gripe. Being with Rook forced her to straddle a questionable line. The Fury on one side, her pig family on the other. However, for pigs the Brysons were actually decent people. They didn't harass the Fury unlike when the Originals were wreaking havoc. Rook also needed to remember the Brysons were customers at the garage. Good ones. His father would be pissed if Rook chased away both their personal business and the fleet business the PD gave them.

"Unless you made a fuckin' mistake and are changin' your mind? That what you're doin', Jet? Havin' second fuckin' thoughts? Those fuckin' regrets I warned you about?"

Whip could tell by Rook's tone alone he was starting to come undone. Tonight had been hard on them all. They were all exhausted and on edge. And it wouldn't take much to send any of them over.

But Whip knew there was absolutely no way the man

wanted to lose Jet. It would drop the man to his fucking knees and he might never get back up.

"Yo," Whip said as quietly as possible. "This ain't the time or the place, you get me?" He moved his head in a circle, indicating the packed bar. "It ain't a secret how you two work shit out. So, brother, since you've already been seen here havin' a beer, why don't you two go and do what you gotta do to fix this? I'll cover for you if Trip has a fit."

Rook and Jet stared at each other for a few more tense seconds, then Rook grabbed her arm and pulled her away from the bar. Whip watched them disappear through the crowd toward the back door where most of them had parked their sleds.

Whip wouldn't doubt if they all heard another explosion from the direction of the farm within the next twenty minutes.

The pressure that had been clawing at Whip's throat during Rook and Jet's exchange quickly disappeared. He grabbed his beer and decided to make his rounds since this was supposed to be a celebration of him becoming another fucking year older.

Happy fuckin' birthday to me.

He hoped to fuck he never had another birthday like this one again.

Chapter Twenty-Two

WHIP ROLLED over and with a muttered curse, punched his pillow into a different shape, hoping that would help him sleep.

He doubted it would. His face still hurt, his muscles were sore, and his brain was still full of swirling shit he couldn't scrape free. From the moment Fallon rode away from him on her Scout... to the disagreement between Rook and Jet at Pete's... to the knife sticking out of Scar's throat and the man's surprised face.

Surprised because the fucker hadn't expected Whip to have the balls to do it.

He'd killed before. Only not someone he'd actually known.

Not someone he'd had conversations with. Shared a beer and a meal with. Shared his club colors with.

Earlier this afternoon the club went on a run—one not on the schedule—so it looked like nothing was out of the ordinary. They stayed away from the mountain, even though they were all curious about what was left.

But it was all over the news with some footage from

overhead helicopters showing a view from above of what was left of the charred, scarred and still smoking terrain.

They didn't have to watch TV to see the area was crawling with feds, including the ATF, and local and state pigs. Not to mention, a shitload of news vans. It was obvious the second the formation pulled out of the farm and onto County Line Road.

A bunch of fire departments from the surrounding areas would also be up there for the next few days—if not the next week or so—putting out the hot spots and monitoring the situation.

One more thing he couldn't shake from his melon was the conversation Whip had with Shay Saturday night at Pete's. Ozzy's ol' lady had gotten close with Fallon during the time she was in town and they had actually become friends.

Whip wondered if Shay had heard from her but didn't want to ask. At minimum, he'd like to know if she was okay. On the other hand, he also didn't want to know that answer. That she was doing okay without him.

Because he wasn't doing okay without her.

He'd eventually get over it. But, *fuck him*, it wouldn't be any time soon.

While the shit with the Shirleys had occupied his brain for the past few days, now that was over—and he sure as fuck hoped it really *was* over—Fallon was front and center in his thoughts.

For a fleeting moment earlier, he'd thought about hooking up with one of the sweet butts—maybe even asking Billie—to try to wipe Fallon from his mind. But he couldn't.

He fucking couldn't.

He didn't want anyone else but Fallon.

And that was a problem.

"What happened with Fallon? Why didn't she stick around until after tonight?" Shay had asked him when she cornered him alone later in the night. It was after The Synners had finished their last set—and was finally able to relax and enjoy the party—and Pete's crowd had thinned out to mostly the Fury. "She told me she planned on staying until after your birthday."

"Birthday was Thursday."

"And she left Wednesday night."

That she did. "You didn't talk to her before she left?" *You didn't talk to her since she left?* was what he was dying to ask.

"No. She dropped off your stuff in the office while Maddie was filling in at the front desk. She never said goodbye."

Shay actually sounded hurt. Unfortunately, that wound was all his fucking fault. "Sorry."

"Why would you be sorry?"

"'Cause I know you two got close in the last few weeks."

Shay's head tilted as she stared at him as if trying to see deep into his soul. Her dark brown eyes softened. "She was great. It was nice to hang out with someone close to my age. She was smart and funny, and we had some great conversations. It didn't make sense she would simply up and leave without at least saying goodbye."

Whip closed his eyes and waited until the pain radiating from his heart and spiraling through his chest passed. "Don't take it personal. Wasn't you, Shay."

"No, it was you."

He opened his eyes. He should walk away right now. Avoid this conversation completely. But he didn't because he wanted to punish himself.

He deserved it.

He should go back to The Barn, grab The Punisher and get Judge to use it on him.

Get the enforcer to break him completely.

Then once he healed, maybe he could move on. Or at least go back to the way things were before he came across a disabled sled with a stranded rider on Copperhead Road.

"Women just don't up and leave like that without a word unless there's a reason, Whip. So, what did you do?" The tone of her question wasn't sharp, but deceivingly soft, which made dealing with her accusation even harder.

"Fucked up."

"That's a given. On purpose or by accident?"

Shay was ten years older and much wiser than him. She was strong without being loud. She was observant without being directly in someone's face. So damn opposite of Ozzy.

Just like Fallon and Whip were complete opposites, too.

Shay and Ozzy were two halves that shouldn't fit together at all, but managed to fit perfectly. Their personalities complemented each other.

He couldn't imagine they'd ever have a disagreement in public like Jet and Rook did earlier. Those two were more like two matchsticks being struck together and igniting.

Jet and Rook were thunder and lightning, while Shay and Ozzy had the push and pull of a tide. "On purpose."

"To chase her away." Shay didn't make that a question because she was smart enough to know that was the answer.

"Yeah."

"Why?"

She was still going to make him explain it. "For the reason we're all gatherin' at Pete's tonight," he answered truthfully.

"For your birthday? Because you think you're too young for her?"

"No." He shook his head. "Not that."

"Because you don't want her to know the truth about the Fury," she concluded.

"That…"

"And?" she prodded.

"Wanted to keep her clear of this mess. Wanted to

protect her. Didn't want any of this shit splashin' back on her. You all chose this life, bein' an ol' lady and bein' a part of the sisterhood, and what goes along with it. She didn't."

Nodding, Shay tucked a long strand of her dark brown hair behind her ear. "That's understandable. However, she's mature and self-aware enough to make her own decisions about it."

"If I'd been truthful, the outcome woulda been the same."

"Even if it was, you should've let her decide that."

You should've let her decide that.

Since they were lobbing truth bombs... "Oz don't deserve you, Shay."

"You know, he tells me that every morning and every morning I tell him he's wrong." Shay smiled up at him. "We don't choose our soulmates, Whip, they're chosen for us. Usually for a reason. The second we meet them we just know in here." She pressed her hand against his chest over his heart. "We recognize who they are but we need to open our eyes to see it. To see them faults and all. That doesn't mean it'll come easy. But, if you let it, it'll come."

Whip growled at that memory from Saturday night and punched the pillow one more time before giving up. He flipped over, sat up, leaned back against the wall and reached for his tin on the folding table next to his bed. Grabbing his cell phone, he used it as a flashlight to dig out a joint and locate his Bic.

Once lit, he took two long drags, hoping the Kush would clear his brain and help him fall asleep.

Or at least take the edge off.

Tonight after the run, everyone had gathered in The Barn, but it wasn't rowdy, or even fun, like normal. It had been subdued since nobody had been in the partying mood and everyone had been uneasy. But hanging together was a way for the brotherhood to stay connected as they waited.

Unfortunately, what they waited for was the feds and law enforcement to bust down the doors and drag them out in handcuffs.

It didn't happen yet, but that didn't mean it still couldn't.

An extensive investigation would begin—if it hadn't already—once the hot spots from the fire were dealt with and the ATF went over the clan's compound with a fine-tooth comb, gathering evidence.

Once they took statements and did interviews.

Once Manning Grove PD and the state police's fire marshal put out feelers, poked and sniffed around.

Until they found enough answers to satisfy them.

So really, it wasn't over.

It wouldn't be over until the investigation was closed. Or it went cold.

None of them were truly safe until then.

Including Fallon.

Being involved with him could take her down with the rest of them.

But maybe once that last *I* was dotted and the last *T* was crossed in the investigation…

Maybe…

Just maybe…

Or maybe by then it would be too late and their chance to be together had passed.

But what if he didn't let it?

What if he reached out to fix that connection? Even if it was only held together by a thread. A thin line of communication kept open for the future.

Something was better than nothing, right? That was Trip's personal motto.

One day when she was done traveling the world, when she was tired of being alone, when she was ready to settle in one spot…

She might come back to him. Forgive him for pushing her away.

And understand why he did it.

He just didn't want to lose her to someone else in the meantime.

To lose that chance.

To snap that thin thread so nothing remained to tug on, to encourage her to return to him.

When he was finished smoking, he licked his fingertips and pinched out the end of the joint before tucking it back into his tin. Then he leaned his head back against the wall and stared at nothing but darkness.

The bunkhouse was quiet and that made the voices in his head deafening.

The one urging him to call her. To reach out. To do whatever he had to to get her back.

The other voice telling him not to do it. Warning him that it wasn't smart. Telling him to be patient and wait to see how things shook out with what happened Saturday night. Once he knew the club was in the clear, he could make an effort to fix what he fucked up.

That would be the right and smart way to do it.

"Yep. Sure fuckin' would," he answered himself as he reached for his damn phone anyway.

He closed his eyes and pressed the top edge of his cell phone against his forehead, blowing out a breath.

It's late and she's probably asleep. Don't fuckin' do it, dumbass.

She probably don't wanna talk to you. Don't fuckin' do it, dumbass.

Don't fuckin' do it, dumbass.

He sighed. Of course he was going to be a dumbass.

He scrolled through his contacts, found her name and hit Send.

One ring.

Go to voicemail.

Two rings.

Go to voicemail.

Three rings.

Go to—

"Hello?" Her question was scratchy and a bit sluggish since he probably woke her.

He closed his eyes again at hearing her voice in his ear and his heart began to thump a little faster.

He had so much to say.

He said nothing.

He wanted to explain.

He gave her nothing.

The silence stretched across what he assumed were hundreds of miles between them.

If he didn't say anything maybe she'd hang up.

"I know it's you, Whip. Your number's programmed into my phone, remember?"

The fact she hadn't deleted it gave him some hope.

But only a very thin sliver.

WHY WASN'T he saying anything? Did he butt dial her or accidentally hit the wrong button? She should simply hang up.

Truthfully, she shouldn't have answered in the first place. But she was weak and her heart had won out over her head.

"Whip, I'm hanging up if you don't say anything. *You* called *me*. There had to be a reason for it."

More silence.

"I'm hanging up," she warned again.

"Don't."

His voice.

God, it made her heart ache with how much she missed him.

It made her heart break for a man she'd only known three weeks.

The first man who ever called her "babe" without it coming off like an insult. The first time in her life she ever welcomed that kind of endearment.

"Didn't mean to wake you."

"You didn't." After she'd turned off the eleven o'clock news, she hadn't been able to sleep. Ever since she'd first heard the reports this morning, she had actually reached for her phone several times throughout the day to call him.

To ask him if he was okay. If everyone in his club was all right.

What had happened in a quaint, normally quiet town called Manning Grove in northern Pennsylvania had hit the national news.

The news anchors talked about the death and destruction. The footage showed some of it. It had been both heart stopping and heartbreaking.

So, yes, she was more than relieved to hear his voice. To know he was alive and hopefully not injured in any way.

But she hadn't forgiven him.

Not because of what he said but because what he said had been a lie.

"That's the problem, Fallon, you think too much. You're too goddamn independent. In my world to be an ol' lady you'd be my property. That means when I tell you I don't want you goin' somewhere you'd listen. When you don't listen, you make me look weak and less than a fuckin' man. I can't fuckin' have that. I'd lose all goddamn respect from my brothers."

She'd heard plenty of lies in her thirty-six years. Too many to count, really. Some worse than others.

But for some reason, coming from Whip... That lie... It more than hurt. It more than disappointed. It left a mark.

At the time she didn't know why those words devastated her more than others.

Now she knew.

Somewhere within those three weeks she had fallen in love with the man. It had snuck up on her so unexpectedly that she couldn't protect her heart before he stole it.

He stole it, probably not even aware of it.

He stole it, then held it in his hand and crushed it within fingers.

He stole it and, *goddamn it*, he *still* held it captive.

It belonged to him now.

A man who was a mechanic and biker living a lifestyle so unlike what she had ever lived, from what she'd ever known.

At first, she only thought his world was different.

Now she wondered if it was dangerous.

With all the down time she had during the day while Whip worked, she had done the research. Asked Shay general questions. Got online and read up on various MCs.

She found some clubs were good. Brotherhoods who helped their community by doing charity work. Some of them protecting victims.

Then there were the bad. Violent. Trafficking guns and drugs. Treating women like shit, like nothing more than objects. Even trafficking women and children for profit. Basically organized crime. No different from the mafia.

She had thought the Fury was the first type, but perhaps they were the second.

"You lied to me."

His soft, steady breathing filled her ear, but no words.

If he wasn't going to speak, she would take the opportunity to have her say and then hang up.

And, if possible, take her heart back. This way she could plug it back into her chest, hope it healed and then move on.

"Do you know how I know what you said to me was a lie, Whip? I spent time with the ol' ladies. You know, the sisterhood that you reminded me I didn't belong to since I was only a guest in your world. But in the short time I spent with those ladies, I discovered something. Something important. Every damn one of them is strong. Every one of them is independent. Even the quiet ones like Red, Syn and Shay. You know how I know? And I'm not talking about seeing it with my own eyes and hearing it with my own ears. It's because they have to deal with the men they love. Men who have strong, very possessive, very protective, sometimes overbearing personalities. I know because while staying at the motel, I got to know Ozzy and Shay better than the rest. If Shay wasn't strong, Oz would steamroll right over her, crushing her spirit and her personality."

She didn't give him the opportunity to respond. She mustered on.

"You said those women were property, when that's the farthest from the truth. None of them *need* their men, they *choose* to be with them. The truth is they are equal and hold power in their own right. On the surface it might appear differently to outsiders, but it's smoke and mirrors, just like the 'Property of' cuts they wear by choice and not because they are forced. Deep down at the very center, the very core of your club, Whip, they are equals. Those women are loved, cherished and respected by men not afraid of being called weak for it. And that…" She blinked away the sting in her eyes and cleared the thick in her throat. "That's how I knew what you said was all a lie."

He lied for a reason and she wanted to know why. She was at least owed that much. But the other end of the line remained quiet.

Disturbingly quiet.

"Why, Whip? *Why* did you drive me away?"

She counted the heartbeats between her question and his answer.

It took three. Three heartbeats. One for every week she spent with him.

"Wanted to keep you away from… this mess."

No, that answer was a cop-out and unacceptable.

"What mess?" Her chest tightened and she rubbed absently at it. "Whip, what mess? You owe me that much."

"Was tryin' to protect you."

"But you didn't protect me. You hurt me by lying."

"That hurt ain't nothin' compared to what else coulda happened."

"Like what? Why couldn't you be honest with me? Why can't you be honest with me now?" She slowly drew in a breath. "Were you trying to protect me from the Shirleys? Or the truth about you and your club?"

Her questions hung between them for far too long.

She should hang up. Delete his number. Never look back. It would be for the best. Probably for both of them.

"Both."

Shit. The fine hairs on the back of her neck stood. The news stories this morning. The news flashing across the screen in her Airbnb tonight. All of it.

All of it.

She knew it.

She *knew* it.

She had hoped it wasn't true.

"What happened on that mountain… It was your club, wasn't it?"

He sucked in a sharp breath. "What're you talkin' about?"

Was he going to play dumb? Lie to her again? "Were you involved in that? Blowing up homes where families lived?"

He hissed out a breath. "Don't assume with shit you see on TV. You don't know the whole story, Fallon."

She wasn't sure if she wanted to know all the details, either. But she did need to know one thing… If he was involved, if he was capable of creating that kind of devastation and destruction. The deaths and disappearances of a whole group of people.

While he hadn't admitted it was his club yet, he also didn't deny it.

An omission versus a lie. Which was worse?

"We got a long history with them, Fallon. They ain't victims."

She squeezed her eyes shut and clamped her hand tighter around her phone.

The news had touched on the history of the Guardians of Freedom. Should it matter if that clan was full of the horrible, dangerous people? The MC had taken it upon themselves to annihilate them from the Earth. They had acted as judge, jury and executioners.

And what about the women and children who had been up on that mountain? They were still searching for them in both the ashes and elsewhere.

Children who were innocents. Children who didn't have a choice to be born into that crazy clan.

She had thought Whip was a good guy. Sweet.

Had she been so completely wrong? Maybe she didn't know him at all and he was everything negative that an MC cut stood for.

Violent. Even deadly. Full of lies, secrets and deceit.

Had the Whip she fell in love with even existed? Or had it all been an act?

Her voice cracked when she whispered, "You kept telling me and I didn't listen. It turns out I was mistaken. "

She could actually hear him swallow through the phone. "'Bout what?"

"You aren't who I thought you were."

A noise came from what sounded like the back of his throat. "You're right, Fallon, I never was. You just didn't believe me."

"I believe you now."

"Wasn't like you were plannin' on stayin' anyway, right? You weren't stayin' here for me no matter who I was."

That was true. She hadn't been ready to settle in one spot yet. She had plans for her and Agnes to explore the country. "I—"

"Right. What I fuckin' thought. I was just someone to occupy your time on your forced detour."

"I never once lied to you, Whip. I was upfront from the beginning. My goal of this trip was to see everything I missed. What I was too busy to see. What I was too busy to experience. For years I was so occupied by looking upward, I never paused to look around. I couldn't do that if I stayed, but..." She pulled a long breath in through her nose and slowly let it out along with, "That didn't mean I couldn't return."

Silence once again filled her ear. Long, torturous dead air.

Finally he whispered, "Were you goin' to, Fallon? Or is it you who's now lyin'?"

"Does it matter now?"

"Yeah, it does. It fuckin' matters to me, Fallon. It matters to fuckin' me. Not once did you say shit or even hint about that. Not fuckin' once."

"Because I didn't know... I didn't realize..." Now it was her turn to not speak, to hold on to her secret. Because what good would it do now to let him know?

It was too late.

"What didn't you know, Fallon? How I felt about you? What didn't you realize? That I wanted you? What?"

Oh God. She couldn't tell him because it would make all of this even more difficult.

A stray tear slipped from the corner of her eye and she quickly batted it away. "How did you feel about me?" He might not be able to see her tears but he could hear them in her voice.

382

"That you belonged to me. That you belonged *with* me. You're mine, Fallon."

You're mine, Fallon.

That claim should disturb her.

What disturbed her was that it didn't.

Another tear escaped and her throat was so tight, she had to force out, "That's not your choice."

"No, it's yours." He exhaled loudly enough for her to hear it. "Lied to protect you, Fallon. Lied 'cause... Fuck! 'Cause I love you. For fuck's sake, didn't realize it at the time 'cause I've never loved a woman before. Didn't realize what it was. Now I do. Now I know. So, ain't gonna lie. I'm puttin' it out there and you do what you gotta do with it."

"I don't know if I can get past what you and your club did, Whip."

"Know you don't know the reason behind it. Know you don't know the history. But know this, the rest of the sisterhood knows all that and more. And all of them, every fuckin' one, is still standin' by their ol' man. They wouldn't if what happened wasn't warranted. Promise you that. Did they like it? Fuck no. Did they realize it was necessary? Fuck yes." He paused. "Bottom line is we do what we gotta do to protect our own. That included you. Still does. Always will."

She pressed a hand to her forehead, trying to make sense of his words. To make sense out of having to do something so extreme to protect the people you loved and cared for.

"I don't want you to do things like that for me. Not ever." She would never want to be the cause of death and destruction. What made her life worth any more than theirs?

"Fallon, here's the truth... I would die to protect you."

"No!" burst from her before she could stop it. She dug her fingers into her hair and grabbed a handful, pulling. Was she awake? Was this real life? "Don't say that!" She sniffled because now, not only were tears streaming down her face, dripping off her chin, her nose had started to run.

"Why?"

"Because you don't mean it," she insisted.

"Mighta lied to you that night but ain't lyin' about this. Promise to never lie to you again. Even if the truth's gonna hurt."

"Whip…" she whispered. A sob was trying to roll up her throat, but it got caught along the way.

"Would never think twice about it, babe. If it was you or me, I'd always choose you."

"No, Whip. That doesn't make sense."

"Don't it? While you were here… You saw it. You said it yourself… About how my brothers love and cherish their women. That also means they protect them, too. The Fury protects the people they love. Again, we do what we gotta do. No matter what it is. And that's one thing I'd do for you."

The man she had fallen in love with, despite their differences, just confessed he would die for her simply because he loved her and wanted to protect her.

He'd sacrifice his *life* for the woman he loved. What would the woman he loved be willing to sacrifice for him?

Chapter Twenty-Three

SHE SPENT hours with the women. Hours talking. Hours listening.

It started with Autumn and her story. Fallon was certain sordid details had been omitted but she'd been given enough info to fill in the blanks on her own.

Her heart ached for the woman. For everything she suffered through at the hands of the Shirleys and the Guardians of Freedom.

But it also swelled with how the Fury came together to help her. With how Sig, a broken man himself, rescued a broken woman he nicknamed "Red." How he took care of her until she could function again.

How he loved her intensely when no one thought he'd be capable of that emotion.

How he and the club were supportive while she was pregnant with Levi. How they protected her from the evil she escaped. How they risked everything and rescued her a second time when the Shirleys stole her back. How they were understanding when it came to her decision to allow the Brysons to adopt her baby.

How they welcomed Red as part of the Fury family when her own had betrayed her.

And now, how they welcomed her three young half-brothers into their lives, into their family, into their "village" to help raise them.

Taking in Ezrah, Noah and Cyrus was a risk they were willing to make because, by way of Red, they were family. They freed those boys from a life of harmful cult-like behavior and thinking. They planned to nurture and protect them as their very own until they were old enough to take care of themselves.

Jemma spoke about what happened to her that day in the public parking lot in town when Dyna, Cage's daughter, was stolen from her and used to bait the men up the mountain. To draw them into a deadly trap.

She heard it all in the attempt for the sisterhood to help her understand the Fury's fears and their actions. Tears were shed. Hugs were given. And later laughter when they began to share the happy moments they cherished that made being a part of the Fury, being an ol' lady, all worthwhile, in an attempt to relieve the heavy cloud overhead, in an attempt to beat back the ugliness.

In a way, that time spent inside The Barn was healing for all of them.

Even Fallon.

She now understood the threat the Shirleys had been. To the club. To the women. To the Fury children.

Not to mention, to the surrounding community.

She wished Whip had been honest with her from the beginning but now understood why he hadn't been.

She wasn't one of them.

She wasn't a part of that sisterhood.

She wasn't a part of that tight-knit community.

She had been just passing through. An outsider.

No one expected her to stay.

More importantly, no one expected her to come back.

But here she was.

Whip hadn't asked her to spend that time with the sisterhood. Instead, to help her understand the situation and her conflicted feelings, she had asked him if they were willing to spend that time with her.

They agreed. However, the sisterhood didn't do it for her. They did it for Whip, their brother. Not one of blood but of Fury.

The women understood her concerns. Her shock at what the Fury was capable of.

But Whip was right. So damn right.

Each and every one of those women supported their men one hundred percent along with the decisions they were pushed to make.

Seeing them with their babies—Stella with Rush, Jemma with Dyna, Reese with Dane, Red with Cyrus, and a pregnant Cassie—she realized how much those men had to lose. And those weren't all the Fury kids, just the ones too young to understand the stories being told.

To the men, family came first, whether family by blood or by Fury. And it hit home what Whip had said. They were going to do what they had to do to protect their own.

No matter what.

Even if they had to die doing it.

Fallon hoped to hell that never happened. Now that the biggest threat to the Fury was gone, it hopefully never would.

As she pushed open the side door and stepped out from The Barn, she glanced across the courtyard. The late afternoon sun blinded her for a moment, forcing her to shade her eyes with her hand. Her heart squeezed as she spotted him.

Alone and waiting.

. . .

WHIP'S EYES locked on Fallon while he ground the end of his joint out on the picnic table. Her expression was unreadable as she trekked across the grassy courtyard once she spotted him sitting on top of the table under the pavilion.

He realized he'd been holding his breath since the second she stepped outside. She'd been in The Barn with the women for fucking hours.

Hours.

Every fucking minute of those hours had been pure torture.

Too many times he wanted to go inside and check to see what was going on. What was being said. To witness Fallon's reaction to it all.

He had to force himself to sit back down. To wait it out.

To try his fucking best to be patient.

To not claw out his heart, burst into The Barn and hand it to her.

It was difficult.

What the women said could change everything. His future... *Hell*, his and Fallon's future relied on it.

He had left it in the sisterhood's hands.

And that was fucking terrifying.

Unfortunately, he had no idea if she was coming over to say goodbye.

Or if after everything she heard, she was willing to give them a chance.

He'd seen some of his brothers struggle at the thought of losing their women forever. He never thought he'd be in their boots.

But here he was.

Waiting impatiently to find out if this was the end or the beginning.

He climbed off the picnic table and turned to face her as she stopped in front of him. He studied her face closely, trying to get a read on her. To prepare for the worst.

When her blue eyes hit his, they locked and held for a few silent moments.

In his head he heard the same ticking as he had while on the mountain before the blasts.

"It was a lot," she said softly.

"Yeah," he breathed.

"Those women are amazing. I said they were strong but they are so much more. The sacrifices they made. Jemma raising a daughter that wasn't hers. Chelle taking on Jude. Autumn taking on three young ones. Reese, at only eleven, taking on the very adult responsibility of raising her baby sister. Syn and Reilly and…" She shook her head. "So many stories bond those women together. That bond them to their men. This might not be what's considered a typical lifestyle but it works for all of you. You all support each other, love each other, protect each other and help raise the children as one big family."

When she paused he wasn't sure if he was supposed to respond or not.

"But it isn't all light, Whip. Darkness also lurks beneath the surface. I know the stories I heard in there aren't the only ones. Secrets swirl around you all whether they're personal or involve the whole club. But I'm an outsider and I understand they went against the club's 'code' to tell me as much as they did. I'm thankful that they were as open as they were."

He closed his eyes for a second because he was waiting for the other fucking boot to drop and the tightness in his chest had become unbearable. "Fallon…"

When she reached up and cupped his face, he opened his eyes. "They love you, Whip. They want you to be happy."

"Fallon…" She needed to know what he was truly capable of before she made any decisions, even if admitting it hurt him in the end. Because if he didn't tell her now, she might find out in the future and he didn't want to hurt her again. "I stabbed our prospect in the fuckin' throat."

"I know and I also know why. You do what you have to do to protect your own," she said, repeating his own explanation from the other night on the phone. "But you also do what you have to do to protect the vulnerable. Gabi's proof of that. Ezrah, Noah and Cyrus are, as well."

"What I did don't bother you?"

"Of course it does. But what Scar was doing to Gabi disturbs me more. There was a consequence for his depravity. You just served him that consequence."

"Got there too late to save her from what he did."

"But you stopped it. You also saved her from what would've continued if she remained with that clan. You gave her a chance to heal and finish growing up. If she had remained with them, she would've been forced to become a mother by men who would've continued doing what Scar did. She would've had the same fate as Autumn."

"Just so you know… Don't regret what I fuckin' did and would do it again if I had to."

She nodded. "I wouldn't expect anything less of you."

"So, what does this mean, Fallon? I don't got much to offer you. Me. My club. Hell, my mother." He released a dry, stilted laugh at that last one. "That's it. Ain't enough for you."

"Why don't you let me make that decision, Whip? And did I ever indicate that it wasn't enough? That I was looking for more? I had more. I walked away from all of that to have a simpler life. I walked away to find my happy, something all that money I worked for can't buy. What I need is simple and I found it."

Holy fuck, she was killing him. "What are you sayin', Fallon?"

"When I gave up everything I had, it showed me that I don't need a lot, Whip. After driving away from Mansfield that night, I realized I had finally found my happy. With you. That's why when you lied to me it ripped my heart out."

"And now?"

"And now? I'm standing here. Again, with you."

He stared at her as he processed what she just said. "You wanna be with me?"

"Yes, but I still want to see the world. Only now I want to see it with you. I want you to join me on that journey. Not to find happiness but to finish discovering myself."

He wasn't sure what to think. He wanted to be relieved but while he'd love to see the world with her, it wasn't that easy. "Got responsibilities here, babe. Can't afford to just hit the road. Got a job, my mother," he swept his hand out, indicating the farm, "my family. Just can't up and leave like that. Not sure if I wanna, either."

As soon as her expression closed and she stepped back, he grabbed her arm and pulled her back to him. "Don't want you to ever regret givin' up your dream just to be with me, Fallon. Want you to be happy, too. If that means you need to go explore for a while, then do it. As long as you come back to me, I'm good with it. If I can swing goin' on a few of your adventures, I'll go. If I can't, then," he shrugged one shoulder, "just promise to come back to me afterward."

Her eyebrows shot up. "You won't care?"

He tucked a chunk of her blonde hair behind her ear and traced his fingertips along her delicate jawline. "Promised you I ain't gonna lie, so… Yeah, I'm gonna care. Also gonna worry every fuckin' second you're away from me. But ain't gonna tell you no 'cause you just told me yes. To me that's a gift I ain't gonna return. One thing I learned from bein' around my brothers and their ol' ladies is compromise is important. Also learned that what works for one couple don't work for another. We gotta do what's gonna work for us. If that means you do a bit of travelin', then you do it. Just know, I'll always be here waitin' for you when you return."

She planted a hand between his cut and onto his chest. "You'll be my home."

He grinned at her and pressed his hand over hers, holding it there. "Yeah, babe, I'll be your home. And you'll be my forever."

He snagged her wrist and pulled her into him, taking her mouth until they were both panting and desperate to make up for the week and a half they were apart. Ten days that seemed like an eternity.

"Just gonna ask for one thing," he murmured against her lips, his dick now throbbing and pressing painfully against his zipper.

"What?"

"Want you to stick around for a little while before you head back out. Need to get my fill of you, so I can survive the time between the second you leave 'til the second you come back to me."

She smiled up at him, her blue eyes soft. *Fuck*, she was beautiful.

"I can do that."

Thank fuck she was able to forgive him for his fuck-up.

"How 'bout we start now." He lifted his open palm.

Her eyebrows pinned together as she stared at it. "What?"

"Need the key to your sled."

"Why?"

"Couldn't feel how hard I was for you?"

"Yes, but…"

"Been dreamin' about havin' a threesome with you, me and Agnes and what a perfect way to celebrate you comin' home."

"Home," she repeated, her voice as soft as her expression.

He shrugged. "Ain't the sayin' 'home is where the heart is?'"

"That's true. But an actual home also has a roof."

He smirked. "We'll figure it out. 'Cause rumor has it that my woman knows how to make dough rise."

She laughed, shaking her head. "I don't know how to make bread."

"Yeah, you do. The kinda bread you don't eat."

She grabbed his shirt at his gut and pulled him until they were toe to toe. "Oh, I see. You want to be a kept man, huh?"

He snorted. "Nah, babe." He lifted his hands between them to show her. He wiggled his fingers. "These are skilled, workin' man's hands. It would be a waste not to use them."

She *hmm*'d as she pulled her key fob out of her pocket and pressed it into his palm. "You're right, that *would* be a waste of talent, so we can't have that. And anyway, Agnes has been feeling kind of lonely."

"Then, let's go keep her company." He grabbed her hand and headed to where their sleds were parked side by side near The Barn. "This gonna be your first threesome?"

She squeezed his hand. "Yes. How about you?"

His step stuttered.

As she tugged him along, Fallon burst out laughing. That sounded so damn good.

He hoped to hear that laugh every damn day for the rest of his life.

He also hoped to fuck she was the last thing he saw when he closed his eyes for the very last time.

He had found his forever.

Epilogue

FINDING FOREVER

A year later…

FALLON SAT ON THE BALCONY, her face turned up to capture the warmth of the sun. While inhaling the salty air, the bright orange, red and golden globe took its good old time lowering behind the horizon. She closed her eyes and the call of seagulls along with the turquoise waves crashing against the white sandy beach filled her ears.

She had rented the penthouse in the private condo complex on the Gulf side of Florida. They were high enough not to hear anyone on the beach, so it felt like they were alone. Just the two of them.

She smiled when the glass door behind her slid open. She didn't have to open her eyes because she could feel his presence. She opened them anyway because, while the sunset was beautiful, her ol' man was even more breathtaking.

Especially since he was shirtless and only wearing a loose pair of knee-length nylon shorts that clung to one of his many impressive assets.

He set the chilled bottle of spring water on the small table next to her lounger along with his beer.

"See what you've been missing?" she asked, tipping her head toward the horizon.

He came around to face her and lifted her bare feet from where they were propped on the railing to plant them onto his tattooed chest. "Yep. See it clearly."

"I meant the sunset over the ocean. Well, technically this isn't the ocean, it's actually the Gulf but close enough."

"Yeah, it's beautiful but not as beautiful as you."

She tilted her head and studied his face. "I know you try not to be sweet, but you just failed."

He grimaced and mouthed a curse in jest. "Just don't tell anyone."

She made a locking motion at her lips and tossed away the invisible key. "Secret's safe with me."

They were so opposite but they also fit perfectly, like a matching lock and key. Two different pieces that, when put together, created something functional and complete.

"Was just talkin' to Trip. They got the area cleared and will break ground for the foundation next week."

It had been a crazy year.

Last April she had stuck around Manning Grove for a month while they helped move Sig, Red and the kids into one of Shelter from the Storm's temporary double-wide trailers on the farm. Then she and Whip had moved into Sig's apartment.

After they settled in, she took one week each month to travel to somewhere new. A couple of times, Whip had gone with her. But mostly, he stayed home.

And every time she left, she felt more and more alone.

Every time she left, she missed him that much more. Like she left behind a big chunk of her heart.

Every time she left, she couldn't wait to go home.

This would be the last trip she would take for a while and she had convinced him to come along for his birthday.

In the time she was home, she had worked with Reese to do the research. They went to the county and found that the deed to the Shirleys' mountain property had been titled under the Pennsylvania Guardians of Freedom, Inc. That news surprised everyone since the clan had to deal with lawyers and the government to make that happen. And since they were a self-proclaimed sovereign nation they usually refused to deal with any kind of government entity.

But what wasn't so surprising was the amount of back taxes owed on what now was only land. Since the club's account had been wiped clean from hiring the Shadows, Fallon used some of her money to buy the property for a fraction of the owed taxes.

Even though she purchased the land, she had the deed put in the Blood Fury's name. With her now acting as the club's unofficial financial advisor and making the Fury's money work for them by investing it smartly, Fallon had no doubt the club would pay her back in a short amount of time.

Her only fee? Allowing Whip to pick the spot on that mountain where they would build their forever home.

"Good. I spoke with the architect and he'll have a few designs for us to look at when we get back," she informed him.

They hadn't rushed to begin construction on the property to allow the land—and the Fury—to start healing first.

"Wanna build my mom a little place up there, too."

"Sweet like taffy at the shore," she teased.

"Stop it, woman," he growled.

She sighed when he began rubbing her feet. Leaning her head back against the chair, she got more comfortable. She was still stiff and sore from traveling this morning. Like Whip, she preferred the open road and the wind in her face while they rode their sleds versus being packed like a canned sardine into a plane, breathing in recycled air and hoping the person coughing three rows behind them wasn't contagious.

It had been his first time flying and, even though they had flown first class and he had never experienced the cramped quarters of economy, the whole trip south he kept saying it was going to be his last. She refrained from telling him that it wouldn't be and some of the places she wanted to take him in the future were only accessible by air, and those would be a much longer flight. She'd break that news to him at a later time.

She had other news to give him first.

She released a long moan and pointed her red painted toes into his pec as he worked the sole of her foot to the point where she almost could orgasm. "Thirty. It's a milestone."

"Yep. Gotta say, babe, so far, this birthday's been way better than the last one."

"I'll agree with that."

As she reached for her water, her attention got caught on her inner wrist. Exactly one year from the day Whip found her along Copperhead Road, they both took the trip to In the Shadows Ink in Shadow Valley and had the Dirty Angel named Crow give her her second tattoo. It wasn't what she originally thought it would be.

She decided on an infinity symbol with Whip's name incorporated into one loop and "my forever" incorporated into the other.

When Crow asked why she chose that symbol, she simply smiled at Whip and explained, "He's my forever."

She took a long sip of water since her mouth was super dry because of what she was about to tell him. When she was done, she put the bottle down, leaned forward and grabbed his hand.

"Help me up," she urged as she dropped her feet from his chest. He pushed off the balcony railing and, using their clasped hands, pulled her to her feet. "I have a birthday present for you."

"This trip was more than enough, babe. Don't need anythin' else. I got you."

"I can't return this gift so you're just going to have to accept it. However, you should sit down before I give it to you."

His eyebrows pinned together. "Should I take my shorts off first?"

She pinned her lips together for a second, then managed to say, "It's not necessary."

He lifted one eyebrow. "But it's an option?"

"Well, if you want to shuck them right here on the balcony, I'm okay with it. I'm not sure if some of the snow-birds walking the beach will be."

He sat on the edge of the lounger she just exited and shot her a smirk. "Lettin' loose my monster might scare them so badly that they keel over."

"Mmm hmm."

When she stepped between his parted thighs, his smirk turned into a crooked smile as he looked up at her with confusion filling his blue eyes.

"Let me see your tattoo." She grabbed his hand, turned it over and brushed her thumb over the design that matched hers on his left wrist. An infinity symbol with her name and "my forever" incorporated into the design.

"My forever," she whispered, pressing a kiss to it.

"For infinity," he answered like he normally did.

She took a deep breath and pressed his hand flat against her stomach. "Happy birthday."

He lifted his gaze from where their hands were planted on her belly to her face. His brow furrowed and confusion once again filled his eyes.

She waited and gave him the time needed to process.

Without blinking once, his expression slowly changed to shock and back to confusion.

The man was struggling. She should help him.

So, she did. "Happy birthday, Daddy."

"F-fallon…" He closed his eyes and took a breath to get his emotions under control.

She now knew all about his stutter and when it occurred. Usually only when he was angry. On rare occasions, when he became very emotional and wasn't prepared to deal with it.

Like with this surprise.

"You okay?" she asked.

His Adam's apple jerked as he swallowed. He nodded as his eyes opened again.

"I know you just turned thirty and in a perfect world you'd wait. But you chose to love a woman who recently turned thirty-seven. Waiting isn't much of an option."

Leaving their joined hands on her lower belly, he wrapped an arm around her hips and pulled her close enough to press his forehead against her middle.

She brushed her free hand through his hair as he simply stayed there and breathed. "Our forever."

After a few quiet moments, he murmured, "My mom's gonna freak the fuck out."

"We should wait to tell anyone. It's early yet. Let's make sure this kid sticks first."

"Babe, he's gonna stick." He tipped his face up to hers. "What about your travelin'?"

She shrugged and gave him a smile. "I wanted to go out and see the world," she brushed the back of her fingers down his cheek and then cupped it, "but I was lucky and the world came to me instead."

Turn mistakes into invaluable lessons and valuable moments into memories...

———

**Turn the page to read the prologue of
Blood & Bones: Easy (Blood Fury MC, bk 12)**

———

Sign up for Jeanne's newsletter to learn about her upcoming releases, sales and more! http://www. jeannestjames.com/newslettersignup

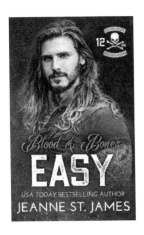

**Turn the page for a sneak peek of
Blood & Bones: Easy (Blood Fury MC, bk 12)**

Blood & Bones: Easy (Unedited)

BLOOD FURY MC, BOOK 12

PROLOGUE

Ashes! Ashes! We All Fall Down

ETHAN TOOK a last drag on his Marlboro, flicked what remained out into the dark and watched it bounce off the pavement, creating a small explosion of embers. His eyes followed the motion as the June breeze spun it into a small glowing arc.

He pushed himself off the brick wall where he'd been leaning and before he could stomp it out, another boot came out of nowhere and did it for him.

"Landry said he scored a case of Rolling Rock."

"Yeah?"

"Yeah. Invited us over. Wanna go?"

E shrugged.

"Said there's gonna be girls there. And his parents are gone for the night."

"Yeah?"

"Is that all you can fucking say?"

"Yeah," E answered with a smirk.

Ben snorted and punched Ethan in the arm. "You're an asshole."

"Yeah."

"Don't you wanna get laid tonight?"

"Yeah."

"Then let's go. You're not going to get your dick wet standing here."

That was true.

It had been a month since Mallory had dropped his ass like a hot coal. He fucked up so he couldn't blame her for kicking his ass to the curb. But still, his easy access to pussy went along with her.

Now he had to work for it.

Yeah, the girls in his class didn't mind flirting but when it came to sliding off their panties and between their thighs, that took a lot more effort. Sometimes more than he was willing to make.

He just needed to find himself a fuck buddy. A girl who wasn't uptight about sex but wasn't a clinger.

Mallory had been a clinger with claws.

She didn't like when he talked to other girls, forget looking at them. She was jealous as fuck. She had even yanked a chunk of hair out of some chick's head when the girl decided to sit down next to him at his lunch table to invite him over to watch a movie on her big screen.

It was all too much damn drama for him.

He liked to keep things chill.

Mallory was far from chill. But her pussy had been tight and she didn't mind sucking his dick, either.

He sighed.

"Yeah, let's go," E finally said. At worst, if he couldn't get laid, he'd get drunk and stoned out of his fucking mind. Landry's older brother usually had some premium green. *If* he was home and willing to share. Though, he tended to ignore Landry and his friends since they were still only seniors in high school.

Whatever.

Not twenty minutes later, he, Ben, Landry and Will were standing around the blazing fire pit in Landry's backyard.

So far not one fucking girl had shown up and Landry's older brother was nowhere to be found. The only thing keeping Ethan still standing there was the cold beer in his hand and the rest of the case buried in ice in a nearby cooler.

Otherwise, this "party" was totally fucking lame.

"Where are the girls, Lan?" Ethan asked him.

His buddy was standing on the other side of the pit, the glow of the flames giving his face a reddish tint.

Landry finished swallowing his mouthful of beer and scrubbed a hand over his mouth. "They said they were coming."

"Yeah, right." Landry probably lied about the girls to get them to come over. Because just a case of Rolling Rock and Landry's playlist on Spotify wasn't going to cut it.

"Know where your brother hides his pot?" E asked him.

Landry shook his head. "We'd be passing around his bong right now if I did."

Ben let out a long, low, "Whoooooooa," under his breath and everyone turned to see what he was staring at.

A hot blonde made her way through two bushes from the line of them that separated the homes. She only wore a fucking tiny string bikini. At nine at night. In the dark. It was far too late to be sunbathing.

But there she was, cutting across the lawn like she was headed to the beach.

"That one of the girls you invited?" Will asked Landry.

"No."

The girl gave Landry a small wave and pointed toward

the cooler on the back porch. Landry lifted his beer and called out, "Help yourself."

Ethan moved to the other side of the pit, his eyes still glued on the thin girl with the generous rack as she headed toward the porch. He elbowed his buddy. "Who's that?"

"My neighbor."

"She cool?" E asked.

Landry shrugged.

"Why haven't I seen her around school?"

"She goes to an all-girls private school. You know, since they are no guys, they do each other." He held two fingers of each hand in a V, and pounded them together to mimic two chicks scissoring. Then he lifted one of the Vs to his mouth and wiggled his tongue between them, pretending he was licking pussy.

Landry probably never ate pussy in his fucking life.

"You hit that yet?" E asked.

Landry snorted. "No, but not for a lack of trying."

"She a snobby bitch?"

Landry shrugged. "Too picky to let me down her pants even for a quick finger bang."

E's eyebrows shot up his forehead. "You asked if you could finger fuck her?"

"Yeah. Why?"

Easy shook his head. No wonder he couldn't score with her. He didn't have any fucking game.

Unlike E.

He could talk the panties off most girls. But, again, sometimes it wasn't worth the effort.

However, the girl snagging a beer might be worth it. Especially after she took her time bending over in front of the cooler, her bikini bottom riding up the crack of her sweet fucking ass.

Yeah, he was going to hit that tonight.

His dick decided it was onboard with that plan, too.

As he turned to head over to where she now stood under the Landry's back porch, her eyes checking out Ethan and his buddies, he heard Landry say to Will, "Watch this. He's going to crash and burn."

Ethan ignored that even though *she*, whatever her name was, had heard him, too, over the loud music.

The blonde tracked him as he took his time on his approach. He wanted to appear curious and casual but not desperate.

Her bikini top was the type with strings that tied at the back and behind her neck, making it easy to release unless she double-knotted it. The bottoms also tied at both hips.

Easy fucking access.

When he went almost boot toe to bare toe with her, he pulled the cold bottle from her fingers and twisted off the top, tossing the cap over his shoulder into the grass. He held out the open beer to her and when she took it, her fingers slowly sliding over his.

With a tilted head, she scanned him from head to boots, making his hard-on do a happy dance in his jeans.

When her gaze lifted to his face again, he wore a grin. "You always visit your neighbors wearing a bikini?"

"I was taking a late swim."

E took his time exploring her from her blonde hair, tossed into a messy knot at the top of her head, all the way to her painted toenails. Along the way, he noticed her nipples asking, "How you doin'?" through the little triangle-shaped fabric struggling to contain her perky, but nicely rounded, tits. "You're not wet."

"Not yet," she said with a wink.

Damn.

What was she? Sixteen or seventeen going on thirty?

"Does it take much?"

"Depends on who's trying," she answered, after taking a sip of her beer.

He smiled. "That would be me."

"Then I guess we'll find out, won't we?" She downed half the beer and when she was done, she smiled back and said, "Grab a couple more. We're about to get thirsty."

He lifted one eyebrow. This was going to be easier than he thought.

After pulling two more beers out of the cooler, she snagged his hand and led him across Landry's yard, back through the break in the bushes and into her backyard that included a large in-ground pool.

"Your parents home?"

She shook her head. "My dad's out on a date."

"He supposed to be home any time soon?"

"Nope. They're at some event that's supposed to run late. Sometimes he stays overnight at his girlfriend's place. He always calls when he's on his way home."

That music sounded much better to his fucking ears than Landry's lame playlist. He wouldn't need much time anyway. He'd dip and dash long before her father came home.

"You a virgin?" he asked as she opened one of the French doors on her back deck.

She released a husky laugh. That was all the answer he needed.

Without freeing his hand, she tugged him inside and slammed the door closed behind them. As soon as they were in what looked like some sort of library or office—he wasn't sure and didn't fucking care—she turned to him and asked, "Are you?"

"Nah."

Her lips curled up at the end. "Good."

When she finally released his hand, she turned and walked away from him, giving him a great view of that ass in the light. After setting her beer down on the side table, she reached behind her neck, she untied the top bow, then moved to the center of her back and undid that one next.

Just like a fucking gift.

Hell yeah. Christmas in July.

Before her bikini top could even hit the floor, she continued rounding the long leather couch that faced the fireplace. She stopped, locked gazes with him, then slowly loosened the bows at each hip, holding her bottoms in place for a moment as he stared at her sweet fucking tits. Perfect and perky.

He held his breath, waiting.

Her, "What are you waiting for?" got him scrambling to put the beers down.

After ripping his T-shirt over his head, he threw it to the floor as he moved to the other side of the couch. Sitting on the end, he quickly shucked his boots and socks, then surged to his feet to unbuckle his belt, shove his jeans and briefs down, freeing his erection. The second he stepped out of his jeans, and before he could say a damn word, she was dragging him down onto the couch and on top of her.

He was liking the way this was going. He didn't have to do any sweet talking or convincing. *She* was the aggressor.

He had no idea what he did to deserve this, but he shouldn't be questioning it. He should just be taking advantage of her generosity.

Shit. He needed to grab a condom from his wallet.

He reached out and stretched his fingers as far as he could. He could barely touch his jeans, but he managed to snag them and pull them closer, sliding his wallet from the back pocket and digging through it until he found what he was looking for.

She—*fuck*, he still didn't know her name—plucked the wrapper from his fingers, tore it open, reached between their sandwiched bodies and rolled it down his hard-on, making his hips jerk at her touch.

Yeah, this girl was no virgin. In fact, her screw count might be a hell of a lot higher than his.

He wrapped his lips around a pebbled nipple, sucking it as hard as he could and pulling a groan from her as she raked her long nails through his shaggy hair.

He rocked his hips to rub his latex-covered dick against her soft inner thigh.

"Hurry up," she encouraged.

He released her nipple with a wet pop. "We got time, right?"

Her nails scraped down his back and dug into his ass. "Yes… but, I'm really horny and want you inside me."

Say no fucking more.

He was trying not to seem selfish and just stick it inside her without any prepping but, *hey*, if that was what she wanted, he wasn't going to argue. "Want me to kiss you?"

"No, just stick it in."

His kind of girl. He really should ask her name.

But before he could, she sighed impatiently, reached between them, grabbed his dick and put it where she wanted it. That just so happened to be the same spot he wanted it, too.

He decided right then and there he didn't really need to know her name. She didn't want conversation or anything more. She only wanted to be fucked.

Luckily, he was her guy.

He closed his eyes as he worked his way inside her. Since he hadn't had a chance to do any foreplay she was dry as fuck. But he managed. Once he was balls deep, he took a few seconds to suck in a breath. Otherwise, he would begin humping her the same way Will's Weiner dog did to his "special" pillow.

"What are you doing? Sleeping?"

He opened his eyes to find her frowning at him. "No. I—"

"Just hurry up and fuck me."

Hurrying up wasn't the problem, making her come before he did, was. "Damn, you're demanding."

"I have every right to be."

He stared down at her. "Do you really think you're all that?"

"Is there a reason you're still talking?"

Damn. "My bad."

She bugged her blue eyes out at him.

Yeah, one fuck with her would be more than enough.

He clenched his teeth and began to pump his hips, hoping she'd get a little wetter to make it easier.

He was three pumps in as she laid there like a fucking dead fish and he was starting to regret this whole thing when he heard a noise come from the front of the house.

He turned wide eyes to her. "You said your father wasn't coming home any time soon."

"I don't think that's my father," she said calmly.

Way too fucking calmly. The tiny hairs on the back of his neck stood. "Who is it?"

She shrugged. "Probably my boyfriend."

Her what?

"You using me to piss off your fucking boyfriend?" When he tried to roll off her, she grabbed him with her legs around his hips and held him there. "Let me fucking go."

He heard footsteps and a male voice call out, "Sarah!"

"Let me fucking go!" he hissed, trying to pull free.

He surged up, breaking her hold. He hit the floor with a grunt when he rolled off her and the couch in one shot.

He scrambled to his feet, trying to locate where he threw his T-shirt. "You're a fucking cunt."

"What the fuck?" came the deep voice from the doorway.

He glanced up from yanking his jeans up his legs, sacrificing his briefs and socks. What he saw made him mutter, "Holy shit."

If that was her damn boyfriend, he was huge. Like football player big. Ethan was *not* a football player. Not even close.

The guy quickly took in the situation and the second his face changed, Ethan knew he was fucking dead.

He finished buttoning his jeans and held up his palms. "Had no idea, dude. She tricked—"

With a yell, the guy rushed him and Ethan could only brace for the impact.

The fucker probably *was* a linebacker because it felt like a damn train hitting him. He stumbled backwards, trying to catch his balance. If he went down, he was done. He needed to stay on his feet and do his best to fight the guy off so he could get out of that damn house.

His head snapped back as he got hit with a sledgehammer under his chin. And then it whipped to the side as he was punched in the jaw with a right hook.

He tried to catch his breath and steady his feet, but he couldn't...

Not before he was struck again. He couldn't stop the backwards motion or his arms windmilling as he was knocked off his feet with help from a two-handed shove to his chest.

He went airborne and when he landed on his ass, his head barely missed the corner of the brick hearth.

By a damn cunt hair.

Fucking son of a bitch.

But before he could even attempt to get back to his feet, the boyfriend was on him, grabbing Ethan's hair and using it to try to rip him to his feet. E reached out and his fingers curled around the closest thing he could find.

He gripped the handle tighter and swung the poker with

everything he could muster, cracking the guy upside the head.

A dull thud could be heard over his ringing ears and E grimaced as warm blood splattered across his face and bare chest.

He blinked several times to try to clear his vision as he watched the boyfriend crumple to the ground in slow motion like an accordion.

Holy shit.

Did Ethan just kill the fucker?

He blinked again and then he finally heard it.

The girl's screams. The continuous shriek that wouldn't stop. He didn't even think she took a damn breath. She just kept wailing as she stood there with her hands on her face, her eyes wide and her mouth gaping open.

That fucking bitch. She caused all of this.

It was all her damn fault.

He should...

No, he needed to get the fuck out of there while he still could.

He struggled to get to his feet, almost falling over because he was so freaking dizzy. Once the spinning slowed a little, he pressed a hand to the side of his face and glanced at his fingers.

Blood. Not only the boyfriend's but his, too.

His head throbbed like it was about to pop off his neck and he could only breathe through his mouth since his nose had to be broken.

But none of that mattered. He needed to escape.

He stumbled as he headed toward the back door, only catching himself in time by planting a hand on the wall. He stared at the bloody handprint left behind for a only second before spotting his T-shirt. He almost fell over as he leaned down to grab it. He didn't even bother to pull it on before he continued to head toward his closest route of escape.

His heart was pounding so hard he wondered how it remained contained in his chest. The voice in his head was telling him to get out of that house as fast as he could.

As he tried to turn the knob, it slipped in his hand so he scrubbed his bloody fingers down his jeans. Finally, he could yank the door open and when he stumbled outside, he paused only for a few seconds to glance over toward Landry's house. He could hear the music still playing and see the glow of the fire pit through the line of bushes, but fuck if he was sticking around to tell them what happened.

He might have just killed that asshole.

He needed to get the fuck out of there.

To go home.

Forget tonight ever happened.

Hope he'd soon wake up from this nightmare and be relieved it wasn't reality.

That the bitch hadn't just used him to piss off her boyfriend. Or make him jealous. Or whatever she had been trying to do when she used him as a tool in her fucked-up plan.

He yanked his T-shirt over his head as he made his way around to the front of the house and began to jog down the sidewalk barefoot.

He not only left his boots behind, he also left his freaking wallet.

By the time he got home, two miles away, his feet were cut up and a bloody mess, just like his face.

He let himself into basement door at the rear of the house and quickly locked it behind him. Leaning back against it, he took a few seconds to catch his breath, to try to slow the pounding of his heart.

He wouldn't be surprised if his parents could hear his heart all the way in their room on the second floor.

He struggled to smother his scream as he relived in his

head what just happened, realizing it wasn't a fucking night-mare at all.

Well, it was, but not the kind you woke up from.

Thank fuck his parents had let him move into the base-ment last year. This way they wouldn't see his face right away.

He stumbled into his bathroom and glanced in the mirror over the sink.

Holy shit.

How the hell was he going to avoid having his parents see him like this? He couldn't hide how fucked up his face was. He needed to think of a good excuse for his appear-ance. He would have two black eyes. The right one was already swollen shut and turning a dark purple.

Running the water in the sink, he washed it as best as he could, trying to ignore the throbbing, the sharp pain and the burning as he scrubbed off the blood and put some butterfly bandages over the worst cuts, like the one seeping under his right eye.

He grabbed toilet paper off the roll and shoved some up both nostrils to try to stop the bleeding. The pain was so damn unbearable he almost blacked out.

He stripped off his bloody shirt and jeans, burying them at the bottom of his overflowing hamper. He dug through his dresser next to find clean shorts and a T-shirt.

Once he managed to put them on, he climbed into bed.

He wanted to close his eyes but the way the adrenaline was still rushing through him, he knew he'd never find sleep tonight with the way his body was shaking and his teeth were chattering.

Worse, if he closed his eyes, he'd keep seeing the side of that fucker's head after being struck with the fireplace poker.

He'd only defended himself. He was forced to do it. That guy would've killed him without a damn thought, he could see it in his eyes. The uncontrollable rage.

No pussy was worth that. None.

And definitely none was worth jail time or even dying.

Especially that selfish fucking bitch.

It was all her goddamn fault.

She caused it all.

She should be the one to pay. Not Ethan.

It didn't take long until the pounding came at their front door.

He wasn't surprised that it happened but just how soon it did.

He could hear his parents' voices and footsteps as they came down from their bedroom.

Don't open the door.

Please, don't open the damn door.

Voices. Not his mom or dad's. Men. More than one.

Then his mom and dad's.

Lots of talking.

He couldn't make out the words.

He didn't have to know what was being said.

His heart was now thumping in his throat as the door from the kitchen to the basement opened and boots descended the steps. Not one set. No. Multiple.

Not cautiously, but with determination.

Shit.

He would go to jail for murder and never get out. He would die in there.

He'd never smell fresh air again.

He'd never get pussy again.

He'd never graduate high school.

Then everything happened in a whirlwind.

Ethan was dragged out of bed.

Pulled to his feet.

Spun around and cuffed. His arms practically yanked from his shoulders.

They were all talking but he didn't know what they were saying.

Words. Too many words.

He couldn't stop his brain from spinning to figure out those words.

He just knew his life was over.

It was over.

He couldn't undo his fuck-up.

He couldn't go back and stay at the fire pit with his friends.

He couldn't tell Ben he didn't want to hang out at Landry's.

He couldn't go back and wake up all over again to start the day over.

It was too late.

Too late.

He'd never forget seeing his mother's face. Her eyes wide. Her hand covering her mouth. Tears streaming down her pale cheeks as the cops dragged him up the steps and out of the house.

He never once stepped foot into that house again.

Get Blood & Bones: Easy (Blood Fury MC, book 12) here:
mybook.to/BFMC-Easy

If You Enjoyed This Book

Thank you for reading Blood & Bones: Whip. If you enjoyed Whip and Fallon's story, please consider leaving a review at your favorite retailer and/or Goodreads to let other readers know. Reviews are always appreciated and just a few words can help an independent author like me tremendously!

Want to read a sample of my work? Download a sampler book here: BookHip.com/MTQQKK

———

Sign up for Jeanne's newsletter: http://www.jeannestjames.com/newslettersignup
Join her FB readers' group for the inside scoop:
https://www.facebook.com/groups/JeannesReviewCrew/

Also by Jeanne St. James

* Available in Audiobook

Made Maleen: A Modern Twist on a Fairy Tale *

Damaged *

Rip Cord: The Complete Trilogy *

Brothers in Blue Series:

(Can be read as standalones)

Brothers in Blue: Max *

Brothers in Blue: Marc *

Brothers in Blue: Matt *

Teddy: A Brothers in Blue Novelette *

Brothers in Blue: A Bryson Family Christmas *

The Dare Ménage Series:

(Can be read as standalones)

Double Dare *

Daring Proposal *

Dare to Be Three *

A Daring Desire *

Dare to Surrender *

A Daring Journey *

The Obsessed Novellas:

(All the novellas in this series are standalones)

Forever Him *

Only Him *

Needing Him *

Loving Her *

Tempting Him *

Down & Dirty: Dirty Angels MC Series®:

Down & Dirty: Zak *

Down & Dirty: Jag *

Down & Dirty: Hawk *

Down & Dirty: Diesel *

Down & Dirty: Axel *

Down & Dirty: Slade *

Down & Dirty: Dawg *

Down & Dirty: Dex *

Down & Dirty: Linc *

Down & Dirty: Crow *

Crossing the Line (A DAMC/Blue Avengers Crossover) *

Magnum: A Dark Knights MC/Dirty Angels MC Crossover *

Crash: A Dirty Angels MC/Blood Fury MC Crossover

Guts & Glory Series:

(In the Shadows Security)

Guts & Glory: Mercy *

Guts & Glory: Ryder *

Guts & Glory: Hunter *

Guts & Glory: Walker *

Guts & Glory: Steel *

Guts & Glory: Brick *

Blood & Bones: Blood Fury MC®:

Blood & Bones: Trip *

Blood & Bones: Sig *

Blood & Bones: Judge *

Blood & Bones: Deacon *

Blood & Bones: Cage *

Blood & Bones: Shade

Blood & Bones: Rook

Blood & Bones: Rev

Blood & Bones: Ozzy

Blood & Bones: Dodge

Blood & Bones: Whip

Blood & Bones: Easy

COMING SOON!

Everything About You (A Second Chance Gay Romance)

Double D Ranch (An MMF Ménage Series)

Blue Avengers MC™

About the Author

JEANNE ST. JAMES is a USA Today and international bestselling romance author who loves writing about strong women and alpha males. She was only thirteen when she first started writing. Her first published piece was an erotic short story in Playgirl magazine. She then went on to publish her first romance novel in 2009. She is now an author of over fifty-five contemporary romances. Along with writing M/F, M/M, and M/M/F ménages, she also writes under the name J.J. Masters.

To keep up with her busy release schedule check her website at www.jeannestjames.com or sign up for her newsletter: http://www.jeannestjames.com/newslettersignup

www.jeannestjames.com
jeanne@jeannestjames.com

Newsletter: http://www.jeannestjames.com/newslettersignup
Jeanne's FB Readers Group: https://www.facebook.com/groups/JeannesReviewCrew/
TikTok: https://www.tiktok.com/@jeannestjames
Audible: https://www.audible.com/author/Jeanne-St-James/B002YBDE7O

facebook.com/JeanneStJamesAuthor

twitter.com/JeanneStJames

amazon.com/author/jeannestjames

instagram.com/JeanneStJames

bookbub.com/authors/jeanne-st-james

goodreads.com/JeanneStJames

pinterest.com/JeanneStJames

Get a FREE Romance Sampler Book

This book contains the first chapter of a variety of my books. This will give you a taste of the type of books I write and if you enjoy the first chapter, I hope you'll be interested in reading the rest of the book.

Each book I list in the sampler will include the description of the book, the genre, and the first chapter, along with links to find out more. I hope you find a book you will enjoy curling up with!

Get it here: BookHip.com/MTQQKK

Made in the USA
Columbia, SC
06 February 2022

55449719R00262